PENDRAGON

BOOK 2 IN THE CHRONICLES OF ARTHUR

PETER GIBBONS

Boldwood

First published in Great Britain in 2024 by Boldwood Books Ltd.

Cover Design by Colin Thomas

Cover Images: Colin Thomas, Thomas Gun and Wikimedia Commons

Map designed by Irina Katsimon

A CIP catalogue record for this book is available from the British Library.

Paperback ISBN 978-1-83518-240-6

Large Print ISBN 978-1-83518-241-3

Hardback ISBN 978-1-83518-239-0

Ebook ISBN 978-1-83518-242-0

Kindle ISBN 978-1-83518-243-7

Audio CD ISBN 978-1-83518-234-5

MP3 CD ISBN 978-1-83518-235-2

Digital audio download ISBN 978-1-83518-238-3

This book is printed on certified sustainable paper. Boldwood Books is dedicated to putting sustainability at the heart of our business. For more information please visit https://www.boldwoodbooks.com/about-us/sustainability/

Boldwood Books Ltd, 23 Bowerdean Street, London, SW6 3TN

www.boldwoodbooks.com

For my family, as always.

Men went [...] with a war-cry,
Speedy steeds and dark armour and shields,
Spear-shafts held high and spear-points sharp-edged,
And glittering coats-of-mail and swords,
He led the way, he thrust through armies,
Five companies fell before his blades.
[...] He fed black ravens on the rampart of a fortress

— FROM 'Y GODODDIN', A WELSH POEM WRITTEN BY THE BARD ANEIRIN IN THE SIXTH CENTURY

BRITAIN, C. 540
N
PICTLAND
DAL RIATA
LOTHIAN
GODODDIN
BERNICIA
RHEGED
DEIRA
ELMET
SAXONS
GWYNEDD
POWYS
DEMETIA
GWENT
DUMNONIA
KERNOW
Kingdoms of Dumnnonia

THE GREAT SIXTH-CENTURY KINGDOMS OF BRITAIN

After the collapse of the Roman Empire in 400AD, the legions left Britain to descend into a place of constant, brutal warfare. By the sixth century, the island is ruled by fierce kings from behind crumbling Roman strongholds and menacing hilltop fortresses. The south-east and western kingdoms have fallen to marauding Germanic invaders known as Saxons. The Saxons are a warlike people from across the sea, first invited to Britain by Vortigern, a weak king of a small kingdom, to aid him in his wars against the rival kings of Britain.

Rheged – Located close to Cumbria in modern-day England. Ruled by King Urien from his seat at the Bear Fort. Warriors of Rheged carry the bear sigil upon their shields.
Gododdin – A kingdom in Britain's north-east, close to modern-day Northumberland and East Lothian. Ruled by King Letan Lyddoc from his fortress Dunpendylaw. Gododdin's warriors march under a stag banner.
Dal Riata – Kingdom on Scotland's west coast, covering what is now Argyll.

Dumnonia – Ruled by King Uther Pendragon. Dumnonian warriors march to war with a dragon sigil upon their shields. Located in Britain's south-west, mainly in modern-day Devon, Somerset and Cornwall.
Gwynedd – Ruled by King Cadwallon Longhand. Located in north Wales and Anglesey.
Elmet – Ruled by King Gwallog. Located in the area around modern-day Leeds, reaching down south to the Midlands. Elmet's warriors wear the *lorica segmentata* armour and red cloaks of the Roman legions.
Bernicia – Lands lost to Ida, the Saxon conqueror. Covers what is now south Northumberland, Tyne and Wear, and Durham. Its warriors once fought beneath the proud banner of the fox.
Deira – Lands stretching along much of Britain's west coast, which fell to Saxon invaders in Vortigern's Great War.
Lothian – Ruled by King Lot, encompassing what is now south-east Scotland.
Powys – Ruled by King Brochvael the Fanged. A large and powerful kingdom in what is now central Wales.
Pictland – Lands occupied by the Picts in Scotland's north.
Demetia – Lands in the south-west of what is now Wales. Ruled by King Morholt and his Irish warriors who took the kingdom by force.
Gwent – A kingdom between the Rivers Wye and Usk, in what is now south Wales. Ruled by King Tewdrig.
Lyndsey – A Saxon kingdom lying between the River Humber and the Wash, ruled by King Cwichelm.
Benoic – A Brythonic kingdom on the borders of Armorican Brittany and Gaul, ruled by King Ban.
Cameliard – A Brythonic kingdom in Brittany, neighbour to Benoic. Ruled by King Leodegrance.

1

542AD, BRITAIN

Arthur brought war to the Saxons.

He led his savage black-cloaked warriors ranging deep into the kingdoms conquered by Saxon invaders a generation ago, hunting the enemy in the lands the Britons called Lloegyr, the lost lands. A man of no kingdom, Arthur was a lord of war without subjects, lands, hall, wealth or title. Arthur had nothing but his reputation and one hundred warriors oathsworn to fight and die under his command, and Arthur fought to push the Saxons back and stem the tide of their inexorable advance. His men called him lord, as did the kings and warlords who ruled Britain's other kingdoms born in the wake of a decayed, collapsed and withdrawn Roman Empire. The title of lord was a mark of respect, an honour bestowed upon him not because he was the son of a great *comitatus* or war leader, but because he was what they needed him to be. A brutal warlord to strike fear into the hearts of the ruthless Saxon invaders. The raiders and killers who had come to Britain's shores with their ships, flaxen hair, axes and an unquenchable thirst for battle, land, slaves and glory.

On a spring morning when frost steamed from heath and

meadow like the breath of Arawn, Lord of the Underworld, Arthur led five score warriors across a wide pasture. He was a tall man of twenty summers, but already bore the marks of battle on his lean, scarred face. Wet grass soaked through his boots and with each breath clouds came from his mouth in billowing gusts. A boy had rubbed Arthur's chain-mail clean with sand and its links shone like a dragon's scales beneath his night-black cloak. Heavy shields of linden-wood boards bossed and rimmed with iron clanked against ash-wood spears as Arthur's war band marched across the eerily still meadow. A dog barked in the village beyond, wandering amidst Saxon pit dwellings, their hovels dug into the ground and walled with wattle and topped with grey winter-soaked thatch.

'Flank them,' Arthur said, turning to Dewi, a lugubrious veteran and capable captain. 'The women and children can go. The warriors die.'

'Forgive me, lord,' said Dewi with an upside-down smile. 'The women and children will fetch a good price at the slave markets and we need food and ale.'

'No slaves. Women and children will spread word of what they see here. Take whatever food and livestock we can find.'

Dewi nodded and barked a well-practised order. Two score warriors loped off east and west to surround the Saxon settlement whilst Arthur marched straight towards its middle like an arrow.

'This place is home to the men who raided Rheged's borders last summer,' Arthur called to his men. 'You all remember the village with the twins. Now is the time for vengeance.'

The sight of a pair of small girls, twins with chestnut hair and milk-white skin left butchered in a blood-spattered barn, would never leave Arthur's mind. Another horror to join the army of dead folk who lived on inside Arthur's head, their fetches haunting him, demanding vengeance, urging him to strike on behalf of the sheep fallen to vicious Saxon wolves. His men needed little reminding, but Arthur wanted that memory burning in their hearts as they fought an enemy on stolen land Britons had once called home.

Arthur touched the bronze disc at his neck and the silver cloak pin he wore inside of his belt for luck as he splashed through a babbling brook and strode up its shallow bank. Two dozen Saxon hovels lay between older, timber-built British houses. Smoke rose from thatch and earth-clad roofs, and the same dog continued to bark, straining at a hemp rope tied to a wooden post. A woman came from a dark doorway with a greasy fur about her shoulders and long, braided hair. She carried a clay pot towards the brook and shrieked as her eyes fell upon Arthur in his bright helmet topped with a plume of raven feathers, his chain-mail coat of armour, heavy shield and the sword belted in a red scabbard at his waist. The sword. Excalibur. A gift from Merlin the Druid. Once named Caledfwlch by Neit, god of war, when she was forged in the distant mists of time. Ambrosius Aurelianus had wielded her glorious edge during the Great War, and now she belonged to Arthur.

The woman dropped her clay pot and ran. She slipped in the mud and scrambled to her feet, diving into the darkness of her hovel. Arthur took two more strides and a big man burst from the same leather-covered doorway, his golden hair long and his beard hanging in two great braids across his bare chest. He carried a Saxon war axe in one hand, the seax which gave his people their name in the other. The Saxon bellowed at the top of his voice, rousing his people, warning them of the war band come to kill them on a bright and frosty morning. Balin of the Two Swords hurried past Arthur, reaching for the blades strapped to his back. Balin drew a sword across each shoulder and approached the axeman, blades held wide. The Saxon bellowed a rumbling guttural challenge, and he swung his axe in a mighty blow to take Balin's head from his shoulders. But Balin ducked beneath the bearded axe to open the Saxon's belly with his sword's edge. The Saxon fell to his knees, clutching at the gaping wound, holding in his insides with bloody hands. Balin reverse swung the blade in his left hand and cut off the man's head with one clean blow.

Arthur drew Excalibur. Its ancient blade scraped on the wooden throat of its fleece-lined scabbard. He caught a whiff of the lanolin smeared upon the sword to protect its god-forged blade. He pointed Excalibur towards the village, and his warriors whooped for joy, exultant at the chance to kill their enemies. More Saxon men stumbled from their homes, eyes bleary with sleep, clutching axes, seaxes and spears. They came to defend their stolen village and the families within. A grey-bearded Saxon with a mouth full of brown teeth came at Arthur, his spear levelled and hate in his pale blue eyes. Arthur batted the spear point away with the flat of Excalibur's blade and let the Saxon's momentum take him into the blood-hungry black cloaks, who cut the enemy down without mercy or hesitation.

Arthur left the slaughter to his warriors, to his hard men who had spent the last two years in constant warfare. They were the Saxon-killers, the men who hunted the enemy beyond Lloegyr's borders, taking the fight to a foe who would otherwise spread like a plague into the Britons' borderlands of Rheged, Elmet and Gododdin. The howling of terrified women melded with the furious war cries of their warrior husbands. Men from across the narrow sea who had crushed the Britons and conquered the eastern coastline, casting its kingdoms to ruin and enslaving populations with their devastating Saxon war-cunning.

Arthur marched through the snarl of hovels, barns, pigsties, chicken coups and mud-slathered pathways. Ahead, a Saxon hall loomed above the smaller dwellings, little more than a barn topped with a ship's prow badly carved to resemble a rearing eagle. A dirty-faced woman clutched an urchin into her skirts and then ran, following her people towards the perceived safety of their lord's hall. Saxon chiefs lived in such halls along with their retainers, his hearth troop of oathsworn warriors. It was the same in every Saxon village Arthur destroyed. He had a question for their headman, their chief, their lord. The same question he had asked a dozen such men in the last year, and he would not stop searching until he found the answer.

Six Saxon warriors charged from the hall. Men with drooping moustaches and hard-baked leather breastplates. They carried heavy shields and leaf-shaped spears and they charged at Arthur, eyes full of fear and faces set hard towards their enemies. Arthur flexed his hand around Excalibur's hilt, the blade perfectly balanced, the sword singing its blood-lament to him above the sounds of the dead and dying. He hefted the heavy shield in his left hand, fingers curled around the wooden grip within the bowl of its iron boss. Balin of the Two Swords rushed to Arthur's side, and they met the Saxons head on. At the last moment, when he could see the ale stains on their breastplates and smell the acrid stink of their sweat, Arthur surged forwards. He drove his shield into the enemy opposite him, crashing its rim into the bottom half of the Saxon's shield. It tilted forward and banged against the man's shins, and he gasped in horror as one of Balin's swords snaked over the shield's edge and tore out his throat. Arthur turned, smashing Excalibur through a spear shaft, and drove his shield rim into the spearman's face, crushing his nose and smashing teeth.

Arthur left the remaining enemy warriors to Balin. Swords rang and men howled in pain as Balin lunged, parried and cut with the precision of a master swordsman. Arthur went to the hall, catching glimpses of his men charging from the flanks, roaring their attack with a fury to dim the sun. He reached the hall's steps, fallen logs set into a grass-covered knoll upon which the hall perched, its eagle prow glaring down at Arthur with hateful, white-painted eyes. He kicked the door open, and a warrior charged him clutching a long-handled war axe. The axe scythed through the air, cutting through the stink of smoke, stale ale and curing meat. Arthur caught the axe on his shield and the impact jolted up his arm and shoulder. He let go of the shield, and the axeman kept moving, bullying Arthur back with his broad shoulder so that Arthur's sword hand became trapped under the Saxon's arm. Arthur reached down with his left hand and pulled the heavy stone sceptre, as long as a man's arm from elbow to fingertip with three wicked faces carved into its bulbous head, free from his belt. He whirled the sceptre around and slammed it into the Saxon's head, crushing his skull with a loud crack. The sceptre came away with the cruel faces carved into its head dripping with blood, matted with hair and bone.

Arthur stepped into the gloomy hall, lit sparingly by a mean hearth fire and two spluttering rushlights. Wide-eyed women stared at him from the room's edges, and men cast their eyes down, unwilling to meet the eyes or challenge from the blood-spattered warrior who had turned their morning to ruin.

'I am Arthur of the Britons,' he shouted in Saxon. Arthur had learned the invaders' language to better understand his enemy, and the people crammed into their lord's hall gaped to hear a Briton speak their mother tongue.

The women and old folk in the hall screamed as a tall warrior spat at Arthur and, in response, Arthur flicked Excalibur with his wrist, slashing open the Saxon's cheek. Holding Excalibur and the bloodied sceptre out before him, Arthur made sure all the people inside the hall could witness the horror. They saw the terrible face of a war that Arthur's people had been subjected to ever since King Vortigern invited the Saxons to Britain's shores to fight against his fellow kings in a war for overlordship.

'How dare you attack us?' said a croaking voice. A heavypaunched man in a yellow cloak limped towards Arthur from the hall's dark recesses. He wore a bronze circlet upon his brow and a thin silver chain wrapped about his sagging jowls. 'I am Othere, and these are my people.'

'Your people raided across the border last summer. They stole cattle and sheep, slaughtered three families, and left murdered children to rot in the ashes of their parents' homes. I have come to you for those people. I am their vengeance and their wrath.'

'Take cattle and sheep. Take horses if you wish, but still your blades, young warrior. Let my people be.'

Arthur stalked between the Saxons, who shuffled and cowered away, leaving a pathway upon the rush-covered floor between him and village leader. 'You gave the order for last year's raid, Othere?'

'I did. All men raid. Your people raid. We are warriors.'

'You came to Britain from across the narrow sea?'

'Just so. I came with Horsa, one of the first of our warlords to set foot on these shores, with nothing but my axe and have built for myself a lordship.'

'You have grown fat and rich on stolen land, and built your wealth on a mountain of corpses. I seek a woman, Othere. A woman with blue eyes and hair the colour of a crow's wing. She is a young woman of my people, a nobleman's daughter captured by Saxon warriors two summers ago when your people lost a battle at the river Glein.'

'I remember it well. My son died that day, and my nephew.'

'The woman?'

'There are many *Wealas* women with blue eyes and black hair, young warrior. How should I remember one slave girl amongst a flock?'

Wealas. The word sent a shiver of anger across Arthur's shoulders. It was the term Saxons used to describe Britons, and in their cruel tongue it meant slave. The missing girl was Arthur's foster sister, Lunete. Saxon warriors had captured her on the eve of Arthur's glorious victory over a Saxon horde beside a glistening river, and he had searched for her ever since.

He held up the heavy stone sceptre. 'I took this from King Ida of Bernicia when I cut off his hand. I killed his son, Ibissa, and laid waste your army. Has anybody in this hall seen a girl of my people with blue eyes and black hair?' Arthur realised he was shouting, and that Balin and Dewi had entered the hall.

The Saxons stared at Arthur with hateful eyes and mouths twisted in contempt. He sighed. Othere breathed heavily, like a cow waiting to be milked. His rheumy eyes flicked from Arthur to the sceptre, and a pale tongue licked across thin lips. Arthur turned on his heel and marched towards the door.

'Kill the headman,' he said to Balin as he brushed past the fearsome swordsman. 'Cut the hands off the menfolk so they can never kill another Briton and send the women and children into the wilderness to tell their people of the black cloaks and what happened here.'

'What of the village, lord?' asked Dewi.

'Burn it. All of it.'

Arthur left the hall, and Othere screamed like a pig as Balin sent him to the afterlife. Despite two years of searching, Arthur had found few hints or tracks of where Lunete's captors had taken her, if she still lived. On cold winter nights, when Arthur was alone beneath his cloak, huddled beside a dwindling campfire, his dark thoughts would intrude. He would ask himself if it were better that Lunete was dead, her beautiful, innocent soul looking down upon him from the afterlife. The alternative was bleak. Bile rose in Arthur's throat and he swallowed it down. The girl he had grown up beside, running through the fields of Caer Ligualid with Arthur and her brother Kai, become a slave. Lunete's fate haunted Arthur, visions of her in fetters, enslaved to a Saxon warlord, subject to the brute's every whim. It sickened him. Arthur slid Excalibur into its scabbard and stared at the sceptre's stone faces, for the thousandth time wondering who they were, and if Ida's weapon and symbol of authority brought him good luck or ill.

Thatch burned, and weeping women took to the hills with their bairns and whatever possessions they could carry. Arthur's black cloaks gathered bread, meat, wheat, barley, eggs and cheese in a wagon and hitched it to a sad-faced donkey who brayed at the fire and smoke. Green abounded in a forest of ash and elm stretching westwards away from the burning village. Spring was time to sharpen blades, to wake men from a winter spent huddling beside a warm fire. Ever more ships crossed the narrow sea, Saxons and brutal warriors from Jutland and the Angle, following tales of lush valleys and weak kingdoms on the island of Britain. More came every spring, a never-ending tide of axes and conquest. Warriors with enough courage to leave their lands in the far north-east, where the fall of mighty Rome turned the land upside down like a shovel in the soil. They braved rolling waves and howling sea storms to bring their desperate fury to Britain and carve out kingdoms of their own. Saxons came for reputation, silver, land and women, and Arthur must prepare to meet that dreaded enemy. He must take his band of black-cloaked avengers and rouse the disparate kingdoms of Britain. It was time to find Merlin. It was time for war.

2

Arthur marched his war band through deep dales, dark, creaking forests and across the high crags of Britain's mountainous north-west until they crossed the badlands between the conquered Saxon kingdoms of Bernicia and Deira, into Rheged. The Briton-ruled kingdom of Arthur's birth. He rode his white stallion, Llamrei, and Balin his roan mare whilst the rest of the black cloaks marched in column, winding their way through the charred timber skeletons of burned borderland farms and villages, and the crumbling stone remnants of Roman walls and way stations left to rot by the departed empire.

After days of hard marching, the company made camp in the ruins of an old Roman pottery. Earthenware shards littered a courtyard overgrown with wild grass and weeds, whilst the building itself comprised three crumbled stone walls and a carpet of blood-red shattered roof tiles. Dewi had the men sweep the place out with birch branches and then set a fire inside the old building. Five of Arthur's men wore the segmented armour of old Rome, and they slipped it off to clean the leather and iron plates with handfuls of gravel, and one of their number, Hywel, brought Arthur a skin filled with ale to slake his thirst.

'We'll get a broth going soon, lord,' Hywel said, offering the skin. 'Some meat as well. There's no danger with a fire here. We haven't spotted any Saxons tracking us.'

'Set the usual sentries and watches through the night. Make sure the lads eat plenty,' said Arthur. He took a drink of the thick spiced brew taken from the Saxon village and handed it back to Hywel. 'We have hard marching ahead. Tell your men they fought well this winter and share this between them.' Arthur bent and took a handful of hacksilver from a leather pouch. Hywel grinned and took the shards hacked from Saxon silver arm rings and hurried to his men, and they clasped fists to their chests and bowed their heads to Arthur as Hywel shared the silver amongst them. Hywel and his four companions were mercenaries from Elmet, a kingdom south of Rheged where warriors still followed Roman ways and wore the armour of the legions. But Hywel and his men had fallen foul of Elmet's king, Gwallog, in some distant dispute and now wore the black cloak of Arthur's warriors over their Roman *lorica segmentata* armour.

Arthur walked amongst his men, clapping them on the shoulder, handing out more silver to those who had distinguished themselves in battle, or who had taken a recent wound. They had found plenty of silver and gold arm rings amongst the Saxon warriors killed in the village, and as a lord of warriors it was Arthur's duty to keep his oathmen rich in silver. He shared a joke with a warrior from old Deira and took a piece of flatbread from a gap-toothed man from Lothian. Once the men settled and meat started roasting over the campfire, Arthur came across Balin sat beside an old kiln that had collapsed long ago and was now filled with sprawling nettles.

'The meat smells good,' Arthur said as he took off his cloak and wriggled out of his chain-mail coat and its leather lining and draped the heavy armour over the kiln's edge.

'We must decide where to march,' said Balin, never a man for small talk. He frowned, thumbing a nick on the edge of one of his swords. He had a lean face framed by a dark beard and close-cropped black hair, tinged with grey. A jagged scar cut through the left side of Balin's face, from forehead to jaw. His eye drooped because of the scar, and the skin around the old wound appeared puckered and tight, as if stretched too thin across his strong cheek-bones. 'The Saxon borders reach to the southern sea, and we do not know where they will strike next. Ida of Bernicia broods beside the narrow sea in Dun Guaroy and can raise a thousand spears if he or his son pushes westwards. Octha is still active south of Elmet, and the southern Saxon kings are ever greedy for more land. We can expect them to push towards Dumnonia this summer or the next.'

'Too many Saxons to fight, and too few men to fight them. It has been two years since we fought Ida at the river Glein. Since then, he hasn't ventured west, though he and his son Theodric certainly hunger for revenge. Further south, Octha has one and a half thousand men and strives to win himself a kingdom. We should know, we have fought them often enough in the last year. To do that, he must kill another Saxon king, or strike at one of our kingdoms. Most likely are the kingdoms bordering lands already fallen to Saxon blades. Perhaps Elmet, Dumnonia or Rheged. He brought three thousand men across the narrow sea, and has but half that number left. Octha has lost men to war, and to his fellow Saxon warlords, and he will lose all of his warriors if he cannot deliver them the victory, spoils and land they hunger for. They'll drift away to join other more successful lords who can furnish them with luck, victory, rings and women. He might even try his hand at Gododdin again, if Ida permits him to cross Bernicia. The southern Saxon kings seem fat and happy. Perhaps they will continue to settle families and farm the land, grow fat on their conquered kingdom's bounty. Men say their days of war are over.'

'Over? What men say that? Fools? They will never be over. A Saxon always wants more. We have fought Octha, that's true enough. But even though he has lost much of his force, we can only carry out hit-and-run attacks. We kill his foragers and sack his supply train. We fall upon his warriors at night and then flee to the forests and mountains to hide. Octha has to feed three thousand men, and to do that he must either rely upon his fellow Saxon kings, or raid. Fifteen hundred warriors eat a lot of food. Look how difficult it is for us to keep one hundred spearmen in food and ale. If we are ever going to recover Lloegyr, we need an army. First, we crush Octha and his roving army, then we push into Bernicia and Deira, then south to drive the rest of the invaders out or into the ground. Octha is desperate now, like a starved bear. What kind of warlord is he if he cannot conquer a kingdom for his men, like Ida, Hengist and Horsa before him? Octha will fight harder than ever. This is his last throw of the knucklebones.'

Arthur sighed and watched the men spit a side of cured beef taken from the Saxon village. They placed it over the campfire next to a smaller flitch of bacon already sizzling over the flames, and the smell of roasting meat made Arthur's mouth water. 'We have chewed over this many times this winter, you and I. With one hundred spears, what can we do but hit, run, hide? That is how we fight the enemy, and though it might seem like we are but bees stinging the hide of a boar, without us, there would be nobody to keep the Saxons in check. I know you crave a war to win back the lands taken from your people. There are but a handful of your Bernicians left amongst us, men who remember when you were a lord, men born on land which once belonged to your people where Ida and his people now rule. But who will fight that war? We need an army of Britons, twenty or thirty times the few brave men in this company. These are but warriors who have sworn to fight for you or I, men who know nothing but war. Most of them came to us fighting in the borders wars, skirmishers and raiders who raid Saxon lands as often as the Saxons raid ours. To fight Ida and return Bernicia to your people, we need an army. It would take three or four thousand men to throw the Saxons back into the narrow sea. To storm their fastnesses and meet them in battle. For that, we need to unite Rheged, Elmet, Powys, Gwynedd, Dumnonia and the rest of the British kingdoms. Only the Pendragon, the high king, can order such an army to muster, and King Uther of Dumnonia will not commit to battle. He and the other kings hide behind their hilltop fastnesses and hope the Saxons don't attack them. They raid, yes, and sent their war band to skirmish on the borders, but they will not commit to war. War takes will, silver and risk. You know all of this, Balin. So we fight with what we have and make a difference where we can.'

Balin took a whetstone and worked out the nick from his sword. The stone scraped along the blade, and Balin eyed it carefully, as though it honed both his thoughts and the edge. 'I know it. Where are my people, anyway? We are too long thrown out of our eastern home. A lost people scattered to the corners of Britain like dandelion seeds in the wind. My country is gone. Land my people tilled and harvested since before the Rome folk came. Uther is old, his days of war and glory are long behind him. If the Pendragon will not muster the kingdoms to march, then what hope do we have?'

Uther was king of Dumnonia, Britain's largest and wealthiest kingdom set in the island's south-western bread basket. Long ago, he had led a combined army of Britons in the Great War against the first Saxon invaders, Hengist and Horsa. Uther was the Pendragon, high king of all the kings of Britain, and none would march without his order. Britain's kingdoms rose from the ashes of the Roman Empire, founded by strong men and Roman auxiliaries in the days when the legions left with their law and the safety provided by their legions. Roman governors, tribunes, legates and centurions left Britain a land where the strong ruled and the weak suffered. The descendants of those warriors who profited in the wake of Rome's departure ruled now as kings, and each was suspicious and warlike towards one another. The kings of neighbouring kingdoms constantly argued over land boundaries, cattle and access to rivers, leading to a never-ending cycle of raiding, feuding and seeking revenge. Each king and warlord kept oathsworn retainers, professional warriors who served their lords in return for rings, silver and the promise of combat to fuel their thirst for reputation. So kings dispatched their men to raid neighbouring kingdoms each summer. They sought horses, livestock, grain, control of fords and access to rivers, tin, salt and anything of value one war band can steal from another.

'There is always hope.' Arthur smiled at his taciturn friend, and Balin shook his head. They had fought beside each other countless times over the last two years, bled together, won together, lost brothers of the sword and shared too many campfires not to know each other's thoughts and dreams. They sat back in companionable silence and waited for the meat to roast. The men japed and jostled each other, some playing at knucklebones, others taking care of their kit. A young warrior stacked spears together, butt ends down, so that they were easily retrievable in an emergency. They stacked shields and spread out cloaks for sleep. Men stretched an old wool sailcloth across the pottery's ruined walls for shelter, and others gathered branches and bracken to make awnings around the ruins. Night drew in with an orange glow on the horizon as the sun waned and the moon waxed.

A sentry came loping from the descending dark, spear in hand

and boots crashing through the brush. Men stood to alert as he approached, reaching for spears or drawing knives.

'Two strangers approach,' said the out-of-breath sentry.

'Are they armed?' asked Dewi.

The sentry shook his head and held up a hand to apologise for his breathlessness. 'I can't tell from this distance, but they come in this direction.'

'From east or west?' asked Arthur.

'From the east, lord.'

'Two strangers cannot subdue one hundred warriors, even if those warriors are callow young men like us.' The men laughed at Arthur's jest. 'Let them approach, but if they wait in the undergrowth or lie in wait for us, seize them and bring them to me.'

'Probably beggars, or worse, priests.' Balin's lips turned in disgust. The Christ faith grew ever more popular amongst the Britons. Most kings allowed a priest in their hall to preach to their people, not because they worshipped the nailed god, but out of fear of his wrath. The religion firmly rooted itself in the southern kingdoms, where wealthy benefactors donated land to priests and bishops who grew fat upon it.

Arthur's black cloaks waited for the strangers to approach camp, and the smoke from their campfire swirled above the old pottery to join the rising crescent moon in the night sky. Arthur and Balin shared cuts of roasted beef and pork, and wooden bowls filled with steaming broth. Men drifted off to sleep, their snoring melding with the clicks and bustling sounds of night animals hiding in the briar and wild grasses.

'Is there food here?' called a voice, as sonorous and clear as a war horn. Arthur sat up and laughed, and Balin looked at him as though he had lost his mind. 'I hope you lazy gluttons haven't eaten it all, sleeping and laying about here in the heather like pigs, with not a care in the world.'

Two figures emerged from the night, both wearing long, hooded black robes. One carried a black staff with a fist-sized lump of polished amber at its top. The amber seemed to glow in the twilight like an egg-shaped drop of sun.

'Merlin,' said Arthur, and he rose to meet the most powerful druid in Britain.

'Ah,' Merlin cried out from the depths of his hood. 'Young Arthur, and Balin of the Two Swords. Two rogues amongst a nest of rogues. Is this what passes for hospitality in your camp? Not an offer of food or drink? No soldier to help carry an old man's bags?'

The young scout scurried toward Merlin and held out his hand to take the satchel slung across the druid's back, but Merlin shooed him away with a click of his tongue and shake of his staff. He pushed back his hood to reveal keen grey eyes in a face creased and weathered with age, though no man knew precisely how old the druid was. Ector, Arthur's foster father, had once said that Merlin was old even when he was a boy. Merlin was bald save for a ring of snow-white hair around his ears, which he wore in a long braid. Faded tattoos covered the old man's scalp, strange symbols, clawing beasts and writhing patterns. His beard was close cropped and beneath his black cloak he wore a long grey tunic. Merlin flashed a quick smile, revealing his astonishingly white teeth.

'Welcome, Lord Merlin,' said Arthur, and bowed his head in respect. The warriors rose to their feet and did the same, a hush falling upon them, broken only by the crackle and hiss of what remained of the meat roasting over the campfire.

'Enough of that,' said Merlin. He turned to the young scout. 'Fetch me a plate of meat and some ale before I turn you into a maggot.' The boy ran to the fire so fast that he fell twice, and the warriors laughed at his nervous fear.

'I thought you would have more men,' said the second stranger in a familiar, heavily accented woman's voice.

'Lady Nimue,' said Arthur, offering the same respect as Merlin.

'I am no lady. The night draws in, and soon the fetches, trolls and wood faeries will come to rust your blades and steal your hair for their spells.' Nimue threw back her hood, and the warriors turned away in fear of her terrible appearance. Even Balin straightened his shoulders as he gazed upon her full-lipped, sharp-eyed face. Nimue had wide hips, and might be beautiful, but for the black ash she wore smeared across the top half of her face so that her eyes were like dark, powerful pits. She covered the bottom half of her face with white paste, so that she looked like a demon of Annwn, and men feared her power. Nimue wore a necklace heavy with iron and stone charms fashioned into crude hammers, phalluses, spears and fish. 'We have news, and you must tell us what you saw this last year in the borderlands, for it was summer when last met.'

Arthur gestured for Nimue and Merlin to sit upon a cloak. Her use of the word 'we' had not gone unnoticed. Nimue had grown in stature and power since Arthur and Balin had captured her two summers ago. Back then she had been a *gwyllion*, a witch who marched with the Saxons, and now she was stuck to Merlin like a limpet. Nimue travelled the length of Britain with Merlin, enjoying the hospitality of kings and lords in every kingdom as was the right of a druid: the holy men, healers and wise men of the old gods who had neither church nor lands. Arthur left Balin in charge of Merlin and Nimue while he made sure that food and ale were brought. He also instructed two men to bring a burning faggot and start a smaller fire for him, Balin and the new arrivals to sit around as they talked.

'Make sure you bring some of the good ale for Merlin,' Arthur said, leaning in to whisper to Dewi. 'You know how he can be.'

Dewi smiled nervously and went to get the good ale the war

band kept for special occasions. They carried their supplies of ale, food, spare spears and shields in a horse-drawn wain.

'That's really Merlin?' asked the young scout, sidling over to Arthur and wringing his hands. He peered over Arthur's shoulder, half hiding and half peeking at the strange figures of Merlin and Nimue.

'That's him. One of the last true remaining men of his kind.'

'Does he really know magic?'

'I don't know, but I wouldn't try him if I were you.'

'No, lord. Is it true what they say, though? That he can turn a man into a toad and make potions to make a woman fall in love?'

'Perhaps. But hurry with that fire before he gets a chill. Or you might find yourself changed into a piglet.'

The scout gulped. 'And the woman is the *gwyllion*, Merlin's witch?'

'That's right, lad. She is Irish. Captured as a girl by Saxon pirates and raised as one of their own. Her Irish name is Nimue, and the Saxons call her Vivien. Raised in the secrets and old knowledge deep within Ireland's mountains and black pools. Irish druids taught her the secrets of their dark mountains, of dwarven smiths and elfish magic. The Saxons realised her power, and they taught Nimue the ways of their gods, of Woden, Thunor and the rest. She hears our gods and the Saxon gods in the trees, flames and rivers. Nimue listens to their commands. She can augur the fate of battle in the guts of a goat or the blood of a raven. She can speak Saxon, Irish, Roman Latin and our own tongue. Nimue knows the nine spells of Woden, of Manawydan, Maponos, Arawn, and has visited Annwn in a dream state, or so men say. Be careful around her, for she has power beyond the reckoning of simple warriors like you and I.'

Arthur winked at the scout and he busied himself with the fire. The lad's name was Becan, and he was one of so many boys orphaned by the Saxon wars. Lads Arthur found on his marches across the borderlands, families dead, nowhere to go and with nothing but hearts full of hate and vengeance. Becan was perhaps fourteen summers old, and a bright lad. He used the faggot to light a small blaze within a rough circle of rocks, and Merlin warmed his thin fingers before the dancing flames.

'Look at me, boy,' said Nimue, and Becan swallowed hard as he met her implacable gaze. She smiled, revealing the precious stones set into her teeth. 'I see strength in you, though you are yet young. You have a stout heart.' Nimue reached forward and Becan shrank back. Nimue laughed cruelly. She reached beneath his jerkin and flicked out a wooden cross. 'Ah, a worshipper of the nailed god. He will not help you in the wars to come, boy. It is to our gods you should look, wear their tokens at your breast. They are of the soil and the sky, the rivers and trees of the land we walk, sleep, and die upon. Here.' Nimue reached into a pouch at her belt and drew forth a small iron harp. 'This is the symbol of Maponos. He will protect your young soul and help you in battle. What will your Christ do when the Saxons come to kill you?'

'The Lord Jesus will show me the way to heaven...'

'Ha! Then you will already be dead. What use is a god who cannot protect his people? You are an orphan of this war, no? Did he protect you then? Serve Maponos, boy, as you serve Arthur here. Arthur is beloved of the gods. How else could he have achieved all that he has? He wields Excalibur and is the only Briton to defeat the invaders since Ambrosius during the Great War. Believe in our gods like you believe in Arthur. Maponos will protect you; wear his token and you shall also have my protection. Give me your hand.'

Becan hesitated and glanced at Arthur, and he inclined his head to show the boy that Nimue would not hurt him. Becan gave her his shaking hand, and she snatched it, yanking him towards her. Nimue spat in his open palm and clapped her own hand over it. She mumbled in words too low to hear or understand, and then let Becan go. He scrambled away and opened his hand to find the little harp there.

'Remember the gods, boy. You will need their help in the war to come.'

'Go, Becan,' Arthur said. 'That's enough of the gods for tonight.'

Becan hurried away and Arthur felt Nimue's fierce eyes upon him. He avoided her stare and took instead a mouthful of hot beef. She would be exultant at turning a Christian soul to the old gods, but her talk of Arthur as beloved of the gods irked him. He had not felt their presence when Ector died, nor when he had lost so many men rescuing Princess Guinevere from Dun Guaroy's formidable crag. Men already looked at Excalibur as though they expected it to crackle thunder at the enemy or split the ground in two whenever Arthur drew its blade.

'What news of the kingdoms?' asked Balin, sensing the awkwardness between Nimue and Arthur.

'We came from the east,' Nimue said, leaning forward so that the firelight twinkled on her stone-set teeth, 'and found your trail in the mountains. The Saxons march. War is upon us, red war. Octha leads fifteen hundred warriors towards Elmet. Your brother is with them, Balin of the Two Swords. Dread Balan, who joined with Vortigern to betray our people. Your own brother who slew your wife and children.'

3

Nimue's dark tidings hit Arthur like a gut-punch. He, Nimue, Merlin and Balin talked long into the night, sat around a crackling fire, feeding the flames with fresh branches just as the Saxons fed the flames of war with their bellicose ambition. Warriors slept in the ruins, snoring and complaining as fellows woke one another to change the watch. Merlin spoke at length of how he and Nimue had spent a year travelling the kingdoms of Britain, seeking support from the kings and warlords for the fight which must come.

'Too many of our kings are old and withered,' Merlin said with a sour twist of his mouth. 'I know not why they linger in this world, clinging to life like limpets. Most of them should have gone to their barrows long ago with younger, fiercer men now sat upon their thrones. Uther, Urien, Gwallog, Letan of Gododdin, Brochvael of Powys, Cadwallon of Gwynedd. Old men who would rather laze beside their hearth fires, tickling slave girls, than march to war. Uther convinces himself that the Saxons will never reach Dumnonia, that they are satisfied squatting on our south-eastern coast far from his stronghold at Durnovaria. He grows foolish in his old age. The Saxons eye his kingdom like slathering wolves, waiting for the right time to strike into Dumnonia's fertile fields. Uther's sons are dead, and he leaves no heir. He has taken a new wife, a pretty, young thing he hopes to whelp a prince upon. Even if he can summon his loins to perform one last time, the child will surely be but a babe when he dies. It will need a steward, a protector, a king in all but name to rule the kingdom until he comes of age. There will be war between Dumnonia's lords when the old boar finally breathes his last. I tried to speak to him of the succession, but all Uther would say was that the strongest will succeed him. Whatever that nonsense means to him, it means nothing but war to me. A war between Dumnonians, a war to win a throne, when our spearmen should march east. Letan is too busy keeping Gododdin's borders safe from Ida's raiders. And like Uther, Brochvael and Cadwallon are too far from the Saxons to feel the heat of their wrath.'

'If the other kingdoms will not fight, Elmet stands alone?' asked Arthur.

'Not alone. You will march to their aid. Nimue and I have sowed the seeds of war across Britain. The kings won't hear of it, but the warriors and churls do, for it is truly they who will feel the wrath of the Saxons when the blades, fire and slaughter come from the east. A legend spreads across Britain, a flicker of hope in a man who wields an ancient sword, who defeated Ida at the river Glein and rescued a princess from a hilltop fortress. We have prepared the way for you to raise an army, even though the kings will not rouse themselves to fight. We cannot lose another kingdom. Not whilst I yet live, and not whilst you wield Excalibur.'

'You and Nimue?' asked Balin, not bothering to conceal the surprise in his voice.

'Yes,' Merlin said, pinching his eyebrows together as though Balin's comment were foolish. 'There are few left with the knowledge we possess. The lore of our land, the understanding of our plants and poisons, the memory of each kingdom's lineage, of how Britain came to be and how the gods created the very soil we sit upon. She has the knowledge of Ireland, and of the Saxons, and that, combined with my own learnings, makes us formidable.'

Nimue's hand brushed Merlin's, and the druid smiled at her. *They are in love*, Arthur realised. He wasn't sure if he should welcome or fear that revelation. Nimue was much younger than Merlin, and she possessed an unmatched fervour and energy. Merlin held power in the influence he had over churls, warriors and kings alike, perhaps greater power than any king. So it was obvious why any woman would be attracted to it. A druid could demand hospitality and succour from any king in Britain. Attacking a druid was forbidden, and doing so would not only anger the gods but also the warriors of Britain.

'How can we raise an army if the kings won't march?' asked Balin. He tossed the remnants of his food into the bushes and didn't bother to hide his frustration at the conversation. 'Rousing warriors behind the backs of kings is a good way to get yourselves killed. Druid or not, there are ways to kill a man without taking the blame. A knife in a dark forest, an old man strangled in his bed, poison in a horn of mead.' He pointed at Nimue. 'You, I think, seek to turn men's hearts away from the nailed god and banish that worship from our lands. I remember when we found you, marching with the Saxons, hair spiked up with mud like a wild woman. Now, you travel at Merlin's side as though you were his equal.'

'Mind your tongue,' hissed Merlin.

Balin waved a frustrated hand. 'I was also there when you gave the sword to Arthur. He did not draw it from a stone, as I have heard men tell. Nor was it placed in that stone by the gods, or a lake spirit, which I have also heard men say. You carried it in a sack and handed the blade to Arthur beside Dun Guaroy's crag. The men who join our ranks come with heads full of stories of Arthur, of magic swords, and a man who is already becoming a legend. We lose many men to Saxon blades, and we need the fresh spearmen your tales bring to our cause, so I do not tell them the truth of things. But who created those legends? Who could spread these stories across the land but folk who wander the realms, filling men's heads with god-favoured warriors and a war between our gods, the nailed god and the Saxon gods?'

Balin didn't wait to hear Merlin's answer. He rose sharply and went to join the men in the old pottery.

'Balin is too twisted by his longing for vengeance to see the warp and weft of what lies before us. But he is right about one thing. Word spreads,' Merlin said, leaning towards Arthur with a glint in his eye. 'The flame kindles. Bards and scops talk of Excalibur, and both men and boys listen beside their hearths of how Britain awakens to fight the hated invader. The old kings cannot live forever. Elmet will be the next kingdom to fall if we cannot muster an army from across Britain. It is the only way. And they will come, Arthur. Warriors will flock to your banner if they believe we can win.'

'They came to us at the river Glein because Uther ordered it,' Arthur said. 'Why do we not press the Pendragon harder? If he commands it, the kingdoms will march. They must. Or another king must challenge Uther and become Pendragon. Persuade Uther to march. Use your druidic power, your spells and tricks to convince him. That surely is simpler and quicker than filling the land with stories and legends?'

Merlin stared into the flames, his face slackening. 'I used my power once before, for Uther and Igraine. It cannot be so again.' His mouth moved silently, flames dancing in the dark of his eyes as his mind pored over those old memories of the Great War. Of

Igraine, Gorlois and how Merlin's conniving and Uther's lust shattered the last alliance. Nimue squeezed Merlin's hand, and he snapped from his trance. 'I know Uther of old. He is a cunning man, but a jealous one. He is already wary of you, Arthur. As your power grows, so does his suspicion of you. You are a man without land or title, a warrior with a hundred spears at his back. Uther is a king without a son, and he can feel support for you growing.'

'He won't fight because he fears I will usurp him?' This was something new. Something Arthur had not considered. Perhaps he was a threat to the kingdoms, he supposed. A warlord commanding one hundred spearmen, a man of no nation, becoming more powerful with each victory. He imagined the old kings slumped upon their thrones swathed in heavy cloaks and furrowed brows, listening to tales of Arthur's legend, suspicion festering, hate growing, fear setting in. How long before Arthur fancied himself a throne of his own? Arthur had no desire to rule, nor to sit upon another man's throne. All he desired was to find Lunete, aid Balin's quest for vengeance against his brother and fight the Saxons. Beyond that, there was nothing. But in a dark corner of Arthur's thought cage, another desire menaced. The lust for war, the joy of battle, the thrill of combat. There was nothing to compare to it. When blades clashed and men danced on the precipice between life and death, a heightened sense of being descended and Arthur yearned for it more than glory, silver or reputation. It was a thing unspoken, hidden like a caged beast in the depths of his soul. The recognition of it in that moment made Arthur stiffen, a guilty thought, and he shook it off, burying it deep within.

'Uther's men came back from the battle at the Glein full of stories of Arthur and Excalibur. All kings fear young men with reputations. But his warriors grow fervent with tales of your glory.

All we need is a spark to light that kindling, and they will flock to your banner like sheep.'

'But to do that, I must go against the Pendragon?'

'They are leaving the nailed god in droves,' said Nimue. 'Soon, our land will be as it once was. A place devoted to the old gods, and the more souls we bring back to Maponos, Neit, Arawn, Manawydan, Gwydion and Lleu Llaw, the stronger we shall be. Once our gods grow strong again, the Saxon gods will tremble and fall before them. That is how we win this war. Elmet is a kingdom devoted to the nailed god, and that will be its ruin. But we can change that, restore the old faith. The gods will grant us victory if we can but bring souls to their worship.'

'Spears and shields will win the war. And I will not go against any king. I need their help, not their enmity. Our kingdoms are fractured enough without your god-fervour setting them against me and each other. We march for Elmet in the morning. Help us by filling my men's hearts with courage and looking for a way to help King Gwallog throw the invaders from his borders. If we try to turn Gwallog away from Christ, it could go ill for us. We march to defend Elmet, not to fill Gwallog's warriors' heads with Maponos and Arawn.'

'They are one and the same thing, young warrior. Your destiny awaits you, Arthur ap Nowhere, whether you like it or not.'

Arthur knuckled at tired eyes and swallowed his rising anger. Merlin sought redemption for all that had gone wrong during the Great War, for how he had hurt Igraine, Uther, Gorlois, and how his meddling had destroyed the old alliance of Britain. Because of that, the Saxons grew stronger. A druid's duty was to protect Britain and its people, and Merlin was Britain's greatest druid. He would do anything to right those wrongs, and Arthur found himself at the centre of that maelstrom. He needed Merlin because the druid was right. So much of what Arthur had become depended on Excalibur's power and Merlin's support. How else could a warrior of no kingdom command one hundred spears? He wanted to tell Merlin he knew the truth about his birth. Ector had told Arthur the tale before he died, of how Merlin had brought a child of Igraine and Uther into the world and placed the babe in Ector's care to raise in secret. A son of Uther, an heir to Dumnonia's throne. That baby had died, and Merlin gave another baby to Ector in its place. That babe of no known parents was Arthur. Arthur held that knowledge deep inside of him, a secret best left beneath the surface, like an animal sleeping in winter. Part of him wanted to tell Merlin he knew and to ask who his actual mother and father were. Was he the child of slaves? The son of a blacksmith, woodsman, thatcher or warrior? The other part did not want to know at all. Perhaps it was a thing better left unknown. Let the druid work his deep cunning. That had seen Arthur rise from nothing to a man others called lord. He glanced at Merlin and Nimue, who were staring deep into each other's eyes. *They yearn for this war*, he thought, *they need it. Merlin for his redemption, and Nimue for her obsession with the gods who give her power.* How long before Merlin spread word that Arthur was Uther and Igraine's son, irrespective of the truth? Arthur realised his fingers toyed with the bronze disc at his neck, a gift from Queen Igraine on her deathbed. Tragic Queen Igraine, sent to marry Urien, the brutal king in his coarse, stark Bear Fort, to atone for her forbidden love of Uther Pendragon. So many had suffered because of Vortigern's treachery, and the plans and ploys of Merlin.

'It's time for sleep,' Arthur said, and left them to their deep cunning and their love. Arthur covered himself with his cloak and a heavy wool blanket. He stared at the stars and wondered how Elmet would survive Octha's onslaught. One and a half thousand warriors would soon swarm into Elmet's farms and villages, savage Saxons with axes and malice. They would burn, steal, rape and murder. So many warriors, too many warriors. He wondered where Lunete was, and if she was suffering. Then he thought of Guinevere, the princess of Cameliard. He closed his eyes and tried to remember her copper hair and eyes the green of a summer sea.

The black cloaks woke early the next morning. They grumbled and yawned, stretched and coughed as they rolled up their woollen sailcloth and gathered their belongings. Arthur and Balin took a breakfast of leftover meat washed down with a mouthful of ale. Arthur rubbed Llamrei down and gave him a sack of oats to eat before pulling on his heavy chain-mail and sword. He found Merlin and Nimue stood before the Roman pottery ruin preaching to Arthur's men, and the warriors gawped at the druid with wide eyes and slack jaws.

'More tales of the sword and the legend of Arthur,' said Balin, tying back his greying hair with a strip of leather at the nape of his neck.

Arthur shrugged his shoulders. Choosing to ignore it rather than let himself become rankled with tales of his own adventures. 'Your brother Balan marches. We shall seek him out. Find him in battle.'

'Aye. Let us hope he is there, and not skulking in the south with his Saxon overlords. He raped my wife and killed my children. My own brother. He must die, and I would drench the land in blood to do it.'

'To Elmet, then.'

Elmet stretched from the southern borders of Rheged, along the mountainous backbone of northern Britain and down into the flatter, rolling midlands. It took two weeks to cross the highlands and come around Elmet from the west, when it should have taken one. Arthur led his men west to avoid running into Saxon scouts and foraging parties, for fear of losing men before the real fight for Elmet had begun. Balin rode ahead to scout the approaches to

Elmet's heartland. At each village the company visited, folk lined the paths to welcome the warriors with bowed heads. The people at hamlets, farmsteads and riverside fishing villages marvelled at the sight of Merlin and Nimue. Nimue delivered two babies during the march and cured a horse with a lame foot. Merlin expelled a demon from an unruly child, pulled teeth, and preached at every village of the gods and their war with the Saxon deities for control of the heavens and the souls of Britain. Boys looked upon Excalibur with awe and fell to their knees whenever Arthur drew the blade to show people the dragon smoke forged into its bright blade. The stories of his legend made Arthur uncomfortable, for there was no magic that he could see. Just a sword, luck and hard fighting. But legend has its uses.

4

Arthur gained a dozen warriors on the road. Lads who fled from their homes and villages in the night to swell Arthur's ranks and follow Merlin's dream of glorious combat. Arthur avoided those gatherings, where Merlin talked in his sonorous voice, which carried across pastures, cattle byres, barns, meadows, enrapturing simple folk with his tales of gods and heroes. His druidic reverence and water-smooth words caught fire in the hearts of young men who could not expect to travel further in their lives than a day's walk from their village. Nimue stalked amongst them, whispering her tales of war between the gods, and after every such gathering, small crosses on leather thongs lay cast aside in the mud, replaced by iron symbols of Britain's old gods she had pressed into their unresisting palms.

On an afternoon where morning rain left the fields damp and where cows huddled together in pastures, Arthur stood with his warriors in the shield wall. Merlin preached to a flock of eager churls beside a fast-flowing river, and Arthur waited for Balin and his scouts' return before deciding upon which direction to march. So, stripped to the waist, he stood with a heavy Saxon shield in his left hand and a spear in his right. They practised the shield-wall techniques Arthur had learned fighting Saxons. The brutal Saxon method of shield-wall fighting which had crushed Britain's armies for a generation, and which Arthur had adopted, drilling his men daily so that it was as familiar to them as grinding grain. Each black cloak carried a large Saxon shield, rather than the smaller shields favoured by the Britons. A Saxon shield protected a man from neck to knee, and in combat Arthur's warriors locked their shields together, overlapping iron rims, each protecting his neighbour as he struck with spear, axe, seax or sword. Men lay their ash-shafted spears upon the shields' edges to punch into enemy faces and necks left exposed by the front rankers who dragged down their shields with axes. Arthur's men practised how to advance in formation, how to wheel, to withdraw sections of the shield wall so an enemy pressing against them would stumble into their blades.

'Advance!' Arthur ordered, and his men took five paces forward. Each man's left foot moved in time, and they grunted together at each right-footed step to keep time. 'Hold.' The men stopped, iron rims clattering together as they stiffened the wall of linden wood. 'Spears.' Arthur laid his own spear across the rim of his shield, and twenty more along the front rank followed. The second rankers passed their spears over the front rankers' shoulders and the third ranks and beyond readied their spears. If a front ranker lost his spear, a rear ranker would pass his forward. Likewise, if a front ranker fell in battle, a man from behind would take his place. Driving forward into the enemy, relentless and mercilessly stabbing, hacking, killing.

Arthur turned to Dewi and gave a nod for the captain to take command.

'Feign retreat on me,' Dewi ordered. Every man in the shield wall turned and ran as though they fled for their lives. 'Shield wall!' he bellowed, and the warriors instantly halted, turned on their heels and remade the wall as solid and threatening as ever.

'Gets 'em every time,' said a warrior along the line. Enemy warriors would see the Britons flee, and believing their spirit broken, would abandon battle order and pursue them. Few men died in the shield wall clash. It was a shoving match where blades slid between shields, men packed as close as bedfellows, too close to swing sword or axe. But when one line broke, when the frightened men broke and one side fled the field, the slaughter began. Saxons would pursue the backs of Arthur's retreating men with wild abandon, maddened with the chance of massacre, and then Arthur's men would reform and crush the surprised enemy with heavy shields and sharp spear blades. Too often, armies of Britons had fallen to the Saxon shield wall. So Arthur worked relentlessly to match the invaders' superior tactics.

'That's enough for now,' said Arthur, sweat dripping from his brow. 'Rest, eat, and then prepare to march.'

The men cheered and clapped one another on the back, running to seek ale or water. Arthur let his shield drop and handed his spear to Becan.

'I might win my first death ring this summer,' said the lad, smiling at Arthur's bare forearms, so tattooed with warrior rings they were almost entirely blue.

'One for every man you kill in battle,' said a burly warrior with a grizzled beard. 'I put two on Lord Arthur myself. Now he has so many he doesn't bother any more.'

Arthur left them to their talk of death rings. It reminded him of Kai, his childhood friend. All Kai had ever wanted was to be a warrior and earn his death rings. But there were enough Saxons to kill to cover every warrior in England's arms from wrist to shoulder, and the tattoos had lost their lustre for Arthur. They were just another memory of the friends and loved ones he had lost. Of

Ector and Lunete. The sound of hooves thudding on the meadow caused a commotion amongst the men, and they parted to let Balin of the Two Swords ride towards Arthur.

'What news?' asked Arthur.

Balin slid from the horse's back and patted her neck. 'Saxons to the east, as thick as flies on a corpse,' he said. 'They march towards Loidis, broken up into small war bands as they advance.'

'Can we approach from the north?'

'If we march today, we can be in Loidis before dark tomorrow.'

Just as Balin had predicted, Arthur and his black cloaks reached Elmet and King Gwallog's stronghold at Loidis on the evening of the following day. King Gwallog's hill fortress sat within ancient Roman walls. Crumbled but repaired over the years since the empire's departure with stone taken from other decaying Roman buildings so that the entire town was ringed by stone walls an arm's length higher than a man is tall. Newer wattle and thatch buildings mixed with the Roman constructions. The Britons had forgotten how to move and carve such monstrous blocks of heavy rock, if the Romans had ever imparted that wizardry to the people of Britain, so dirty brown wood and thatch replaced gloriously white stone, granite and marble.

Two warriors came from the gates to meet Arthur's war band. Each warrior wore a red cloak faded to light pink by weather and use, and the segmented cuirasses of the Roman legions above iron-studded leather kilts. The evening was balmy, and they sweated beneath shining Roman-style helmets with an iron peak at their top. They carried heavy oblong shields bearing the Christian cross, wore short swords on their right hips and carried Roman-style pilum spears with long, thin ash shafts topped by a matching length of iron. Hywel and his men of Elmet hid their Roman gear beneath their black cloaks, for they had left Elmet long ago for reasons they had not shared, and Arthur had not asked.

'Welcome to Loidis, Lord Arthur,' said one of the Elmet warriors with a grin. He carried a scar upon his forehead, above a long nose and wide mouth. Arthur was surprised to be recognised without introduction, but Balin of the Two Swords was a man of reputation, and Arthur supposed his black cloaks were fair famed enough to the men of Elmet.

'Lord Merlin,' the second guard said in a surprised voice. He bowed low, as did the first guard.

'We shall require food, ale and somewhere comfortable to sleep tonight,' said Merlin in his usual haughty tone. 'Is Gwallog here?'

'The king is in his hall, Lord Merlin, preparing for war.'

'And Idnerth?'

'The Primus Pilum is here as well.'

Merlin sighed dramatically at the use of Idnerth's official title as first spear, or commander of King Gwallog's legionaries. 'You men of Elmet and your fondness for the Romans. They are gone, young man. Departed our shores in your grandfather's father's time, and yet you cling on to their ways like children. They conquered us, and they left us.'

'King Gwallog's grandfather—' started the scar-faced warrior until Merlin raised a long finger to halt him.

'If you are about to tell me that Gwallog's grandfather wore the purple, I shall have the ground swallow us all up and cast us into Annwn.'

'Perhaps if you brought us to the king, we could move along?' said Arthur, rescuing the young warrior from Merlin's ire.

'Yes, lord, of course. Your men can camp outside the city gates and we will bring them food and drink.'

Arthur thanked him, and Dewi led the bulk of Arthur's company to make camp outside Loidis' stone walls. Arthur followed the Elmet warriors through the tall gate. Balin, Merlin and Nimue followed as they made their way through cobbled streets and tall buildings, some built by the Romans themselves, and others crudely fashioned from the rubble of their fallen grandeur. Timber and thatch propped up and supplemented what had fallen under the weight of time. Straight dressed stone joined with roughly hewn oak and pine posts and roof lintels, and buildings once topped with ceramic tiles now held sodden thatch or crudely cut wooden tiles, which rotted and leaked water into the ancient buildings.

Gwallog's hall was a huge Roman building, its stone rising three times the height of a man, each slab cut perfectly straight and laid one on top of the other. No man knew how they had cut such heavy stone, where they had quarried it, how they had moved the impossibly heavy blocks and eventually laid them atop one another. The building was as cold as a cave, and iron braziers warmed the entrance where two tall soldiers in Roman armour stood guard. More braziers lit and warmed the interior, and voices echoed around the high stone ceiling. A soldier bade Arthur and his company wait beyond a set of heavy doors, beyond which men shouted and argued. The soldier slipped inside the doors, and the arguing stopped abruptly. The door creaked open wider, and Idnerth appeared. He was broad shouldered and tall, with a long, clean-shaven face and short, close-cropped hair. He wore the *lorica segmentata* of the legions and a red cloak pinned at his shoulders.

'Arthur, welcome,' Idnerth said, and took Arthur's forearm in the warrior's grip. He greeted Balin warmly and bowed his head in reverence to Merlin and Nimue. 'We are in war council, but King Gwallog bids you enter.'

Arthur followed Idnerth through the heavy doors and into a wide chamber lit by more braziers. Four men stood around a long table, upon which lay Idnerth's helmet with its red bristling horsehair crest, a jug and five cups.

'King Gwallog,' said Idnerth, looking at a wiry, bald man who stood at the head of the table. 'May I present Lord Arthur and Balin of the Two Swords? You already know Lord Merlin and Lady Nimue, of course.'

'I have heard of you, Arthur,' said Gwallog, his voice slow and drawling. White hair grew from his ears in clumps and his eyebrows were as pale and wild as heather. 'And of you, Lord Balin. Merlin, the moon has not waxed since your last visit. We talked of war when last you came before me, and now Saxons descend upon my land like ravenous wolves.' The king gestured to a thin young man clad in Roman armour, the heavy iron-plated cuirass hanging from his bony frame like it belonged to a much bigger man. 'This is my son, Ceretic.'

'I thank you, King Gwallog, for the men you sent to the river Glein. They fought bravely and we could have not won without them. Prince Ceretic, I am honoured to meet you,' said Arthur.

'Aye, well. That was a battle for Gododdin's survival. Where are the Gododdin men now that my kingdom is under attack?'

'Have you sent riders north to Gododdin?'

'We did. Three days past. Let us hope that King Letan is as generous with his spearman as I was in his hour of need.'

'Men will come,' said Merlin, striding forwards. He reached for the jug on the table and tipped it forwards so he could peek inside. He sniffed and curled his lip. 'Wine! Your coffers must be full of silver if you can afford to ship such luxury across the narrow sea.'

'My coffers are thin enough, Merlin. Though what business that is of yours I do not know.' Gwallog stiffened and adjusted the white cloth robe he wore wrapped about him, hanging over one arm like a too-long cloak. Purple patterns trimmed the cloth's edges, and Gwallog wore a silver cross at his breast, hanging upon a fine silver chain.

'I have brought Arthur, Balin, and their hundred black cloaks,

Gwallog, and I am a druid. If I want to discuss the contents of your treasure hoard, I will do so. I hear that Octha and fifteen hundred Saxons muster on your borders. You have sent word to King Letan. That is good. We must also go to the other kings. To Uther. Have you sent more riders?'

'Not yet.' Gwallog frowned at Merlin. 'We have set our kingdom to prayer and have roused the men of Elmet to bring spears and shields.'

'Your nailed god will not help you in this fight,' said Nimue, the corners of her mouth drooping in contempt.

'How many men can you march to war, lord king?' asked Arthur, ignoring Nimue's spite.

'Idnerth commands three hundred legionaries, and we can muster another thousand warriors.'

'The thousand are farmers, potters, smiths, weavers and herdsman,' said Balin, and Gwallog fixed him with an icy stare.

'The men of Elmet are made of stern stuff, Lord Balin. We have withstood Saxon attacks before and my kingdom yet stands.'

'Where are the Saxons now?' asked Arthur quickly, before Balin had time to take offence at the king's barbed response. Bernicia was one of the first kingdoms to fall to the Saxons, and Balin did not need reminding of it, nor would he take kindly to the subtle inference that his people fought less stoutly in defence of their lost kingdom than the men of Elmet.

'They mass on our western borders, marching in war bands. Attacking farms and villages to keep themselves supplied and come slowly, burning and destroying. They are perhaps four days away,' said Idnerth. 'Our army is already mustering, and we should be able to field a thousand men, including my legionaries, by the time Octha reaches Loidis.'

'You would let Octha attack here?' asked Arthur incredulously. 'He will be halfway across Elmet by then.'

'Mustering men is no simple matter,' said Gwallog. 'You are but young and have no lands. Do not presume to tell me how to defend my own kingdom. How long do you think it takes to send riders to every corner of Elmet and summon men to war? Men have fields to till, flocks to move to higher pastures. Should I send Idnerth and his warriors to die so that we can keep Octha away from Loidis? Let him come. We can defend these walls for weeks whilst his warriors throw away their lives trying to assault Roman stone.'

'I will take to the field then, lord king. My men at least can harry Octha and slow his advance.'

Gwallog sighed and kneaded his furrowed brow. 'I spoke hastily, young commander. I thank you for bringing your warriors to Elmet. Yes, harry them, keep them back from our walls as long as you can whilst we muster our defences. Every day, more of my people arrive at Loidis, each with their own tale of horror, rape and slaughter. Mothers wailing inconsolably at the enslavement of their daughters, fathers bereft of sons and wives. My commanders and I talk of nothing but war. We must make the hard decisions. Our hearts bid us march whatever warriors we can muster this very day and meet the enemy in our fields. I long to drive my spear into the hearts of our enemies and ride to war as you do. But I am king, and my duty is to my kingdom and my people. Running headlong into battle is not always the right decision. We must plan, prepare, set our minds to be more cunning than our enemies. If Loidis falls, then so does Elmet. If I march before I have enough warriors to defeat Octha, then I fall and leave Loidis unprotected. The hard choice, but the necessary decision, is to watch my people arrive at my gates, with tears and blood staining their faces, and still hold fast. These are dark times we find ourselves in. Everything is at stake if we lose. This is no game, no summer cattle raid. We fight for our very survival. The Saxons threaten us with slavery and death. If I make the wrong decision, all my people will suffer. They look to me to lead and do what must be done.'

'Dark times indeed,' said Merlin. 'Nimue and I shall go to Urien of Rheged and Cadwallon Longhand of Gwynedd in search of warriors. Send a rider to Uther. Let the Pendragon know the Saxons attack.'

'Uther?' Gwallog spat. 'He will not stir himself for Elmet, nor for any other kingdom. All he craves is wine and women, and that has always been his weakness. As well you know, Merlin. He sent men to the river Glein, but a mere token force, not the full strength of Dumnonia. Uther rules the largest and wealthiest of our kingdoms and yet his warriors are untested and unmolested by the Saxons.'

'The gods will save you, not the Pendragon,' said Nimue. She stalked around the hall, hissing at the crosses Gwallog and his men wore. The warriors shrank away from her jewel-encrusted teeth and fiercely painted face. 'Look to the old gods, and they shall reward your devotion with strength. Look at your god, bleeding and weeping upon his cross. A weakling. A god for the meek, for those who see suffering as the pathway to the afterlife. Our gods are gods of war, of power. They are the thunder, the mighty sea and the howling wind. The Saxons worship terrible gods, one-eyed gods of battle and death who demand war and blood. How can your weeping god stand up to the horror of the Saxons?'

'We are God's people here. I tolerate Merlin because he is a druid, and ancient law demands it. But what are you, *gwyllion*, but a witch who would spread your pagan filth amongst my people and damn their souls to hell? Do not talk so of the Lord Jesus Christ in my presence again, or it will cost you your head. You are no druid, witch, and I abide you only because you are Merlin's plaything.'

'Filth? Plaything?' gasped Nimue, and just as she turned and snarled at the king, Merlin slammed his black staff on the stone floor.

'Enough!' he bellowed, and his voice echoed around the hall. 'I shall leave you dull-witted warriors to talk of marching and defence. I shall try to raise an army.' Merlin turned on his heel, his white cloak billowing behind him as he strode from King Gwallog's hall. Nimue hurried after him, and Gwallog's men exhaled collectively, shoulders relaxing. Nimue had that effect on men. She was fearsome to behold, and her power made them uncomfortable.

'Steward,' Gwallog called over his shoulder. 'Bring wine for Arthur and Balin.' A man hurried from the shadows and offered Arthur and Balin small cups filled with wine the colour of blood.

Arthur sipped at the strong-tasting wine and Idnerth told them of the fighting on Elmet's borders. The Saxons had first sent raiding parties deep into Elmet, striking into the valleys and dales, probing for any sign of armed resistance. Then, war bands came with war dogs, spears and shields, killing and foraging, leaving piles of food and ale for the hundreds of warriors who followed behind them. Idnerth himself had taken two hundred men to push the enemy back, but had become overwhelmed by the sheer number of enemy warriors.

'We cannot afford to lose our warriors,' Idnerth said, 'for we have so few. Two hundred of my legionaries can hold the walls of Loidis. But if we die fighting skirmishes in forests and riverbanks, then it falls to Elmet's farmers to stand against Octha's blood-mad warriors. So we must pick our time to fight and not commit our finest men until we can land the decisive blow.'

'Keep your legionaries here, Idnerth,' said Arthur. 'Balin and I will take our men to your borders. We shall harry the enemy, destroy their stores of food, make them earn every step they take into Elmet.'

'There are too many. How can you hope to stop so vast a force?'

'They say my brother is with them,' said Balin. 'I shall hunt for him, and we shall kill as many of the enemy as we can. They shall fear our black cloaks and come to know what it means to fight against Britons.'

'Gododdin will come,' Arthur said. 'Merlin will bring warriors, I am sure of it. We just need time, and I will buy us that time. Gather provisions inside your walls, lord king, and we shall join you here when we can fight no more. Then we shall stand together and fight them from your walls, and the Saxons will have to march over our corpses before Elmet falls.'

5

Three days after leaving Loidis, Arthur rode Llamrei through a creaking forest. The stallion picked his way amongst fallen bark and rotting leaf mulch, and Arthur ducked beneath sprawling branches of birch and elm. True to his word to King Gwallog, Arthur hunted the Saxon war bands who crept like a slithering plague across Elmet's borders.

Octha's army came split into small contingents, bands of one hundred warriors, as they swarmed through the forests and valleys, feeding themselves through raids and slaughter. To march fifteen hundred warriors from the heart of Lloegyr into Elmet required an immense amount of food, water and ale. Unless Octha had spent a vast sum of silver and a year gathering a mountain of supplies, his men needed to forage as they went. That meant scouts and foraging parties marching ahead of each war band, seeking farms, villages, places to camp and fresh water. Elmet was not their home. These were hard men from across the narrow sea striding out into an unknown land, where every hillside, river and wood provided both opportunity and challenge.

Arthur and Balin ambled their horses along a brook, its

babbling waters splashing clear over moss-covered rocks. Lush, wild grass grew around shallow banks in a clearing blooming with primrose and violets. Arthur stroked Llamrei's mane and patted his powerful neck. The horse dipped his head and took a drink from the cool water. Arthur wore his mail coat, Excalibur hung from his belt in her red scabbard, and King Ida's sceptre nestled against his hip. Balin slid from the back of his horse and stroked his mare's rump as she also took a long drink. Three magpies flew from the forest to Arthur's east, and Balin watched their black wings beat across the clearing.

'One for sorrow,' Balin said, reciting the old rhyme, 'two for mirth, three for death, and four for a birth.'

'Are they coming?' asked Arthur, trying not to look in the direction from which the magpies had flown, disturbed from their nests by hidden warriors tramping through the undergrowth. Arthur knew they were there, big men clad in fox and wolf fur, axes and spears in their fists and murder in their hearts.

'They are coming.'

Balin smiled up at Arthur, and Arthur almost laughed, even though one hundred Saxons approached from the deep forest, weaving their way through the tangle of ancient woodland. Balin rarely smiled, but the chance to kill Saxons brought a lightness to the grim warrior and his levity took Arthur by surprise. Llamrei whickered and Arthur shushed him, patting the horse's neck again. Balin's horse also became skittish, and Balin stroked its ears to calm the beast. Arthur's black cloaks had tracked the Saxon war band since morning, spying on them from high ground as the enemy advanced into the woodland on Elmet's eastern border. They carried spears and shields, and led donkeys pulling wains filled with grain, cuts of meat, churns of milk and barrels of ale. If the Saxon war band marched a day further west, they would come upon a settlement of small houses set about a sprawling oak tree. Those people grew wheat and barley, paid their tithes to King Gwallog, worshipped the nailed god, and prayed for protection by both. The Saxons would take their lives and their food. They would slaughter the menfolk, rape the women and enslave the children. That was the war Octha brought to King Gwallog's people, and only Arthur and his black cloaks stood in their way. Arthur had come upon three such villages since leaving Loidis, where folk had received word from the king to leave their dwellings and seek safety behind Loidis' high walls, but still they tarried. They worried about their fields, crops, livestock, and how they would feed themselves through winter if they left their farmland untended. But better to be hungry than dead.

'Remember, let them see us before we ride,' Arthur said, allowing his mind to imagine the village aflame and its people screaming and dying.

A rotten branch broke underfoot as the Saxons came close, the crack sending unseen forest animals scurrying for cover in the undergrowth. Arthur and Balin had left their cloaks with the men, so that their mail coats and weapons would shine beneath the golden sun. Arthur's warriors waited in silence, hidden by bough and leaf, by bracken and fern. He and Balin were just two wealthy men watering their horses, alone in a forest. Their armour and weapons would be irresistible to men hungry for wealth and plunder. Octha's warriors were violent men bent on pillage and destruction, emboldened by their numbers and by the promise of war.

The first of them came striding from the trees with axes resting upon their shoulders and hungry looks on their bearded faces. A dozen of them, clad in leather and furs, with naalbinding cloth strips tied around their calves. Some wore helmets and others carried shields. More followed, coughing, sniffing and mumbling as they drifted from the trees towards the brook. Balin jumped lithely onto his mare, wheeling the horse about as her hooves splashed in the water.

Barking erupted behind the Saxons, and Arthur understood why the horses were so skittish. Saxon war dogs. He dug his heels into Llamrei's flanks and turned just as an arrow whipped across the clearing to tear through the air between him and Balin. Six dogs followed the arrow. Monstrous, muscular beasts wearing iron-spiked collars. Arthur rode hard away from the Saxons, urging Llamrei into a gallop. The stallion reared and surged forwards as Balin's mare splashed through the brook. More arrows whistled past Arthur and he clicked his tongue to urge the horse on, bending low, the wind whipping his hair as Llamrei raced away from the enemy.

The Saxons whooped for joy at the prospect of hunting two wealthy lords with gloriously expensive weapons, and Arthur ducked beneath a branch as Llamrei entered the woods. Vengeful black cloaks waited for him there, men who had seen the suffering of common folk too many times. They peered over the rims of their shields, hard eyes set upon the enemy. Dewi handed Arthur his helmet as he climbed off Llamrei, and he pulled it on, quickly fastening the chin strap. Anthun, a stocky warrior with bowlegs and barrel chest, took Llamrei's reins and led the horse away from the front line. Becan handed Arthur a spear, and Balin came thundering through the trees, dogs snapping at his horse's hind legs.

One monstrous war dog leapt and sunk its teeth into the mare's rump and the horse screamed in pain. Balin leapt from her, pulling a sword from his back in one fluid motion. He landed and brought the sword down hard, hacking into the war dog's neck. The beast fell dead and five more of the monsters circled Balin, slathering and baying with their great teeth bared. He backed away, moving towards the safety of the front line, slowly drawing his second sword from across his right shoulder.

Another war dog snarled and leapt at Balin, jumping, jaws open, ready to tear out Balin's throat until a dozen arrows flew from Arthur's men and peppered its muscled body with goose-feathered shafts. The rest of the dogs charged at Arthur's line, more arrows twanged from bowstrings, but the archers aimed too high and the shafts sailed above the running dogs to disappear into the trees. Black cloaks cried out in terror as the dogs tore into them, barking, snarling, jaws rending shields and sinking into flesh. The shield wall sagged as men fell away from the enormous beasts, each one as tall as a man's waist.

'Kill the monsters!' a warrior shouted.

More cries of pain. The dogs whined and shrieked as Arthur's men stabbed them with spears and knives. Two of the beasts peeled away from the battle line. They whimpered and ran about the trees in confusion, limping, hides matted with dark blood. The dogs' ferocious attack had jolted the line, and Dewi barked orders, urging the men back into formation. Four injured warriors shuffled to the rear, their legs savaged by the marauding war dogs. The dogs struck horror into the men. The animals would never be enough to crush a shield wall, but they were terrifying, and Arthur worried what a score of the beasts would do to an advancing shield wall.

'Reform and advance,' Arthur shouted to his men. 'The dogs are gone, before us are just men. They come in ragged formation. Kill as many as you can and take the food carts. Don't follow those who flee. Stop when you hear the carnyx.'

His men clashed spears on shields to show they understood Arthur's command. The carnyx was a war horn. A long, curved bronze tube the size and shape of a spear shaft, topped by a magnificent bronze wolf's head with its mouth agape and snarling.

'No mercy. Strike hard, strike fast. These men are killers, slavers and murderers. These are the Saxons who come to take all we have. On me!'

Arthur strode out of his line of men, and Balin went beside him. The first dozen Saxons came running into the clearing, chasing the sound of their war dogs. Arthur tested the weight of his spear and drew the weapon back. He used his left hand for balance, took three quick steps and hurled the spear with all of his might. The leaf-shaped blade soared through the trees and slammed into a Saxon's chest, hurling the man from his feet to die writhing and choking in the rotten leaf mulch. The charging Saxons paused, stunned to see their comrade dying so brutally. Arthur drew Excalibur and held the sword aloft so his men could see the gleaming blade. He let the war-rage flow through him, embracing it, becoming one with it. Then went to kill the enemy.

The Saxons came on too quickly, too eager for the kill to notice the Britons waiting for them in the dense forest. They believed they chased two warlords into the trees and came howling after their prey. The Saxons raced into the trees, leaping over low branches, axes held in their fists, teeth bared, believing their dogs had brought down the two wealthy riders and that an easy kill and rich mail coats and weapons awaited. By the time the dozen Saxons noticed three ranks of iron-shod shields, held by growling, helmeted Britons, it was too late. Balin killed a man with lethal slashes of his swords, the blades flashing in the half-light beneath the leaf canopy and blood-spattered crimson on dark tree bark. Arthur came from behind a thick trunk with Excalibur levelled and a bushy-bearded Saxon ran onto the blade, and Arthur drove it home. He gaped at Arthur, his breath stinking of garlic, staring down at the sword stuck through his midriff. Arthur yanked the sword free and waited for his warriors to envelop him. Ten more Saxons died quickly, crashing into an implacable line of shields and spears.

Scores of Saxons charged into the fray, rushing to the chase, hurrying to see what had become of their quarry in the forest. They paused, faced with five ranks of Britons marching in step, boots crunching through the undergrowth, spears pointing, a wall of iron and wood, solid and deadly. The Saxons charged into the shield wall with howling ferocity and Arthur's men struck with practised efficiency. Saxons hammered into shields and died as spear points tore out their throats and jabbed at their eyes. They screamed as they fell, and Arthur felt no pity, for every scream reminded him of a slave captured or a family slaughtered. More Saxons burst into the clearing, and Arthur's men kept up the steady march, pushing them back with shield bosses and stabbing with their spears. Two score Saxons fell by the time their leaders called to them to halt and form up, and as they tried to bring shields from their rear, Arthur ordered his men to attack.

The forest filled with the roar of Arthur's black cloaks as they broke ranks and charged at the enemy. Arthur went with them, as did Balin, and they thundered into the Saxons with vengeful fury. Arthur killed two men with sweeps of Excalibur's blade, chaos sweeping the Saxons asunder before they could form themselves into a defensive line. Balin battered into them, his two swords driving into the centre with astonishing skill.

An enormous man with a scarred face and long, greasy hair came at Arthur with an axe in one hand and a seax in the other. Arthur parried an axe blow and swayed away from a vicious seax lunge aimed at his groin. The axeman came on, furiously swinging his axe and seax in savage sweeps, all the time roaring at Arthur, spittle flying from his maw in wild fury. Arthur parried and backed away from the onslaught until the big man tired. When the axe swings lost their strength and the Saxon had spent his power, Arthur struck. He let a tired axe-slash sing past his shoulder and grabbed the hair at the back of the Saxon's skull with his left hand.

He stamped his left foot into the crook of the Saxon's knee, driving him to the ground. The Saxon tried desperately to stab at Arthur with his seax, but he had spent his strength in the wild attack, and Arthur drove Excalibur down into his throat and pierced his murderous heart.

Balin fought beyond the shield wall, whirling his two swords about him, deep amongst the enemy. They shrank back from him, unable to match his skill and ferocity. Balin fought like a man possessed by a demon, pure hate driving him on. He slashed open men's throats, smashed their knees to ruin, driving the point of his sword into their chests and stomachs. These were Saxons, men who had taken everything from Balin. He fought like each man he faced was one who had slaughtered his wife and children, as though every Saxon who raised a weapon against him was a man who lived upon land once owned by Balin and his lost people.

The Saxons retreated before Arthur's shield wall; a bald man with a bulbous nose and bare, muscled arms fought at their centre. He struck at Arthur's shield wall with his axe, roaring at his men to fall back. He was their leader, their captain, and once he was dead, the Saxons would break and flee. Arthur bullied his way through his men, shouldering through their shields and spear points until he came to the front rank. The Saxon leader's axe hammered into a black cloak's shield and the muscled enemy reached over the shield rim and punched the black cloak hard in the face. The Briton shuddered, nose broken and blood sheeting down his face, and the Saxon dragged his axe free and the black cloak tottered forward. Arthur leapt into the space and brought Excalibur up just as the Saxon brought his axe down in the killing stroke. The axe haft struck Excalibur's blade, jarring up Arthur's arm. Arthur grabbed the falling black cloak with his left hand and hauled him back amongst the shield wall and barged his shoulder into the Saxon, driving him backwards.

Battle is a ferocious clash at full force, and Arthur punched Excalibur's hilt into the Saxon's face, but he swayed away from the blow and brought his axe haft up to clatter into Arthur's cheek. The blow thudded against Arthur's helmet and rung his head like a bell. Men jostled him as they fought against the Saxons, shoulders barging him, boots stamping on his feet, war cries filling his ears. Arthur struck out with Excalibur but found only air. A heavy Saxon hand grabbed the neck of his chain-mail and dragged Arthur away from his men. He stumbled, the heat of terror burning his gut. A killing blow came for his neck before Arthur could react, but a black cloak caught it on his shield. The shield rim banged into Arthur's back and he fell to one knee. To fall was to die beneath the crush of blades, shields and boots. So Arthur roared like a beast and grabbed Excalibur in two hands. He slashed it about him, connecting with flesh and bone, and a Saxon cried out in pain. Arthur drove himself to his feet and, just as the muscled Saxon was about to drag his axe blade across Arthur's throat, he plunged Excalibur's point into the man's stomach.

Arthur leant into the blow, driving Excalibur deep. The Saxon jerked on the blade, thrashing to twist away, his eyes clenched closed, teeth gnashing together. Arthur roared at him and took two steps forward, sawing the sword back and forth into the enemy's innards. He stopped and wrenched the blade free with a terrible sucking sound, leaving the Saxon to fall to the mulch screaming at his terrible death-wound.

'Arthur, Arthur, Arthur!' the black cloaks cheered. Just as Arthur had hoped, the Saxons broke into an all-out run at the sight of their dying commander.

'Sound the carnyx,' Arthur ordered, his breath coming in ragged gasps, muscles burning with exhaustion. A burly black cloak lifted the gleaming carnyx so that the wolf's head towered above the warriors. The carnyx blared fearsomely to call the halt, undulating and high-pitched like a metallic beast. Only Balin disobeyed the horn's order. The lord of lost Bernicia chased after the enemy, hacking at their backs with his swords. The fight in the clearing had been short, savage, brutal and bloody. Men fell to their knees in exhaustion, but Balin fought on, driven by his hate-filled need for vengeance. He plunged his sword into the fallen, ran on, brought another man down, and then another.

'Where is Balan?' Balin shouted into the trees after the fleeing Saxons. 'Where is Balan of Bernicia?'

The black cloaks looked away from Balin. They had seen his relentless fury before, but the younger warriors stared at him with horror. Warriors followed a code of honour. It was why the churls and common folk respected the warrior caste. Warriors risked their lives to protect the people. The common folk paid tithes of wheat, barley, meat and cheese to their lords so that great men could keep households of professional warriors. A warrior was above the common man, outranked only by kings and lords. He took an oath to serve his lord and fought to the death for the men in his hearth troop. He should protect the weak and fight with bravery. Hacking at injured men went against that code, but no man would accuse Balin of dishonour. He was a man torn by grief, who struck at the enemy like only a man who hates with utmost intensity can.

'Balan of Bernicia?' Balin growled, kneeling over a fallen Saxon. The man sat against a tree trunk, bleeding from wounds to chest and leg. Balin repeated his question in the Saxon tongue, but the enemy just stared at him with frightened eyes. 'Have you seen Balan of Bernicia?'

The Saxon licked dry lips and nodded.

'Where? Where did you see him?'

'With my lord Octha. He marches with Octha,' the Saxon gasped in his own tongue.

'What does he look like?' Balin grabbed the man by his jerkin and levelled his sword at the man's face.

'Like you.'

'Is he here? Is he close to here?'

'No, lord, he is south of here, with Octha's war band.'

'South where?'

'I do not know. Please, lord. Let me go, I don't know where. I am just a spearman. The headmen don't tell me anything.'

Balin stood and shook his head. He turned to walk away, and then as an afterthought he back swung his sword to cut the injured Saxon's throat open in a deadly slash. Balin caught Arthur's eye and held the gaze for a heartbeat. Arthur looked away. When he had first marched with Ector, his spear father, Arthur had been naïve of the ways of war. He had balked at killing, and was at first shocked by Balin's actions. Though Arthur was still young, he was a man of war and war was cruel. It was an unforgiving slaughter. Prisoners must be fed and cared for, and so Arthur's black cloaks took no prisoners. Balin was who he had to be. He was the face of what Elmet stood to lose. The personification of the Britons' struggle against the Saxons and Arthur would never criticise his friend for wreaking his vengeance amongst the enemy. They sailed their dragon ships to Briton's coast. Death and slaughter their ambition. Saxon brutality made men like Balin and Arthur possible. War had brought them renown and power, and as the dying groaned and slithered in their own entrails Arthur took a moment to temper the joy he felt, the thrill of battle, the exhilaration of one hundred warriors chanting his name.

'South, then,' Arthur said, and Balin nodded. Their job was to harry the Saxons and keep their war bands at bay for as long as possible so that King Gwallog could muster his army and defend his kingdom. Arthur found Dewi amongst the warriors, the captain busy checking dents in his shield's iron boss. 'Take the food carts, strip the enemy of weapons and anything of value. We march away from here soon, heading south.'

'Here's a few of the fur-wearing bastards who won't kill any more Britons.' Dewi grinned.

'Let's hope we have bought enough time for the villagers to flee to Elmet before this war band regroups, or the next one marches this way.'

A whining caught Arthur's attention, and he followed the sound to a fallen, rotting tree trunk. Becan crouched there, stroking one of the surviving Saxon war dogs. Its tongue lolled and its tail wagged as Becan stroked its short, wiry fur. Arthur levelled Excalibur to kill the monster, but the dog stared up at him with big, sad eyes. It whined again and Becan glanced up at Arthur.

'He's hurt, lord,' said Becan, and pointed to a cut on the dog's flank.

Arthur frowned and lowered his sword. The dog slunk over to him and nuzzled Arthur's leg. He bent and scratched his ear, and the dog licked Arthur's hand. He smiled. It was only a dog, twisted and tortured into a killing monster by the Saxons, but still just a dog.

'He likes you,' said Becan, grinning. 'Can we keep him with us?'

'You can bring him along,' Arthur said, 'but he only eats after every man in our company has eaten his fill. If he bites anyone, you will be the one to kill the beast.'

'Yes, lord. What shall we call him?'

Arthur smiled despite himself. He stroked the dog again, and it sat upon Arthur's foot. It had been a day of carnage. Five of Arthur's men were dead and more injured. But they had driven off a Saxon war band, and though those men would surely regroup and continue their advance, it was the best Arthur could do. Steal their food and kill their warriors. The dog calmed him, brought him down from the high of battle.

'Cavall. Like the Rome folk's word for horse. We are in Elmet, the last bastion of the Romans, and the beast is almost as big as a horse.'

Becan smiled at the name, and Arthur left him with the wounded animal. Anthun and Dewi saw to the wounded, and Arthur knelt with the men who rocked and clutched at bleeding limbs, arrow and stab wounds. He held Loka's hand, a dying man whose stomach pulsed dark gouts of blood through his clutching fingers. With his free hand, Loka held Arthur tight, staring at him with fervent eyes. He mouthed something which Arthur could not hear and fat tears rolled down Loka's strained face. The man tensed, rocked his head violently and died. This was the price of war, the cost of meeting the Saxon threat.

The black cloaks buried the dead and loaded the injured into the captured wains, leaving the Saxon dead to stay where they lay. Donkeys brayed as men led the Saxon supply wains away from the clearing. They headed south, in search of Balin's brother and more of Octha's Saxons, for the war between Gwallog and Octha had begun, and Arthur and his band of black cloaks fought to hold back a tide of bloodthirsty Saxons.

6

Arthur and Balin led their black cloaks south and east, away from Loidis. They fought almost daily, skirmishing with Saxon foragers and stragglers, beating back the dozens of war bands pushing east into Elmet's frontier. They traversed the borderlands for seven days, sweeping away the Saxon scouts of Octha's vanguard, pushing them back but never pressing too far eastwards where the hordes of Octha's army mustered for war. To wander too far east was to risk becoming surrounded by the enemy when Arthur's numbers permitted only hit-and-run fights, not full-blown engagements. The captured wains filled with food kept Arthur's men fed, and to elude Saxon scouts they slept in the lee of rocky outcrops, hollows and deep fissures in the landscape. Arthur's own scouts ranged ahead of the marching column. They returned regularly to report of increasing numbers of Saxon warriors loose in the borderlands with tales of burned villages, slaughtered livestock and common folk enslaved or murdered. Arthur's men laid in wait for those advancing war bands, ambushing the enemy when they stopped to make camp, where they ate and slept, attacking like ghosts from the cover of woodland, valley and riverbed.

The black cloaks entered a flat land, filled with dykes, ditches, marshy bogs and waterlogged fields heavy with foul brown water. This was the land to Elmet's eastern border, close to the broad and winding river Dubglas. The river began at the confluence of the Ouse and Trent and cut a wide tidal swathe deep into southern Deira and out into the narrow sea. Arthur kept his men to the byways and shepherd paths, avoiding the old Roman road the Saxons used to march through Lloegyr's fens and marshes. Ermine Street ran north from Londinium, crossing Britain's east coast until it met the south bank of the river Dubglas before leading on into Deira's heartland. The road cut through the bogs and fens and allowed merchants and warriors alike the luxury of travelling the lowlands without fear of floodwaters. The Roman legions had built Ermine Street, just as they had the Fosse Way, Watling Street and many other such important highways which criss-crossed Britain. Twice as wide as a man is tall, with ditches on either side of a raised, curved bank fortified with sand, gravel and stone, Roman-built roads lived on as another reminder of empire's glory long passed and Britons had not the skill nor knowledge to build such constructions of their own.

Cavall, the Saxon war dog, seemed a little swayed by the wound taken in battle. He took to loping along beside Llamrei and would sit beside Arthur whenever the column stopped to rest. The dog's fondness for Arthur dismayed Becan, but Arthur made the lad responsible for caring for Llamrei and Balin's mare, and that kept him busy and happy. On a morning where driving rain pounded from a dark, heavy sky, Arthur led the black cloaks down a shallow valley towards a border farmstead, little more than a drystone roundhouse roofed with turf beside a wooden barn. On a rise above the farm, sheep wandered in green pastures, and a thin trail of smoke came from the farmhouse roof to be snatched away by a brisk wind and swallowed by the rain.

Cavall barked at a farm dog standing guard before the barn, and Arthur whistled at the war dog to be quiet. Cavall ceased his barking and jogged beside Llamrei, glancing up at Arthur with its red tongue lolling. A small man in woollen trews and a green jerkin came from the barn, wringing his hands in fear at the sight of so many warriors stalking towards his home through the rain.

'We seek shelter,' Arthur called to the farmer, raising a hand in greeting, and to show that he came in peace.

The churl wiped his hands upon his trews and called over his shoulder. He stood in the muddy courtyard between barn and house, and squinted at the approaching black cloaks. He bowed his head in deferential respect when Arthur and Balin's horses reached the barn and then helped Becan tie the horses to a fence post. A heavy woman came bustling from the farmhouse with two small girls clutched to her skirts, and she too bowed her head, fussing at her clothes and hair.

'Your men can use the barn to get out of the rain, my lords,' said the farmer, ushering the men into the long building. The barn smelled of fresh wood and damp grass, with sheaves of hay stacked at its edges and golden sawdust littering the ground where the farmer had been busy whittling at a new milking stool. The pale wood and whittling knife were left lying on the hard-packed earthen floor. His wife brought the warriors some cheese to share between them, but the farmer apologised for not having enough ale to share.

'I only have enough ale and bread to feed my family, and surely not enough to share with so many hungry mouths,' he said, wringing his gnarled hands. 'Are you going to take my food?'

'No,' said Arthur. 'Bring the man some meat, and some of that mead from the wains.' Anthun took the farmer to the captured wains, and the man laughed with delight as he took a side of smoked ham.

'Thank you, my lords,' said the woman. She beamed at Arthur and Balin, and shooed the children away from her side.

'You should leave this place,' Balin warned her. 'Saxons are on the march and will be here within days.'

She frowned. 'Leave? Where should we go?'

'Loidis,' Arthur said. 'The safest place for your family is behind the city walls.'

'I've never been to Loidis. My sister lives in the next glen over yonder, and my father's place is just beyond at Bunny Hollow. What would happen to our home if we left?'

'You cannot stay here. It's too dangerous.' Arthur's eyes flickered to the children and then back to the woman.

'I can't leave here. I've never left.'

Balin took a handful of hay and handed it to Becan so that he could brush the horses down. He turned to the woman and fixed her with a hard stare. 'Tomorrow, maybe the day after, Saxons will march into your house. They will rape you and cut your throat because you are too old to enslave. If they have enough food to feed them, they will take your daughters as slaves. If not, they will kill them too. Your husband will die and your farm here will be nothing but ash and ruin. So stay, if you wish, and wait for your doom.'

The woman began to cry, and she clutched at a crude wooden cross hanging at her neck. She gathered the children and hurried towards her house. Arthur stared at Balin, but the hard warrior just shrugged.

'Better to tell her how it will be, than for her to find out for herself,' he said, which Arthur supposed was true enough.

Relentless rain battered the farmyard, fat droplets splashing in the mud and dripping through the barn's leaking roof. The black cloaks huddled inside the building, one hundred men hiding from the miserable weather, wringing out their clothes and cloaks to get out the worst of the wet. Arthur stared eastwards, at the sheep in the pasture, and wondered again where Lunete was and if he would ever find her. A figure moved amongst the sheep, a blur at first, too hard to see because of the hard rain. But it came closer, a man running through the fields towards the farm.

'Is it one of ours?' asked Balin, assuming it was one of their scouts returning with news. But as it grew closer, they realised the figure was too small to be a warrior.

'Father, father!' the figure cried out. He glanced over his shoulder, twisted too far, and tripped over in the meadow. He rose and stumbled on, hurtling towards the farm.

'Ewen!' the farmer called, running from his house to meet his distressed son.

Arthur stood and walked out into the rain. His leather chainmail liner lay wet and cold against his body as he followed the farmer. He hoped that the heckles rising on the back of his neck were wrong, and that what had so terrified the boy was something other than enemy warriors. Then Arthur's heart sank, because over the sheep pasture came a score of men. Something flew from their ranks, flying high through the driving line like a soaring bird. It seemed to pause high in the gloomy sky and then plummeted too quick to see. The arrow hit the running boy in the back, sending him sprawling mere paces from his father's arms. He couldn't have been over twelve summers old.

'Saxons!' came a cry from inside the barn. Arthur's hand dropped to the stone sceptre in his belt. His thumb rubbed across the cruel, carved faces and the sobs of the poor farmer were like knives in Arthur's ears. His mail was suddenly heavy, like a dead weight dragging his shoulders down. He had barely slept since leaving Loidis. Each night his warriors slept under the stars, and Arthur lay in the dark waiting for the watch to cry out and warn of approaching Saxons. When he did sleep, he often woke in a panic, checking about him to make sure the enemy had not sneaked in under cover of darkness to kill his men. Too much death. Too much blood.

The rain soaked the farmer, who cradled his dying son. The boy choked and gasped and then died in his father's arms. Blood ran in rivulets through the mud and puddled at Arthur's feet. More Saxons appeared, their axes and spears waving in the distance as they tramped towards the farm. They shouted and whooped in their guttural tongue. They would descend on the farmhouse and tear it apart. Could there ever be an end to this war? Were there enough Britons to throw back the invaders who seemed to multiply each summer, whilst the Britons suffered and shrank behind their hilltop fastnesses?

Arthur grabbed Excalibur's hilt, and the moment he touched the leather-wrapped grip, the melancholy fell from him. He drew the blade and pointed it at the Saxons, the farm boy's blood pooling at his boots, vengeful anger filling his muscles with strength.

'Prepare to fight!' Arthur called to his men. 'Get the family out of here, send them west or north, but get them gone.'

'Bastards are everywhere,' growled Balin, coming to Arthur's side with a sword in each hand. And so they were.

The black cloaks trudged from the barn, their usual vigour and cheering at the chance of battle replaced by bowed heads. They dragged their spears through the mud and stared with blank faces at the Saxons on the hillside. Riders appeared amongst the Saxons, a dozen men on large horses. They swirled on the hills and then urged their mounts to canter towards the farm. More men came with them, dozens of them carrying axes, spears and shields.

'There are too many,' said Arthur, almost to himself, trying to count how many warriors massed beyond the house and barn. The riders came on, and yet more Saxons followed, scores of men with weapons massing in the driving rain.

'We can fight them.' Balin twirled his swords and smiled mirthlessly at the enemy.

'We can. And we might defeat them, but how many warriors would we lose to defend this place? We have already lost twenty men since we left Loidis. There are at least one hundred Saxons there, probably more. We could lose thirty men here to win, and sixty if we are defeated. There is no defensive position here, and if we lose too many men, our mission to slow the Saxon advance is over.'

'So we run like whipped dogs?'

Arthur turned and grabbed Balin's arm. 'Would you rather kill a few Saxons today and die gloriously, only to lose the war and see Britain become a Saxon kingdom? Or live to fight another day? Who is fighting this war but us, Balin? Our kings wait behind their walls for the war to come to them. We are the only ones who take the fight to the enemy. Just us with our hundred spearmen. We all want to charge into the Saxons and strike at them and avenge the dead boy. But there is no cunning in dying today. Our deaths here are a waste of our spears. Spears we can drive into the enemy when the time is right and we can win. Would you have Elmet fall just as Bernicia did?' Arthur turned to Dewi and sheathed his sword. 'Order the retreat. We make for the ditch yonder.' Arthur pointed south of the farm, where the high grassland fell away into bog and wetland, where a small wooden bridge crossed the waterway to grazing fields on the far side.

Balin roared at the sky and swung his swords in frustration, but he followed Arthur towards the barn. Still more of the enemy breasted the rise, and Arthur formed a dozen of his men in a retreating line, shields towards the enemy, Arthur at the centre. The farmer's wife wailed like a night fetch as she hugged her dead son, and Arthur's men had to pull away and drag the desperate mother towards the marshes. Retreat into the waterways was Arthur's only hope of escape. To stay was to die. He could lose the enemy in the marsh. Then return and strike at them in a different, more favourable location.

'Can you navigate the bogs?' Arthur asked the farmer, but he just stared blankly at his son's corpse and the advancing Saxons. Arthur shook him by the shoulder. 'Can you guide us through the flood lands?' Arthur shouted, and the man snapped from his daze. He nodded, part of his consciousness locked in shock at his son's death, the rest aware of Arthur's question. He nodded again and pointed towards the lowlands. Anthun helped the churl and his wife hurry towards the bridge and timber walkway which straddled the flooded marshland.

'The riders, lord,' said Dewi, and pointed his spear to where the enemy riders galloped their horses around the farm's flank.

'They want to cut us off,' Arthur said. 'Hurry.'

The black cloaks ran towards a flooded field surrounded by tall reeds. Becan led Llamrei and Balin's mare towards the walkway and Cavall followed. The field's brown water shook and rippled beneath the heavy rain and the riders came about the farmhouse, whooping for joy at the prospect of a fight. Across the rise, two hundred Saxons came on in ragged formation. Arthur swallowed the gnaw of fear in his gullet. To be caught here was to die, and he moved faster, urging his men onwards.

'Any sign of our scouts?' Arthur called.

Balin shook his head. 'Saxons must have killed them.'

Arthur never camped without scouting the surrounding territory and he cursed at the thought of more black cloaks fallen to Saxon blades. Boots banged on timber as the black cloaks ran across the walkway made of pine laths over stakes set deep into the mire. The walkway covered the deepest stretch of marshland leading on to a raised island of wildflowers and brush. From there, other walkways spread out in different directions, connecting eyots and islands rising from the stale brown water like the backs of sea beasts. The boards rattled as warriors ran into the bog and that thudding mixed with the jangle of iron, the screams of the farmer's wife, her children's wailing, the patter of rain and the baying howl of two hundred charging Saxons.

Arthur and a dozen men formed a protective ring of shields around the bridge and walkway to protect the retreat. Half of his men were across the walkway to the safety of the island beyond, when hoofbeats rocked the earth beneath Arthur's feet like a tremor.

'They are not Saxons,' said Becan, pointing at the twelve riders reining in twenty paces away from Arthur. They howled and shook their spears in frustration at not cutting off Arthur's retreat. The riders carried smaller shields than usual for Saxons, and one of those shields bore a familiar sigil.

'Britons fighting alongside Saxons?' Balin spat. 'Wait...'

The riders fanned out and urged their mounts towards Arthur's line of shields. Their leader wore his silver hair long and loose and his face was a mass of scar tissue around a missing left eye. He carried a faded shield, and Arthur peered at the sigil just as the scarred man threw his spear with lightning speed. Men rarely fought on horseback. It was a precarious business, with only a horse blanket and reins to keep a man steady. But the scarred warrior launched his spear overhand, with barely any back lift, and the weapon sliced through the air. The spear thudded into the warrior next to Arthur, crunching into his chest, killing the warrior instantly.

'Balan,' Balin said, as though in a trance. He stepped forward with his two swords levelled, and then Arthur saw it. The sigil upon the scarred man's shield was the fox of lost Bernicia, the same sigil Balin and his few surviving Bernicians wore with pride. It was Balin's brother, come at the head of a Saxon war band to attack Elmet and destroy Arthur's warriors.

Balan slid from his horse and drew his sword. His scarred face twisted in what could have been smile or snarl. His twelve riders followed, each one clad in bright chain-mail and carrying fine swords. Their shields all bore faded sigils, the beasts of lost kingdoms, the birds and growling predators of once proud realms fallen to Saxon invaders. They were all big men. Silver glittered at their arms and necks, and their forearms were tattooed blue with warrior rings.

'Brother,' Balan said, flicking the tip of his sword in salute at Balin. 'Still a masterless man? Roaming the countryside with beggars and brigands? Are you ready to die?'

'Bastard,' Balin hissed. Saxons thronged the farmyard. Too many for Arthur's ring of shields to fight. But a strange look fell upon Balin's face. As though the world stood still, as though everyone and everything disappeared except him and his brother. 'I have searched for you. Many years I have waited for this moment.'

'Do you remember Father's sword?' Balan held up his sword for Balin to see. 'He would have preferred you to have it. I was never good enough for him. But now the old bastard rots beneath the earth with slugs and snails crawling in his skull and I have his blade. Me, the black sheep, scorned and whipped by a father who showed me nothing but cruelty. I am the one who carries the blade of our forefathers in my hand. Come then, brother. You hate me, and with good reason. Here I am.'

'Balin, no,' Arthur warned. Every black cloak had made it across the bridge and walkway, all save Arthur, Balin and the ten black cloaks in the protective line. If they ran now, they could defend the walkway as they went and escape. Arthur looked out at the Saxons, some already ransacking the farmhouse and barn, the rest massed before Arthur and his men, murder in their eyes and weapons in their fists. 'We must go, now.'

Balin took two steps towards his brother, and Arthur hauled him back. Balin tried to shake Arthur off, his eyes never leaving his brother's ruined face.

Balan laughed. 'Do you need your lover to hold you back? You were always weak, brother. Just like our father, just like our people. Why do you think I joined with Vortigern?'

Balin thrust Arthur away from him and raised his swords. 'Because you are a traitor, a raping whoreson too frightened to fight for his people.'

'I am a winner. I joined with the victors! Now I own vast estates in the kingdom of Kent, and sit on the councils of kings! What do you own? What do you do but scrabble around in the dirt fighting thieves and vagabonds? When Elmet falls, Octha will pay me a fortune in silver and slaves. That is my price to bring my men to his fight. My warriors, my victorious fighters who will make him a king. You are a fool who fights for a dying dream. What do the people care to whom they pay their tithes? What difference does it make to them if a tenth of their surplus goes to Gwallog, the idiot in his rusty Roman armour, or Octha? You think the common folk yearn for Gwallog, or Urien, or Uther? You are as much of an empty head as our father was. Are you ready to meet your wife and daughters in the afterlife, brother?'

Arthur sheathed Excalibur and leapt at Balin just as he lunged to strike at his hateful brother. He wrapped two arms around the warrior's shoulders and dragged him towards the walkway.

'No!' Balin roared, and he bucked in Arthur's arms like a wild horse. The black cloaks folded around Arthur and Balin as Arthur struggled to drag his friend backwards towards the marsh. Balan gestured to his twelve men, Britons all, and they advanced towards

Arthur's protective shield wall. Balan lunged at a black cloak, feinting low and then striking high. The man took the blow upon his shield, but at the same time, Balan kicked the black cloak's legs out from under him. The warrior fell with a grunt, and Balan's sword snaked out with lightning speed, stabbing hard down into the fallen man's gullet. Balan's twelve traitors attacked, throwing their bulk at the black cloaks in a furious assault. They fought like demons, bullying Arthur's men across the walkway. They were the last survivors of dead kingdoms, men who had turned their cloaks to fight for the hated invader. Warriors whose long-dead lords lay beneath the earth with the twelve traitors' broken oaths rotting beside their corpses. They hacked at shields and their blades struck with precision and strength.

Three of Arthur's men died in that brutal assault, splashing into the filthy water and eking their lifeblood into the bog. Men Arthur knew like brothers. Brave warriors who had fought with honour for their people. Six more fell back injured, so that the fight to retreat became a desperate battle for survival. Arthur tried to strike at them, but the twelve traitors used their shields and swords with precision, defending every blow and lashing out with strikes of their own. His men pulled back, and the twelve traitors dragged the injured black cloaks from the walkway. Arthur and his men wailed in agonised frustration as the twelve bastards gathered about the captured warriors. They pulled them from the walkway, made a circle around them and beat them mercilessly with iron-banded shields. They hammered at Arthur's wounded warriors, kicking them, spitting at them and battering them to bloody ruin. There were too many of the enemy for the black cloaks to advance, though the enemy taunted them to do it, the twelve rogues beat Arthur's wounded men to death to provoke Arthur and Balin to charge and it was a monumental effort to keep back and protect the walkway so that the bulk of Arthur's men could get away.

'Come and fight me, brother,' Balan taunted, waving his bloodied sword. He stalked to where Arthur's injured warriors lay dead, their bodies beaten to bloody heaps of meat. Balan put his boot on the chest of a man still breathing, a young man, breath whistling from his shattered mouth and chest. Balan laughed at him. He swung his sword with such force that it sliced through the young warrior's neck as if it were made of cheese. Balan kicked the gory head towards the walkway and spat upon the headless corpse. Arthur gasped at the horror of it, the sheer brutality and disrespect. His men broiled, first one man surging forward, only to be dragged back by his comrades, and then another as Balan and his twelve traitors goaded them. 'You fear me, Balin, you always did. I was always the stronger brother, you always the lickspittle, grovelling to Father like a slave. Your children screamed like pigs when they died, and your wife moaned as I took her. She would have come with me, I think, so much did she enjoy my loins. But I killed her. She was a fool of a whore and she got what she deserved.'

'Bastard!' Balin screamed, a heart-rending sound of utter pain and hate. He broke free of Arthur's grip. Balin charged through the shield wall and hurled himself at his brother. The brothers clashed in a whirl of blades. Balin roared with visceral hate, forcing his brother backwards. Balan parried each blow with sword and shield, and Balin fought on, swords striking with impossible force and speed. Arthur ran after his friend, but Balin pressed forwards. He battered Balan's shield with his two swords until his brother fell to one knee, and for a moment, it appeared Balin would claim his vengeance. Then, Balan whistled like a shepherd to his dogs and his traitors surged forwards.

Balin had not realised how far he had driven his brother back, and before Arthur could react, the twelve treacherous Britons closed in around Balin with their shields. They battered him, clattering and driving Balin down. They pinned him with linden wood and iron so that his arms became trapped and he could not raise his swords. Arthur charged towards him, but Balan darted around his trapped brother and swung his sword with such speed that Arthur had to fling himself to the ground to avoid it. The sword point came again, stabbing at Arthur's midriff, and he rolled away. Balan kicked Arthur hard in the groin, and he fumbled at Excalibur, unable to draw the weapon whilst on the ground, sprawling in the rain-soaked mud. Just at the moment Arthur thought he would fall to Balan's blade, black cloaks swirled around him, and their large shields forced Balan to retreat.

'I'm coming for you, Arthur ap Nowhere. Ector's whelp,' Balan snarled, his single eye shining in triumph. 'I will crush your legend under my boot. You are the shit which clings to a sheep's arse, pigs' vomit and toad gristle. Merlin's pet, who brings men to his banner with lies. I want your sword and I want your soul. I'm coming for both.'

Balan backed off. He turned and cracked the hilt of his sword off Balin's skull, and Arthur's friend went limp between the press of enemy shields. Balan and his twelve traitors dragged Balin away from the fight, his boots dragging in the dirt. Arthur's own men hauled him across the walkway, fighting furiously as the Saxon horde descended upon them. Arthur drew Excalibur and fought with them, striking across the shields at an enemy who came on in a wall of fearsome axes and stabbing spears. The black cloaks retreated, taking small steps backwards as they fended off overwhelming enemy numbers. Saxons jumped into the foul marsh water and tried to hack at the legs of Arthur's men, and Arthur cut at their faces and necks with Excalibur's blade until they came no more. A long-handled Saxon war axe clattered onto the walkway as Arthur cut through its owner's wrist. He sheathed Excalibur and hefted the heavy weapon in both hands.

'Get back. Now!' Arthur ordered his men. Four had died on the walkway, whose timbers were now slick with blood. The dead slumped in the dark waters, and as Arthur's men surged away, he chopped the mighty axe down hard, shearing through a Saxon's boot and on into the lath beyond. He hacked until the walkway broke and its planks collapsed into the floodwater. Saxons howled in frustration and tossed spears at Arthur's men, who escaped onto the island. The Saxons could not follow. The waters were too deep to cross, and if they tried to swim, Arthur's men would cut them down as they came.

Arthur ran with his men, fleeing for his life across the brush-covered eyots, chopping through walkways as he went to hinder the enemy's pursuit. There were too many Saxons, always too many, and Balin was lost. Arthur's comrade of the sword captured by his hated brother, his greatest enemy, and Arthur ran from battle with a head full of sorrow and a heart full of hate.

7

The black cloaks retreated through the night, stumbling through bogs, briars, thickets and marsh. Arthur trudged through the darkness with ice-cold feet in sodden boots as relentless rain lashed them like a cold whip. The Saxons followed. They skirted the marshland, coming wide around its southern edge until darkness fell and Arthur's scouts reported the Saxons camped for the night on a knoll ringed with silver birch trees. Arthur pushed his men on in the dark, though they slipped on unsure footing, squelching into mud. Men fell into foul water and huddled together, shivering in their soaking clothes. The heavy ground stole their strength and drank their hope. They went in grim silence, stunned by the attack on the farm, the night seeming to last an eternity.

Eventually, morning broke. The rain stopped, fat drops dripping from leafy boughs as Arthur ordered his men to rest within a hilltop grove. The lowlands swept away before them, fields half flooded where birds waded in the high waters, and their song filled the chill morning air. Arthur sat heavily beside Dewi and Anthun, clothes clinging to his shivering flesh, teeth chattering and hands shaking. Anthun, his single, long eyebrow bent into a frown, fumbled at his striking stone and knife, trying to scrape a spark into a pile of damp kindling.

'Balin,' Dewi whispered, staring as Anthun's knife scraped down the stone over and again. 'I thought no one could beat him. He was the greatest swordsman in Britain.'

'Is,' said Arthur. 'Is the greatest swordsman.'

'Yes, lord.'

Cavall whined and nudged his muzzle into Arthur's shoulders, and he draped an arm around the hound. He couldn't believe Balin was gone either, captured by the very man he hated above all things.

'Saxons,' said Becan, pointing south with his spear. The black cloaks groaned, because Becan was right. A hundred Saxon spearmen loped through a distant field, splashing through the floodwaters towards where Arthur's men rested.

Arthur pushed himself to his feet, bones weary and aching from lack of sleep and the terrible night march. His shoulders ached and his eyes itched like nettle stings. His men sat with heads hung low, their cloaks, weapons and armour filthy. In the desperate flight from the farmhouse, they had left the wains and supplies behind, so that there was nothing to eat or drink for men who had marched for a day and a night through grim conditions.

'Fall back to Loidis,' Arthur said, his gaze fixed on the Saxon war band. 'March north from here, and march hard. If you can keep ahead of this pursuing war band, you shouldn't meet any more Saxons on the road. The marsh protects the way, and the enemy is still in the east.'

'Yes, lord,' said Dewi, and he began to rouse the men. Nudging the last warriors to rise with his boot. 'Stay and die if you wish, you lazy curs. On your feet, come on. Time to move.'

'Take my shield and spear to Loidis, and the farmer and his family.'

'Where are you going?' Dewi paused, glancing at the Saxons and then back at Arthur. 'It's impossible, lord.' He suddenly understood Arthur's plan, but before he could object any further, Arthur placed a hand on his shoulder.

'We have done as much as we can to slow Octha's advance. Get the men into Loidis and I will join you there. I cannot leave Balin with the enemy. The fight for Loidis will be a siege of the city. Defend it, Dewi. I will return, and we shall fight together on the walls.'

'Let me go with you.' He paused and then threw his hands up as Arthur stayed stoically silent. 'At least take a score of the lads with you?'

'Best if I go alone. Protect the men, Dewi, don't stop. March all day and you should reach Loidis tomorrow.'

Dewi gaped at Arthur and seemed to struggle to get words to form in his mouth. He frowned down at the labouring warriors, then dragged a warrior up from his haunches and kicked another up the arse to get them moving.

'Don't die out there,' said Hywel, wiping rainwater from his Roman armour with his cloak. 'The men need you, lord. Elmet needs you.' Hywel glanced nervously at Arthur, and then back to the men. 'I was nothing before you came. Banished from Elmet, for a crime committed whilst drunk. A crime I can never find forgiveness for. I was a masterless man, wandering with those banished alongside me. We were lost, fighting for pay, raiding, stealing, and worse. You found us and gave us a cause. We are men again, warriors with pride and reputation. Come back to us, Lord Arthur.' He bowed to Arthur, then joined the rest of the black cloaks as they wove their way down from the hillock in single file. Hywel scooped up one of the farmer's daughters and placed her on his shoulders.

'He said it better than I could,' Dewi said. 'I know we can't leave

Balin out there to die, but if you fall, then I fear Elmet will, too. If you are going after him, why not take us all? One hundred spearman stand more chance than one man alone.'

'Gwallog is a fierce warrior, and Idnerth's legionaries are more than a match for any Saxon warriors. Elmet can make a stand. Octha has to attack Loidis' walls, and that will cost him hundreds of warriors. If Gwallog and Idnerth can hold the wall, Elmet will survive,' said Arthur.

'Idnerth has a few hundred trained men to protect Loidis, and each of his three hundred legionaries is perhaps worth two Saxons. The rest are men like the farmer there. Churls with spears. They can't stand up to a horde of Saxons. Men believe in you, lord, they believe in the sword.'

'And yet they'll fight anyway, for their homes, wives and children. Whether or not I am there.'

'But with you there, they'll believe they can win.'

'Take the sword, then. Take Excalibur to Loidis and let the people see it. Merlin has their heads filled with horse shit and legends.' Arthur reached for Excalibur.

'You'll be needing that, I think. It's not the sword or the legend. It's you they believe in. A man of no nation who fights for all Britons. One of us. A man who wins, and who doesn't fight for any king or kingdom. You fight for all the people of this land, and so do I. What becomes of us black cloaks without Arthur or Balin? We have no country, no king or lord save you. Take us with you. We all want to get Balin back. It makes no sense to go out there alone where cursed Saxons are as thick on the land as flies on shit.'

'If we all go in search of Balin, we travel slowly and on foot. The Saxons are already upon us. We would have to fight those men before us before we even begin to cross the marsh. There are Saxons everywhere, you have seen them. To march back into that country is to die. I go alone. Llamrei will carry me around this approaching war band faster than they can pursue me. I can skirt around the bog and find Balin. One man alone might just get into their camp and get Balin out. As a war band, we stand no chance.'

'You know best, lord. Stay alive, and I hope you find Balin.'

Arthur watched them go, understanding that what Hywel and Dewi had said was true. His men looked to him now, and perhaps so did the common folk of Elmet, Rheged, Gododdin and the rest of the British kingdoms whose borders butted against lands lost to the Saxons. Merlin would scold him for going after Balin. A ruthless commander would let the Bernician die and instead go with his men to where he was needed most. That was surely wielding Excalibur atop Loidis' high walls. Arthur's head pounded behind his eyes. The weight of command lay heavy upon his shoulders. Arthur's men needed him. He was their lord, their ring-giver, who gave them purpose, wealth and reputation. To have one hundred warriors dependent upon his decisions was a burden which Arthur normally wore lightly. But Arthur was a man as well as a leader. He was the foster son of Ector, hero of the Great War, and Balin had risked his own life countless times following Arthur's orders. Balin was a great lord, a fair-famed warrior known and respected throughout Britain, and yet he followed a man half his age, a man without land or title. Arthur could not leave Balin to his brother's tortures, not whilst he had the strength to wield a sword.

Llamrei whickered as Arthur threw a riding blanket over his back. It was still damp from the heavy rain, and smelled of wet dog.

'Carry me swiftly, my friend,' Arthur whispered into Llamrei's ear. The horse was as hungry and tired as Arthur, but he needed the mighty stallion to carry him far and fast. Arthur climbed onto Llamrei's back and gently tapped his heels against the stallion's muscled flanks. He started down the hill and Cavall followed, keeping pace with Llamrei as Arthur urged him to a canter. He rode towards the oncoming Saxons, and they shook their axes at him. One man nocked an arrow to a bow, but the string was wet and the arrow flew only a dozen paces. Arthur rode around their flank and their calls and cries of angered frustration died in the wind. The black cloaks marched ahead, and Arthur had eluded the enemy. There was no sign of Balan or his twelve rogue Britons in the pursuing force, and Arthur riding behind them would give the Saxon war band's leader a problem. Balan had despatched them in pursuit of the black cloaks with orders to find and kill Arthur. He had said as much at the farmhouse. Balan wanted Arthur and Excalibur. The war band's leader must now decide if he should pursue the black cloaks, or turn and follow Arthur. He couldn't press too close to Elmet or too far ahead of the main Saxon force for fear of being caught by Elmet skirmishers beyond the city walls. Arthur glanced over his shoulder and ground his teeth with satisfaction as the Saxons abandoned their pursuit of the black cloaks and came after Arthur. Dewi and his men were safe. For now.

The Saxon war band had left a trail of footprints across the wetlands. A hundred men had churned rain-sodden fields to brown muck, and Arthur led Llamrei along that track towards the farmhouse. He came about the marshes from the south-east, on a route leading across low-lying hills and grazing pastures. He rode until the sun descended into the west, a sliver of gold in a heavy grey sky. Arthur rested Llamrei and walked beside the great stallion, following the footprints with Cavall padding along beside him. The tracks led him in a wide loop around the boggy floodplain and back to where the Saxons had first breasted the horizon to surprise Arthur and his men. Arthur saw sentries posted around the barn and roundhouse, and he waited in a thin coppice of birch, blackthorn and ash. He kept low, tied Llamrei off and watched the Saxons through a tangle of briar. Firelight shone through open window shutters where men laughed and talked loudly inside the house and barn. Arthur grimaced at the sound of Balan and his traitors laughing with the Saxons, mocking Balin, Britain and the fate of its people.

Arthur waited, crouched in the tangle of bush and thorns, nestled beneath crooked trees until darkness enveloped the land in its shadowy embrace. Llamrei grazed on the wild grass and Cavall curled up beside Arthur as he watched the enemy enjoy the spoils of their victory. Arthur's damp clothes stiffened as they dried, his leather mail liner stinking and his hair lank. The time passed slowly, and Arthur tried to occupy his mind by counting how many warriors came and went as they pissed behind the building or fetched a new barrel of ale from the captured wains. But always the intrusive thoughts would barge their way in, taking over his mind like a charging shield wall. The way the twelve traitors had beaten his injured men. How Balan had cut the head from a fallen warrior. Balin's capture. The farmer's boy killed by a Saxon arrow. The face of war was dark, a long way from the days of his childhood spent running in the fields of Caer Ligualid with Kai and Lunete. That seemed like a different life, and he a different person. Arthur glanced at his calloused hands, traced the scar upon his face and the beard around his jaw. The boy was gone, living only in memories. That child still ran in golden fields with Kai, his foster brother. He climbed trees with Lunete and laughed at her wildness. He practised spear, axe and sword with his spear father, Ector the noble hero. The boy lived, locked forever as he once was, inside Arthur's thought cage: treasured memories which seemed like someone else's life amidst the blood and death of his war of resistance against the Saxons. Another man's dreams of an idyllic life.

The Saxons changed the watch, and the warriors who replaced the four men at each corner of the farmstead came from the barn on unsteady legs. One held a chunk of steaming meat in his hand, and another came holding his belly, and belched so loudly that Arthur could hear it from his hiding place. One even sang a sad dirge as he leant upon his spear, staring out at the marshes. Too much ale or mead for men about to take a turn on night-sentry duty, and it wasn't long before the singing man sat down and hunched over his spear, drifting off into drunken slumber. Arthur hid in the gloom until he was sure the man had fallen into a deep sleep. He took off his mail coat, boots, sword belt and scabbard. The steel and iron would catch moon and starlight, and Arthur wanted to move like a night demon, like one of Nimue's spirits or the hidden folk who came out at night to haunt the hills and valleys and steal away naughty children. Arthur left Llamrei and Cavall and made his way slowly from the trees. He kept low, crawling across the grass like a night animal, attuned to the creaks and sounds of the night. He crawled with Ida's sceptre in one hand and his seax in the other. Arthur took a handful of soil and smeared it over the seax blade until it was filthy with earth, and slowly he edged closer to the farm, hoping that Balin was alive within.

A shape shuffled in the darkness and Arthur stopped still. At first, he thought it was a night demon, but quickly realised it was only a badger and the beast shuffled away quickly when it caught Arthur's scent. Arthur went slowly and carefully, crawling through the rain-soaked grass and mud, keeping low as he approached the sleeping sentry. He had seen nothing of Balin during the long hours watching the farmhouse, so his friend could be in either the barn or the house. Ten men had come from the building to piss, and Arthur had marked them all by their Saxon furs, their long hair or how they braided their beards so that he would not double count them. He listened to their laughter and sounds of their voices and tried to guess how many were inside. The men who had marched in pursuit of Arthur's black cloaks had not yet returned, and Arthur hoped they had camped for the night in the wild before returning to Balan at the farmhouse. The twelve traitors were there. Three of them had come outside to piss, so Arthur assumed Balan himself was inside somewhere.

The sentry snored like a snuffling pig, slumped forward over his spear, reeking of ale and sweat. Arthur crawled towards him, slowly and carefully. If he woke, the Saxon would raise the alarm and Arthur thought there could be fifty men sleeping between the barn and farmhouse. If he was a competent commander, Balan would have the rest of his men scouting in all directions. He was in enemy territory and would need to know quickly of any approaching Briton forces. Fifty men would cut Arthur down in the time it would take a man to pull on his boots. He paused. There was still time to crawl back through the mud and rain-soaked grass, to clamber onto Llamrei's back and ride away. Nobody would know. He could say Balin was already dead. They wouldn't judge him for it. At least Arthur had tried to rescue his friend. Arthur rubbed his fingers across the cruel stone faces etched into his sceptre, seeking strength in their harshness. He suppressed those weak thoughts, mastering himself and his fears. Leaving his friend to a terrible fate was not the way of the warrior. Not the way of the hard men, the ones who led warriors, won victories. He closed his eyes and asked Andraste, the goddess of war, to make his blade swift and his enemies slow.

Arthur crawled forwards, sceptre in one hand and mud-slathered seax between his teeth, the iron taste of soil claggy in his mouth. The snoring Saxon coughed in his sleep and slumped slightly to one side. Arthur shifted his knee and the mud beneath it squelched. The guard woke with a groan, and Arthur scrambled towards him. He looked right into Arthur's face, his flaxen beard and blue eyes clear beneath the moonlight. The Saxon's mouth opened in ale- and sleep-fuddled surprise and Arthur smashed the sceptre into his face. The Saxon fell and dropped his spear. He gasped, hands clutching at shattered teeth and broken nose, and Arthur leapt on him. He slapped his left hand over the man's mouth to prevent him from crying out. Blood oozed between Arthur's fingers where the sceptre had smashed the guard's nose to pulp. The man clawed at Arthur, kicking, fighting for his life with the strength of the desperate.

Arthur clung on, steeling himself with the knowledge that it is not easy to kill a man. Men cling to life like limpets on a ship's hull. The bards tell of single sword strokes and bloodless deaths, but all of Arthur's experience told him that the reality is grim and blood-slathered. Arthur tried to hit the Saxon again, but he caught the sceptre and fought to wrestle it from Arthur's grip. Arthur pushed the man's face into the dirt, putting his weight behind his arm to drive the flaxen beard into the stinking mud. They struggled together, grunting, scratching and shoving. It was too noisy, taking too long. Arthur let go of the sceptre and grabbed the seax from his mouth, its antler hilt cool and sure in his hand. He drove its broken-backed blade into the Saxon's groin, feeling resistance and pushing the weapon deep into flesh and muscle. He jerked and shook, twisting away from Arthur as the blade sank into his innards. Arthur ripped the blade free and punched it six times into the Saxon's guts and chest in short, powerful, murderous blows. The Saxon wept and moaned as death came for him, and Arthur only released his hand from the man's mouth once his body had gone limp.

Arthur lay back, his chest heaving from the exertion. He forced himself to rise, grabbed his sceptre and tucked the seax into his trews. He took the Saxon's spear and walked towards the barn, trying to look like a Saxon, making himself stroll confidently despite the fear gnawing at his belly. It was deep into the night, the moon more than halfway across the sky, and the sounds of laughter and boisterous shouting had dwindled to a few voices and only the occasional drawl of tired laughing. Arthur made it to the barn doors and peered inside. He drew back immediately. It was hard to count the men sleeping in the hay beneath cloaks, but at least two score warriors lay in the barn, and four huddled around a small fire, drinking the last of their captured ale. Arthur risked another peek, but there was no sign of Balin, Balan or his dozen traitors. Arthur pressed his back against the barn, wondering again if Balin was dead and if he was a fool for entering the Saxon camp, risking his own life for nothing. He tightened his grip on the spear and made for the farmhouse.

Halfway there, a horse snorted and Arthur remembered that Balan and his twelve bastards had come on horseback. He had escaped the war band beyond the marshes because of Llamrei, the stallion's speed far out-matching their marching pace. If he freed Balin and returned to Llamrei, they would need to ride double and Balan and his men would easily follow Llamrei's tracks and eventually ride them down with Llamrei weighed down. Arthur skirted the roundhouse and found the horses tied to a fence post. There was another sentry out there in the darkness somewhere, so Arthur carefully untied the horses. He slapped their rumps and waved his arms, and the horses moved lazily away from the farm.

Light flickered through open window shutters, and the roundhouse shifted with shadows as men moved around inside. Two men spoke in the language of the Britons, words mixing with the sounds of snoring as Arthur approached cautiously. The farmhouse door was half open, wooden laths fixed to leather hinges creaking slightly as the light breeze shifted the door back and forth. Arthur risked a look through the narrow opening. A score of men lay asleep in the tight space, and two of the traitors sat around a fire, lazing in the farmer's chairs, mugs of ale in their broad fists.

Arthur's eyes widened, and his knuckles whitened. Because Balin sat between them. He was naked and bloody, his greying hair hanging loose about his bowed head. One of the seated men cuffed Balin around the head, and the other laughed.

'Perhaps he will join Vortigern?' said one of the Britons, his voice deep and gruff. Arthur wasn't sure what he meant by that. Perhaps he meant Balin's fate was to be tortured and killed like the hated evil king who had begun the Great War by inviting the Saxons to Britain's shores.

'Or Balan will flay the skin from his bones and cover his shield with his brother's hide?'

'Won't be long now until this place falls. Octha will be king of Elmet.'

'And we will be rich men.'

'Richer men.' Another bout of cackling laughter. Their voices slurred as they spoke.

'I haven't had a woman for days. There had better be some good pickings when Loidis falls.'

'There'll be whores for everyone, old friend. Don't you worry. Fine women in Roman clothes, they might need breaking in, mind, but they'll be nice and soft.' More cackling.

Arthur turned away from the door. There were too many men inside for him to creep around, and there was no way he could get to Balin whilst the two Britons sat about him in their cups. He bit his bottom lip. There had to be a way in. He could not leave Balin to be humiliated and murdered by Balan and his bastards. Arthur waited, because there was nothing else he could do. A heroic charge into the farmhouse could end only in death, so he did nothing. Eventually, the voices died down, and Arthur risked another look inside. The two Britons were asleep in their chairs, ale cups fallen to the floor and Balin still huddled between them, his bare skin pallid in the dwindling firelight.

The sun would soon appear over the horizon, and the Saxons would wake to continue their murderous advance into Elmet. It was now or never. Arthur braced himself and opened the door. It creaked loudly as the leather hinges struggled with the door's weight and Arthur winced, expecting the sleeping warriors to wake. But too much ale in their bellies kept them in a deep sleep, and Arthur tiptoed around their snoring forms. He stepped over one of the twelve traitors, an enormous man with red hair, and Arthur could so easily have killed the bastard with his spear, or cut his throat whilst he slept. But the risk was too high, any struggle and the rest would awake and hack Arthur to death. He took two more long strides through the sleeping men until he was in the house's centre, surrounded by deadly enemies. Balan slept on a pallet bed, the farmer's bed of dry straw and woollen blankets. To get to him, Arthur would have to cross a dozen bodies, and so his death must wait for another time.

A man groaned and shifted on Arthur's left. He stopped, still and silent, but the man did not wake. Another Saxon coughed and turned over, but also stayed fast asleep. Arthur continued until he came to Balin, so white that his skin was like candle wax. He crouched beside the veteran warrior and laid the spear across his own shoulder. He shook Balin gently, but he did not stir, so he shook his arm harder. Balin's head snapped up like a striking snake, his face a mass of swelling and bruised flesh. He recognised Arthur and his eyes became wet with surprised joy. Arthur placed a finger to his own lips and gestured at the sleeping enemies. Balin nodded his understanding. Arthur took his seax and cut the hemp rope, which bound Balin at wrist and ankle.

'Can you walk?' Arthur whispered, leaning close to Balin so that the words were as quiet as a summer wind.

Balin's dry tongue licked his swollen, cut lips. 'I'll bloody walk out of here,' he mumbled. Arthur helped Balin to his feet, and

Balin hunched, leaning heavily upon Arthur's arm as they made their way slowly, painstakingly, through the sleeping enemy warriors. They reached the door and Balin glanced backwards at Balan and the rest of the enemy, but Arthur shook his head. To kill even one of them was to die, and Arthur had to get back to his men. He owed it to them as much as he owed vengeance to Balin. Balin's eyes squeezed shut and a single tear rolled down his cheek.

'My wife. My sons,' he whispered, and it was the only time Arthur had heard Balin mention his dead family. Balin shuddered, his body sobbing. The horror of his dead family and his brother's unspeakable betrayal was raw and blistering now that Balan had returned. Arthur hurried to the door. He had one arm around Balin, and the spear in the other, and with that weapon, he pushed the door open. There, staring at him with surprise, was a ruddy-faced Saxon. Arthur let Balin go and drove the spear forward. He drove the point into the Saxon's open mouth and pushed him backwards. The Saxon toppled and fell, and Arthur kicked him hard in the face. The sound of the man hitting the damp earth in the night was like a tree falling. Arthur struck again with the spear, tearing out the dying man's throat as he rolled in the dirt, clutching at his ruined mouth.

Arthur rushed to Balin and hauled him upright. Men stirred within the house, and the door banged as Arthur dragged Balin out into the darkness.

'Keep the bastard noise down,' grumbled a man in Saxon.

'What's all the row about?' said another voice, accompanied by the creak of leather clothing.

Arthur dragged Balin's naked form with him, running across the farmyard, past the barn and out towards where Llamrei and Cavall waited.

'You, there,' called a voice. A sentry from the farm's far side. Arthur ignored him and kept dragging Balin on.

'Wake up!' the sentry called. 'The prisoner! Wake up!'

Heat bloomed in Arthur's chest, fear burning like a furnace. More voices erupted behind him, but Arthur could not turn to look. He had to keep moving. The trees emerged from the darkness like long black fingers and he was almost there. Balin's breath came in ragged gasps and he dragged the Bernician through the wet grass. Almost there. But the sound of boots came crashing behind him, coming close, moving faster than Arthur. Too close. He dropped Balin and spun around, and a spear drove into Arthur's shoulder. It was like being kicked by a mule, and Arthur fell backwards. It was the sentry, his black-bearded face wild with anger. He pulled the spear back to strike the killing blow, and more of the enemy came streaming from the farmhouse, pulling on jerkins, stumbling from sleep. The spear point hovered above Arthur's face, but as it came down Arthur parried the haft with the sceptre. The spear came back again and Arthur fumbled for the seax, but it had fallen out of his trews when he fell to the ground and was not within his grasp. His shoulder roared with pain and warm blood soaked his upper body.

Arthur whistled, long and loud, and was rewarded by the sound of barking. He parried the spear again, and the sentry kicked Arthur in the chest. Then, just as the spear came to pierce Arthur's heart, Cavall came bounding from the darkness like a nightmare. The war dog leapt upon the sentry, barking and snarling, his monstrous teeth rending and tearing. Arthur stood and grabbed Balin's arm. He ran for his life, dragging Balin's naked form with him. They reached the trees and Arthur untied Llamrei. He heaved at Balin, but his wounded shoulder screamed in pain. He tried again, but could not lift his friend.

'Balin!' Arthur shouted. 'If you want to live, if you want to kill your brother, get on the horse. Help me, Balin, and I swear your brother will die screaming. Do it for your family!'

Balin came alive as though imbued with God-given strength. He clambered onto Llamrei's back and Arthur shoved him over the horse's rump, and then climbed on himself. He urged Llamrei on, and the stallion surged into a canter just as two score enemies charged at the coppice. Arthur whistled and Cavall came bounding towards him, and they rode into the darkness with the sounds of the enemy roaring in their ears. Arthur sat behind Balin, holding Llamrei's reins with one hand, and keeping Balin upright with the other.

'Thank you,' Balin croaked, his voice barely audible, but the words found their way into Arthur's soul and he held tight on to his friend, knowing what it meant for the proud warrior to understand what Arthur had saved him from, and the risk he had taken to do it.

Arthur rode into the darkness, heading westwards, away from the advancing Saxon war bands, who now filled Elmet's eastern lands. Balan marched with Octha, and they came to destroy Elmet and crush the Britons beneath their boots and their blades. But Balin was alive, and though Arthur's shoulder bled and throbbed with blinding pain, he rode on to King Gwallog, to defend its Roman walls from an army of bloodthirsty Saxons, and Balan's treacherous Britons.

8

Arthur arrived at Loidis half dead with exhaustion. Llamrei trotted slowly, head bowed and nostrils flared as his hooves clip-clopped on the Roman road leading to the city gates. White lather flecked the horse's belly with patches of it turned pink by Arthur and Balin's blood. Arthur had ridden hard, pausing only to wrap Balin in a cloak to cover his nakedness and taking no time to tend to his or Balin's wounds. King Gwallog's scouts, out searching for Saxon skirmishers, had come across Arthur a half-day's ride from Loidis and escorted him to the old Roman city. They provided spare clothing for Balin and shared what food and ale they possessed, which Arthur ate hungrily. Balin, however, could not eat and only managed to slurp ale through the corner of his mouth. Balan had beaten his brother so badly that his face was unrecognisable, swollen to twice its usual size across his jaw and eyes. His body was a patchwork of lurid purple bruises, jagged cuts, and burns where Balan had heated a knife and slashed at his flesh and cut away part of Balin's ear as he probed his brother with questions about Loidis' defences. Balin, of course, had revealed nothing.

Idnerth came to meet Arthur and Balin at the gate in his Roman finery and led them both to his own quarters. Idnerth lived in a cool, marble-lined villa within the city walls, and he brought a bent-backed priest to care for Arthur and Balin's wounds. Arthur was relieved to find his men had arrived in the city without further harm, and King Gwallog had provided them with quarters and food. Becan came to clean Arthur's gear and take care of Llamrei, and Dewi and Hywel came to visit Arthur as he sat upon a couch in Idnerth's garden.

'Priests might be silver-hoarding weasels,' said Dewi, examining Arthur's wounded shoulder, 'but they know their healing.'

'I once saw a priest cut open a warrior's head to relieve the pressure from an axe blow he'd taken to the skull. The man's head had swollen up like a drunkard's bladder,' said Hywel.

'You don't say. Did he live?'

'No. He died that same day.'

Dewi glanced at Arthur and then back to Hywel. 'Maybe keep your interesting stories to yourself next time. Our lord is at the mercy of the black crows here. So is Lord Balin. The last thing they need are tales of priests killing men during their healing.'

'How is Balin? Can we see him?' Hywel looked about to see if there were any priests in the villa, and then pulled a skin of ale from beneath his cloak and winked at Arthur. The holy men would disapprove, but a drink would do Balin good.

'Balin suffers,' Arthur said. 'His brother was not gentle.'

'Aye. That brother of his is a bastard and no mistake. He and his band of traitors. How could a man fight for the Saxons against his own people?' Hywel leant forward, his face opening with excitement. 'Is it true, Lord Arthur? The men say that you killed a dozen men to free Balin from his brother. They say you struck them down with Excalibur, and the sword made you invisible until the first blow was struck?'

'What news of the Saxons?' Arthur asked, to change the

subject. Merlin wasn't even in Loidis, and the cursed legends grew. He hadn't the heart or the strength to tell Hywel the actual story of Balin's rescue, but the seeds of Merlin's legends and stories grew legs, spreading on their own now that the druid had laid the foundations.

Balin had stayed abed for two days and would not speak to anyone. Arthur feared that his friend's wounds were as much of the mind as of the body, and that hate devoured Balin alive from the inside out. The best thing for Balin was to heal quickly and return to the fray. The longer he spent recovering, with nothing but thoughts of his brother and their terrible history, the closer he came to madness.

'All the lands east of Loidis have fallen to the Saxons. King Gwallog ordered all of his warriors and any churl who can carry a spear to report to Loidis. The city is full of men with soil under their fingernails, onions in their satchels, and spears in their hands. We think Octha brings one and a half thousand men to war, and then Balan brought two hundred of his mercenaries north. They'll be here within two days. Scouts report the Saxon war bands are joining in the western marches. Octha's army is preparing to march as one force.'

'Two days. So soon. We have our men, Idnerth's legionaries, and an army of churls?'

'No sign of Merlin yet neither,' said Dewi, edging slightly in front of Hywel and frowning at him. 'See to the men, Hywel. Make sure they have enough to eat.'

Hywel glanced at Arthur, thought about protesting at being dismissed, and left the villa following Dewi's orders.

'Problems?' Arthur asked.

'Only that bloody upstart Hywel getting too big for his boots. Or his silly Roman sandals. He's grown cocksure since we came to

Elmet. Seems King Gwallog's forgiven him for whatever his previous transgression was.'

'He has never said what caused Gwallog to banish him and his comrades from Elmet, but they are stout fighters, and we are lucky to have them with our black cloaks.'

'They are. Hywel just needs to know his place. That's all, lord. You have our oaths, and I'm the captain. That's the end of it.'

'How many of our men are fit to fight?'

'We've lost a dozen men. Some killed outright, and another five died from the wound rot. Some stout fighters, too.'

'Did you bury them?'

'Aye. Some were Christians, and the priests here said the words and sang their songs over the dirt. The rest we buried in the usual way, with their spears and knives, nails clipped and hair trimmed.'

'Good. Well done, Dewi.'

'Thank you, lord.' Dewi's shoulders straightened at the compliment. 'Good to see you up and awake. The men would like to see you. If you feel up to it, that is.'

Dewi clapped a fist to his chest and marched out of the villa. The clash was close, war falling upon Elmet with the inevitability of the flood tide. Arthur had to get to the walls and help with the defence preparations. Dewi was right, his men needed to see him. He sat up on the couch and stifled a shout of pain as the wound in his shoulder shifted and burned. A priest had cleaned the spear wound, and sewn the flaps of skin together, and used clean cloth to bind the wound with honey and herbs. Every time Arthur moved, the skin pulled at its stitching. He stood and bit his bottom lip, leaning over heavily, the movement painful. Once up on his feet, Arthur found he could move around easily enough once he didn't move his upper body too much or twist his head.

Cavall stirred from where he slept beside Arthur's couch. He rose and wagged his tail, licking and nuzzling Arthur's leg. Despite the pain, Arthur bent and gave the war dog, who had saved his life, a scratch behind the ear. The dog yawned and curled up to go back to sleep and Arthur straightened, grimacing again at the stabbing pain in his wounded shoulder. The stone floor was cool beneath Arthur's bare feet, and Idnerth's villa was fresh with the smell of freshly cut rushes. Arthur found Balin in his room, lying on a straw-filled mattress. Closed window shutters kept the room dark, but a shaft of light shone on Balin's still swollen face. His eyes were little more than slits in a sea of purple, and his mouth seemed small with too-large lips.

'Balin, are you awake?' Arthur whispered. Balin needed his sleep to recover from his injuries, and Arthur did not wish to wake him.

'Yes,' Balin lisped.

'I am going for a walk around the walls. Care to join me?'

Balin rolled over and looked away, ignoring the question.

'Fresh air and a stretch of your legs will do you good.'

Still nothing.

'We must prepare the defences. The Saxons will be here tomorrow or the day after. We need to talk to Gwallog about how he intends to defend the walls, prepare our men, make sure supplies are organised, help the churls learn how to wield a spear. There is much to be done, and we need your experience. Unless you want Loidis to fall? For Octha's Saxons to swarm over the walls and take every woman and child as their slaves? And what then, shall Elmet share Bernicia's fate?'

Balin grunted, placed a hand on the mattress, and pushed himself up. He groaned, rising gingerly, clutching at his ribs. Arthur took a step forward, intending to help Balin rise, but he raised a finger to warn Arthur off. Balin struggled to his feet, paused, and then slowly pulled on a leather jerkin and trews.

'Come, then,' Balin said, words muffled by his injured mouth.

They left Idnerth's villa, walking at a slow place through the cobbled streets. Common folk shied away from Balin's appearance, and one toothless old woman clasped a hand to her mouth and hurried away down an alley. Loidis' streets ran along straight Roman lines, laid out by the legions long ago. Stone buildings lined those streets, houses, smithies, potteries, grain stores and merchants' shops. A tangle of muddy pathways cut through the streets, weaving and winding between the principal thoroughfares, lined with rough timber and wattle houses. The people who lived between the streets were dirty-faced, thin, mean folk who scratched a living from the wealthier of Loidis' inhabitants. They were the labourers, women who swept houses, whores, thatchers and beggars. Stout timbers propped even the old Roman buildings up, their tops roofed with thatch. It was as though Gwallog's people lived inside a tomb of ancestors long dead, doing their best to maintain the façade of imperial grandeur, but every year the old stone crumbled a little more, cobbles came away from the streets, more oak lintels were required to prop up ancient ceilings and keep walls from tumbling down. The city moved ever further away from the majesty of Roman stone and tile, falling into a world of rotting timbers, wattle and thatch.

Balin and Arthur walked in silence, just as they often sat quietly together whilst in the field. Arthur was comfortable with it, satisfied that his friend was beside him, with no need for idle chatter. He felt no need to ask Balin about his brother, for the horror of that was clear enough, as was Balin's incandescent rage and burning desire for revenge. Six of Idnerth's legionaries marched along the stone-cobbled street coming in Arthur's direction. They marched in time, *lorica segmentata* gleaming, clean-shaven faces, faded red cloaks swaying as they moved, helmets polished and gleaming. The legionaries saluted Arthur and Balin and went on their way.

Arthur reached the western wall to find it a hive of activity. Idnerth stood tall on the summit, bellowing orders, the red horsehair crest upon his helmet glorious as the sun caught his armour. Arthur and Balin made their way up the wall steps at a slow pace, and as he climbed higher, Arthur was taken aback to hear men calling his name. He turned, having to move his whole body to avoid tearing the stitches in his shoulder. He raised his good arm and waved to the men who flocked from the streets.

'Arthur, Arthur, Arthur!' they chanted. Men with tousled hair and spears in their hands who had come from the fields and meadows of Elmet's environs to answer King Gwallog's call to arms.

'Back to work,' Idnerth roared, and the calls of acclaim stopped as Idnerth's legionaries stomped amongst the crowd, shoving men and shouting at them to fetch this or carry that. Arthur turned back and climbed again, catching sight of his black cloaks high on the wall. He and Balin met them at the summit, and the warriors gathered around, grins splitting their faces as they rejoiced to see their two leaders up and about after their injuries. Arthur met them warmly, clapping men on the back, commending certain of them for their bravery, or asking about a recent wound.

'How go the defences?' he asked.

'We gather rocks and anything else we can find to hurl at the Saxons when they come,' said Anthun.

'We have men coming to us every day, wanting to join our ranks,' said Hywel as he stacked a piece of stone rubble onto an existing pile. 'Let us fight for Arthur, they say. Did he pull the sword from a stone, they ask.'

'And what answer do you give them?'

'We say yes! Of course he did. We have already replaced the men we lost, and our ranks swell. Dewi had to ask a woman to make us more black cloaks to keep up with demand.'

'Send a boy to look after Llamrei so that Becan can return to his duties, and make sure the horse has clean hay.'

'Yes, lord.' Hywel clapped his fist to his chest. Arthur was about to walk away when Hywel stepped in front of him, leaning close so that he was out of the other warriors' earshot. 'I'm ready to give orders, Lord Arthur. You just tell me what needs to be done, and I'll get the lads moving. I was almost a centurion, you know, when I fought for Idnerth and King Gwallog.'

'Dewi is the captain. He relays what Balin and I command to the men.'

'I know that... but he can be a grumpy sod. His ways upset the younger lads.'

'Dewi is captain. That's an end to it. You are a capable man, Hywel. See to your duties and who knows how things might change in the future.'

'Yes, lord. Thank you, lord.'

Arthur stepped around him, and he and Balin walked towards Idnerth. Arthur peered over the walls out on to the fields before the thick forest to the west. Dense woodland covered much of Elmet, interspersed here and there with farmsteads and villages beside streams and along the fast-flowing river Aire which meandered around the city's southern wall, bending south before turning west.

'I hate that story,' Arthur said, as much to himself as to Balin. 'The sword in the stone. Merlin fills men's heads with nonsense.'

Balin said nothing, his eyes fixed on the woods, where soon Octha's horde would come with ladders, axes and spears to attack the walls. Balan was out there too, somewhere, killing his way across the countryside with his twelve traitors.

'Primus Pilum,' Arthur said, hailing Idnerth using his full title.

'Healing well, I see,' Idnerth replied, and turned to bark at three young men. 'Don't drop that, or I'll have you marching around the walls with your shield above your head until dark.' The young men heaved a vast cauldron between them, which they had already hauled up the stone steps and now struggled to set above a firepit atop the walls.

'For boiling water?' Balin asked.

'Pitch and tar first.' Idnerth sniffed and bent to look beneath the cauldrons. 'Then fire arrows. Burn 'em on the ladders. They can't scrape it off. It melts their skin. Bastard next to them will burn as well. They'll hear their screams across the narrow sea.'

Arthur nodded appreciatively, imagining the horror of hot tar burning his flesh. 'Can we defend the entire wall?'

'No, not all at once. But Octha can't attack every part of the wall at once either. We'll shift our men to wherever he attacks.'

'Sallies,' said Balin, voice still mumbled by his injuries so that the 's' became a 't'.

'What was that?'

'Sallies. We can march out from the gates at night, or from walls not under attack and hit them. Destroy their ladders, kill as many as we can and return the way we came.'

'Much experience of sieges, have you?'

'Yes.'

Arthur shook his head just enough to warn Idnerth not to press the issue, but not enough that Balin would notice the gesture. Arthur had seen Balin attack men who brought up the fall of old Bernicia at the wrong time. Balin never spoke of it, but Arthur had parts of the tale from the few other surviving Bernician warriors, and knew Balin had fought for and lost many towns to the Saxons before the old kingdom fell.

'The king!' hissed a legionary, and every man on the battlements stood to attention. King Gwallog marched along the wall, arms clasped behind his back. He wore a hard leather cuirass shaped to resemble a muscled warrior's body, silver gilding showed beasts fighting across his chest and a purple ribbon tied about its middle. He wore the same studded leather kilt as Idnerth and his legionaries, and supple calf-length boots.

'Scouts tell me the enemy will arrive tomorrow,' Gwallog said in his slow voice, after inclining his head in greeting to Idnerth, Arthur and Balin. White scars criss-crossed his wiry arms as a testament to the king's liking to fight in the front lines as a younger man.

'We'll be ready, lord king,' said Idnerth.

'Shall we? Is any man ever ready for war? We can be ready with our rocks and our cauldrons, but are the men ready for the blood and the suffering? We know all about that, but we are warriors. The common man thinks he knows of war from the bards who come to his home and tell him stories of Lleu Llaw, Bran the Blessed and Ambrosius Aurelianus. But they don't know.'

'Half of them won't fight. They are only useful to stand on the walls and shake their spears and show the Saxons how many spearmen we have. Of the other half, one in ten will discover himself to be a fighter, will revel in the blades and the combat. The rest will throw missiles and defend themselves well enough.'

'A pox on the Saxons for bringing their greed to my kingdom. God protect us from their pagan brutality.' Gwallog reached for a gold cross hanging over his cuirass and seemed not to care that Arthur and Balin were not Christ worshippers.

'When they come, they will attack with everything they have,' said Balin. 'They will besiege us. Their warriors won't put up with the wait to starve us out, and they don't have enough men to keep a tight ring around the walls and blockade the river.'

'It will be a hard fight,' said Idnerth.

'We'll defend the city with our lives,' said Arthur.

Gwallog fixed him with an icy stare. 'We thank you for keeping your word, Arthur. You harried the Saxons and bought us precious time to gather men and provisions. You returned with your black cloaks, and we shall need their experience when Octha attacks. But where are the others? Where is Gododdin? Rheged? Powys, and the rest?'

Arthur had no answer to that. Between Idnerth's legionaries and Arthur's black cloaks, they had four hundred warriors to defend Loidis. Gwallog had hoped another thousand churls would arrive from the countryside to answer his call, but time was too short to get the message out through the forests of Elmet's far corners, so that barely six hundred farmers had reported to Loidis to take up arms. It would not be enough to repel Octha's and Balan's warriors. Arthur knew it, but he could not say it. Every man who fought had to believe they could win, or they would flee the moment a Saxon axe swung atop Loidis Roman walls.

'Riders approach, lord king,' called a warrior from along the wall. 'Riders and a marching column.'

'More farmers?' asked Idnerth.

'They come from the north, Primus Pilus.'

Arthur's hope lifted as he peered across the northern fields. Banners flew before the column of marching men, and even from the walls, Arthur could make out the stag of Gododdin. These were no mere farmers.

'Strike me down if that's not Bors of Gododdin,' Arthur said, unable to keep the smile from his face. Bors was a huge man, a champion of his people, and he and Arthur had once stormed a Saxon fortress to rescue a princess and prince.

'Merlin is with them,' said Idnerth, shielding his eyes with his hand, 'and his *gwyllion*. But I only count fifty men?'

'Fifty spearmen,' Gwallog spat. 'Is that all the Britons can muster to come to Elmet's aid? Not even the number I sent with Idnerth to save Gododdin at the river Glein.'

'More will come,' said Arthur, wishing he hadn't, because he didn't believe it. Though he wanted to trust in Merlin's dream of a united Britain, the kingdoms would not march unless Uther Pendragon commanded it.

'Is that women I see with them? What force is this Merlin brings to my gates? His mad witch and women in skirts. If this is all the druids can muster, then we are truly right to look to God for succour. Saxons come to slaughter my people, and Merlin the druid brings me women and stories of dead gods.'

Arthur stiffened at Gwallog's criticism of Merlin and the old religion, though he kept his council. The old druid had helped Arthur, trusted him, imbued him with power. He might not like Merlin's tactics and how he stirred up enthusiasm amongst the Britons, but without him Arthur would still be a spearman of Caer Ligualid and Gododdin would certainly now be a Saxon kingdom. Arthur and King Gwallog watched the column approach, and Arthur's cheeks flushed as the two women who rode at the front of the column came closer. He did not recognise the woman on the roan gelding, but the woman riding a dappled mare, straight-backed, copper hair ruffled by the wind, could only be one woman. Princess Guinevere of Cameliard, the most beautiful woman Arthur had ever seen.

9

'Yes, I brought thirty warriors with me. But we are men of Gododdin and no ordinary fighters. And I am here,' said Bors loudly, his voice echoing around the stone walls and pillars. 'I wrestled three bears on the journey south, pulled up two trees, rode a bolt of lightning, leapt three rivers, caught three eagles and drank a dozen barrels of ale. And I have only been on the road for seven days. I expect to slay at least a hundred Saxons in the first assault, in which case my presence is worth a score of Elmet's finest warriors.'

The men inside King Gwallog's hall laughed and Bors laughed with them, all except Gwallog himself, who brooded angrily upon his throne. The king of Elmet had greeted Bors, Merlin and the new arrivals with angered challenge, frustrated at the lack of support for his embattled kingdom. Bors was the leader of King Letan Lyddoc of Gododdin's forces, who were at constant war with the Saxons of Bernicia and the Scots of Lothian. Gododdin lay to Bernicia and Rheged's north, isolated from southern Britain by Saxon rule in Bernicia and Deira. Bors was the biggest man Arthur had ever seen. He was head and shoulders taller than any man in the hall, with a chest as thick around as a trunk of stoutest oak. Bors wore a leather breastplate with pieces of chain-mail draped around his boulder-like shoulders and thick neck. He carried a Saxon war axe tucked into his belt, where a long knife also hung from an ornate sheath. Bors had a heavy black beard beneath a completely shaved head and a round, heavily scarred face.

King Gwallog scowled and raised his hand for the hall to fall silent. He cleared his throat and said, 'Mighty you may be, Lord Bors, but I had expected Letan's commitment to at least match the force I sent north to support your war against Ida of Bernicia.'

'War comes again to Gododdin,' said Merlin, striding into the hall's centre with his black staff held before him. 'Ida's son Theodric raids deep into Gododdin, with five hundred spearmen. He raids, burns and turns the borderlands into a nightmare. So, King Letan is hard-pushed to defend his own borders, and yet even amidst such challenges, he sends his greatest champion south to fight for you.'

Arthur listened as he leant against a marble pillar, doing his best to keep his attention on Bors and Gwallog, but it was all he could do to keep his eyes from Guinevere. Her hair shone like burnished gold in the torchlight, her face was long and gentle with full lips, and her eyes the green of a summer sea. Men's voices blended with their echoes, so that the discussion was merely background noise beside Guinevere's startling beauty. She was like a red rose amongst warriors clad in steel, iron and leather. She glanced at him, sensing his stare, and Arthur looked away quickly, unable to stop his cheeks from flushing with embarrassment.

'What news then of King Urien and Rheged?' Gwallog grumbled.

'Urien has committed to send warriors south, and his warlord Kai of Caer Ligualid will lead them.'

'Let us hope they can stir themselves from their beds before

Elmet burns to ashes. And who are these fair ladies you bring to us in time of war?'

Merlin cleared his throat. 'We met Princess Guinevere and Lady Morgan on the road. They travel from Rheged south to Dumnonia and must pass through Elmet, but the road is too treacherous with Saxons on the march. So they joined our company.'

'Ladies travelling across Britain without escort? Has King Urien finally lost his wits, as well as his courage?'

A murmur ran through the crowd gathered inside Gwallog's hall to hear the king openly criticise a fellow ruler so. The discussion suddenly caught Arthur's attention, he being born of Rheged. King Urien was a fair-famed warrior and a powerful king, and his son Owain was one of the finest warriors in Britain.

Merlin slammed his staff down hard on the slate floor, and the sound of it shocked everybody in the hall to silence.

'You are a king here, Gwallog, and so I choose my words carefully,' Merlin said, his voice suddenly earthquake hard. 'Your kingdom is under attack and people die on Saxon blades. You may speak as you wish in your own hall, and can be forgiven for speaking hastily in this dire situation. But do not speak so of the lord of the Bear Fort. Urien will provide warriors, but not if he hears how you disrespect his reputation. The attack upon Elmet came swiftly, and it takes time to muster warriors to send south. Surely you, above all men, can appreciate that? Even the levy of Elmet has not yet fully gathered here to heed your call.'

Gwallog waved a hand in angry acknowledgement of Merlin's scolding words.

'Kai will come,' Merlin continued. 'I have Urien's word, and whatever he may be, he would not break a promise to a druid. The two ladies who came with us left Rheged in a hurry and came without escort. Their business is their own, but I would ask you to give them succour until the road to Dumnonia is safe to travel. Princess Guinevere is the daughter of King Leodegrance of Cameliard across the narrow sea. Lady Morgan is the daughter of King Gorlois of Kernow and Lady Igraine, born to Gorlois before his unfortunate demise in the Great War.'

Gwallog narrowed his eyes at Merlin. 'You are welcome here, ladies, and of course we shall try to make you as comfortable as possible, though we are shortly to come under siege by our enemies and this will be no place for gentlefolk. We all know of King Gorlois, and how he died, Merlin. I haven't forgotten the part you played in Gorlois' demise and Igraine's marriage. I was there, remember? And I played my part in the Great War.'

Merlin growled and shook his staff at the king, face contorting with rage. The gathered men shrank back in the shadows as the druid and the king eyed each other with open hostility. Arthur once again tore his eyes from Guinevere, drawn to Merlin's fury. For the first time that Arthur was aware of, Gwallog had openly challenged Merlin for his role in destroying the alliance of Britons in the Great War. Men said Merlin had sent King Gorlois to fight a battle he could not win, knowing the king would die, so that Uther Pendragon would marry Gorlois' widow Igraine, said to be the fairest woman ever born in Britain. That was the price Merlin was prepared to pay for victory over the Saxons, for Uther would not commit to war unless Merlin gave him Igraine. The alliance of kings discovered the plot, and their pact to fight together against Hengist and Horsa and the Saxon hordes shattered. Merlin salvaged part of it by sending Igraine to marry Urien of Rheged instead of Uther, and Igraine had suffered a life of misery at the hands of Rheged's brutal king. Arthur himself had sat with Igraine upon her deathbed, and she had gifted him a bronze disc that night in her dark chamber, which he had worn around his neck ever since.

'The hour grows late,' Merlin growled, mastering his anger. 'And the Saxon forces wax. We are done here, King Gwallog. Tomorrow, we look to your defences.'

'And may God protect us,' Gwallog said, twisting the knife. 'Bishop Emrys, give us a blessing so that we may sleep sounder tonight knowing that God hears our prayers.'

A fat bishop in a tall mitre shuffled out from the crowd, hand held high with two fingers extended. Merlin turned on his heel and stormed from the hall, and Nimue hissed at the holy man, mirrored his two-fingered gesture of blessing but then inverted her hand and drove the fingers into her throat. The Bishop spluttered and swallowed hard, before beginning his liturgy. The men of Elmet in the hall fell to one knee and made the sign of the cross, and Guinevere, Morgan, Bors and the men of Rheged left the Christians to their prayers.

Arthur hurried, eager to catch up to Guinevere and take a chance to hear her voice or see her smile. He reached the oak doors to Gwallog's hall and found Bors waiting on the other side.

'Lord Arthur,' said Bors, his voice deep and rumbling. 'Spear or arrow?'

Arthur peered around the Gododdin warrior's bulk as Guinevere and her green dress disappeared around a corner. He bit his lip, desperate for a chance to speak to her once more. His fingers brushed the pin she had gifted him, a silver brooch pin he wore behind his belt. He held that pin every night before sleep, thinking of her green eyes, her smile, and how she made him feel whenever he was around her.

'What was that?' Arthur replied, realising that Bors would not shift his vast frame.

'Your wound. Spear or arrow?'

'Spear.' Arthur rolled his injured shoulder and snapped himself out of his thoughts of Guinevere to give Bors the respect he deserved. Arthur held out his hand and Bors took his forearm in the warrior's grip, shaking it so hard that Arthur stumbled. 'Glad to have you with us, Lord Bors.'

'You've filled out since the battle at the Glein.' Bors clapped Arthur's good shoulder and squeezed his bicep. 'Perhaps even grown a little taller. You are a man now, full-grown. Though you were a man that day also, and what a day it was.'

'It's good to see you, though I wish it were under better circumstances.'

'Better circumstances? Ha! We are here to kill Saxons, lad. What better circumstances could there be? Unless we fought them with horns of strong Gododdin ale in our fists. The ale in Elmet tastes like cat piss, and their mead stinks of fat men's farts. Too many priests here, too many prayers.'

'Get some rest then and don't drink too much.'

'Don't drink too much? You have been in Elmet too long, you are going soft. Soon you'll be talking about the Rome folk every waking moment and wearing a bloody leather skirt. I heard what happened to Balin. Where is the grim old beast? I want to see how he is.'

Arthur directed Bors to Idnerth's villa, waited as casually as possible until the giant left the corridor outside Gwallog's hall, and set off at a run after Guinevere. He ignored the throb of his shoulder and sprinted down the stone hallway, turning left and right through pillared colonnades, until he rounded another corner at full tilt and crashed into Guinevere and Morgan, sending both ladies staggering from their feet.

'My ladies, I am sorry,' he said, the stab of embarrassment worse than any blade he had faced in the shield wall. Guinevere recovered herself, for she had stopped herself from falling by leaning into the wall, but Morgan lay sprawled on the cold floor. Arthur reached down to help her, and Morgan smiled up at him with big blue eyes, her golden hair tumbling about her shoulders, fallen out of its tied-up style.

'In a hurry, Lord Arthur?' asked Guinevere, a smirk playing on her lips.

'No lady... well, yes... that is, I...'

'Shall we forgive him, Morgan?'

Morgan tapped a finger against her chin thoughtfully. 'We shall. I don't believe we have been introduced?'

'Lady Morgan of Kernow, this is Arthur of... where is it again?'

'I was born in Rheged, but I am not oathsworn to King Urien nor any man.'

'That's it, Arthur ap Nowhere they say. Isn't that it?'

'Some men say that, yes, my lady.'

'I have heard of you, of your victories, that is. Is that Excalibur?'

'Yes, it is.'

'The sword in the stone. How exciting to meet two heroes in the same week. First Bors and now Arthur. Merlin was right about you.'

Arthur smiled, and fought to not let the disappointment show upon his face, wondering what nonsense Merlin had filled the ladies' heads with on the march south.

'You are finally travelling south to Dumnonia?' he said to Guinevere, ignoring the talk of legends and Merlin's tall tales.

'Yes, finally we travel to Uther's court as my father intended.'

'And how is it that you travel without warriors to guide and protect you, and that a lady of Kernow is your only travel partner?'

Morgan and Guinevere exchanged a quick glance, and then Guinevere flashed her disarming smile. 'King Marc of Kernow sent Morgan north to serve as a lady at King Uther's court, just as we ladies have to do before our fathers find us a suitable husband. King Marc is Lady Morgan's foster father. We travel south together to leave the Bear Fort and join King Uther's court in Dumnonia.'

'The Bear Fort is not to your liking?'

'Is it to anyone's liking? There cannot be a colder, harsher place in all of Britain. It rains more than it's dry, winter dark seems to last forever. I spent more time in my chamber than I did riding or walking outside.'

'I am glad that you are here,' Arthur said, and ground his teeth as his face again flushed red and he could not control it. 'Though King Gwallog was right, it is not safe to be in Loidis now.'

'I am also glad.' She smiled, not the least bit bashfully, staring confidently into Arthur's eyes. 'We had to leave the Bear Fort in a hurry and thought not to come to Loidis until we met Merlin and Bors on the road. They persuaded us to ride with them, otherwise we should fall prey to marauding Saxons.'

'The hour grows late, and you must be weary from your travels. Sleep well, ladies. I will see you tomorrow, and hopefully there is more time to talk together before the enemy arrives.'

Guinevere and Morgan bowed their heads, and as Arthur took his leave, the sound of their laughter haunted him all the way back to Idnerth's villa. He worried he had made a fool of himself, barging into them like a clod, talking like a fool. Arthur was suddenly aware of his rough clothes, stained and soiled from the wild, and wondered how a lady of any court could entertain a rough soldier without the practised airs and graces of courtly life.

Arthur found Bors and Balin at the villa sharing a cup of ale, though it was Bors doing most of the talking. Arthur slumped in his bed and lay staring at the ceiling, cursing himself for a lackwit. His mind spun again with how Guinevere must think of him, of how he should have run a comb through his hair and beard and polished his mail before talking to her. Arthur tried to sleep, tossing and turning on his bed of straw, but always he came back to Guinevere. He feared what would become of her and Morgan should Loidis fall, and that steeled his desire to defeat the Saxons.

She was stuck in his head like a thorn, and all concerns of the advancing Saxon army slipped away. It was as though the war was over and the Saxons had been cowed into submission by Guinevere's beauty.

But he was wrong about that, because he awoke the next morning from a fitful sleep to the sounds of war horns.

10

Arthur raced from Idnerth's villa through cobbled streets crammed with warriors. Centurions with red-plumed crests traversing their helmets bellowed orders, chivvying frightened-faced farmer-spearmen into groups. Arthur wove his way between them, strapping on Excalibur's scabbard and its thick leather sword belt. He ran up the stairs to the east-facing wall and found Idnerth and Bors staring out over the battlements towards the forest.

'They are here?' Arthur asked.

'They've been blowing war horns since the crack of dawn, but no sign of the furry whoresons yet,' said Bors.

'Nothing from our scouts, either,' said Idnerth.

'I can smell the bastards. They are in the forest, swilling stolen ale and eating raided meat. The fight comes today, Idnerth. Is your army of churls ready?'

Idnerth glanced down below Loidis' walls where hundreds of men milled about the gap between buildings and wall, nothing but spears in their hands and fear in their eyes. No armour, just simple jerkins. Some carried clubs, grain flails and wood axes. Arthur saw one man with no weapon save a rusted shovel resting upon his shoulder.

'Ready as they'll ever be.'

'Look,' said Arthur, pointing across the field between Loidis and the thick wood, where a lone rider ambled from the treeline on a bay horse. The rider let his horse have its head, and it picked its way lazily into the green field, stopping here and there to crop at the grass whilst the rider stared at the warriors atop the city walls as though he had not a care in the world.

'Octha,' Nimue hissed, making Arthur and Idnerth jump. She seemed to arrive from nowhere, and Merlin stood beside her, glowering at the enemy. The legionaries made the sign of the cross to ward off their fear of the druid's pagan power, and both Arthur's and Bors' men bowed their heads to the Merlin and the *gwyllion*.

Beyond the wall, the Saxon rider slowly shook off his fur cloak to reveal his bare chest. It was Octha himself, the Saxon warlord who had come to slaughter, burn and conquer to make himself a king. He carried a war axe in one hand and he pointed the weapon at Loidis. Octha sat astride his horse confidently and without fear, controlling the beast with his knees alone. One man alone facing a city and its walls thronged with warriors.

'I saw him, at Dun Guaroy,' said Arthur, recalling the Saxon fortress that the enemy now called Bebbanburg, where he had saved Guinevere. Octha's face left a lasting impression on his memory, as it was not an easy one to forget. Octha was a monstrous man, almost as big as Bors, heavily muscled with a face so flat it was as though a boulder had crushed it. 'He fights like a maddened boar.'

'I should march out of the gate and challenge the bastard,' said Bors. The warriors about them agreed, murmuring with excitement at the prospect of single combat between Bors the champion and Octha.

'Why? He has an army out there waiting. Octha won't face you and risk death when he is about to win himself a kingdom.'

'Then why come and parade around like that? If he wants to fight, fight me.'

'He wants to fight, Bors, but not with you alone. He wants to kill us all and sit on King Gwallog's throne.'

'Get the legionaries up here,' Idnerth said to a centurion on his left. 'Keep fifty men below with the levy. I want the rest on the wall. Now. Ready bows and bring sheaves of arrows. Get the fires going. I want the pitch, tar, and water boiling before they reach the walls.'

Octha shouted something, but the morning breeze snatched his words away. He was too far away to be heard clearly, but the warriors on the walls fell silent, leaning in to listen, a heady mix of fear and anticipation fixing their gaze on the lone Saxon commander as he bellowed and shook his axe in belligerent challenge.

'Doesn't the fool know we can't hear him?' said Dewi, and the black cloaks chuckled as they marched up the stairs to take their place on the walls beside Idnerth's legionaries. 'Maybe his ears are full of fur.'

'Or wool from the sheep he's been humping. Saxon bastard,' said Anthun, and the men laughed again.

'Do not mock him,' Nimue said. She stalked amongst them, her face painted half black and half bone white. The warriors shuffled to get away from her as she moved through their ranks. She slunk about them, staring into men's eyes, moving with a cat-like prowl. 'Of all the Saxons, Octha is the one most feared by his own people. Even powerful men like Ida, Aelle of the south Saxons, Ida of Bernicia, Cwichelm of Lindsey and Clappa of Deira fear Octha's fury. Men who have won kingdoms by sheer will, battle, seax and blood. Feared warriors and champions would not cross Octha. And you mock him?'

'If you wish to stand with the warriors, Nimue, use your *seidr* and imbue us with battle-luck,' Arthur said. His men didn't need to hear about Octha's prowess, they needed bravery. 'Put your magic into our blades and let our gods show us the way to victory over the Saxons and their gods.'

'Just so, young Arthur,' she said, smiling to reveal her teeth and the precious stones set within them. She began to chant in her strange, ethereal-sounding native Irish. Arthur picked out the names of Arawn and Andraste as she called upon the gods to bring their favour to the defenders. The men closed their eyes, allowing her undulating song to seep into their souls as Nimue tapped them on the shoulder, or caressed their weapons with her long fingers to pass the gods' power into iron and steel. Even the Christian legionaries felt it, glancing nervously at one another, frightened by Nimue's paganism but her power rousing their heckles.

A war horn trumpeted from the forest and three men broke from the treeline across the field, running like hares from baying hounds. They ran desperately. Stripped naked with pale skin gleaming beside the dark forest and green fields. The running men repeatedly glanced over their shoulders as they ran with such terror that they almost tripped themselves up. They skirted wide of Octha's horse, running for their lives, arms flailing and faces contorted into rictuses of terror.

'Those poor men are our scouts,' Idnerth said. 'God save their souls.'

The three men passed Octha, and then the Saxon warlord dug his heels into his horse. It lurched into a canter and then a gallop.

'Come on, run,' called one of Idnerth's men. The rest of the legionaries took up the call, and soon all the men on Loidis' walls shouted encouragement, desperate for their countrymen to reach the city gates. Arthur found himself cheering that the three would close the distance, but Octha's horse gained on them, closing in too quickly.

'By the gods, we should send men out to rescue them,' said Bors, barging his way to the front of the wall.

'They wouldn't get there in time,' said Idnerth, knuckles white around his Roman pilum spear.

'Then we would at least slay Octha. I'm sick of looking at the Saxon turd. I'll go by myself. Get me a horse!' Bors disappeared from the battlements, but Idnerth was right. There was no time to save the desperate souls who ran for their lives.

Octha's horse raced between the fleeing scouts, and as he passed the foremost runner, Octha held his axe out wide to his side so that the blade sliced open the man's back, sending him spinning to the grass. A man cannot swing a heavy weapon on horseback without losing his balance, with only the reins and his knees to keep him mounted. So Octha leapt from his horse and buried the axe in the scout's skull as he struggled to get to his feet. The second scout tried to run wide of Octha, but the big Saxon ran him down and plunged his axe into the man's back with a loud thud. The warriors atop the walls groaned with dismay, and Bors milled about below the wall, yelling for someone to bring him a horse.

'He's going to make it,' said a hopeful legionary as the last scout ran clear of Octha's murderous war axe. But the monstrous Saxon took two steps and hurled his weapon. It turned over in the air, morning light catching its blade, and took the scout between the shoulder blades, sending him tumbling to the ground.

'Archers,' Idnerth growled. His three hundred legionaries laid down their spears, and each took a bow from boys who hurried amongst them, carrying armfuls of the yew-carved weapons. Each man also took a quiver of a dozen arrows. 'Nock.' They rested the arrows upon the bows and took the strain, stretching the bowstrings back to their right ears, bow staves creaking with the effort. 'Loose.'

Three hundred arrows soared into the morning sky, like a flock of white-feathered birds soaring high before whistling down at murderous speed towards the Saxon warlord. Octha held his massive arms out wide, as though he waited for the arrows' embrace, but the shafts fell short, slapping into the field in front of him. He laughed at the men on the walls, strolled to his horse and leapt upon its back, and rode back towards the forest. Horns blared from the woodland, and men appeared from the treeline. They came first as lone warriors, with silvery-grey furs about their shoulders and chests, then in groups of ten, then hundreds until an army of Saxons came from the trees.

'The Lord Jesus is with you, brave men,' said a faltering voice. It was Gwallog's bishop, Emrys, two fingers raised high, making the sign of the cross before Idnerth's warriors. The king was beside him, clad in his muscled Roman breastplate and a short Roman sword in his hand.

'God save us,' Gwallog gasped as he took in the size of the force arrayed against him. There were too many to count, and Arthur could not tell if it was one or two thousand warriors coming from the trees like ants in summer. Their spears and axes glinted beneath the sun like a shimmering lake. Octha's army was vast, war horns blared and Octha rode along the front of his warriors, hollering and waving his arms like a madman. They shook and sang an undulating war song, beating spears upon shields to make a war-din to shake Loidis' walls.

'Your god won't save you, King Gwallog,' said Merlin. 'Today you need the gods born of this land, our gods. Cruel gods of war and blood. You need Andraste and Arawn, Maponos and Lleu Llaw. Did your Jesus ever take up arms?'

'The Lord God shall cause thine enemies that rise up against thee to be smitten before thy face: they shall come out against thee one way, and flee before thee seven ways,' Bishop Emrys shouted at Merlin.

'Will you renounce your nailed god and support the true gods, King Gwallog?'

'I am a man of God, Merlin. This is not the time to speak of turning my back on the one true god!' Gwallog snapped. 'Where are the forces you promised us? Where are the warriors of Rheged, Powys, Gwynedd and beyond? We stand alone, with but a paltry force from Gododdin and Arthur's black cloaks. If my city falls, it will not be because of your pagan gods, or my true god. It is because the Saxons attack my city in overwhelming numbers and nobody, not the Pendragon nor any of my so-called allies, came to our aid.'

'Very well. Nimue, we are neither wanted nor needed here. Arthur, Bors, I shall await you at the southern gate.'

'Merlin, wait.' Arthur stepped away from the parapet and leant close to the druid. 'Take Guinevere and Morgan with you, and Balin, for he is still too badly injured to fight. If the city falls, get them to safety.'

Merlin frowned and then grinned wolfishly. 'There are too many Saxons, even for you and Excalibur. The king is right, support from other kingdoms did not arrive, and he cannot win against so many of the enemy. Do not waste your life on these walls. Great battles await, battles than can save our country. Gwallog's doom is set. If he cannot, even in his hour of need, return to the gods of his ancestors, then there is no hope for Elmet.'

Merlin turned on his heel and strode from the walls with Nimue trailing in his wake. Arthur took a step to go after him, but then realised that the men on the walls and beneath the stairs all watched and heard the druid. Most of them might be Christ worshippers, but they were still in awe of Merlin's power, and

Arthur's heart dropped at the looks of desperate fear in their eyes. Merlin had abandoned them, scorned by King Gwallog and his love of the nailed god.

'Look to God, he will protect your souls. We have no need of pagan wizards,' Bishop Emrys called, and Arthur shook his head in disbelief.

'Lord king,' Arthur said to Gwallog. 'This is not the time to worry about your men's souls. Octha comes to take everything you have. You need Merlin. The men believe in his power. Look at them!'

Gwallog waved Arthur away with his hand, and it was too late to persuade the king to at least ask Merlin to stand with the warriors rather than leave them to their doom. Arthur joined Bors and his black cloaks as a Saxon army advanced on Loidis. They came in a mighty wave with Octha at the centre. Countless warriors marching across the eastern plain, carrying ladders so freshly constructed that their timbers shone like gold. Horns continued to blare, and now their own shamans pranced before the Saxons. They capered with hair stuck up into points by dung, shaking their talismans and howling their curses up at the walls.

'How can we withstand their magic without Merlin?' asked Anthun, and the surrounding black cloaks murmured their agreement.

'Believe in your spears and your shields, men,' Arthur said, and he took his place amongst them.

The Saxon horde seethed across the field, and the moment the mass of fur, iron, leather and roaring warriors stepped across the lines of arrows his men had loosed at Octha, Idnerth ordered his men to loose. Each man let fly a dozen arrows, shooting one after the other in rapid succession, their shafts blackening the sky like an enormous murder of crows. The Saxons raised their shields, and the sound of iron arrowheads pounding into the linden-wood boards rattled like thunder.

'Spears!' Idnerth bellowed, and his men cast aside their bows and took up their Roman pilum spears. The Saxons lowered their shields and let out an almighty roar, clashing their weapons in defiance at the Britons. Many of the Saxons howled in agony, clutching at arrow shafts in their limbs and guts, but most of Idnerth's arrows had struck the wall of shields rather than the flesh beyond.

Two ranks of Saxons ran from the front lines, bows in their hands. The first rank knelt, and both loosed a volley of arrows at the walls. Arthur ducked as the shafts skittered against the stone and whistled over his head. One of Idnerth's legionaries gasped as an arrow slammed into his eye, and he toppled from the wall to send the Saxons into a joyous fury. More arrows peppered the walls, and the defenders shrank behind the parapet for cover. Arthur ducked, volleys of arrows flying overhead.

The arrows suddenly stopped, and Arthur stood.

'There they come!' Dewi called. The arrows had been a screen to allow Octha's men to charge at the walls with a score of ladders and Saxons streamed up them like squirrels.

'Yes,' Bors rumbled. 'Let them come. Let them come and die.'

'Spears and rocks!' Idnerth ordered. 'Aim for the first man on the ladder, always the first man.'

Idnerth himself leant over the wall, his red horsehair plume swaying. He tossed his spear down and the iron tip punched into the leading Saxon on the ladder below him. The spear thumped into the gap between neck and shoulder, and the Saxon tumbled backwards and dragged the men below him on the ladder down into the mass of baying warriors below.

The black cloaks grabbed the rocks and chunks of rubble piled around them and hurled the missiles down at the Saxons. Men with desperate eyes scrambled up the ladders, knives between their teeth and axes in their hands. Rocks smashed their skulls, and they fell howling into their comrades, only to be replaced by another warrior on the ladder whose rungs became slick with gore. Idnerth's men tossed their pilum spears into the enemy and down into the shields below. A Roman spear was different to a normal ash-shafted spear and its leaf-shaped point. A pilum was longer than a man is tall, and heavy, with a long iron shank fixed to a wooden shaft. The tip was a small arrow shape, and the iron shank was softer than the spear Arthur's men carried.

'Your spears are bending,' Dewi called to the legionaries. The iron shafts bent and twisted as they struck men and shields in the welter of Saxons below the walls.

'So the bastards can't throw them back at us,' grinned a legionary, and Dewi laughed. Arthur threw a handful of old Roman stone down at a yellow-bearded Saxon and it crashed into his teeth, sending the man sprawling. The warriors on the walls shouted with joy as they pounded the Saxons with missiles, but the Saxons kept on climbing, fresh warriors replacing any who fell from the ladders.

'There are no more rocks,' a warrior called, and the same shout was echoed by warriors all along the wall as they ran out of things to hurl at the enemy.

'Time to burn the sons of whores,' growled Idnerth. 'Fetch the cauldrons.'

Men groaned as they slid timber poles beneath the broiling cauldrons' rims, and hauled them to the wall's edge. Steam billowed, the stink of pitch and tar burning Arthur's throat, and the men balanced the massive bronze cauldrons on the edge. Idnerth swept his hand down, and the warriors tipped boiling tar, pitch and water over the climbing enemy. The Saxons screamed, and the sound was like nothing Arthur had ever heard. They howled like demons as the flesh burned from their bones and they fell into their comrades, splashing them with the terrifyingly hot liquids. One cauldron slipped from the wall, and the whole thing tumbled over the edge, ringing like a bell as it clattered against stone and smashed two ladders. Boiling hot pitch splashed over the Saxons and they ran away from its horror like scuttling mice.

'Fire arrows,' Idnerth said, his face set hard and pitiless against the enemy. The legionaries picked up their bows once more, and the bow-boys ran amongst them with arrows wrapped in wool and pitch. Other boys carried flaming torches, and they lit the arrows so that the top of the wall crackled with flame. 'Loose,' Idnerth ordered, and his men shot their fire arrows down towards the ladders. A whoosh of sound popped in Arthur's ears, and he flinched away from the horror of hundreds of Saxons bursting into flame. They screamed in incomparable pain, running like madmen as their hair and skin burned, reeking of foul, roasting meat. They clawed at themselves and rolled in the field as their friends tried desperately to get away and avoid their own clothes catching fire.

'Now they know they're in a war,' Gwallog bellowed, waving his short Roman sword about his head. 'Let them come. Let them see what it means to fight the legions of Elmet.'

The warriors on the walls cheered as though they had won the battle, clapping each other's backs and laughing with the joy of survival. But Arthur peered again over the edge, and Octha himself appeared below the wall, clearing burning ladders away with his axe, and his men joined him, inspired by his brave determination. They brought fresh ladders to the walls, and climbed again with renewed ferocity, the number of their warriors teeming in the field as though those already killed and maimed had barely dented the size of their horde.

'Kill them as they come, boys,' Bors said, and drew his axe.

'Wait until they reach the top,' Arthur told his men, 'then strike at their heads. Don't lean over the edge or they'll hack up at you.'

Saxons streamed up the ladders and Idnerth drove his Roman sword into a Saxon's eye as he popped up above the battlements. More Saxons came; the real slaughter began. Arthur swept Excalibur into the neck of a climbing Saxon and blood slapped against stone. A Gododdin man leaned over the edge, trying to sweep a ladder away with his spear and Saxon hands grabbed him and hauled him wailing over the edge. Arrows flew from below, trying to push the Britons back from the edge, but they fought on. More ladders came, and dirty Saxon hands grubbed over the parapet, hauling themselves over as not enough Britons tried to defend too much wall. Arthur hacked and stabbed, and his shoulder ached from killing Saxons. The battle raged all morning, and even Bors had to take a rest of swinging his axe, stepping away from the front to swig ale ladled from barrels by frightened-faced boys. The Saxons relentlessly attacked, and for every two Saxons who fell from their ladders, one struck his axe or seax at a Briton until a steady stream of wounded and dying men limped from the walls to priests waiting below to tend to them.

A great cheer went up from Arthur's black cloaks, because Balin appeared on the wall. His face was still the blue-purple of a thistle, and he carried a spear in his hands. Balin of the Two Swords, one of the few surviving warriors of a fallen kingdom, had come to kill the enemy and his presence imbued the warriors on the wall with renewed vigour. He charged forwards and drove his spear point into a Saxon's throat and the black cloaks fought like savages, as though the battle had only just begun. Balin struck over and again until his spear shaft shivered, then he picked up a Saxon axe from the battlements and struck again.

'You are not yet healed,' Arthur said as he surged to fight at Balin's side.

'Nothing could keep me from this fight,' he said, and cracked a Saxon's helmet apart like an egg.

A wild-eyed Saxon swayed away from Excalibur's point and jabbed a wicked bladed seax at Arthur's chest. The point drove him backwards, and would have killed him if his chain-mail hadn't absorbed the blow. Hywel killed the Saxon with a thrust of his spear and Arthur fell back from the front line, hands on his knees, sweat dripping from his brow. His wounded shoulder ached, and he could feel blood moving beneath the leather jerkin under his mail. Battle raged all along the east-facing wall with a thousand Saxons yet to join the fray. Arthur wondered how long the assault could last. A day? Would there be rest when darkness fell only for fighting to begin anew at first light? It was a desperate thought. It was the first time Arthur had defended a city, and he could see no way for Octha to sweep the high walls clear of defenders while Octha's men were forced to fight balanced atop ladders.

As though to answer Arthur's thoughts, a horn blared from the south, but not a Saxon horn. The sound came from within Loidis, and Arthur turned, trying to see who had raised the sound. At the same time, a great crash thundered beneath the eastern wall. Arthur felt its tremor in his boots and his men looked to him with fear-stricken faces.

'They have brought up a ram,' Idnerth said. His lean face was bloodied and smeared with filth, his short sword black with blood. Gwallog fought beside his Primus Pilum, the king hacking at those who came to take his city and slaughter his people. 'Boil more pitch! Refill the cauldrons!'

Arthur dashed to the wall's edge and risked a glance over the side. Amongst the throng of baying Saxons, a score of raised shields protected a long tree trunk, twice as thick as a man. The Saxons held the trunk by stout boughs and they hammered its weight into the eastern gate, smashing into the oak doors, slowly taking four steps back, and then charging again.

'Look to the south,' said Becan, tugging at Arthur's sleeve. 'They are attacking from the southern wall, lord.' Arthur peered south but could see nothing. 'Come, lord, I beg you.' Arthur followed Becan, sword in hand, as they crossed the eastern wall and turned south onto the stretch of wall which faced towards the wide bend in the river Aire. A dozen men guarded that wall, and each of them pointed towards the river as they saw Arthur approach.

'There, lord, look,' a burly man said.

Arthur peered towards the river and noticed three boats moored against the bank. Men streamed from the ships, charging towards the south gate which Gwallog's people used to fetch water from the river. It was a small gate, only wide enough for two people to walk through abreast and certainly not wide enough for an army to charge into.

'How many men?' Arthur asked.

'Fifty, lord. We only saw them as they came ashore, so I blew the horn.' He was a man of Gwallog's levy, a farmer in a stained woollen jerkin with a curved war horn in his hand.

'Why did you not see them as they approached?'

'We were told to carry more rocks and bricks to the eastern wall, lord. So we did, then we were told to come back here and keep watch.'

Arthur peered over the parapet but could see no sign of the enemy. He turned and ran to the stone stairway leading down from the wall. Then he stared in horror, for below him Balan and his twelve traitors ran in through the southern gate, followed by more Saxons. They had found a way in. Arthur knew not how they had opened the river gate, but the enemy was inside Loidis, and Balin's brother had come to the slaughter.

11

Balan and his warriors charged from the south gate and reached the east-facing wall before anybody fighting above could react. Arthur had the burly farmer who had sounded the alarm blow his war horn until his cheeks were ready to burst, but such was the din and fervour of the fight over the eastern gate that neither Gwallog, Idnerth, Balin nor Bors heard it. Arthur charged down the steps and ran along the cobbled street as the men of Elmet's levy simply moved aside to let Balan's men through. Hundreds of men pressed into the narrow space between the city walls and its buildings, and Arthur slammed into the crowd, shouldering and clawing his way through to get at Balan and his traitors.

'Stop them, stop them!' Arthur bellowed, but the churls were confused and had let the enemy run through their massed ranks and reach the eastern gate without challenge. Balan and his traitors were Britons. They wore their hair like Britons, dressed like Britons and carried shields emblazoned with the fox and other familiar symbols, all of which made them look at home, running towards where the fighting was thickest. Bors and Balin heard the horn at last and came charging down from the wall with the black cloaks and the men of Gododdin at their backs. Balan's warriors met them with locked shields and a furious battle unfolded beneath the stone archway, where twin oak gates stood against the Saxon battering ram.

Arthur could not get through the crowd to join that fight and he roared at the surrounding men to get out of his way. Men came stumbling from the southern gate with bloodied noses and wounds. They were levy men and Arthur reached out and grabbed one by the arm.

'What happened? How did they get in?' he said, shaking the man, who stared at him with glassy eyes as though in a daze.

'One of our lot opened the gate for them, lord,' said the man, a thin churl with a heavy jaw and blood seeping from a wound on his scalp. 'He was a Briton, dressed like me. We protested, telling him to keep it closed, but he beat us and opened it, anyway. When the men from the river came through the gate, he joined them and ran to the other gate. He was one of them, an enemy already inside the city walls, waiting to let the buggers in. We were bloody and beaten. I didn't know what to do.'

Arthur left him and ran to join Balin and Bors at the eastern gate. One of Balin's traitors must have come into Loidis, feigning to be a churl answering the levy call. He had opened the small southern gate and let Balan's men in. Arthur's stomach churned at the sickening simplicity of it. No one would have suspected it or looked for it. A Briton coming through the gates in the days before the battle with hundreds of others answering their king's call. When Octha attacked the eastern wall with full force, the man simply opened a gate beneath a wall manned by too few guards. There were just not enough defenders to cover every stretch of Loidis' perimeter wall, and Balan had sailed up the river Aire with fifty men, a traitor's heart and a cunning plan.

The fight beneath the eastern gate was ferocious. Arthur threw himself into it, fighting with Bors on his left and Balin on his right. They faced a shield wall of huge Saxons, men with big shields and war axes who had followed Balan through the river gate. Arthur tore out the throat of one, only to see him replaced with a bigger, stronger enemy. Bors fended off blows with his axe, and tried to grab the enemy shields and rip them away, but the enemy was strong and they battered the Gododdin giant until he fell back. Arthur hacked at them with Excalibur, fighting until his good arm screamed with exhaustion, but there was no way through their shields. Four warriors died in that furious fight, cut down by Saxon axes and smashed to ruin by their iron-shod shield rims.

Behind the protection of that shield wall, Balan and his twelve traitors hauled at the heavy spar bracing the oak gates. They lifted the spar free and Arthur's heart almost burst with despair. Balan turned, saw Arthur and Balin, and a wicked grin split his one-eyed, scarred face. He pointed at Balin's axe and laughed, holding aloft their father's sword in mocking triumph. The spar was free, and nothing remained to stop the enemy horde from driving through the gates into the city. Balin roared with impotent fury as Octha's monstrous frame pushed open the gates and howled his ear-shattering battle cry.

Octha's Saxon army flooded in through the gate. The force of their charge drove Arthur, Balin and Bors back, their sheer numbers overwhelming the defenders. No blows needed to be struck. It was a tidal wave of Saxon bodies hurling Arthur and the defenders out of the way by sheer pressure of numbers. The black cloaks and the men of Gododdin fled down cobbled streets, unable to resist so many Saxons. Arthur ran, as did Bors and Balin, and a heavy cloak of descending shame drowned out his battle-fury as Arthur ran for his life. They lost sight of Idnerth and Gwallog and the brave men of Elmet. Roman buildings blurred past him as Arthur made for the southern gate.

Merlin waited there, with Nimue, Guinevere and Morgan, and Arthur, Bors and Balin followed them out of the gate towards the river, where the ships left by Balan's men waited in the water. They moved in silence, clambering into the boats and casting off. Black cloaks and Gododdin men took up the oars and rowed westwards, upstream, and away from the Saxons. Balin stood in the prow, staring back at Elmet with tears upon his bruised face as the first pillars of smoke rose from the city and screams came from behind the walls, wailing a terrible lament to begin the story of fallen Elmet.

'Look,' said Guinevere, rushing to the stern and pointing ashore. People poured from the city's western gate. Legionaries amongst them, hundreds of men, women and children fleeing their conquered home and city. The river carried the boats away from Loidis, and Arthur turned to watch the fugitives flee, wishing he had a dozen more boats to carry them all to safety.

'I hope Gwallog, Ceretic and Idnerth are amongst them,' whispered Bors. The big man sat in the bilge, gaping at the lost city, as ashamed as Arthur at their defeat and the manner of their escape.

'Another city fallen to Woden's people,' said Nimue. She perched feline-like upon an empty rowing bench, head cocked to one side as she stared at the city where Saxon warriors marauded through the streets and lanes, and where the women and children of Loidis suffered terrible fates.

They rowed along the river's wide turns, defeated and disconsolate. Guinevere came to Arthur and helped him check his wound. She pulled the mail and leather liner over his head, leant over the side and cupped her hand with water to wash the wound. Some of the stitching had burst, and she gently wiped the blood away with her wet hands.

'You did all you could,' she said. But Arthur could say or do nothing except stare back, his mind full of regret and despair that more warriors had not come to defend the city and its people. Darkness fell, and they hauled the ships ashore, camping in the lee of the vessels' hulls, pulling sailcloths out over oars stuck into the riverbank like makeshift tents. Seventy-two black cloaks and twenty-nine men of Gododdin survived the battle. Many of the men had sustained injuries in the ferocious fighting. Merlin and Nimue spent the evening tending to the wounded, cleaning and treating their wounds. The most serious wounds Merlin closed with a knife heated to glowing red in the campfire. Nimue walked along the riverbank, plucking herbs and plants which she mashed with river water in an upturned helmet, and heated the brew over the fire. She had the warriors drink the tea to help them sleep and recover their strength, and made another thick paste to smear on wounds to keep the cuts free of infection.

Balin sat alone on the camp's edge, brooding, staring out into the river. Arthur knew him well enough to leave the man alone. He could only imagine the thoughts milling through Balin's mind, memories of other cities he had tried to protect but had seen fall. Balin knew first-hand the horrors which awaited the people of Loidis now that Octha's men rampaged through the houses, churches, lanes and royal buildings. He would not want to discuss those feelings with anyone, nor his unquenchable hatred for his brother, who had been the architect of Loidis' downfall.

'Is Elmet now a Saxon kingdom?' Guinevere asked, helping Arthur back on with his leather jerkin.

'Octha certainly rules in Loidis and Gwallog, hopefully, has fled. But it is only a Saxon kingdom if Octha can hold on to it, and whilst Idnerth and King Gwallog live, that fight will never be over,' Arthur said.

'Is it still your fight?'

'It is all our fights. If the Saxons settle in Elmet, it won't be long before their greedy eyes turn to the next kingdom, to Elmet's borders, to see what new lands they can conquer.'

'Will you stay here in Elmet and fight alongside King Gwallog?'

Arthur took a sip of Nimue's tea. 'Perhaps, but first I shall go to Rheged and implore Urien to send warriors to help King Gwallog.'

'Rheged.' Guinevere said the word as though she had a piece of rotten food in her mouth.

'Yes, Urien's kingdom is the only one close enough to feel genuinely threatened by Octha's victory. The threat is too remote for the rest to march without the Pendragon's order.'

'I must continue south. I cannot return to Rheged.'

'The road is too dangerous. It is safer for you to stay with us. I'm afraid your journey to Dumnonia will have to wait.'

'I cannot return to Rheged because I fled from King Urien.'

'Fled? Why?'

'He tried to marry me.'

Arthur almost dropped his tea. 'Urien?'

'Yes, he pawed at me for months. Calling me to his hall, inviting me to his chamber or to ride in the dales around the Bear Fort. He sent word to my father, who would be only delighted for me to marry a great king and renowned warrior like Urien. I, however, certainly do not wish to marry the old brute. All women know how he treated Queen Igraine. How he beat and humiliated her.'

'You must go back to him, Guinevere. You cannot choose who you marry, that is for your father to decide. Do you really wish to make an enemy of King Urien of the Bear Fort?'

'I know that. Do you think my head is full of smoke? But I won't allow two old men to determine my life. I will decide who I marry and what becomes of me. So, I ran away and Morgan came with me. We are for Dumnonia, warmer weather, and far away from that slathering old man drooling at my skirts every time I turn around.'

'Urien is not a forgiving man, Guinevere.'

'And he shall never be my husband. I would rather die. The gods grant us but one life, and it is not my destiny to rot in a dark chamber in the Bear Fort, in a land damp and hard with rock and rain.'

'Life is not that simple. When you get to Dumnonia, if you get to Dumnonia, and Uther hears how you fled from Rheged, he will send you straight back. This is not a game. Bards fill folk with tales of brave warriors, beautiful princesses, battles, heroes and fair maidens, but they lie. This is a land of war, of blades, murder, slaves, fortresses and murderous Saxons. What woman of royal blood has ever chosen her husband for love? Kings use their daughters to marry for alliance, for strength, or for more land. I have learned much since I left the safety of my spear-father's home to take up the spear. There is no forgiveness in this world. No right to anything you cannot protect with a stout spear or a sharp sword. Whatever it is you think the gods owe you because you are a princess, you are owed nothing. Destiny and fate are words used by those would fill our heads with dreams. Legends and dreams are how we drive young men to the shield wall, how we persuade women to marry men they have never met to strengthen their fathers' positions. There is only this—' Arthur tapped his hand upon Excalibur's cold pommel '—and this.' He tapped his forehead.

'What of this?' Guinevere touched Arthur's chest, her slender fingers pushing at the chain-mail and leather over his heart. 'Our hearts can be free if we have the courage to strive for what we truly desire. Why should we submit to the will of others? Does Merlin? Octha? Do you?'

He stared into her green eyes and had no answer. The weariness of battle was still heavy upon him, though Guinevere had washed its filth from his face and body.

'I have kept this with me.' Arthur leant back and took the silver cloak pin she had given to him, and which he always wore inside his belt. 'It brings me luck.'

Guinevere smiled. 'I am glad. I think of you, out there in the wilds. Wondering if you are safe, or if something terrible has happened to you.'

'You think of me?'

She blushed and looked away, and then flashed a cheeky grin. 'But you do need a bath.'

'Really? I washed...' He could not remember the last time he had bathed, for it had not occurred to him amongst the problems of war and worries about the Saxon threat.

'You smell like an old goat.'

'Come now, go easy on a soldier.'

'An old goat who has rolled in a pigsty and ridden through a bog.'

They laughed together, and it was a strange feeling. The surrounding warriors stared in disbelief. How could anybody find humour at a time like this? But Guinevere transported Arthur away from war and the concerns of men, supplies, marching and battle. She brought a lightness to him, a bright possibility of something different. Another dream running alongside his dreams of victory and reputation, a simpler dream. They sat there for a moment, just looking at each other. Arthur longed to lean forward and kiss her full lips, to hold her soft, warm body close to him. For a guilty moment, he allowed himself to wonder if she might feel the same. Could a princess of Cameliard fall in love with a wandering warrior? In those green eyes flecked with gold, Arthur saw a fleeting vision of himself without a sword, living with her in a warm valley beside a cool stream.

'It is time to talk, Arthur,' said Merlin's harsh voice, snapping Arthur from his dream.

'Yes,' Arthur said simply, and smiled at Guinevere as he stood to walk with the druid.

Merlin marched between the sullen warriors and around Nimue, who was still busy tending to the wounded. He walked with his hands clasped behind his back and a hard look creasing his lined face. The wan light flickering from the camp fire caught the tattooed shapes on the druid's skull, and strength emanated from him like warmth from the blaze. Arthur could not guess how old Merlin was, and would not ask him for fear of his cutting wrath, but he was at least as old as Urien and Uther, and Ector had once said that Merlin was old in the days of the Great War, the kingdom-shattering events of which unfolded a generation ago. They left the firelight and walked beside the river, its flowing waters sighing in the darkness as unseen beasts shifted and croaked in the brush.

'Has she bewitched you, too?' Merlin cocked an eyebrow at Arthur and cackled as he struggled to find a response. Merlin halted beside a gnarled willow tree. Its trunk twisted and folded around itself and the branches stretched over the water, drooping and dripping long, sad boughs into the river. Merlin laid his hand upon the trunk and closed his eyes, as if he could feel the tree, converse with it, soak up all it had seen during its long life.

'She was to marry Urien. Did you know that?'

'He desired to marry her. There is a difference. I knew her father, Leodegrance, in the Great War. A stout fighter. But Cameliard is as hard-pressed by enemies across the narrow sea as we are here. He would welcome Urien as his son-in-law, once Rheged committed to send warriors to fight for Cameliard.'

'Would Urien send men across the sea?'

'He might. He could send his son Owain with a company of warriors.'

Arthur stroked a hand down his face. 'We need Owain and his

warriors here, not across the sea. If Owain, Kai and five hundred men of Rheged had marched to Elmet, we would celebrate a glorious victory this evening, not sleep beneath an old sailcloth running for our lives.'

'Just so. You are starting to use your head, as well as the sword I gave you. She will not marry Urien.'

'Then who?'

'What do you care? I have seen you mooning over her. She is beautiful, is she not?'

'She is kind, gentle, and clever, and…'

'Ha! I knew it. She is one of those things, surely, but what daughter of a king is kind? You have lost yourself in that flowing copper hair and bright eyes. But pull yourself together. Quickly. Before you make a fool of both of us. She will marry some poor lackwit with land and silver, but not until this war is over. There is a chance to recover Elmet before Octha overruns the kingdom. He has taken Loidis, and he will remain there for weeks whilst his men enjoy the fruits of their labour. He is their lord, and his men are bound to him only because he promises them glory, spoils and women. They have those things now. That is the very reason they came to Britain, risking everything to leave their homes and families. They want to enjoy it, to bask in their victory. The time for us to strike back is now. But we need more men. You shall go to Urien and return with Owain and Kai. I shall find Gwallog and Idnerth and see about gathering as many men as we can to recover the city.'

'And Guinevere?'

'Did I give you that sword so that you could succumb to the whims of that pitiful little crustacean between your legs, or so that you can use your head and your heart to return this land to our people? Do I busy myself for nothing spreading word of your exploits, sowing the seeds of legend in men's heads so that they are ready to rise to your banner when the time is right?'

'I did not ask for any of that.' Arthur snapped a twig from the tree and tossed it into the river.

'Asked for it? Petulant boy! Ingrate!' Merlin snarled, his face twisted with anger. Arthur shrank back, feeling the druid's power like a furnace. 'You yearned for it, and do still. Do not act so coy. I know what lives within that dark heart of yours, the inside of your thought cage, which you share with no one else. You crave the adulation and the glory. You are a leader of men, as prideful and vainglorious as any of our kings. Do you not bask in triumph when men call your name? Or feel like a giant when you slay your enemies and drive them from the battlefield?

'It was I who gave you to Ector, I who ensured you were raised by the finest warrior in all Britain. Do you think what was a mistake? Mere folly? You talked to me before of Igraine's child, who you are or were and could become. Your little sweetheart back there is a princess, a noblewoman. She is the daughter of a warrior king, as brutal a man as the rest of them. Would she marry the son of a slave woman? Be careful what you say to me, Arthur ap Nowhere, for I can easily crush what I have created. Treat me with respect, for I am the father of all you are and ever will be. Only I know the truth of your birth. How do you know that Ector did not lie to protect you when he spoke to you of Igraine and dead babies?'

Arthur gaped at Merlin. The druid's hard eyes bored into Arthur's skull like hot coals. Arthur fumbled for words, to find some way of pushing back against Merlin's harshness. But everything he said was true, and the truth burned like a whip.

'Yes... now you begin to understand. Do not ask me if you are the Pendragon's son, a fishwife's brat, or a slave's whelp. I hold the truth of it, and you do not need to know. Accept what you are and what you want. Allow me to make you into the warlord of Britain, and kings will bow to you before we are done. To unite the kingdoms of this island and muster enough men to throw the Saxons back across the sea, we need more than a warlord, more than a king of some shit-stinking hill fort atop a midden heap. We need the battle-king of Britain, a man who wields Excalibur and leads an army of men drawn from every corner of our land. That is what I strive for and what must be. You are that man, Arthur, and you wish for it as much as I. Admit it to yourself and embrace the work I do, accept the legends and men will come. With five hundred more men, we could have saved Loidis. Imagine what we could do with five thousand? For that to happen, men must believe in the legend. It must kindle a fire within them. Then they will flock to the sword and the man who wields it. Let the screams of the dying within Loidis stay with you. I hope their fetches haunt your dreams, for they shall live forever inside mine. We owed it to those people to raise an army. It is our duty! Become who you must be. Let me show you the way and we shall defeat the Saxons. Is that what you want?'

Arthur stroked his thumb across Ida's sceptre where it hung from his belt. Ida had brought the stone symbol of his authority across the sea and it had helped him win a kingdom. Arthur believed the harsh, snarling faces carved upon its head belonged to cruel, long-dead kings of the Saxon people. They knew what it took to be a commander of warriors, and so did the Saxons, who risked everything to come to Britain. To be a leader, to be a commander of men, required hardness, cruelty, ambition and strength. That is what Arthur had learned since he had left Caer Ligualid to become a man. Merlin had peered deep within Arthur's secret heart, where nobody else could see and where Arthur himself feared to look and admit who he was and what hopes kindled there. He wanted it. Arthur wanted power, glory, reputation. He burned to see the Saxons defeated, to hear his name called by armies, and have kings grovel at his feet. Arthur wanted Guinevere. He wanted it all. That was it laid bare, and the knowing of it shocked him.

'Yes,' Arthur whispered. 'Yes,' he said again, this time with belligerence. Jaw set, shoulders back.

'Good. Then let's get to work.'

12

Arthur reached the Bear Fort after a week of riding alone through the forests and hills of northern Elmet into southern Rheged. He took a wide path, avoiding the Roman roads and wagon paths which wound their way through valleys and dales. Instead, Arthur kept to the creaking woods and bleak high places. He came alone because every man was needed in Elmet, and took the hard road because his mission was too important for him to fall prey to a roving Saxon war band.

Balin took charge of the black cloaks and gave his word to protect Guinevere and Morgan. Merlin and Nimue remained with Bors and his Gododdin men as the two war bands split up to find Gwallog and the survivors of Loidis. Their aim was to fight the Saxons, to attack any of them who left Loidis to raid and burn local villages. Merlin and Nimue gave the men belief. They blessed them with the old gods' favour and went from village to village, stirring up support and gathering any who had not mustered to join the fight for Elmet's survival.

Cavall bounded along at Llamrei's side and Arthur reached Rheged on a grey morning. The Bear Fort loomed on its high promontory glowering down at the river Eden, and Arthur followed the river's meander and up the steep-sided approach to King Urien's fortress. A stiff wind whipped in from the western sea and billowed around the hill to whip Arthur's hair away from his face. Cold drizzle seeped from the sky like fog to soak his cloak and armour so that Arthur shivered his way up the hill to the sharp, fang-like stakes of the Bear Fort's timber palisade. The gate which bridged the gap across the fortress' ditch was down and Llamrei's hooves clattered on the dark wood as he whickered at the smell of civilisation after so long travelling in the wild.

The fortress stank of smoke, shit and damp thatch as Arthur dismounted in a wide courtyard surrounded by wattle houses, smithies and potteries. A guard came and helped Arthur with Llamrei's reins, and the warrior clapped his fist to his chest in salute.

'Welcome, Lord Arthur,' said a second guard, and Arthur inclined his head.

'I come to speak with King Urien.'

'He is at home, lord. You are in luck, for Prince Owain and Lord Kai are also here. I can escort you to the great hall.'

Arthur followed the guard, a short man with ratty grey hair, through the tangle of the Bear Fort's mud-slick streets. Folk bowed to Arthur because of his mail and sword, though he doubted any recognised him as the boy from Caer Ligualid. Arthur ran over and over in his mind what he would say to Urien when they came face to face. To ask a king for warriors was not like asking a churl for a mug of cow's milk. Urien's warriors were the men who protected his kingdom and made sure his subjects paid and delivered up their annual tithe. To lose warriors jeopardised a king's hold upon his kingdom and left him vulnerable to attack. Arthur mulled over this as he stepped around a pile of donkey shit and tried to accustom himself to the gut-churning smell inside the fortress.

'Lord king,' the guard called as they entered the Bear Fort hall. Arthur glanced up at the enormous bear's skull hanging above the door, and steeled himself, preparing to meet the famous King of Rheged. Arthur had met Urien before, and was born and raised in Caer Ligualid, a stronghold within Urien's kingdom. But Urien was a powerful man known for his harshness and Arthur would have rather faced a Saxon shield wall than face Urien in his hall.

The king slouched on his high-backed throne, glowering, malevolent like a dragon atop its pile of treasure. The roof was high and smoke-blackened. Torches flickered in iron crutches set high on support posts which stretched from floor to rafters. Shields with Urien's bear sigil hung on the walls, along with the shields of enemies Urien and his warriors had slain in battle. The skulls of five men killed by Urien himself adorned his throne, and the king ran a heavy hand down his braided iron-grey beard. A scar ran from the top of Urien's head down through his eye to his jaw. He was broad and thick-necked, with a round face and clever eyes, and Arthur shivered to think of the grim old king pawing at Guinevere, her soft skin shuddering beneath his calloused hand.

'Well, we are honoured,' said Urien, his voice as cracked and full of gravel as the gulley beside a Roman road. 'The great Lord Arthur is here, fresh from slaying Saxons by the hundred, pulling swords from stones, and shitting water faeries from his arse.'

'Lord king,' said Arthur, forcing himself to show only a face of stone, and not blush at the king's mockery despite the sniggers from Urien's gathered warriors. A dozen feasting benches spread amongst the floor rushes and rushlights, where courtiers and hearth-troop warriors ate bread and cheese and drank ale around the crackling hearth fire. Smoke hung heavy in the air as it waited to seep through the thatch, making the wan light shimmer and Arthur's mouth dry.

'What brings you home to Rheged? This is your home, though

you have never sworn me an oath or shown me the respect a king deserves.'

Arthur ignored the slight again, anger rising inside him. 'I come from Elmet with dire news. Octha has taken Loidis, and King Gwallog fights a desperate war to cling to his kingdom's survival.'

'I imagine old Gwallog regrets his cattle raids now, then. I hope he enjoyed the beef his skulking raiders have stolen from my borders every summer since I was a boy. I expect he wishes he had been a better friend to Rheged and the other kingdoms, instead of prancing around in his foolish white toga as though he were a tribune of Rome.'

'I was at the attack on Loidis. I fought on the walls against Octha and his horde. With more men, we could have defended the city and defeated Octha.'

'Could you, now? With more men, I could rule the entirety of Britain, boy. Are you a boaster, as well as Merlin's pet?'

'I am not a boy, and nor am I your subject to be spoken to in such a way.' The sniggering stopped, and a hush fell upon the Bear Fort's mead hall. 'I am Arthur, wielder of Excalibur and leader of over one hundred spearmen. I come to ask you, King Urien, to send warriors south to join the surviving warriors of Elmet in the fight against the Saxons. Against the enemies of Britain and of us all.'

'Mind your tongue whilst you are a guest in my hall. I know why you have come. Merlin sent you. He would weaken me, drain my kingdom of warriors until I am as weak as Gwallog. Then, when Rheged is on its knees and I must beg my fellow kings for help, the druid will have as much power over me as he does you. That will not be my fate. I have experienced Merlin's meddling before, long ago, and am wise to his cunning.'

'Bors of Gododdin fights with Elmet. King Letan supports the war.'

'King Letan,' Urien scoffed and took a drink of ale from a curved horn. 'Safe now in his mountains, after we all sent our warriors north to save his kingdom from the Saxons. But of course you know that, because you are the hero of the river Glein.'

'I know it. I lost Ector, my spear-father, that day. I see Lords Kai and Owain here, men who fought like bears and won a great victory. But the fight continues, and if Elmet falls, surely Rheged is next.'

'Men from Gwynedd raid my southern borders, and ships from Lothian raid my western coast. I have gathered my captains here today to talk of how we should strike back at them. How can I spare men to fight Saxons when my fellow kings steal my livestock and burn my villages? The Pendragon does not command the kingdoms to muster, so who are you and Merlin to ask us to fight for another kingdom? We marched to the river Glein because the men of Dumnonia came north with Uther's dragon banner and the Pendragon's fasces. I see no dragon banner now?'

Arthur searched the hall and found only grim faces staring back at him. Words would not come, as though his voice was a prisoner inside his throat. Elmet needed Urien's men. It was as simple as that. But Urien was right, and the Pendragon had not given the order to march. Kai caught Arthur's eye. His foster brother smiled sadly. He was Urien's oath man and had succeeded Ector, his father, as lord of Caer Ligualid. Kai ruled the Caer at Urien's pleasure and so would not, could not, speak in support of Arthur against the king.

'The Lady Guinevere is with Merlin and my black cloaks in Elmet,' Arthur said, the words escaping from his mouth before he could hold them back, before the idea of using that gaming piece had fully formed in his mind.

Urien leant forward, the leather of his iron-studded jerkin creaking as he beckoned a gnarled finger for Arthur to approach the throne. Arthur strode through the hall, the eyes of veteran warriors following him, drinking in his mail, sword and the death-ring tattoos which stained his forearms blue. Arthur rested his hand on Excalibur's hilt, letting the sword imbue him with confidence he did not feel. Owain ap Urien sat on a feasting bench beside his father's throne, and the prince met Arthur's gaze with a flat stare which gave nothing away. His long black hair framed a strong face which remained impassive, showing neither support nor enmity, though Owain had fought bravely at the river Glein and earned much renown. Before the battle, Owain had questioned Arthur's right to lead and had despaired of Arthur's battle plan, but they had fought side by side and defeated Ida's army together.

Arthur stopped before Urien and his skull-framed throne, and he met the king's icy stare with his stone face. The last time he was there, Arthur had been a boy, a young spearman of Caer Ligualid. Now, he was a warlord in his own right. Winner of a great battle, and a killer. Arthur had felt like an imposter upon first entering the hall, but even under the withering strength of Urien's gaze, Arthur wrestled his fears into submission and mastered himself. He was Arthur, and he would not look away from King Urien, no matter his reputation or his ferocity.

The skulls seemed to stare at Arthur, cavernous black holes where eyes once lived, souls snatched from life by Urien's hand. Their grey bone and the memory of the men they had once belonged to a symbol of the king's brutal ruthlessness.

'Guinevere is in Elmet?' Urien asked, his voice a low growl, almost a whisper so that the men in his hall would not hear.

'She is with Balin and my black cloaks, along with Merlin and Nimue. She came to us in Loidis before the city fell.' Arthur stopped short of letting Urien know she had told him of his intentions.

'And Lady Morgan, Gorlois' daughter?'

'She is there too.'

Urien slumped back and drummed his fingers on the arm of his throne, eyeing Arthur carefully. 'You should have brought her back to me.'

'Why? Guinevere was a guest at your court, and makes her way to Dumnonia. Which, she says, is where her father intended her to be when he sent her across the sea. Before her ships were waylaid and I rescued her from Dun Guaroy.'

'She should not have left here without my leave. Return her to me.'

'The lady does not belong to you and can go where she pleases.'

Urien leaned forward and squinted at Arthur, the corner of his lip curling with distaste. 'Do not anger me, lad. You come into my hall strutting like the cock in the henhouse because you've won a battle and killed a few Saxons. I was killing my enemies before you were born. My arms were thick with death rings before you sucked a nursemaid's tit. I know war, and I know Merlin. Do not think the druid will protect you from my wrath. My wife is dead, and Guinevere will be mine. I have sent word to Leodegrance with an offer of marriage, and he will accept it. So bring her back to me, Arthur, or I will fetch her myself.'

'Elmet is a dangerous place now that Loidis has fallen and there are but few warriors to keep the roads safe for maidens who wish to travel. If she left the protection of my black cloaks to ride north, Saxons could waylay her. It's best if she goes south, to the safety of Dumnonia and Uther's court until the war for Elmet is over.'

'She will be my wife!' Urien barked, and slammed his fist hard onto his throne. 'Uther will force her to his bed faster than a hare running from a hound. I want her, and she will be mine.'

'I came here to ask for warriors to fight our common enemy, not to talk of an old king's lust. I must return with all haste to fight for King Gwallog's kingdom. But if you were to send an escort of warriors south with me, an escort large enough to protect Princess Guinevere from the dangers of the road, I would make sure she returns with your men when the fighting is over.'

'I want her here before the moon wanes.'

'After we recover Loidis.'

Urien grumbled and glanced at his son, Owain. Owain smiled at Arthur and nodded his head in agreement. 'Your oath on it.'

Arthur kept his stone face, but inside his mind churned like a stormy sea. He had not intended to use Guinevere as a bargaining piece to persuade Urien to send warriors south. Entering the fort, he had hoped that his plea might suffice, that the victory at the Glein could be enough to show Urien, with support from Owain and Kai, that they could defeat the Saxons again. Guinevere occupied Arthur's head as much as the war against the Saxons. Every night he fell asleep thinking of her, and every morning he woke and wondered where she was and what she was doing. He could not hand her over to Urien. The king licked his lips and smiled, revealing a set of broken yellowed teeth behind his beard. He was scarred, hard and cruel, and the thought of him taking Guinevere to his bed made Arthur's stomach heave. But he needed warriors. If Elmet was to survive, and to throw Octha out of Loidis, Arthur needed spearmen. Uther's bloodshot eyes bored into Arthur, and he hated the wily old king at that moment. He wanted to draw Excalibur and drive the blade into Urien's rotten heart, but that was a boy's thought, the uncontrolled wish of a fool.

'I will need four hundred spearmen to keep the princess safe.'

'One hundred, and you must pay them each a pouch of hack-silver for their trouble.'

'Three hundred and fifty, and I'll pay their commanders a pound of silver each.'

'Three hundred and you'll pay every man. Otherwise, they come back to me hungry for silver and gold. That is what it means to be a lord, young commander. Men expect silver, rings and glory. You take them, you reward them.'

'Three hundred spearmen, then.'

'Owain and Kai will lead them, and you can march in two days' time.'

'Thank you, lord king.' Arthur clapped a fist to his chest and turned on his heel, feeling sick for making a promise he could not keep.

'Wait,' Urien rasped, and Arthur closed his eyes and sighed. 'Your oath to return the princess?'

Arthur turned, knelt and placed his hands inside Urien's hands. 'I give you my oath that I shall send the princess north once the battle for Loidis is over, and I will pay your men for their service.'

'Good, good. Now, eat, drink. Owain and Kai will ready my men for the road. Keep my betrothed safe, Arthur. I need her in my bed.'

Arthur gave another salute to Urien, and one to Owain, and then went to Kai's feasting bench, where the men made room for Arthur to sit beside his foster brother.

'Brother!' said Kai, and took Arthur's forearm in the warrior's grip before pulling him into a warm embrace. 'It has been too long.'

'It has. I have missed you. You look well,' Arthur said and punched Kai on the shoulder. Kai was both taller and broader than Arthur, and always had been. He wore his rust-coloured hair long and tied back in a tight braid. His beard, once thin and wispy, had grown thick and fell full and bushy onto Kai's chest.

'You look tired. And older.'

A warrior handed Arthur a wooden platter and a cup of frothing mead, which he took thankfully. There was bread, cheese and golden butter on the table, and Arthur tore a chunk from a steaming loaf and took a drink. 'Too many nights spent sleeping in the open. Not like you, brother, sleeping in Caer Ligualid every night on a soft feather-filled bed with stewards and maids to answer your every whim.'

'If only that were true. I barely get a moment's rest between collecting the tithe, judging disputes, riding out with my men to protect our borders. It is not easy ruling the Caer.'

'Is he a fair ruler?' Arthur asked the men around the table, and they smiled.

'Sometimes,' said an older warrior, with two fingers missing from his left hand. 'He can be as hard as his father...'

'But as soft as fresh shit on the training field,' Arthur cut in, and the warriors laughed and raised their cups. The jest settled the men down and they talked amongst themselves, leaving Arthur and Kai to talk in peace.

'How goes the search?' asked Kai.

'There is no word of Lunete anywhere in the borderlands. For two years I have searched for her, across the mountains of Bernicia and Deira, north into the border with Gododdin and south into the wetlands and fens of Elmet and Lindsey. I cannot find any trail of our sister. It is as though she completely vanished that day.'

Kai placed a hand on Arthur's back. 'Maybe Lunete is dead. That she died that very day when the Saxons took her.'

'I cannot believe that. She is out there somewhere. I have asked Merlin, and he and Nimue both augured it for me. Merlin searched flame and ice and Nimue in the entrails of a boar, and both believe Lunete lives. But where can she be?'

'If she was in lands ruled by Britons, she would be at home in

Caer Ligualid by now. If Merlin says she lives, then Lunete must be in Saxon hands. Which means she is a servant, slave, or worse. In that case, it would be better if she had died that day.'

'I miss her. Her wildness. She brought smiles to the darkest of halls, and every man in Caer Ligualid loved her like a daughter.'

'What can we do but keep searching?'

'Never give up looking for her. One day, we might catch sight of her crow-black hair in a village, a mead hall, or riding through a forest on a fast mare. That is my hope, at least.'

Kai raised his cup and Arthur touched it with his own and both men drank deeply. 'So we march together again?'

'Aye, south to Loidis, where Gwallog fights to recover his city and save his kingdom.'

'How many men does he have?'

'Gwallog had three hundred legionaries commanded by Idnerth. Bors has thirty men from Gododdin left, and I have seventy black cloaks left after the battle for Loidis. Gwallog has his levy, which could be as many as a thousand men or as few as three hundred. Many of those farmers will have died in the fighting, or melted away in the night to join the families and flee before the Saxons leave Loidis and ravage the rest of Elmet.'

'And Octha?'

'One thousand five hundred men. Balan is with him, Balin's brother, along with a band of two hundred mercenaries and twelve Britons.'

'Britons fighting alongside Saxons. How can they do it?' Kai made the sign to ward off evil.

'It was Balan and his twelve traitors who breached the gate at Loidis. Entered the city disguised as a levy-man of Elmet and opened a small gate from within. We could have defended the walls against Octha for days. Perhaps until Octha's numbers dwindled so badly that he was forced to give up the assault and run back to Lloegyr.'

'But he has one thousand five hundred men, and you have at best five hundred warriors.'

'We both have less than that following the battle, and Octha lost many men beneath the walls.'

'He still has three times Gwallog's force, not counting the levy. What man of the levy can stand and trade blows with a trained Saxon whose life revolves around war and combat?'

'Well, now we have three hundred men of Rheged to swell our force. And the mighty Kai.'

Kai laughed. 'It is not enough.'

'No. It's not. We need more warriors, we need an army of Britons. That is what it will take to defeat the invaders once and for all. But we do have Merlin.'

'Then perhaps it is time for the druid to show his magic. Turn the Saxons into worms or pigs, or make the heavens spit lightning at them.'

'It might just take something like that, brother.'

They embraced again and drank Urien's mead and ate his bread. Arthur listened to the warriors reminisce about the battle of the river Glein. He showed them Excalibur and let men hold its god-forged blade. They marvelled at the markings on the silvery-grey sword, and at the dragon carved into the pommel's iron ball. Arthur told them the tale of the blade, of how Merlin had taken it from the war god Neit, how it had once been called Caledfwlch when it was forged in the mists of time. They asked him about the legends, and Arthur did not dispute Merlin's tales, but wriggled his way free of confirming them.

It was a bawdy night with too much mead, song and laughter. Then, two days later, when Kai and Owain had mustered their warriors, Arthur rode Llamrei at the head of three hundred spearmen. They marched to a war few believed they could win, to oust a larger enemy from behind stout Roman walls. He had warriors to help Gwallog's cause, but Arthur's head broiled with guilt, for he had given an oath to King Urien of the Bear Fort to send the fair Guinevere north once the fighting was over. North, into the hands of a grim king and a life of misery. That was the price for three hundred spearmen, and Arthur doubted he could do it, not to the woman he loved. For he did love her. It was a drowning thing of longing and obsession. Arthur could not get her green eyes or her smile out of his head. He longed for her, to hear her laugh, to simply be close to her.

Cavall barked and chased a rabbit across the downs, and Arthur's left thumb caressed the bronze disc he wore at his neck. He remembered Igraine upon her deathbed and the life of cruelty she had endured at Urien's hands. How she had loved a young Uther, and how that dream had died amongst the warp and weft of the Great War. That could not be Guinevere's fate. But the oath hung about Arthur like a fog, and he fought to cast it out of his thoughts. He had a war to fight and Saxons to kill, and hard times called for hard decisions. Octha and Balan lingered in Loidis, and they had to be thrown out of the old city. Thrown out and fought with sharp blades and stout warriors. Octha and Balan were ferocious men, cunning warriors driven by ruthless ambition. Men to fear, but Arthur must face them. He must be the man to stand before them with sword in hand and face their wrath, and suffer the withering onslaught of their axes, swords and spears. Arthur steeled himself to that fight, and rode towards it full of anger, with himself as much as his enemies.

13

Arthur returned to Elmet to find Balin and Bors camped with King Gwallog's legionaries and his levy on a steep hillside below a lofty pine forest. The trees stretched high and deep across a high range, and the sound of saws and adzes scraping and hacking filled the valley. Idnerth welcomed Owain and Kai and found a place to make camp by a thin river which traversed the rocky valley basin. Arthur caught sight of Guinevere the moment he reached the sprawling mass of tents, lean-tos, men, fires and work gangs. He gave Llamrei to a camp boy with instructions to brush and feed the horse. Arthur skirted around the camp's edge to avoid Guinevere, heading instead to find Gwallog, Bors and Balin.

'Merlin has finally lost his mind,' King Gwallog said, sat on an upturned log whilst one of his men set a fire around which the camp commanders gathered. 'Though we are lucky to have him with us. I had to force Bishop Emrys to apologise for the ugly scene atop the wall. A regrettable affair.'

'What is he doing?' Arthur replied. They watched Merlin striding across a strip of hillside turned golden by sawdust. He had fifty men working with tools, hacking and trimming long tree trunks, alongside piles of already trimmed and cut trunks set aside in organised piles. Others worked at lengths of hemp, twisting and plaiting it into thick rope laying long and pale on the sloping grassland.

'He has had fifty men working in the trees for three days. We can't stay here much longer. We need to find more food for the men. Saxon scouts found us yesterday, lingering in the distance, watching and counting.'

'I have brought three hundred men from Rheged to help your cause, lord king.'

'Three hundred is better than nothing, I suppose,' said Gwallog with a shrug. 'Though another thousand would be better.' He seemed to have lost his grim demeanour, his shoulders slumped and his eyes distant. Like a grandfather sitting with his grandchildren, rather than the fierce king of Roman Elmet. 'Thank you, Arthur, every spear is welcome.'

'Is Merlin building something?'

'Who knows what the old druid is up to? Even after I made Emrys grovel, Merlin won't talk to me, because of this, you see.' Gwallog held up the cross he wore around his neck. 'But the men look up to him, so...' He waved his hand.

'And the Saxons?'

'Still in my city. And we must get them out. Merlin says he has a plan, but he won't share it. You talk to him, Arthur. He listens to you.'

'I'll talk to him. Lord king, I am sorry. For Loidis and for your people.'

The levity suddenly dropped from Gwallog, and he stared into the clouds. 'We fought well, and the walls held. For a while I thought Octha would waste his army against us.' Gwallog inhaled sharply and clasped a hand to his mouth. 'God save us. The people we left inside the city. Their screams. We had to run. There was no choice. They overwhelmed us. Perhaps I should have stayed and died to defend the city to the last, but what use is there in us all perishing inside Loidis?'

'And we live to fight again, and avenge those who suffered at the hands of Octha and his horde.'

'We do. But the screams, Arthur. I can hear them now. So much pain. So much.'

Gwallog fell silent, staring blankly out at the sky. Arthur waited for a moment in case the king would speak again, but he did not. The calmness descended and Gwallog smiled wistfully as he stared into nothing. It was unnerving to watch the king slip from the horror of his people's destruction to serenity, and Arthur wondered what the defeat had done to the old king's mind.

Arthur left Gwallog and waved to Bors, who was busy practising with his spear along with his warriors of Gododdin. Arthur marched through the camp, weaving between warriors on the hill who sat talking in groups, repairing spears, stringing bows and playing knucklebones. Merlin raised an eyebrow when he noticed Arthur approaching and waited for him, hands on hips and a fervent gleam in his eyes. The hillside stunk like a boatyard, and columns of smoke swirled above the treeline as though men made pine tar to caulk a ship.

'Back already,' said Merlin. 'Urien sent Owain and Kai, I see.'

'He did. And warriors.'

Merlin scratched beneath his beard. 'What did he weasel out of you, I wonder? What did it take to get the old boar to give you his men?' He stared at Arthur, boring into his soul, and then a sadness sagged Merlin's face as though he saw something occurring way off in the future.

'What is it?'

'Nothing, nothing.' Merlin recovered and waved his hands impatiently, frowning at his work gangs. 'No time to talk of that nonsense now. We are working against time here. You can put Urien's men to work. Bring them to me, and have them bring their axes or whatever they can find to cut trees.'

'Why are you cutting down trees?'

'Because in three days' time, we are going to take Loidis back.'

'How?'

'I have spoken to the gods. In three days, they will help us open the city gates. So have your men ready to march and fight.'

'But...'

'No more questions. No time for it. Nimue!' Merlin shouted, and the Irish *gwyllion* popped up from behind a pile of trimmed logs, her face paint as unnerving as ever. 'Arthur, I need you to assign a company of fifty men to Nimue. Good men. Men you can trust. And you'll go with them. But I can't tell you what it's for.'

'They will need to know if they are to follow Nimue. The men are wary of her.'

'Afraid of her, you mean? And so they should be. Do you trust me, Arthur? Do you believe in the gods?'

'Of course.'

'Then do as I ask and stop being so churlish.'

Merlin strode away, shouting orders at the men who worked at the fallen trees. He swung his arms around, complaining about the size of the cut logs and berating the men to work harder. Arthur left him there and went to find Idnerth. The Primus Pilum was with his men, sorting through spears and sheaves of arrows beside three wagons. The two men greeted each other warmly.

'Merlin says we fight in three days' time,' Arthur said, and nodded appreciatively at the organisation of the legionaries' weapons and armour.

'I only wish we knew what he had planned,' replied Idnerth. 'Merlin is up to something. He invokes the old gods, I think, so I dare not wonder what that means for us followers of Christ. What on God's green land is he making in the forest? Ladders? Some other druid's contraption to help us scale the walls?'

'People underestimate Merlin. He went away for so long after the Great War that people have forgotten what a great druid can do. Let's hope his plan works, for the only hope we have of taking Loidis at the moment is an all-out assault. And we do not have enough warriors to waste dying trying to climb those walls whilst the Saxons rain rocks, blades and whatever else they can find upon our heads. The king seems... different.'

'Aye. He took the defeat hard. The king fell into a deep despair, and no one could talk to him for days. He would neither eat nor drink. But this last week, a calmness fell upon him. He prays a lot, but will not involve himself in any talk of battle. He sends his son instead.'

'Is Prince Ceretic capable?'

'Yes, I believe so. He fought as we fled Loidis and has been trained to fight since he was a boy. He will do well enough. In times like this, boys become men. Is there ever a time to be ready for war? Were you ready when Ector put a spear in your hand?'

Arthur shook his head and recalled his first kill and his first fight. Arthur had failed miserably the first time Ector brought him to war. It was only through Lunete and Kai's encouragement that he finally found the steel within him to do what must be done. 'Merlin asks for fifty men to be ready to follow Nimue when his cunning plan unfolds in three days' time. I'll take my black cloaks.'

'We'll all be ready. I'll pray for victory.'

Merlin's work continued on into the next day as the druid barked and whistled at the men, instructing them to cut this branch that way, or that log another way. He and Nimue were inseparable. They slept together beneath an awning, ate together and talked incessantly. Merlin would bear no questions from any of the leaders in camp, and on the morning of the second day, he told Arthur that he would need one hundred men the following day to shift his logs and stakes through the woods towards Loidis. Idnerth rounded those men up from the countryside levy, whilst the rest of the warriors sharpened blades and prepared to fight.

On the afternoon of that second day, Arthur returned from a scouting party mounted on Llamrei and found Guinevere walking with Morgan along the edge of the pine forest. The sun shone in a warm sky, and the valley hummed with the noise of Merlin's work parties. Birds sang in the woods, and the talk of a thousand men gathered for war rumbled like a distant sea.

'What a fine boy,' said Morgan, a smile splitting her pretty face. 'He must be eighteen hands tall. I love horses. I used to ride often around Tintagel, and King Marc gave me a mare of my own when I was a girl.'

Arthur slid off Llamrei's riding blanket and brought the stallion close so that Morgan could pet his neck. Llamrei snorted and shook his tail, and the ladies jumped back and giggled. Llamrei was an enormous horse with powerful limbs. His size was enough to frighten most people, and Arthur smiled to see Morgan appreciate the horse.

'He could do with a walk to cool him down, and some food, Lady Morgan, if you would like to take him for a while?'

'I would love to.' She took the reins and led Llamrei towards the main camp, talking to him and stroking his ears as she went.

'I hope you and Lady Morgan are not too uncomfortable living in camp,' Arthur said to Guinevere, masking his excitement at being alone with the princess.

'On the contrary, this is a splendid adventure. When would two women at court ever get the chance to go on campaign with warriors? The situation is dire, and I feel for King Gwallog and his people. But Morgan and I are both comfortable and honoured to be with the army.'

'Should we walk for a while?'

She beamed and hooked her arm around his as they set off together. Arthur blushed, and glanced back at the men, worried that they might see him walking arm in arm with the princess. Her hand brushed against his and the thrill of her warmth raced up his arm.

'You met with King Urien?'

'I did. I went to ask for men. Owain is here, and Kai.'

'I saw Owain, though he did not greet me warmly.'

'Urien still wants to marry you, and he wants you to return to the Bear Fort with Owain once the fighting here is over.'

'He can want all he likes, but I will not go.'

'Even if the fate of Elmet depends upon it?'

'How can the fate of Elmet depend on whether I, a woman from a land across the sea with no warriors and no wealth to bring to your war, marry an old man in Rheged?'

'Because Urien says he will send his army south and join our fight if I return you to him.'

Guinevere whipped her arm out from beneath Arthur's and faced him, hands on hips. 'What makes you think you have the power to return me anywhere? And Urien, the haggard old beast, can have any woman in his kingdom. He only wants me because he can't have me. Once he has bedded me and whelped a pup on me, he'll lock me in a dark part of his awful fortress to live out my days subject to his fists, growls and whims. I will not become Queen Igraine. I would rather die. I can find a ship and return to Cameliard if I have to.'

'I fear your father will accept Urien's proposal. Is that not why he sent you to Britain in the first place? To find a husband who can send warriors to help defend Cameliard?'

'Yes. But...'

'And is it not the fate of all noble-born women to marry the man their father chooses?'

'Yes. But not this woman. I thought you understood that. Understood me?'

'I… you are…' Arthur fumbled over the words, her green eyes disarming him. 'The last thing I want is for you to be unhappy. I have thought of you constantly since the first time we met inside Dun Guaroy. But to defeat the Saxons…'

'Please don't. Don't say that to defeat the Saxons I must marry Urien of the Bear Fort. He can bring at most six, maybe seven hundred warriors to your fight. Is that enough to defeat Octha, and then Ida, and then the kings in Lindsey and Kent? And what of the new warlords who come from across the sea? Will it be Urien's men who will slay them each summer until there are no more Saxons in the world? You are a man of admirable qualities, Arthur. And I too have dreamed fondly of you since first we met. But perhaps I was wrong to have thought so highly of you.'

'We must all make sacrifices if we are to defend our land from the invaders.' The words came out before Arthur could think, before he could stop himself. They were ill chosen and poorly considered.

Guinevere pulled away from him, taking two steps backwards. 'Give me a sword then, or a spear. Put me in the front rank and I shall make my sacrifice that way. If I am to sacrifice and suffer to save the people of this land from our enemies, then let it be quick. You men, you warriors. You dream of a glorious death, of the bards singing your name for generations, of your brave deeds living on through the years. What do you know of sacrifice? Are you happy for me to live a life of misery? Decades of suffering under Urien's cruelty? I wouldn't wish that on my worst enemy. Even Octha and Balin's brother deserve a quick death rather than a lifetime of torture. You act as though there is something between us, that there are shared feelings between you and me, and yet you would drag me to a prison where I shall wither and die?'

'Guinevere, wait.' She began to run, and Arthur went after her. 'Wait, please.'

She stopped and turned, arms folded across her chest, chin jutting and eyes blazing. 'I think it's for the best if we keep away from each other until the fighting is over. But mark me, warlord, if you desire glory and victory more than you care for me, then you shall have to drag me kicking and screaming through all the hills and valleys between here and Rheged before I will marry King Urien.'

'I don't want you to marry him. I won't make you go.'

'We'll see about that, won't we?'

She marched away and Arthur's heart burst with regret. He wished Merlin could turn back time, let Arthur relive that moment. He cursed Urien for making him swear the oath, and he cursed himself for a fool. Arthur wanted victory, he wanted to crush Octha and drive the Saxons back. But he also loved Guinevere with a passionate fire. But it seemed the gods would not let him have both, that it must be one or the other. His great love, or the chance to defeat the cursed invader.

Arthur trudged down the valley away from the pine forest, feeling as though he had been gut-punched. He found Kai sat with Bors, Balin, Dewi and a handful of Caer Ligualid men drinking ale and picking at two roast rabbits.

'You've got a face like a slapped arse,' said Bors, and the others laughed, and then quickly stopped as Arthur glared at them.

'I need a drink. Lots of drink. And I don't walk to talk about it.'

'Then you can sit next to Balin. Lads, fetch a fresh barrel so that we can drink. If there's one thing a warrior needs, it's to blow off some steam. Don't bring that Saxon horse piss, bring good ale, frothy stuff. Potent stuff.'

Arthur drank more than he had drunk before. He drank so much that he vomited behind an alder tree and then drank some more. The men laughed and sang, told old war stories and made oaths of how hard they would fight the Saxons. Arthur kept his own council. The men left him in peace as they drank and made merry, respecting his melancholy just as they did Balin's. Arthur drank until he could sup no more, until he remembered that tomorrow he would need to ready his men to attack Loidis, and he got up to walk off the ale. He stumbled on unsteady feet, falling three times before finding Cavall sleeping beside his bedroll. Arthur collapsed beside the great war dog and they tumbled together, rolling and play fighting on the grass.

'You are quite the animal lover,' said a friendly voice, and Arthur looked to see Morgan smiling down at him.

'He's a good dog, loyal and quiet.'

'Like all dogs should be. I took care of your horse. He is fed, watered and resting.'

Arthur hadn't fully appreciated before quite how beautiful Morgan was. She sat beside him and played with Cavall, laughing as she leapt about the grass with the dog. The sun set behind the pines, casting the vale in a golden hue. He talked with Morgan about the war, and Caer Ligualid, and she spoke of Kernow and her life as King Marc's ward. Darkness fell and men found their beds, and Arthur sat closer and closer to Morgan, and she to him. They laughed and touched hands. She looked into his eyes and told Arthur he was brave. Arthur felt good, his problems dulled by ale, and he allowed himself to drift with his ale-fuddled mind. She wasn't Guinevere, but Morgan was softer, gentler, warmer. As the valley went quiet, Arthur fumbled with Morgan's dress and they kissed passionately, and then lay down together, him needing and she willing.

Arthur woke the next morning with a start. He sat up and

clasped his hands to a head ringing as though Llamrei had kicked him in the night. He was naked, but Morgan was gone. Arthur cursed himself. He must find Morgan and apologise. Arthur could not even fully remember what they had done, how far things had gone. He remembered being by the fire with Bors and the rest, and then sitting with Morgan and Cavall. Then he remembered kissing Morgan, and he retched.

Hoofbeats sounded in the valley, and Arthur pulled on his clothes, forcing himself to stand. He would need to make it right with Guinevere. He could not send her into Urien's cruel embrace. But she would surely rebuke him now that he had been with Morgan? Arthur hated himself at that moment. All of his hopes and dreams were rotting before his eyes.

'Riders, lord,' called Dewi, looking as bleary-eyed as Arthur himself.

A dozen horsemen rode into the valley, each riding fine mounts and dressed in chain-mail. Their leader wore a strange cuirass of gleaming fish scales and he had his hair and beard clipped close to his head.

'I have come to fight against the Saxons,' the man called in a clear, bright voice. 'I am Lancelot of the Lake, come from Benoic across the sea to fight beside Arthur and his warriors.'

14

Lancelot wheeled his horse around, its hooves throwing up earth as the morning sun made the dew shine like jewels. Arthur searched for his mail and sword, one hand clutching his thumping head, and dry retched. His mouth was as parched as a riverbed in drought and he grabbed a waterskin from beside his cloak. Arthur gulped it down, the cool liquid gushing down his throat, spilling across his chin and beard. When it was empty, he gasped, searching for more, but could find none. He pulled on his mail and strapped Excalibur to his waist and did his best to walk confidently towards the new arrivals.

'What's all the bloody noise about?' roared Bors, striding from the camp with his hair and beard askew from sleep, and a face like thunder.

'A new arrival. Come with me,' Arthur said, and the two warriors went to meet Lancelot of the Lake. 'Welcome,' Arthur called with a hand raised in greeting, squinting as the sun sent stabs of pain shooting through his eyes. 'I am Arthur, and this is Lord Bors of Gododdin.'

'Ah, the men of legends stood here before me. Long have I

searched for you,' said Lancelot, and a smile split his broad face. He leapt nimbly from his mount and handed the reins to one of his men.

'Big bastard,' whispered Bors, eying Lancelot up as he came closer. He was almost as tall as Bors himself, and broad across the shoulder with a slim waist. He walked lithely like a dancer, gliding on the balls of his feet. His face was flat and broad with a square jaw with flinty eyes. He was a head taller than Arthur, thicker across the chest, and looked like a warrior straight out of a bard's song.

'I heard the songs of your legend across the sea,' said Lancelot. 'Of how you drew the sword from the stone and killed a hundred men to rescue a princess from a Saxon fortress. That must be Excalibur?'

'Yes,' Arthur said, his head still too blurred to offer any argument against Merlin's ever-spreading legend.

'Your fame travels even across the narrow sea,' said Bors to Arthur, and then draped a heavy arm around Lancelot's shoulders and led him away to find some food. 'Did you hear the one about when he farted a gust of wind so strong that it sent a fleet of enemy ships back across the sea?'

Lancelot brought eleven well-armed warriors with him, each one with sword, spear and shields with bright blue painted crucifixes. Their presence was welcome, and King Gwallog invited Bors, Lancelot and his men to breakfast with him inside his tent. Merlin was already busy with his timber work, and as Arthur strode up the hillside to find the druid, he caught sight of Morgan and Guinevere fetching water from the river. They both stared up at him, one full of spite and one with wide-eyed hope, but Arthur looked away and carried on as though he had not seen them. What would Guinevere say when she heard how Arthur had run straight from his argument with her into Morgan's arms?

Arthur found Merlin behind piles of stripped and trimmed wood, and the druid was deep in conversation with Nimue. Great columns of thick smoke billowed from the depths of the forest to fill the air with an acrid stink. Fires burned, glowing between the dense boughs as though Merlin had unleashed Annwn itself and brought the underworld to the forests of Elmet.

'Well, well. Arthur,' said Merlin when Arthur had cleared his throat so as not to surprise the druid and the witch.

'Lord Merlin,' Arthur said. 'You said today is the day that we should prepare for the attack.'

'And so we shall. Are you ready to follow Nimue?'

'I am ready. New warriors have come to join our fight.'

'I saw. More Christians.'

Nimue grinned wolfishly, and her teeth shimmered. 'Are you sure you are ready, young warrior? Are you ready to embrace the power of the gods?'

Arthur shivered, half because of his excess consumption of ale, and half because of the look in Nimue's dark eyes.

Arthur was glad to be busy, throwing himself into anything that would distract him from his guilt over the night he had spent with Morgan. Arthur told no one what he had done, of how in his cups he had taken advantage of the lady of Kernow, when he had no feelings for her. He prayed to Maponos that Morgan would not share their secret with Guinevere. Morgan was a sweet girl, but it was Guinevere to whom his heart was devoted.

Arthur's ambition and need for an army demanded that he returned Guinevere to Rheged, knowing full well what that meant for her future. It was not the act of a warrior. Whenever Arthur caught sight of Morgan approaching, or staring at him across camp, he went the other way, and whenever he stole a glance at Guinevere, she looked away from him. It was a mess, a horrible thing of Arthur's making, and only through work could he push it to the back of his mind. He organised wagons and wains to transport Merlin's timbers and cauldrons of the foul concoction the druid had brewed in the forest. Arthur gathered fifty of his black cloaks to march and follow Nimue's orders, though none of them relished the thought of what she had in store for them. The army struck camp, and King Gwallog led them north towards Loidis. Prince Ceretic rode at his father's side whilst Idnerth marched with the remaining legionaries.

'Like old Rome returned,' said Lancelot, riding alongside Arthur and marvelling at Idnerth's men in their *lorica segmentata* armour and flowing red cloaks. They marched in perfect time, their oblong shields emblazoned with the cross and their iron-topped pilum spears resting on their shoulders at the same angle. 'I hear that fifty men will follow the witch into the battle at Merlin's request?'

'Aye, and I will lead them,' said Arthur. Lancelot had spent most of the day wandering around camp, introducing himself to lords and warriors alike. He was a confident, jovial man with a quick smile, and more than once Arthur heard laughter coming from wherever Lancelot went.

'I request that I be permitted to join that war party,' Lancelot said. He spoke with the same accent as Guinevere, the softer-accented speech of the Britons across the sea influenced as it was by the Saxons, Jutes, Angles and Franks who surrounded their homeland.

'I do not yet know what Merlin and Nimue have in store for us, but there will be hard fighting, and I will go where the battle is fiercest. To take Loidis, we shall need more than whatever Merlin and Nimue have cooked up. I have picked my fifty, but you are welcome to join us and make it fifty-one. What brought you across the sea to our war?'

'Thank you. My father is King Ban of Benoic, the kingdom

beside Cameliard across the sea, and I am his fourth son. My eldest brother is my father's heir, my second brother is a priest and will one day be bishop of Benoic, my third brother trains to fight and is the spare to my father's heir. I, being the fourth son, must find my own way in this world. All I have is my sword and my men. This is not our first time at war. Enemies beset our lands. We fight against the same Saxons as you, along with other wild savages who invaded from the wastelands when the Roman legion withdrew from their northern empire. I have come following the stories, the tales of heroic battles, and a warrior with a god-forged sword. There is a chance here for a man to make something of himself, I think. Or to die in combat, which is a risk all warriors take when we heft our blades across the shield wall. If I win my father's, or my brother's, war, what will it do for me? If I stayed in Benoic, people would remember my name for a few years. They would say there goes Lancelot, who fought to keep Benoic free. But then, when I grow old in a small keep somewhere beside the sea, lord of nothing but a dozen men and a handful of pigs, people will forget about me. If I am blessed with children, they will remember my name when I am dead. But their children will forget me, and then, within two score years, it will be as though Lancelot never lived at all.'

Arthur understood the fear of being forgotten. All warriors craved reputation. Every man with the hubris and belligerence to pick up a weapon and seek combat wanted for other men to know his name and give him the respect due to a champion. It was what drove men to keep their nerve in battle when the blades came, when blood flowed and men screamed and died. 'Can you fight, Prince Lancelot?'

'We shall see when we face the enemy.' Lancelot flashed a broad grin full of white teeth, which turned his hard face handsome for a moment, and Arthur knew that was true enough. If

Lancelot was to take his place in Arthur's fifty, he would soon be in the thick of the war he had sailed across the sea to fight.

Arthur led his black cloaks north with Balin riding balefully beside him. Both had recovered from their injuries, though Balin's face was a scarred mess of misshapen bones, nose twisted flat against it and his scarring terrible to look upon. Nimue offered to fix his nose, but Balin refused, saying he would wear his disfigurement like a ring of honour until he was avenged upon his hated brother. Bors and his thirty surviving men of Gododdin came behind Arthur's seventy-three black cloaks, including the fifty he would place under Nimue's command. Bors bellowed and laughed with his warriors as they trudged through the meadows and pathways leading north. Kai and Owain followed with their three hundred spearmen, and then Gwallog and Ceretic with the Elmet levy and Idnerth's two hundred legionaries.

They marched to retake Loidis with one thousand warriors, though a third of their number were untrained farmers and laypeople levied from Gwallog's kingdom. Many of those who had answered their king's call to arms had since fled back to their families and farms, for it had been weeks since the fall of Loidis. Food was short, and men worried about the fates of their crops and livestock and the welfare of their loved ones. Guinevere and Morgan rode with Lancelot's warriors and seemed content to talk to the men from close to Guinevere's homeland, but whenever the ladies laughed it sent a pang of jealousy down Arthur's spine, and it was all he could do not to turn around and see what, or who, it was that so amused them.

Merlin ordered a halt a few hours south of the city, and Arthur sent scouts north to search for enemy positions around Loidis and to check which approaches were safest. The army could advance on Loidis from east or west, with the east providing cover of deep woodland. To approach Loidis at its south wall would require a crossing of the river Aire in direct view of the city, for there were no shallow fords close to the city itself. The marching warriors gawped at Merlin's carts filled with stripped and trimmed timbers, but the druid chased them away and shook his staff, threatening to turn them into crabs.

Night fell, and Nimue called Arthur to rally his fifty men. She came with her usual face paint, but with a feral look in her eyes. She flitted around the men, hopping from one foot to another, whispering in her native Irish, and then chanting in both British and Saxon tongues. Nimue brought five boys with her, and each carried a sack which jangled as they hurried to keep up with her keen stride. Nimue capered as she walked, whispering prayers and incantations, and led them deep into the forest, skirting east to come about Loidis from the same direction as Octha and his war band had advanced from. Arthur brought Dewi, Hywel, Anthun, Becan, Balin and Lancelot, and picked the rest from the best of his black cloaks. Nimue led them to a dark part of the forest where she instructed Arthur to make camp.

'Sleep well,' she said, wringing her hands with a grin. 'For tomorrow, the gods will come. Merlin has seen it, and we shall witness their might. Our gods will come to show us their power and throw the Saxons from Loidis. We must be ready. Merlin has searched for years, crossed the kingdom, combining his druidic ken with knowledge of the Rome folk. He has read their parchments, he understands their writing and the magic they used to crush the world beneath their marching legions. Merlin will do his part and the gods will do theirs. The gods create a chance for us to strike, a small window shutter ajar in the vastness of time. Your fifty men must use it wisely. You will be terrified, Arthur, your very bones will shudder at the sight of what is coming. So steel your men and make ready. For tomorrow, fifty men will take a fortress and send an army of Saxons to flight.' She disappeared into the twilight, picking at fungus and tree bark and placing the collection in a leather pouch.

Arthur stared after her, feeling the eyes of his men upon him. Understandably, they wanted to know what lay in store for them in the morning. How could fifty men possibly storm a city held by Octha and his warriors? But they knew better than to ask Arthur the questions to which he had no answers. He met their gaze with his hard face, showing them he held no fear. Arthur's warriors trusted him. He was their lord, their ring-giver and they were oathsworn to follow him even into the fires of Annwn if he commanded it. They were good men, brave men, and Arthur went amongst them, reminding them of brave deeds, wishing them luck, listening to their banter as they teased one another around a small campfire. Arthur did not doubt they would do what was required when Nimue revealed her plan of attack.

Arthur slept fitfully, taking a turn at the watch midway through the night to give the rest of the men a chance to rest. He stared out into the darkness, listening to the night beasts grubbing and scruffing in the undergrowth, glad that Nimue had left out offerings from the hidden folk and the demons who lived in the night. Thoughts of Guinevere and Morgan filled his head, as unwelcome as a sore tooth. He was tired of it, sick of thinking of women when he should concentrate on the battle to come. Arthur did not know what Merlin and Nimue had planned, and still he marched blindly to attack a city defended by Octha and his savage Saxons. Guinevere was a distraction, stopping him from thinking clearly. With her face living inside his skull, Arthur could have marched his men to death in a mad attack upon the walls, without a properly thought-out plan of attack, so he was glad to have Nimue's plan to lead him.

A twig broke behind him and Arthur spun, whipping his seax free of its sheath at the small of his back.

'Just me,' said Balin, emerging from the trees like a twisted demon. 'I couldn't sleep either.'

'Are we right to put our trust in Nimue and Merlin?' Arthur said and beckoned Balin to sit. It was the fear he could voice to no other, for his men had to believe that Arthur trusted the druid and the witch completely. But all men swim in the sea of fear, all men worry the night before battle. It is the time when a warrior is alone in the darkness with his mind, when the doubts come. He remembers sights of men with shattered bones, severed limbs, slashed throats and bloody wounds. He worries if his sword or spear will shatter, or if he has put a keen enough edge on his blade. The night before battle is the time to think of loved ones, to regret harsh words, to worry about what will become of them when he is gone. Arthur was glad of Balin's company, and the grim warrior sat down beside Arthur and warmed his hands on the small fire.

'What choice do we have? If their power cannot win the battle, then what hope is there for our gods and our people?'

'What does she bring in those sacks, I wonder?'

'We shall find out tomorrow. Sounds like knives, or spear blades.'

'What do you make of our friend from across the sea?'

'Lancelot? Just like Nimue's sacks, tomorrow will reveal his true nature. Though the men seem to like him well enough. He fell asleep swiftly enough tonight, whilst most men will spend the night rolling awake with their fears.'

'Balan will be inside the city.'

'I hope to find him there. For my fate and his are intertwined and my brother's doom is long overdue. I doubt there has ever been a hate so pure as the fire that runs between us. I will kill him, Arthur, I must. Every day he continues to live is an insult to my family's memory.'

'He will die. For what he did to your family, for betraying our people, and for how he tortured you at the farmhouse.'

'For all those things. We shall send his soul screaming to Annwn to twist and writhe with serpents and foul beasts for eternity. How is it that good men die, and evil ones live on to hurt and make others suffer?'

'Merlin says the gods like to be amused. Perhaps he is right.'

'We shall amuse them tomorrow, if slaughter is what they desire.'

'Who knows what the gods want? But let them grant you your vengeance, and give us the strength to cast Octha out of Loidis.'

'It would be better if we had more men.'

'We always need more men. That seems to be our curse. The Pendragon will not march. Perhaps it will be our doom.'

'You are of grim temperament tonight. Seems like I am the light-humoured one for a change.'

'There is a lot to be concerned about.' Arthur took a twig and poked it in the embers to give the fire a kick.

'True enough. Anything to do with you and the princess?'

'There is no me and the princess. Don't we have more important things to worry about?'

'We do. You were close to Guinevere, that's all. It was plain enough to see. Now you are always on opposite sides of the army.'

Arthur glanced at Balin, his scarred face for once open and willing to talk. 'Urien of Rheged wants to marry her. She fled from him and he wants her back.'

'And she will not go?'

'She will not. Urien sent Owain and Kai here to fight for Loidis and then take her to the Bear Fort.'

'Ah.'

'I gave Urien my oath to send the princess north when the fighting is done.'

'A princess, or Guinevere?' Arthur's head snapped around and Balin held up his hands to apologise. 'I can mind my own business if you prefer.'

'We have to win the fight first. Worry about this later.' Arthur wished that were true, for the unwelcome thoughts of Guinevere and Morgan were like raiders in his mind and he could not cast them out. Balin stayed with Arthur for the rest of his watch, and when it was over, Arthur finally slept a dream-filled, restless sleep until a pallid sun rose, morning came, and it was time to throw Octha out of Loidis.

15

Arthur and his fifty warriors followed Nimue as she splashed through the river's shallows. Her five boys trailed after her heels, carrying hemp sacks which clanked as she ushered them on with joyful songs, capering in the water as though she were going to a springtime feast. Arthur and his men kept low, each travelling on foot. Arthur, Balin and Lancelot reassured them, telling the war band that they were the bravest of the army, hand-picked to retake Loidis. But they ran with pale faces and dry lips, exchanging glances and all the time gaping at Nimue and her out-of-place hopefulness.

Arthur's boots crunched on the riverbed, and the chill water lapped around his feet and calves. He carried Excalibur and the sceptre at his belt and his seax in a sheath at the small of his back. He went without a shield at Nimue's command, as did each man of the fifty. The walls of Loidis appeared as grey and gloomy as the shifting clouds above, as a brisk wind shook trees and bushes and whipped men's hair away from their faces. A handful of Saxons patrolled the battlements facing towards the eastern forest and southern river, but Arthur believed that more walked the west- and north-facing walls, for that would be where Octha would expect any attack to come. To the east lay Saxon-ruled territories, and south lay only the hills and forests of Elmet, but to north and west was Rheged, Gwynedd and Powys. Mighty British kingdoms, and the only powers who could oppose Octha now that Loidis had fallen. Riverside reeds and high, grassy banks kept Arthur's warriors hidden from the city walls, and the black cloaks carried their spears low, so that the points wouldn't reach above the foliage and attract attention.

They had left the forest at daybreak, whilst most men lay snoring beneath cloaks and awnings. Arthur had marched at the front of the column, whilst Balin and Lancelot took up the rear. The men had talked in hushed voices, speculating about what Nimue had planned. Nimue's constant preaching of the old gods' power, and Merlin's mysterious work in the woods which nobody understood, had the men gossiping like washerwomen by a river. The warriors convinced themselves that she and Merlin would cast a great spell and magic the war band inside the walls to open the gates for Gwallog, Idnerth, Bors, Kai, Owain and the army lurking in the deep forest beyond Loidis' eastern wall.

'If Merlin can magic us inside the city walls,' Balin snapped when he heard the warriors discussing their theories on how Merlin and Nimue planned to assault Loidis, 'why doesn't he just magic the gate open, or make our army appear in the city square? For that matter, why doesn't he magic Octha and his entire army back across the sea?' The men had frowned at Balin as though he talked nonsense, such was their belief in the druid's power.

Merlin kept the main force deep in the sprawling, dark forest, hidden within the pine, yew and larch, waiting beneath the same leaves under which Octha's army had approached from Lloegyr. Traces of the Saxon army remained in the woods. Ashes of old campfires, discarded clothing and the bones of their meals. Arthur still had no guess what Merlin and Nimue had planned, though their cunning must reveal itself soon if battle was to be joined on the day Merlin had so confidently predicted it would.

Nimue led them to within a stone's throw of the place where Balan and his traitors had entered Loidis through its southern gate, and from which Arthur had fled using Balan's ships. The gate was closed, and the river flowed free of ships as it meandered lazily within sight of the old city. Spears shifted on the walls as men patrolled. Smoke rose from within and from where Arthur watched, crouched in the shallows. It was as though the battle for Loidis had never occurred at all. Birds sang their summer song, inside the town voices rumbled and dogs barked, as though life carried on as normal.

'Wait now and be patient,' Nimue said, coming to join Arthur, wringing her hands and grinning. She took a sack from one of her boys and reached inside to draw free an iron hook as long as Arthur's forearm. 'When the signal comes, this is how we shall climb the walls.' She showed Arthur the rope tied through a hole at the end of the hook. 'We throw the hooks over the walls and climb like children stealing eggs from high branches.'

'Is that it? That's your plan?' Arthur said, unable to believe the ridiculous simplicity and foolishness of her hooks and rope. 'The Saxons will kill us with spears and arrows before we even reach the foot of the wall to throw those hooks. Never mind actually climbing the walls.'

'You will see. It's coming soon.' She laughed like a child and shook her head as though the secret were too much for her to keep. Arthur stared at her, suddenly afraid that he entrusted his own life and that of his men to a madwoman. Just as that terrible thought dawned on him, a great shout went up from the east.

'Merlin comes,' Nimue hissed, 'he comes!'

Arthur craned his neck. Warriors crouched in the river fell to a hush.

'Woden, hear me!' Merlin called in Saxon, his voice as long and loud as thunder.

Arthur crept to the riverbank and pushed the reeds aside with his spear. On the field before Loidis' eastern gate where Octha had raised his scaling ladders, Merlin stood alone. He held his amber-topped spear aloft and his robes billowed around him, buoyed by the wind. Saxons gathered on the walls, spear-points bristling as they came to see what the strange, tattooed druid was doing before their conquered city.

'Octha, lord of warriors, war-chief. I am Merlin, a druid of Britain. I come to you with the power of Neit, with the fury of Andraste and strength of Manawydan. Begone from this place, or I shall rain down the fury of the gods upon you all.'

Arthur glanced at Nimue and she stood with her eyes closed, mouthing a silent incantation, arms held out wide. A silence descended over the city until a murmur of commotion came from the east-facing wall.

'Get away from here, wizard,' boomed a voice from the battlements.

'Octha!' Nimue hissed.

'Begone, war-crow. Back to your cave. Before I send my war dogs out. I rule here now. Octha. King of Loidis. Bow to me and leave.'

'Prepare to face the wrath of the gods, Octha. I shall bring the fires of the otherworld to cast you out. I shall cast the land into darkness and you will know that you are cursed. Leave the city or the curse will follow you and your people until the end of time.'

'Away! Haggard old crust of a thing. You crow like an addled whore.' Another figure appeared on the battlements, a smaller man with one eye, a scarred-faced Briton.

'Balan,' Balin said, and his knuckles turned white around his weapon's haft.

More figures appeared on the high walls, captives struggling against Balan's twelve bastards as they dragged the sorrowful figures to the wall's edge. Balan lifted his sword high and then used it to cut the throat of a woman with long, dark hair. He shoved her dying body over the edge where she fell silently to die beyond the gate. Balan and his twelve traitors killed ten prisoners that way, their blood staining the grey walls crimson. He killed the honest folk of Elmet, four women, four men and two children. He used Balin's father's sword, and Balin had to look away from the horror wrought by his family's blade. The warriors watched in silence, stunned by Balan's cruelty, by his willingness to kill women and children to drive fear into the Britons' hearts. Arthur forced himself to watch, so that he could keep the memory of the needlessly slain close to him when battle came.

A sudden change came over the land, and Arthur shuddered. The clouds changed colour, shifting, becoming somehow darker. Birds took flight from the woodland, their squawking like the shrieking of women. Starlings dived and swooped in a great murmuration, creating the illusion of evening, but the sun, barely risen to noon, remained hidden behind cloud cover.

'I call to the gods! Hear me now!' Merlin bellowed. His voice changed. Becoming deep and rumbling, loud and commanding, like it came from the depths of the earth. It was as though the sky itself responded to his call. The men around Arthur stared open-mouthed, all kneeling at the river's edge, transfixed by the druid in fearful anticipation of what might happen next.

'I am the wind which blows over the sea,
I am wave of the sea,
I am bird of prey on the cliff face,
I am lake in the valley.'

Merlin's voice roared, impossibly loud. He moved gracefully, like a fish beneath the waves, dipping and gliding through the grass. His staff swung about him and the amber tip glowed as though aflame.

'Behold the shadows,' Nimue howled, and pointed a long finger to the riverbank. 'The gods are coming! The time is nigh!'

Arthur glanced downward, and the previously concealed sun emerged from behind the clouds. It was changed somehow, grown less bright, dimmed so that it cast dappled shadows on the water and high grass. It shone through the trees, but the shadows were not leaf- or branch-shaped, but scores of black crescent moons shimmering in the strange light. Arthur's heart raced, and Merlin continued his dance. Arthur had thought the druid was a master of cunning and deception, able to twist men's minds to his will with words and their belief in his power. But before Arthur's eyes Merlin had changed the sky, and black cloaks, scarred veterans, began to clutch one another's arms, agape at the druidic power unfolding before them.

Merlin paused and raised his staff to the sun.

'Vulture today,
I was once wild boar,
I first lived in the flock of pigs,
Here I am now in the flock of birds!'

The bird flight descended back into the woodland, and Arthur heard a collective intake of breath from inside the city walls. The sky grew darker, and an eerie half-light descended upon the land.

'I curse you, Octha, Saxon from across the sea. The gods curse your warriors and your people. I will cast the sun from the sky and turn your women's wombs to ashes. Your warriors' courage shall dim with the sun. Leave this place or your souls are mine, destined to wander the fires of the underworld for eternity as wraiths. You shall be the slaves of my people until the end of days. I curse you!'

Merlin took up his dance again, and the Saxons inside Loidis shouted and hollered in fear, for, to Arthur's horror, the sun itself grew dark, turning to shadow before his very eyes. Men came from the forest behind Merlin, dragging the great timbers his teams had cut and trimmed in the pine forest. A dozen crews hauled the spars and lintels, and others came with wagons bearing the cauldrons and Merlin's acrid potions.

'Behold! I steal the sun from you, Octha!' Merlin roared, and the Saxons howled in the terror because the sun itself turned black. 'I have the power to cast the sun from the sky. Hear me, O gods of our land. Merlin calls to you, snatch the very sun from above until foul Octha takes his people from Loidis. Curse them! Poison them! I give their souls to you to burn forever in sacrifice!

I have been sow, I have been he-goat,
I have been sage plant, I have been boar,
I have been a horn, I have been a wild sow,
I have been a shout in battle,
I have been a stream on the slope,
I have been a wave on the stretch of shore,
I have been the damp gleam of a downpour,
I have been the tabby-headed cat on three trees,
I have been a ball, I have been a head,
I have been a she-goat on an elder tree,
I have been a well-fed crane, a sight to see,

I command you to turn this land dark. I am Merlin Lord of Druids, darkness comes!'

Arthur's warriors whimpered and stared at Arthur, and he fought to hold his nerve as the sun went black and cast the land in darkness. A spark flashed to life on Arthur's left, distracting him from the horror of the sun's blackness. Nimue dragged a knife across a striking stone, with a torch in her left hand taken from one of her boys' sacks. The flame spat into life and lit up her grinning face in the darkness.

'Now,' Nimue roared, 'follow me.'

Arthur gulped, staring at the dark sky with his men trembling about him. A great wailing came from inside the city, screams and cries of terror as Saxons witnessed daytime turn to darkness.

'Now, I said,' Nimue spat, and shook Arthur by the shoulder. She took the sacks from her boys and threw them to Arthur's men. 'You are under my protection. All of you. Come now. No matter what you see, trust in me. Trust in Merlin, and you shall come to no harm.'

Arthur nodded and followed Nimue as she scrambled up the riverbank and ran towards the city. Some of his men remained rooted to the spot like trees, terror-stricken faces gaping up at the sky. Arthur ran to them and dragged them from the riverbank to follow Nimue. Above them a circle of blinding light appeared from the edges of the blackened sun, and out in the eastern fields torches moved in the darkness, hammers thudded and timbers creaked. Arthur drew Excalibur, seeking comfort in the blade and finding it in the wrapped leather grip.

'Won't they see us from the walls?' he shouted to Nimue.

'Do you think they care about us when they wither and cower under Merlin's curse with the sun stolen from them? There won't be a single warrior up on the walls, believe me.'

Sure enough, they reached the foot of the Roman walls and dragged the hooks and rope from Nimue's sacks. Balin took the first length of twisted hemp and swung it about him in great circles and then cast the iron hook high. It tumbled back to the ground, and he barely leapt out of the way before it crushed his skull. Balin tried again and this time the hook clanked over the wall and he hauled on the rope. The hook held, and more of Arthur's warriors took their turn until they secured twelve hooks over the battlements. A ripping, rending sound tore across the fields beyond Loidis, and Arthur flinched. His men gasped and covered their heads at the crashing sound, magnified by the ethereal darkness so that it sounded like a monstrous demon had clawed its way from beneath the earth.

'By the gods, what fresh magic is this?' gasped one of Arthur's men. A ball of fire flew from the darkness high into the sky and crashed against the walls to send sparks and shards flying in all directions. Yet more fearful cries came from within the city.

'Hold fast,' Arthur said as some of his men fell to their knees and others covered their heads with their hands. He felt the same fear, the same terror as they did. What fell power had Merlin brought to Loidis that he could dim the sun and hurl balls of fire the size of a horse high into the air? It was breathtaking to witness, and the men grabbed their amulets and trinkets for luck and whispered prayers to the gods. In a time where the nailed god fought with the old gods for supremacy, Merlin's awesome power showed them just how formidable the gods of Britain truly were.

'Merlin.' Nimue grinned, her torch flames glinting upon her terrible smile. She grabbed Arthur's arm with her strong, long fingers, staring at him with unbounded glee. 'He uses the sorcery of the Rome folk. Rock throwers, magnificent weapons the legions used to conquer the world. He learned such things during the long years he spent alone on Ynys Môn. He gathered their parchments and scrolls to him, studying the ancient wars and secrets of Old Rome, Greece, and even older peoples. Assyrians, Medes, Persians, races far beyond the world of our understanding. Only Merlin knows these things. Only Merlin can harness old knowledge and make it new. The rules of their war contraptions and means to use them set down by Vegetius live in Merlin's cavernous mind, and now, empowered by the gods, he uses his cunning to rain down wrath upon Octha. Climb now and open the gates, kill them, kill for the gods, kill for Merlin, kill them all!'

Balin made the climb first, and Arthur followed. The rope tore at his hands and the wound at his shoulder burned as he hauled himself towards the summit. Arthur's boots scrabbled against the walls, seeking grip in the gaps between the great stones. Chunks of old rock tore away from the wall and filled Arthur's mouth with chalky dust. He slipped and found his grip again, and almost fell to his death when Nimue clambered up the rope next to him. Corded muscle stood out on her thin arms and she cackled like a madwoman as she hauled herself towards the summit. Arthur's men climbed in silence, fighting to master their fear as more of Merlin's fireballs sailed over the walls to devastate the Saxons within. Many hit the walls themselves, exploding in searing flashes of light, and Arthur focused on the climb, unable to understand how Merlin had conjured up such powerful magic. He reached the summit and hauled himself over, sitting with his back to the battlements and sucking in great gulps of air.

'The walls are empty,' Balin said, holding out his hand to help Arthur to his feet. Bursts of sunlight appeared from the black sun, and Arthur gazed down into a city in panic. Saxons rolled on the ground in terror, clutching to one another in abject fear. They tore their hair, screamed, prayed to the sky with arms outstretched. Others fled about the streets and between buildings without purpose, just running from the carnage raining upon them from above. Buildings burned under Merlin's bombardment, wattle walls crumbled, horses and beasts wailed and screamed and Arthur gripped Excalibur tight.

'To the gate,' Arthur ordered, and his men followed him down the stairway leading from the walls into the city. A cowering warrior peered up at them where he sat with his arms around his knees at the foot of the stairs, and the Saxon died as Balin slashed his axe across the Saxon's face. Nimue laughed with glee, crowing at the sky and spitting curses at the cowering Saxons. Balan had taken his brother's blades, and so Balin of the Two Swords fought with axe and knife, cutting and slashing as he ran amongst the stricken enemy. Arthur ran through the Saxons, not waiting to strike a blow, focused on reaching the gates before the Saxons realised their enemies were inside the city walls. They were too terror-stricken to fight, their minds unable to comprehend what destruction Merlin had brought to their lives, but soon they would awaken from that stupor and Arthur wanted the gates open before the warriors inside the city realised he was amongst them.

They reached the east-facing gate without resistance, and Arthur ordered his men to haul the bracing spar free of its crutches. Ten of them raced to the task, and the spar clattered to the Roman-built road. They heaved the twin oak gates open and their iron hinges creaked as Arthur peered out into the fields beyond. Slithers of light came from the darkened sun and cast a wan light upon Merlin's war machines, two wooden frames like the skeletons of halls without wattle or thatch stood in the field, and Arthur gasped as a huge arm swung over the frame like a man's arm throwing a rock. A fiery ball soared through the sky, crackling and burning across clouds cast in a pallid hue as the sun crept from behind its black mask.

'Have you ever seen anything like that in your life?' said Lancelot, gaping at Merlin's contraptions and shaking his head.

'No,' Arthur replied. 'Nor are we likely to again.'

A war cry erupted from the pine forest, and just as Octha's horde had charged from the woods to rip Loidis from King Gwallog's rule, now an army of Britons came howling from the trees and across the open plain. They ran across the field as sunlight bathed the green grass in warm light, and Merlin and Nimue had done as they promised. They had blackened the sun itself and rained down balls of fire to make the city fall.

'Close the gate!' barked a Saxon voice. 'Close the gate!'

A big man appeared in the gap between Loidis' buildings and the walls, a war axe in one fist, and his hard face stared at Arthur, dripping with malice.

'Octha!' Nimue spat. It was Octha, come to defend his newly won city even though his people howled at the sky as though it was the end of days.

'You *Wealas* dogs would bring the very sky down upon us all,' Octha growled. A band of twenty burly warriors came with him, but each man glanced from Arthur's men to the sky above every few heartbeats, and Arthur could sense fear dripping from them like ice in a thaw. 'You block out the sun and rain down fire, and yet we live. I remember you, witch, but this is far beyond your *seidr*. You could pull teeth and birth horses, and now this? Are you one of them now?'

'I am a daughter of Neit, of Andraste and Eireann. Your people stole and enslaved me when I was but a girl. I glory in your doom, Octha the Cursed. Your strength shrivels and your people scream like pigs.'

Octha took a step forward and snarled at Nimue. 'Rancid bitch.'

'Mighty Merlin has cursed you for eternity, unless you and your people leave the city now. Go, leave by the northern gate. Save your people's souls or condemn to suffer for all time. Woden harkens to my prayers, Saxon. Your own god will turn his back on you unless you leave this place.' Nimue threw her head back and screamed at the lightening sky. The clouds were cast in a rust-coloured hue, and it was mere moments since the sun had turned black and disappeared before the Saxons' eyes. Nimue crouched, her fingers curled like claws and her eyes burning in her painted face. She smiled and pointed to the warriors at Octha's sides. 'Brave warriors. Flee now, or you will be forever denied a place in Woden's corpse hall. I say it, my *seidr* says it, the sky itself says it, Merlin says it and Woden hears. Valhǫll is closed to you unless you leave Loidis now. Stay and wander Niflheim in the fire and ice for all time.'

The warriors around Octha exchanged nervous glances. One of them walked backwards, and then another. Then three of them, big men all, turned and ran away from Nimue's words like scalded cats.

'Stand and fight,' Octha growled. 'It's nothing but tricks and the words of an addled whore. Stand with your lord.' A score of warriors stood with Octha, sweat beading their brows, fingers shifting grip on their axe hafts. Another two score milled about beyond that first band, Saxons flitting about the streets, shouting and calling to another in anguish, torn between fulfilling their oaths to Octha and running before the sky fell down upon their heads.

'But you are cursed,' said Arthur, hammering home Nimue's words. He pointed Excalibur at Octha. 'And now you will die.'

'Where is Balan?' asked Balin, standing beside Arthur.

'Gone.' Octha curled his lip and spat in disgust. 'Fled with his men upon fast horses as the sun went black. A coward. Like all you *Wealas*.' Octha spat in disgust at Balan's lack of courage. He inclined his broad skull to his men and pointed his axe at the black cloaks. 'Kill them.' Octha spoke quietly, eyes fixed on Arthur. The Saxons charged. Their fear suddenly turned to anger, and they bellowed like hungry cows.

'Hold the gate!' Arthur ordered. His fifty black cloaks had to hold the eastern gate until Merlin and the army crossed the field, but Octha himself charged at Arthur and more of his warriors found their courage in their leader's bravery. They came howling with bearded war axes and wicked seaxes with broken-backed blades, warriors who charged into a fight for their lives and for their very souls.

16

Arthur braced himself, Excalibur in hand and fifty black cloaks with him. They faced Octha and his hearth troop, his picked champions who stood with their warlord whilst the rest of his army fled in terror. Arthur's army was still only halfway across the grass field, and if Octha's men could kill the black cloaks beneath the open gate, they could close it and all Merlin's magnificent sorcery would have been in vain. Bors, Owain and Kai must then attack the walls, try to break the gate open with the battering ram and fire whilst the Saxons rained down stone, spear and anything they could think of to hurt a man. That assault could not happen. Octha had attacked the walls with overwhelming numbers, knowing that Balan's traitorous Briton had snuck inside and would open the southern gate. Another of Merlin's fire stones whirred overhead, and the Saxons ducked, peering upwards, whispering prayers to their savage gods. The stone smashed into a building beyond view, and a massive shower of sparks shot into the air, accompanied by hundreds of screams as men fled from the flying balls of fire.

'We hold them,' Arthur said to his men. 'We must hold this

gate until our men reach us. They are coming. Most of Octha's army is in flight, so all we have to do is stop Octha here and the city is ours. Are you with me?'

'Arthur, Arthur, Arthur!' the black cloaks roared as one.

Octha howled at his men, his face contorting with a mix of fear and anger. He had seen things no man alive in Britain had seen before: the sky turning black, great stones tossed over city walls by a druid's sorcery, and yet he had to fight to defend what he had won. So Octha's men charged. A warrior behind him shouldered past Arthur, a figure moving as fast and powerful as a galloping horse. He came in a blur, dashing to meet the Saxon charge alone. It was Lancelot. The prince of Benoic ran straight into Octha's champions, sword in hand and his lamellar cuirass shining. He covered the distance between Arthur and the enemy in five great strides, sidestepped an axe blade and opened a Saxon's guts with a cut of his sword so fast it was almost a blur. Lancelot matched Octha's picked men for size and his broad shoulders crashed into them, his feet shifting in the dust like a dancer, blade singing as it sliced and lunged. At first, the enemy tried to swarm him, to bully him with their shields and their size, but Lancelot was too quick and too strong. He caught a Saxon shield on his shoulder and drove the shield man backwards, hitting him so hard that the Saxon staggered and died with Lancelot's sword in his throat before he could protect himself. Lancelot grabbed a Saxon's shield with his left hand and tore it from the arm of a grizzled warrior. The Saxon's mouth dropped open in surprise at Lancelot's strength, and he died with the Benoic warrior's sword in his maw.

Arthur followed Lancelot and charged into the fray, and his black cloaks went with him. He blocked a seax with Excalibur's blade and kicked the attacker to the ground where he died beneath the black cloaks' fury. Balin fought beside Arthur, hacking at the enemy with his axe, and the fight beneath the gate turned into a furious battle. A Saxon axe chopped into a black cloak's face with a sickening crunch, and another gutted the black cloak beside Arthur with a sweep of his seax. There was no shield wall nor battle strategy in it, just the pure hatred of men who fought to defend their land against an invader, and a band of hardened champions fighting for their lives and their lord. A black cloak behind Arthur howled in pain as a spear thumped into his chest, and a Saxon died in tears as Balin ripped his throat out. Arthur lost sight of Lancelot in the press of battling men. All he could see were the warriors around him as he parried and lunged with Excalibur. The air stank of pitch, burning thatch, iron and voided bowels.

'Our men are coming,' Arthur called to his black cloaks, and as though in response, the onrushing Britons roared as they charged across the field. 'Hold them, fight for your people, fight for Elmet, fight for Arthur!'

A great axe swung at Arthur's neck and he felt its passing ruffle his hair, so close was it to snatching away his life. Arthur shoulder barged the axeman away from him and it was like crashing into pure rock. It was Octha himself, reeking of stale sweat and old leather. He grabbed Arthur's face in his great hand and crushed his fingers into Arthur's eyes and cheek, his strength shocking, each finger like an iron rod, and it felt as though Arthur's skull would burst. White pain seared through his head and Octha was too close for Arthur to bring Excalibur to bear. Balin surged at Octha with his axe raised, but the Saxon warlord clattered him with his axe haft and sent Balin falling into the press of men.

The noise of battle hushed in Arthur's ears, and screams of the dying dulled. There was only Octha's calloused hand, his impossibly strong fingers damp and clawing, digging into Arthur's bones. Panic flooded Arthur's senses. The city was almost taken, Merlin moving sun and moon to retake the city, and Arthur thought he was about to die before the triumph was complete. Octha's bloodshot eyes bore into Arthur, his foul teeth bared in a rictus of hate. Arthur struggled, but could not shake himself free. He reached behind himself and grabbed the antler-hilted seax from its sheath and jabbed the point at Octha. The blade punched at the warlord's hardened leather breastplate. But the armour held, and Octha didn't even flinch.

'*Wealas* whoreson,' Octha growled, spattering Arthur's face with spittle as he leaned in to watch Arthur die. Arthur stabbed again with the seax and this time found something soft, so he pressed the blade and twisted it as Octha crushed his head so hard Arthur thought it could implode at any moment. The pressure relented as Octha drew back suddenly, hissing in pain. Arthur slashed upwards the seax, and the edge caught Octha's forearm, opening a long gash so that the big man released his grip on Arthur's face. Arthur darted away, his head aching as though a smith had pounded it against an anvil. A scream rent the air and Nimue leapt at Octha. She clawed at his face with her talon-like nails and yanked his hair with such force that she pulled a hank from his skull. She capered away, hooting with glee, and showed the hair to the Saxon warlord, whose face dropped in horror. Nimue ran away with the hair and Octha tried to follow, but met only Lancelot and his blood-spattered cuirass.

Lancelot and Octha traded blows and men fell back from them, staring in awe at the strength and skill as their weapons clanged and clashed together. They fought for twenty heartbeats, trading blows, swerving, punching, snarling, and Lancelot was like a god of war. Axe and sword came together and the two men matched each other for strength, leaning in, shoving with all their might, each trying to throw the other backwards. To Arthur's astonishment, it was Octha who gave way, his great neck and muscled shoulders driven backwards by Lancelot's power. A shrill trumpet undulated across the plain beyond the walls, metallic and shrill, followed by a tumultuous war cry.

'The carnyx!' the black cloaks called as one, and Arthur rejoiced, because his army had come. He turned just as Owain and Kai charged through the gate, and Arthur raised his sword with joy. Octha turned and ran and his men followed, charging into the tangle of streets as an army of Britons came to kill them.

'Now he knows fear,' Nimue cackled, clinging to Arthur's arm and grinning up at him. 'I have his hair, and with that I can make charms and curse his luck. He knows it, for it is Saxon magic I learned in his own hall.' She turned to the onrushing army. 'Kill them all!' she called, laughing with mad glee, and followed the warriors as they surged into the city. Arthur sagged, men buffeting and shouldering him aside in their wild charge. He made his way to the walls and leant against the cold stone, his head still ringing where Octha had tried to crush him to death.

'We did it,' said Balin, and took Arthur's forearm in the warrior's grip.

'But the fight isn't over,' Arthur replied. 'Not until Octha and his men are dead. Find Bors and Idnerth. If we let the men run wild, the Saxons will escape. We must defeat them here once and for all.'

Owain and Kai led the army in a wild charge through the streets of Loidis. A thousand warriors pounded through the gate, boots thundering on the Roman stone pathway, voices crying for victory and weapons raised above their heads. Lancelot and Nimue got lost in the throng as men flooded the area between the gate and the city buildings. They could only enter the gate six abreast, so outside the city hundreds of Britons waited in the field, pushing and crushing forwards as they surged towards the fighting, desperate to strike a blow at the Saxons. Arthur sheathed Excalibur, as Balin shrugged in frustration. It was chaos, too many men in too small a space so that it was impossible to give any orders or bring any order to the fight. Bors, Idnerth, Gwallog and the other commanders could be anywhere inside the city, and Arthur dragged a hand down his aching face. He ran alongside the wall and climbed the stone stairs to its summit. Balin followed, and the two friends gasped as they reached the parapet.

Men thronged the field outside the gate, hundreds of warriors baying for Saxon blood. Beyond the warriors, Merlin's great war contraptions stood idle like the masts of two ships; the cauldrons of pitch or tar Merlin had used to light his flaming rocks smoked beyond the golden timbers. The city itself seethed with shifting forms, like rivers of people flowing along the cobbled streets and muddy lanes. The noise was deafening, a great rolling of shouting, screaming and clanging of weapons.

'Arthur, look.' Balin pointed to the north, where the woodland's shadows shifted as hundreds of Saxons fled from Loidis' west and northern gates. They raced for the forest and ran through the trees eastwards towards Lloegyr.

'They are getting away,' Arthur said. He stared down at the warriors still passing beneath the gate below him, and then over his shoulder at the chaos inside the walls. 'There's no way we can stop them.'

A force of Saxons emerged from the trees and dashed towards Merlin's stone throwers, which they had left unprotected in the desperate charge to exact revenge on the Saxons. Those men hacked at Merlin's creations with axes, chopping the wood and rope construction with vengeful fury, and there was nothing Arthur could do about it. To get out of the city, he would need to navigate through marauding warriors and out of a wall gate, all of which were thronged with charging Britons or fleeing Saxons. By the time he could gather a force and make any sort of pursuit, it would be too late. Octha, if he lived, was gone and so were most of his warriors.

With a cracking, creaking groan, one of Merlin's throwers crashed to the ground, and the other sagged to one side like an old horse dying. The Saxons shouted with defiance as they chopped Merlin's creations to firewood and used the druid's cauldrons of pitch to burn the timbers. Smoke rose from the stone throwers to mix with the columns of twisting grey rising from the city where the flaming rocks had smashed into houses and set wattle and thatch to flame. The sky, still scarred scarlet and orange by the disappearing sun, became obscured by dirty grey smoke. Arthur watched the Saxons flee, waving their spears and axes at that final spiteful triumph as they left the throwers to burn with crackling flame. He could not count their number, mere shadows moving beyond the treeline, but there were many of them. Too many. Arthur had recovered Loidis, but he did not feel the elation of victory, only the gloomy understanding that the true battle was not yet fought. The reckoning was yet to come, and it had to come, because Octha's ambition would never be quelled. He would keep on coming, hungering for a kingdom of his own like a starving wolf. So, as Arthur watched the men clad in fur and iron disappear into the vast woodland, he made a simple oath to himself. A promise written in the blood of so many dead Britons. Octha must die.

17

The fight within Loidis raged all day as Britons searched for hiding Saxons in barns, roof thatch and every conceivable hiding place. Idnerth's legionaries and Arthur's black cloaks secured the walls and made a protective ring around the palace and old Roman buildings at Loidis' centre, but the lay and levy folk sought bloody vengeance on the Saxons who had taken their city. Hundreds of Saxon dead fouled the city with their blood, though many more successfully escaped the city to flee eastwards. Song and laughter rang out in the streets as the people of Loidis rejoiced in their victory. They drank Saxon ale and returned to their lost homes, and the work to repair the damage caused by Merlin's stone throwers could begin. Slaves captured by Octha's men were freed from their pens and returned to their families, and the city rang with joy, just as it had wailed in horror when Octha took the walls.

Arthur sat in King Gwallog's hall beside Bors, Balin, Owain, Kai and Idnerth. The king of Elmet fussed about his Roman chamber, tutting where he spotted the Saxons had chipped the stonework, or had damaged his feasting benches.

'The city is recovered,' said Owain, as he used a strip of leather to tie his long black hair at the nape of his neck. 'The Saxons are gone.'

'But the war is not over,' Arthur said, trying to hide the weariness from his voice. 'We have talked this over for an hour already when we should prepare to march.'

'I agree. I shall march my men north in the morning, along with my father's bride.'

'We must march eastwards. You know this, Prince Owain. We have a chance to crush Octha and his army forever. We are on the brink of a glorious victory. A few more days is all I ask of you and your men. March with us, fight Octha, and then return north as heroes.'

'We have already won a victory, one that men will speak of long after we have all left this world. Merlin turned the sun black and tossed great balls of fire over the city walls. The tale of this battle shall be told up and down Britain like the song of Lleu Llaw.'

'But Octha lives. There will never by another chance like this to rid ourselves of a powerful Saxon warlord. We have weakened him and his men are broken and afraid. We must turn this battle into a complete victory.'

Owain shook his head and curled his lip. 'I do not take orders from you, a jumped-up commander of a few dozen masterless men. I am Owain ap Urien, Prince of Rheged, and I have fulfilled my part of our bargain. In the morning you will bring the princess to me and I shall leave and my warriors with me.'

'Kai?'

'I am oathsworn to King Urien and Rheged. I rule in Caer Ligualid at his pleasure, so I go where Owain goes. You know that, brother.'

Arthur sighed and raised his hand to apologise to Kai. Owain smirked and drummed his fingers on the arm of his high-backed chair as if the entire conversation bored him.

'Arthur is right,' Bors said, his mouth half full of cheese, which he ate from a wooden platter on the feasting bench before him. 'If we let Octha go now, we'll have to fight him again next summer when he regains his strength. Could be here, could be Gododdin, could be in Rheged. I say we march and put the bastard down forever.'

'And I wish you good luck in the war to come, Lord Bors,' Owain said. 'But you will do it without my men.'

Idnerth groaned and unbuckled his Roman armour, laying the *lorica segmentata* down over the back of his chair. 'We haven't yet done a full count, but I have just over two hundred legionaries fit to fight. The rest are dead or too badly wounded to follow Octha. Arthur and Balin have three score black cloaks who could fight. Bors, how many men of Gododdin can still bear arms?'

'A score,' said Bors. 'The rest are dead or hurt.'

'Without your men, Owain, it seems we can muster only three hundred warriors to take the fight to Octha.'

'Octha is probably already dead,' said Owain. 'There are dead Saxons everywhere. Even the levy warriors killed a dozen Saxons each. There are dead Saxons in the river, on the streets, in the woods, and in every building in Loidis.'

'Octha lives,' said a harsh voice. Every man in the room stiffened as Merlin entered. His bright eyes glittered, though there was a stoop to his gait and his skin bore a grey pallor. 'He lives and must be killed.'

'Merlin!' called Gwallog. The king moved slowly to Merlin and bowed his head solemnly. 'To think men thought your power had faded. There can be few alive today who have witnessed the full power of a druid as we did today.'

'Thank the gods, Gwallog, not me. Though I see you still wear that cross around your neck?'

'Aye...' Gwallog held the heavy silver crucifix up and stared at it and then shuffled away, scratching his head, still not the man he had been before the initial loss of his city.

'I have done my part. Now it is time for you all to do yours. Prepare your warriors for the chase, for we have a Saxon to kill. Nimue has seen it. She has burned Octha's hair to augur it, and he lives. She can find him and will lead our forces to where he licks his wounds.'

'We have only three hundred men, Merlin,' said Balin.

Merlin cocked an eyebrow at Owain. 'What of Rheged?'

'We return home tomorrow.'

'Why? When there is work still to be done.'

'Fight to return the city to King Gwallog. That was the bargain Arthur struck with my father. It is done. Now, it is time for Arthur to honour his oath.'

'Oath?' asked Merlin, and shot Arthur a murderous glance.

'He didn't tell you, did he?' Owain laughed. 'My father will marry Princess Guinevere and I return north with her on the morrow. You are welcome at the wedding, Lord Merlin, of course.'

'I swore I would send the princess north once Loidis was won,' Arthur said, 'though she will not thank me for it.'

'You would leave us on the cusp of a crushing victory, so close we can smell it. You would give that up so that your father can marry again?' asked Merlin incredulously. 'He has a hall full of women. Can the old bear not wait a few more weeks to be wed?'

'An oath is an oath,' said Owain.

'I moved the very heavens for this war, Owain ap Urien. Is it too much to ask Rheged to fight for our land and our people? Do your warriors not long to kill the enemies of our people? We have a chance, one chance, to slaughter an army of Saxons. We can remove an entire horde of invaders from our land and strike fear into the Saxon kings. Would you give that up? Can you really march away from Loidis knowing how close we are to a victory that will save countless Britons' lives?'

'I do as I am commanded. As does Kai. As do my men. Urien protects Rheged first, and thinks of Rheged above all else. You have your victory, Lord Merlin. You would hang yet more glory around the neck of this thing you have created.' He waved a hand in Arthur's direction. 'How long before he wants his own throne to sit upon?'

'Fool!' Merlin shouted, startling Arthur and the other men in the room. 'You abandon your people and forsake us all.'

'Careful, druid.' Owain stood, the muscles beneath his jaw working. 'You have power, as you have shown, and all men respect you. But Rheged is my home, and that is where my people are. Not in Elmet or Gododdin or fighting for your puppet, Arthur.' Owain marched out of the hall and Kai followed, leaving the rest in a miserable silence.

'We still have the levy,' said King Gwallog in a surprisingly cheerful voice. 'We have five hundred men, at least, who have not yet returned to their homes. Idnerth will march them east beside you, Merlin, and you, Lord Arthur.'

'If we run headlong into Octha's army, we risk annihilation,' said Balin. 'A boar is at its most dangerous when wounded and cornered.'

Gwallog approached Arthur and adjusted the white robe he wore cast over one shoulder and resting in the crook of his arm. 'Just so, Lord Balin. But we have Arthur, a man who has risen from nothing to become the *dux bellorum* of our people. He is our lord of war, the man who defeated Ida at the river Glein and has now cast Octha out of Loidis. So, my *dux bellorum*, can we pursue Octha with the men we have?'

Arthur's hand gripped Ida's sceptre, and he stroked his thumb across its faces. 'We must,' he said. 'We cannot let Octha live. More ships come every spring, their hulls packed to the oars with war-hungry Saxons. We have won today, but in spring Octha will march again with another army, two or three thousand strong. It has to end. We march with the warriors we have along with King Gwallog's levy.'

They spent the evening talking of where to muster, who would take the vanguard and the rearguard, how much food they would need and who would command. All agreed that the army was Arthur's to lead, and he accepted with grim determination. They left one by one, first Balin seeking sleep, then Idnerth and Gwallog. Finally, Bors drank his fill of ale and went to find his warriors. In the end, Arthur was alone with Merlin, and they sat together in the empty stone hall.

'I never knew men could wield such power,' Arthur said. 'To blacken the sun and make day become night.'

Merlin leaned in close with a mischievous glint in his eye. 'What happened today was an alignment of the sun and moon. I had no part in it, other than using the gifts the gods granted me to predict its coming.'

'Alignment?' To Arthur and all the Britons, the sun was Lugh, the god riding his mighty stag across the heavens, and Étaín was the moon goddess to whom folk prayed for help with healing.

'Never mind. These are matters beyond the mind of a simple warrior. You see the sun rise and set, the moon wax and wane, tides ebb and flood, and ask no questions. You care only for the problems of spearmen and battle, so leave the rest to me. Our people have forgotten more about the sun and moon than we shall ever learn again. At the great standing stones in the south-west, us druids celebrate the power of the moon and sun. I knew the moon would block out the sun today, the stones predicted it, and thank the gods for it.'

Arthur was confused, but probing Merlin's vast cunning rarely yielded any greater level of understanding of what the druid held inside his cavernous mind. 'And the stone throwers?'

'The Romans used them to smash city walls to dust. I have spent my life learning, Arthur. Learning countless generations of druidic teachings and knowledge, but also other knowledge lost to our people, like the teaching left to us by the Romans. I have a trove of such scribblings on Ynys Môn, and there are few now who can read their tongue. Vegetius teaches us of war, of training soldiers, or ambush, retreat and attack. His writing is as dull as a Christian bishop's ramblings, but Vegetius knows war, Arthur. He also teaches us how to build Roman war machines. The stone throwers were not, sadly, my invention, nor are they anything new to the world. They are old knowledge, ancient secrets there to be harnessed if we can just pull our heads from the rotting thatch and crumbling rock. The Romans conquered us and left us fragments of their greatness. It's out there, Arthur, for us to learn and make ourselves into something great. Into one person with a country of our own. But we can't, because we insist on fighting one another over stolen cattle, goat paths and grazing rights. The Saxons come across the sea and keep us low with their constant warfare, and unless we can beat them, we shall forever live amongst wood and mud and in fear of the invader.'

'If the throwers can toss burning rocks over the walls and destroy buildings, why not smash down the gate and walls? Why have Nimue lead us over the southern wall?'

'Accuracy, my dear Arthur, is the problem. The Romans could do it. They could crush a sleeping dog from across the battlefield. The secret is their *mathematica*. Numbers. We can count a score of cows, or a dozen spearmen, but most men barely know how old they are, never mind how to count and write a number like ten thousand three hundred and seventy-two. But the Romans could count and write numbers way beyond our understanding. I understand it, of course. But I didn't have time to measure the distance between the throwers and the walls, or calculate the weight of the rock to be thrown, and then use Roman *mathematica* to determine where the thrower should be placed to accurately destroy the gate. So, I used the throwers to strike terror into Saxon hearts.'

'Can you make more?'

'If we have to take a city, yes. But we don't need Roman machines to defeat Octha. We need spearmen. We needed my knowledge today to take Loidis. Without it, our paltry force would have crashed against the walls like the sea pounding at cliffs, making no more dent than a flea on a sow's back.' Merlin paused and took a sip of ale. His long face stared at Arthur, quick eyes flitting over the scars on Arthur's cheek and chin, before fixing on Arthur's eyes. It was hard to return that stare, holding the gaze of a man who knew when the sun would fail and how to build weapons able to toss a rock it took four men to lift. Merlin raised his hand and wagged a long finger. 'What oath did you give to Urien?'

Arthur cleared his throat and looked away. 'That I would send the princess north if he gave me warriors to help recover Loidis.'

'Then she must go north with Owain.'

'Merlin, Guinevere is not like other women. She is...'

'She is beautiful, and you are in love with her. That is as plain as balls on a bull. But don't be a fool. Love itself is foolish, and oft the ruin of many great men. If you break your oath to Urien, he will become your enemy and instead of fighting Saxons, you will find yourself attacked by Urien, Owain and the army of Rheged. No other king of Britain will support you if that happens. You will be alone, beyond even my help. So send the princess north. Do it for Britain and do it for me.'

Arthur's heart sank and a great pit opened in his belly, as though a rock plummeted through his insides. Guinevere had not spoken to him since her hard words and revulsion at the prospect of marrying Urien. But what could Arthur do? It seemed fate was set against him, that it was impossible to have both the woman he loved and lead an army of Britons to victory over the Saxons. Was that to be his great sacrifice, the price to be paid for power and glory?

'It is not for me to send Guinevere north. She is not mine to give,' Arthur said meekly, as a weak attempt to offer an argument against what he knew must be done.

'She follows your army, and your sword keeps her safe. She eats your food and drinks your ale and, without you, she would be a woman alone in a city full of drunken warriors. How long would Guinevere live if she was not under your protection? She might not acknowledge it or like it, but there it is, nonetheless. Guinevere came across the sea with a company of her father's warriors and those men died when she was captured. You rescued her from Dun Guaroy and since then she has enjoyed the hospitality of King Urien's court. She chose to leave the Bear Fort with the Lady Morgan and was lucky to come across Bors and I marching south. Without that, who knows what would have been her fate? Two ladies riding the length of Britain to reach Dumnonia would tempt a hundred brigands and masterless men.

'Don't lose sight of where we are going and what we are doing here, Arthur. Gwallog named you *dux bellorum*, and he is right. He is king of Elmet, but his mind has turned to mush since Octha took Loidis from him. Idnerth is a brave and capable warrior, but he follows your orders without question, as does Bors. Balin of the Two Swords follows you, a warrior of great renown, and you have your own force of warriors. Your wars began north in Gododdin and we move south, fighting the enemy and increasing your renown. All the kings of Britain know of Arthur ap Nowhere who won the battle of the river Glein and cut the hand from King Ida of

Bernicia and killed his son Ibissa. You must look forward, strive towards our aim. The Saxons must be defeated, and to do that, we need a united army of Britons. Men believe the legends I spread because they want to. They crave a hero, they seek someone to lead them in a war against our invader.'

'Then we should use what we have gained to persuade Uther Pendragon to order the kingdoms to muster for war,' said Arthur. Talk of the legends pricked at him, poked and annoyed him. He didn't want men to think a god-forged sword or a druid's power carried Arthur to victory. He wanted to be his own man, who earned his own victories. Not a druid's puppet. Urien's warning of Merlin's cunning lived in Arthur's thought cage, like lingering damp on a wall, festering and poisoning his mind. 'What need of we for legends if the Pendragon orders war?'

'Listen to me and listen close.' Merlin leaned in, his mouth a hard, straight slit and his eyes fierce and bright. 'There is no persuading Uther Pendragon. I have told you before, Uther fears your growing power. He and the rest of the kings are jealous of any new power in the land. It threatens them. Owain said it himself. Surely a man who can win a battle and who leads a company of warriors will seek a throne of his own? Where will he strike? Will he march on Dumnonia, Rheged or Powys? Uther will not support us. He did when you were nothing and his warriors marched north to the Glein. But now? His young wife is with child and he seeks to secure Dumnonia for his heir. He has not the belly for war. So, we grow the legends, spread the word of Arthur and the sword of power. Always we strive for the greater aim. The end of this war.'

'I have no love for your legends and stories, Merlin. They plague me at every turn. Men believe I only win because of you. Arthur's victories are Merlin's victories. Who am I without Merlin and Excalibur?'

'A pox on your pride!' Merlin shouted and startled Arthur. 'We fight for something bigger than Arthur or Merlin. We fight for the survival of our people. Win, and there will always be a Rheged, an Elmet, a Dumnonia and a Gododdin. Lose, and the Saxons will keep coming, keep pushing until there is nothing of Britain but a distant memory. Our kings will be Saxons, our women will marry Saxons and bear Saxon children with Saxon names. Our places will have Saxon names and we shall be forgotten. Whispers on the wind, men who worshipped forgotten gods. *Wealas*. Nothing. A time will come when you must confront Uther, when we must challenge him and force the kingdoms to unite. Otherwise, what are we doing? We can't win this war with your black cloaks alone. When that time comes, you will need the legend, you will need the belief men have in Excalibur and the feats of Arthur ap Nowhere. Men will follow a legend and they will follow the sword. They will follow you.'

'I am tired of your cunning, Merlin. I am a warrior. I can fight battles and swing the sword. But this talk of challenging Uther is too much. You dream too far of a thing which cannot be.'

'It has to be! This is our last chance. Why can you not see that? Ambrosius swung that sword before you, and he came so close to driving the Saxons out. So close we could taste victory. Then the alliance fell apart. Ambrosius died and Uther gave up Igraine to become Pendragon. Only then did the other kings support Uther after Gorlois' death. They believed I was responsible for meddling in Gorlois' death to serve Uther's love for Igraine. To buy the kings' support for Uther, I became an exile on Ynys Môn, Igraine went to Urien, and Uther became Pendragon. Then we won a glorious victory over the Saxons. But we did not follow it up. We did not turn that one victory into the total defeat of the enemy. A truce was made. Saxon warlords became kings. Uther stopped, enjoying his new title as Pendragon, king of kings. The alliance shattered and Saxons grew in power. The very Saxons Vortigern the Cursed brought to our shores to fight in his army betrayed him and overwhelmed his kingdom. King Gwyrangon of Kent fell, Ida came, and now Saxons rule half of our island. Saxons are born here now, people of this land who speak a different language and worship different gods. Uther did not use the title of Pendragon well. He wasted it. Even after Igraine sacrificed so much, after I sacrificed so much. The ancient title of Pendragon, king of kings, must be used to win this war. The challenge is coming, Arthur, and you must be ready.'

'Me? Challenge Uther to become Pendragon? How can it be? Even if I were to win such a challenge, the other kings would never accept a high king who is not already a king. It makes no sense.'

'This is how it must be. How it will be. The kings will accept you because you have the sword, you are the legend, and you have Merlin at your side. This is what we have prepared for. What you were born for.'

'Born for? I am the son of unknown parents, taken by you to stand in for the dead son of Uther and Igraine. I was born for nothing but what I can take by the strength of my sword arm.' Arthur realised he was shouting, teeth grinding, fists bunched. He paced the room to calm himself, whilst Merlin smouldered in his chair.

'You know nothing of those days. Don't believe everything Ector told you.'

'I know enough. Speak plainly, Merlin. Now is the time for truth.'

'Now is the time to press our victory. You must pursue Octha whilst I go south to seek support in Gwynedd, Powys, Gwent and Dumnonia.'

'We are not done here. Am I a son of nobody or not?'

'You are what you must be.'

'Speak the truth, druid! Or take back your sword and your legends and leave me alone.'

'The truth? What is the truth, but what people believe it to be? What was the truth of today? Did Merlin use ancient magic to make the sun disappear, or did he read the old star patterns and know that the moon would block out the sun on this very day? What will people believe? They will believe what I tell them to believe. That is truth. Now, gather your men and march east. Pursue Octha and his men and kill them all. Guinevere goes north with Owain. That is the truth.'

An idea slipped to the forefront of Arthur's mind, something which had grown there like a seed since he had left the Bear Fort. Something cruel born of love, something Arthur craved. It distracted him from the talk of his parentage, slithering like a serpent to take priority. Another secret desire, living in the dark part of him. A thing he desired almost as much as he desired glory and reputation.

'I can be who you want me to be,' Arthur said softly, drawing close to Merlin, allowing the darkness to take over, giving life to his selfishness and ambition. There was an answer to Merlin's problem. It would give Arthur both his greatest desire and feed his ambitious hunger. The answer took away a guilty secret and served a selfish need. It was a cruel solution, not worthy of an honourable warrior, but was worthy of the ruthless cunning of kings, or perhaps of the *dux bellorum*. 'But there is a cost, Merlin.'

'There is always a cost.'

'When I swore that oath to Urien, I swore to send a princess north to the Bear Fort and a princess I shall send. But it will not be Guinevere.'

'Careful, now. Do not trick Urien. He is no fool to be trifled with.'

'I shall send him a princess of Kernow, the daughter of Igraine and Gorlois. Morgan is beautiful and of royal blood. What king would not rejoice in such a marriage? Their child will be a prince or princess of Britain, a royal of both Kernow and Rheged. Guinevere can only bring a flimsy alliance separated by the narrow sea. But Morgan brings prestige, and she is the daughter of Igraine, his dead wife, but no blood relation to Uther himself.'

'What is to be Guinevere's fate in this plot of yours?'

'She will be my wife. And you will marry us before I leave Loidis.'

Merlin seemed to age thirty years in an instant. He sagged, his back curving and face drooping. 'This is how we fail. How we fall to ruin. This is how it went with Uther in the Great War, and now it repeats itself. Women and lust cloud men's minds. They weaken us, take away from our greater purpose. What can an old man do but agree to your demand? I have fought for too long, seen too many disappointments to give up now. Morgan will go north and Guinevere will be your wife. But you will take Excalibur and kill Octha, no matter what it takes, no matter what you must do.'

'I shall.'

'Then Morgan will be wed to Urien, and I shall send word of it to her ward, King Marc of Kernow. I hope her tears and sorrow do not haunt you as she suffers for the rest of her days in the Bear Fort. Urien will not be gentle with her. That is the curse of great men with grand schemes, the ones who suffer reach out to us in the darkness. They blame us and curse us. And so they should. That is the price of power.'

Arthur left Merlin in the hall, but could not find sleep. He walked the battlements alone, stomach sick with guilt and heart filled with hope. Guinevere would be his, but he had traded Morgan into a lifetime of suffering. Morgan who had done him no wrong, whom he had lain with in a drunken stupor to assuage his grief when Guinevere had spurned him. Arthur had thought himself a good man, a noble warrior, one who followed the warrior's path as Ector had taught him. But as the night breeze made him shiver, Arthur knew he had done a black deed. He had sacrificed Morgan at the altar of his own desire and ambition, and he must live with that. He reached for Igraine's bronze disc at his neck, but the cold metal gave him no comfort. Igraine's sadness would now become Morgan's sadness. Worse than that, if what Merlin hinted at was true, and Arthur was in the fact Igraine and Uther's son, then he was also Morgan's half-brother. Which was a horrifying thought. Ector would not lie, Arthur told himself. He was Arthur ap Nowhere and nobody, the son of a forgotten churl of a slave. Arthur had not pressed Merlin on the matter because he did not want to know the truth. He could not deal with it, if truth it was. So, he walked alone and convinced himself of Ector's honesty, for tomorrow he must send a princess to a life of suffering at Urien's hands, and march an army to kill a Saxon warlord.

18

Guinevere and Morgan spent the night in Idnerth's villa, sleeping in the same rooms where Arthur and Balin had recovered after their flight from Balan and his twelve traitors. Idnerth had two legionaries guard them whilst he slept in the Roman barracks with his men. As dawn broke on the day after the battle, Arthur found Kai with the warriors of Caer Ligualid, preparing their supplies to march north. The men coughed and grunted, stumbling about with the bleary eyes and thick heads of men who had spent much of the previous night drinking and celebrating victory over the Saxons. Arthur knew many of them, especially the older warriors who had served Ector in the years when Arthur, Kai and Lunete grew up running wild around the Caer. They greeted Arthur with solemn nods of respect, some clasped fists to their breasts and others called to him by name. Arthur shook their forearms and congratulated them on a battle well fought until Kai appeared from behind a closed-up smithy kneading his forehead with his hand.

'Late night, brother?' Arthur asked.

Kai laughed. 'Late and long. Too much ale and not enough sleep.'

'Somebody get him the hair of the dog that bit him.' The warriors laughed and one tossed Kai a sloshing skin of ale.

Kai took a long pull and grimaced as the golden liquid flowed down his beard. 'It tasted better last night.'

'I need to talk to you, brother.'

Kai noticed the look in Arthur's eye and the good humour slipped away from his handsome face. 'I see. Come then. Let's walk together.'

Arthur talked, and Kai listened. He told him about Merlin and Excalibur and what the druid demanded of Arthur if the Britons were to have any hope of defeating the Saxons. Kai knew most of the tale, for they had met Merlin together and Kai was with Arthur on campaign when Merlin had first handed him the ancient and powerful sword.

'So now we come to the rub,' Arthur said. 'I gave an oath to Urien to send a princess north once the battle for Loidis was over.'

'I remember it well.'

'I will marry Guinevere. Princess Morgan of Kernow will return north with you and Owain and marry King Urien.' Arthur had spent hours on his night-long march around the high walls pondering how to accomplish his plan without enraging Owain or betraying his oath. Kai was his answer. His brother, his best and greatest friend.

'You love Guinevere?'

'With all my heart. The sun rises and sets with her, brother.'

'Then it shall be so.' Kai pulled Arthur into a long embrace. He did not ask why, or how he should break the news to Owain and Urien. He just accepted it because it was what Arthur needed.

'Morgan will travel north in a covered wagon, which I have

men preparing as we speak. By the time Owain realises which princess he has, Guinevere and I will be married. Morgan will go to Urien willingly, and the old bear will be happy to have a beautiful, young queen to squeeze beside his fire.'

'We march before midday, and I will collect the wagon personally. Once Urien is distracted by the curve of her breasts and the warmth of her body, he might settle for Morgan, but Owain will be enraged. He will think you have deceived him.'

'Owain is always enraged, and he likes me about as much as a splinter in the arse.'

Arthur left Kai and crossed the city to Idnerth's villa. The legionaries allowed him to enter, and he found Guinevere in the garden. She walked amongst the flower beds with the sun in her copper hair, and when Arthur saw her, his guts knotted just as they would when he advanced on a Saxon shield wall.

'Arthur,' she said tartly, arms crossed and head tilted slightly, her anger clearly not forgotten and Arthur's words not forgiven.

'Lady Guinevere,' he said, and swallowed at the dryness in his throat. 'I have something to... that is to say that I... we need to talk about...' Arthur paused and squared his shoulders. She smirked at him, which did not help his awkwardness. 'I have angered you, and I was wrong. It is not for me to decide where you go or who you should marry.'

'No. It is not.'

'But I hope you realise how highly I think of you.'

'And I you.' She smiled, and Arthur's cheeks flushed red as they often did when close to her. He could not stop it, and the more he tried to control it, the redder and hotter his face became.

'You are a princess of Cameliard and I am a simple warrior, not worthy of a lady such as you. But I am not without wealth or oathmen, and though I have no lands, and no title to speak of, I would like to ask you, or to send word to your father to ask him, or make it known that...' Arthur stopped himself again, losing the run of what he was trying to say.

'My father gave up being the master of my destiny when he packed me off to Britain amidst a war he knew raged across the island. But for you, I would still be at Dun Guaroy and perhaps a Saxon's bed slave. My father thought of himself and his kingdom before my welfare and placed me in grave danger. I know what you are trying to say, and my answer is yes. You are a man who will go far, I think, Arthur ap Nowhere. I have heard the talk of the *dux bellorum* and how King Gwallog and King Letan Lyddoc of Gododdin honour you. What woman would not want to marry Britain's warlord? Though quite where we shall live and raise our children, I do not know.'

Arthur's jaw fell open, and then she came to him and he kissed her. Her lips touched his, and his body tingled as though struck by lightning. He laughed for joy and held her tight, and then sent her with two of his black cloaks to wait with Merlin until he could join her again. The happiness faded quickly, the joy of requited love replaced brutally by the misery of what must happen so that he and Guinevere could be together.

He found Morgan sitting on a long couch eating a meal of bread and honey. Arthur watched her for a moment, her soft face and the curve of her neck. Urien would paw her and maul her, and when he was done, and she grew too old for his tastes, he would discard her into the dark recesses of the Bear Fort. Arthur was about to send Morgan to that fate and the guilt gnawed at his insides like a serpent. It was the price to be paid for Guinevere and to lead an army into Lloegyr.

'Lady Morgan,' he said, bowing his head respectfully.

'Lord Arthur,' she replied, and sat up straight, forcing a smile to her strained face. 'I am surprised to see you. But pleased. Would you like some bread? I don't have the stomach for it today, I am afraid.'

'No, thank you. I come to you with news, my lady.' He paused, summoning the will to come straight out with the hard news. 'You are to be married.'

'Ah,' she said. She set down the wooden plate and brushed crumbs from her skirts.

'Word has been sent to King Marc in Kernow, and the match is arranged.'

'Who am I to marry?'

'King Urien of Rheged. You are to be a queen, my lady.'

Morgan's lip quivered, and she cuffed a tear from her eye. 'My stepfather, whom I have never met, and whom I helped Guinevere escape. It seems I shall follow in my poor mother's footsteps. I expected King Marc to decide who would be my husband. Not you.'

'It is not I who decided your future,' Arthur lied. 'But it is for the greater good of Britain. You will make a noble queen, Lady Morgan, and your marriage ensures that Rheged keeps its warriors fighting to keep the Saxons at bay.' Arthur bowed. 'You will leave today with Prince Owain.'

Arthur turned on his heel and took a step to leave, relieved that the conversation had been so brief, for he had expected it to be far worse.

'Arthur?' Morgan called after him.

'Yes, lady?' he replied, stopping and turning back to her.

'I feel your child quickening inside me. You should know that before you take Guinevere to wife. I will go and marry Urien, duty demands it, and I cannot go against King Marc's will. But I am no fool. I see and have seen more than you know. You used me like a whore, and I hate you for that.'

Arthur just stared, her words hitting him like a hammer blow.

'You can go now,' Morgan said, hate dripping from her like poison from a serpent's fangs.

He left her there with so much left unsaid. Morgan and Guinevere were close, and she had left Rheged with the princess of Cameliard and knew full well what marrying King Urien meant, and yet she would go, anyway. Arthur watched Owain and Kai leave from the walls, their warriors marching alongside Morgan in her covered wagon. He wondered if what she said was true, that his drunken mistake had turned into a life, a child set to be born into an uncertain future. Just like him. She couldn't know that a baby grew within her so soon after their night together, he told himself. It was a trick to hurt him for sending her to Urien. He hoped that was all it was. Owain would rage and shout when he discovered it was Morgan and not Guinevere in the covered wagon, but by the time they camped and she emerged from the wagon to eat, it would be too late. Owain could not return to his father and complain of Arthur's deceit, for he would look like a fool. What prince returns from war with the wrong bride for his king? Owain's pride and Urien's wrathfulness aided Arthur's ploy. Owain could not lose face and complain that he had brought Princess Morgan north, and King Urien had his princess and Arthur had kept his oath, albeit through a play on words. Arthur had sworn to send a princess north, and so he had. Urien could not spurn Morgan or he would attract the enmity of her ward, King Marc of Kernow, and he would not publicly rebuke his son and champion Owain ap Urien.

The wind swirled across the battlements, its sting dragging a tear from Arthur's eye to roll down his cheek. He realised once again that he was holding Ida's sceptre with his thumb on the cruel faces, and he wondered what spirits were locked within its cold stone. Perhaps it was the sceptre making him so ruthless, the fetches of long-dead Saxon warlords changing him, making him as cruel and hard as they. Arthur shoved it back into his belt and shivered. He hoped it was the sceptre and not his own ruthless soul.

Merlin and Guinevere waited for Arthur in a rose garden close to Gwallog's hall. Balin was there, with Bors, Idnerth and Lancelot. Each had polished their mail to a bright sheen and combed their beards and hair. Bors even looked like he might have bathed for the celebration. King Gwallog and Prince Ceretic presided over the ceremony in their white Roman robes and Guinevere was beautiful in a gown of sea green. Nimue sang an Irish love song in her native tongue, and Merlin said the words to join Arthur and Guinevere together in the ways of the old gods as man and wife. They all celebrated that day, though the fare was not as King Gwallog would have wished. The Saxons had eaten their way through most of his larder, but there was still fresh bread, honey, fish from the river and roast pork.

Arthur held Guinevere close that night and they slept together in Idnerth's villa. But as Arthur lay beside his wife, his thoughts turned to Morgan and her fate. Guinevere mentioned nothing of Morgan, that the woman who was perhaps her closest friend in Britain, so close that they had fled Rheged together, had gone to face the fate that she so despised. Perhaps some things were best left unsaid. Arthur hoped Morgan had lied, and that his bastard was not growing inside her. That would be a heavy price to pay for a victory he had not yet won, and the wife lying beside him.

Arthur listened to Guinevere's breathing, watched the rise and fall of her chest as she slept. He had sacrificed a part of himself to claw closer to victory, and it weighed heavy, like an anchor stone dragging behind him. But the need for victory countered that weight. Octha must fall. Balan must die. Arthur must win. It had to be so, or all the sacrifices would be in vain. Ector's death, Lunete's disappearance, Balin's lost kingdom, Morgan's dreadful fate, the deaths of so many Britons at the hands of the invader. Arthur felt it all. The responsibility to right those wrongs came with Excalibur, with Merlin's favour, with Guinevere's hand. He simply had to win, but to do it, Arthur must march into Lloegyr and slay a warlord. Arthur had to follow the bear into its cave and attack the beast in its own lair, even if it meant his own death.

Octha must fall. Balan must die. Arthur must win.

19

The river crashed and bounced against slick rocks as it babbled and leapt through a steep valley bed, beneath hillsides dotted with boulders amongst yellow wildflowers. The huge wolf-grey rocks seemed out of place amongst the grass, ferns and brush, for there was not a cliff or mountain in sight. It was as though giants had tossed them into the valley in the fog before time began, when giants and monsters roamed Britain beside the gods and the hidden folk. Arthur sat with his back against a smooth stone, listening as hoofbeats thundered down the hillside, feeling the dull thrum through his mail like a drum.

'Wait,' Balin hissed. He lay belly down on a flat slab of rock, hidden from their quarry by its stone lip, eagerly watching their approach.

'How many?' Arthur whispered.

'Six.'

Lancelot grinned at the prospect of a fight like a greedy child offered leftovers after a meal. Arthur and the army were three days' march deep into Lloegyr, beyond the dense forests on the Elmet–Deira border and within a day's march of the marshlands around the river Dubglas. Arthur's army marched a day behind the vanguard led by Arthur himself, ranging ahead on horseback with his black cloaks and Lancelot's men. They hunted Saxons, harrying enemy scouts through the woodlands and hills, seeking news of Octha's retreating army. Lancelot's reputation had grown since the fight beneath the gate at Loidis. He had proved himself a formidable warrior, and the men spoke with awe of his almost unnatural speed and strength.

At first, the Saxons were easy to track because their retreat left a trail of corpses in its wake like the shed skin of a snake. The dead were grey, gaunt and withered things. Saxons injured in the fighting for Loidis, who had steadily succumbed to infection or blood loss in the days following the battle. The Saxons preferred to burn their dead, especially warriors who believed their souls would ascend to Valhǫll, the great hall of their god Woden. At first, Arthur's scouts found the charred remains of men burned with spears and shields clutched to their chests, but over the last two days, they had found a dozen men buried in shallow graves, many already disturbed and gnawed at by animals. The Saxons grew low on food and ale, their retreat becoming ever more desperate as they slunk into the depths of Lloegyr and away from Arthur's vengeful Britons.

It was not hard to follow Octha. A thousand men leave a smear across the countryside like a great worm has slithered across it, leaving a desolate smudge of brown filth. Octha's men left discarded clothing, rotting boots, the bones from their meals, ashes of campfires and heaps of stinking shit and piss buzzing with flies. Octha's scouts ranged behind his retreating force like a skirmishing rearguard, watching Arthur's pursuit and trying to pick off his foragers and scouts if they ventured too far ahead of the marching column. Arthur hunted Octha's scouts to seek information, anything that would help him outmanoeuvre Octha, to surprise him, to pounce when the Saxon was unprepared. To destroy him.

'Just six?' Arthur said with a shake of his head. 'Luckily for us, we are just three.'

'Hush, they are close,' Balin whispered, with a finger to his lips.

Hooves thundered down the valley. The crashing rumbling of Arthur's riders herding Saxons into Arthur's trap. His men had followed the scouts all day as they ranged across the valley heights, searching westwards for a sign of Arthur's army. Octha was no fool, and Arthur had not concealed his pursuit so that the scouts Octha sent ranging to west and south, watching, reporting, waiting, knew exactly where the main Briton force marched and how far they were from Octha's column. What Arthur didn't yet know was how many warriors remained in Octha's army, and where he was going. If he kept pushing east, Octha would move into King Clappa of Deira's lands. Saxon lands. But whether Clappa would welcome an army eating and drinking their way across his land was an important question.

If Octha moved south, he must march across the wet, treacherous fens and marshlands into Lindsey, currently ruled by King Cwichelm, an old Saxon warrior who had come across the sea with Hengist and Horsa. Either of Clappa or Cwichelm might offer Octha succour, or they could see him as a threat and push him from their kingdoms and onto Arthur's spear points. But if the Saxons joined forces, if Octha could persuade Cwichelm or Clappa to bind their warriors to his, then Arthur could see no outcome but defeat for his ragtag army. His force of survivors from Idnerth's legionaries, what remained of Bors' Gododdin warriors, Arthur's black cloaks, and the levy of Elmet.

Guinevere remained behind the safety of Loidis' walls with King Gwallog, Prince Ceretic, Merlin, Nimue and two hundred men of the Elmet levy. Merlin stayed to give the defenders confidence, and he and Nimue tended to the folk who had remained in Loidis and had suffered most at the Saxons' hands. The women they had raped, the children they had whipped and enslaved, and the men they had beaten and abused. The inexperienced men left to patrol the walls and the city's environs were too few to defend Loidis from any fresh Saxon attack, but Arthur could not spare any more from his already perilously small army.

Boots splashed in the water, and six men panted as they fled from Arthur's riders. Horses whickered as they raced along the riverbank and Arthur laid his hand on the cold stone. Its damp hardness seeped into his flesh and he closed his eyes. It was a rock of Britain, whether tossed there by a giant or born of the land itself. It was of the very fabric of his home and Arthur let its strength flow into his limbs.

'Now,' Balin said, and rose to crouch on the rock slab.

Arthur drew Excalibur and stepped out from behind the boulder with the sword in his hand. Lancelot flanked him and together they stood in the rushing river water, facing six charging Saxons. The Saxon scouts stopped dead, eyes flicking from Arthur and back to the pursuing riders. Arthur gestured with Excalibur and his riders turned and cantered away, much to the Saxons' surprise. They wore simple jerkins edged with fur and carried bows, spears and seax blades and saw two mailed warriors with swords standing between them and safety.

'Six of us, two of them,' barked a spindly man with a cruel mouth in his native tongue. 'Kill these *Wealas* turds and we are away.' They hadn't yet noticed Balin crouching on his rock above them.

'They are lords. Look at their weapons,' said another.

'All the better for us when we take all they have. Offa, you, me and Aldhelm will take the big bastard. You three take the pup.'

'How many men does Octha have left?' Arthur said in Saxon, his voice calm but firm. 'Tell us and you may live.'

They glanced at one another in surprise to hear a Briton speak Saxon, but the spindly man sneered. 'Your riders are gone, shit-worm. Throw down your sword and take off your mail and we might let you live. How about that, *Wealas*?'

'Very well. Have it your way. You can tell me what I want to know as you scream with my sword tearing out your insides.'

'Kill the impudent dog.' He charged at Arthur with a wicked bladed seax in his fist and a murderous glint in his eye. The rest of the Saxon scouts also charged, shouting their war cries to embolden themselves, splashing through the river to fight six against two.

Arthur braced himself, setting his feet in the riverbed, tiny stones crunching beneath his boots as the chill water flowed around him. Much of fighting is about understanding distance and space. Arthur had practised with weapons in Caer Ligualid from the time he could walk, taught how to fight by Ector himself, one of the greatest champions in all Britain. Strike when an enemy is too far away and your blade swings wide, or you lunge off balance. Strike too late, and your enemy is too close. The stroke fouls, or the enemy's blade bites first, cold steel slicing into your skin, rending muscle and organs, spilling blood and taking life. So when the Saxon came within the right range, Arthur flicked his wrist, lifting the tip of Excalibur's blade with sudden speed and all the strength in an arm hardened to battle and war. The tip whipped across the Saxon's bicep, cutting through his jerkin and slashing open the skin beyond. He cried out in surprised pain as his blood plopped into the river in fat crimson gobbets, pouring down an arm made useless by Excalibur's honed tip. The seax fell from the Saxon's fingers and splashed in the water and he stared open-mouthed at

Arthur. His mousy beard and straggly hair showed grey at the chin and temples, and the Saxon must have thought Arthur nothing but a boy, perhaps the son of a great lord who had furnished his heir with expensive chain-mail and a sword as valuable as a warship. But he was wrong about that. He faced a scarred and experienced warrior, a warlord and ruthless killer.

Lancelot crashed into the next two Saxons like a maddened bull. His charge sent up great plumes of water as his heavy boots churned the clear water brown. The first Saxon tried to shy away from Lancelot's bulk and speed. His spear lowered and his eyes closed in terror. Lancelot hit that Saxon so hard with the edge of his sword that it clove through shoulder and arm, severing the limb completely. The Saxon cried out in horrified pain as his arm splashed into the river and turned its muddied waters pink with blood. The other Saxons balked then, their attack turning into stunned backward steps. Lancelot drove his sword into the chest of the next Saxon with all the power in his broad shoulders. His blade smashed through the ash shaft of a spear raised to block him, shattering the weapon as though it were made of cinders. Chest bones cracked, and the man shuddered as Lancelot's sword punched through his back and sprayed the remaining Saxons with warm blood.

Balin leapt from his hiding place and landed amongst the enemy, slashing at their legs with his axe like a woodsman pollarding his forest. The Saxons crawled in the shallows, trying to escape the savage Britons who had assailed them with such ferocity. Arthur smashed a golden-haired Saxon's skull with his sword to leave the warrior lying face down in the river. Balin and Lancelot dispatched the rest with similar brutality until all were dead but the spindly man. He sat with his back against a rock dashed with yellow lichen, cradling his injured arm and shaking with fear.

'How many men remain in Octha's army?' Arthur asked again, letting Excalibur hang at his side. The blade dripped blood and gore into the stream and the Saxon's eyes fixed upon it as though the sword was made of gold. 'Tell me now and I'll leave you alive. Hold your tongue and we'll cripple you. Leave you here to die slowly. The wolves and night animals will come and gnaw on you before the end. Ravens will peck out your eyes whilst the dark things of the riverbank crawl into your wound and eat you from the inside out. There is no honour in that, Saxon. It will take you days to die, wailing and screaming like a beast, before your soul travels to the afterlife reserved for cowards, traitors and those who die without honour. Is that the death you want? Is that how your ancestors would wish you to die? Howling in pain and suffering in a foreign land.'

The Saxon snapped out of his daze and locked eyes with Arthur. 'This is not a foreign land. This is *our* land.'

'Very well. Seems like he won't talk. Lancelot, hamstring him, and we'll leave him here for the animals.'

'Wait, wait. Octha has little over a thousand men fit to fight. Then another few hundred slaves, women and children. There, I told you. Please don't leave me here for the wolves and ravens.'

'Good. I'm a man of my word. You can go.'

The Saxon gaped at Arthur, and then at Balin and Lancelot. Arthur washed Excalibur clean in the river water and dried the blade on a dead man's cloak. The spindly Saxon struggled to his feet and stumbled through the babbling waters. He fell and rose and fled like only a man who fears for his life can run.

'You should have killed him,' said Balin. 'We'll have to fight the bastard again before long.'

'Like Redwulf,' said Arthur. He watched the Saxon disappear beyond the valley and recalled the young Saxon he had encountered on the same day he had met Nimue.

'Like Redwulf,' Balin agreed.

'Who by Andraste's tits is Redwulf?' asked Lancelot, his mouth gurning around the Saxon name as though he had eaten a mouthful of rancid meat.

'A Saxon I should have killed,' Arthur replied. 'I captured him, and Balin urged me to kill him. Balin never leaves a Saxon alive. Redwulf lived because I vouched for him, and then he betrayed us. I was naïve, and it was an expensive lesson. Good men died because of it.'

'So why let this one live?'

Arthur shrugged. 'I gave him my word. But I didn't say *you* wouldn't kill him.'

'I'll do the bastard,' said Balin, and set off after the Saxon.

'He hates them,' said Lancelot, watching Balin charge off.

'More than you could ever understand. Balin is the embodiment of our struggles against the Saxons. He has lost more than most men could dream of. His land, his wife, his children. He lives only to kill Saxons, but above all, he lives for the debt owed to his brother. Balin is a thing of pure hate, a man driven to eat and sleep only by his thirst for vengeance. His hate for the Saxons is like the fire in a smith's forge, so bright that it's hard to look upon, so hot that it can sear you to stand too close to it.'

'Can we fight a thousand Saxons with the men we have?'

'We have to, whether or not it is possible. We are two days behind them, and in two more days, Octha will either be welcomed into the bosom of Lindsey or Deira, or must turn and face us. The fight is coming, Lancelot. The chance to make the reputation you desire. The chance to kill our enemies.'

'And if they defeat us?'

'Then we die and the cycle continues to turn like a merchant's wagon wheel rolling along a Roman road. Forever turning, rolling to its destination. We die and our bodies become bones and dung for the fields. Octha rebuilds his army with warriors from across the sea and eventually, inevitably, he will kill and slaughter until he becomes king of Elmet.'

'We must make sure we win, then.' Lancelot smiled, and Arthur wished it was so easy. He wished war was as simple as marching across the hills and lining up to fight Octha's army. But it was not simple. Arthur's men trusted him and depended on him. Their lives, and the lives and homes of their families, depended upon Arthur's ability to win battles, upon his cunning and daring to take the fight to the enemy. That responsibility weighed him down like an extra coat of chain-mail. He had to crush Octha, to beat him so badly that he could never rise gain, to kill him or slaughter so many of his warriors that Octha's dreams were ruined forever.

Three days later, Arthur found Octha and his army. The Saxons had made camp in the lee of a high crag, the last promontory before the river Dubglas slid into lowland marsh and fens, the boggy flatlands which swamped Britain's eastern coast in a vast swathe of fenlands stretching as far south as the Saxon kingdom of Kent. They waited at the border between Deira and Lindsey, waiting to see what sort of welcome Clappa and Cwichelm would offer.

Llamrei whickered and snorted as Balin's mare trotted slowly alongside him. Arthur leant forward and stroked the stallion's ears. Idnerth, Bors, Lancelot and Dewi all sat astride horses, stood in a line staring out at a swathe of land beneath the high, sharp crag.

'There are a lot of the bastards,' said Bors, though with too much glee for it to be a warning. 'They don't look like they want to fight. We might have to wake them up a bit. Kill a few of the turds to get things going.'

'Attack them now before they have a chance to form up,' Balin said. His horse sensed his anger and its hooves pawed at the grass, the mare skittering from side to side.

'They still outnumber us,' Arthur said, 'but they are hungry and tired. They've been marching for days and they left Loidis in a hurry without food or ale. So they have been eating only what they can forage, and drinking from rivers and streams.'

'I can smell their shit from here,' said Bors. 'Their arses are dripping with runny shit from that foul water they have been drinking. Balin is right, charge them now and kill them all whilst we have the chance.'

'They'll just run away again,' said Idnerth. He wore his full Roman panoply of cuirass, studded kilt and shining helmet with its crosswise red plume.

'So we cut them down as they flee.'

'It will be a running battle. They still outnumber us, and that pursuit will turn into a hundred small skirmishes. They'll pick us off in small groups as our levy men get too excited, hacking and flailing with their spears, hoes and adzes. If we aren't careful, we'll find our force destroyed, and when Octha realises that he'll turn around, form up and finish us.'

'And we left only two hundred levy men to protect Loidis,' Arthur said wistfully, his mind imagining Octha's army returning victorious to storm an almost unprotected city. With Guinevere inside its walls.

'So we force them to fight us here,' said Lancelot, as eager for battle as Balin. 'Though it's hard to tell truly how many men they have.'

The Saxons swarmed beneath the crag like ants. Smoke from their fires swirled above them, whipped into a smudge of cloud by an easterly breeze. They hurried to grab weapons, shouting, some barking orders, others rushing to form a ragged line of shields at the foot of the hill between Arthur's men and their encampment. They saw Arthur's army arrayed on a long, flat patch of grazing meadow, shields and spears ready and poised for battle. Arthur had fewer than five hundred men, and though Lancelot was right, Arthur guessed Octha still had close to a thousand men on the hill.

'Here he comes,' said Dewi, pointing to where a big man on a white horse ambled through the makeshift Saxon shield wall towards the Britons.

'Octha,' Arthur said.

'We'd best see what the fur-wearing sheep-shagger has to say for himself,' said Bors, and was rewarded with a laugh from Dewi.

'I'll go alone,' said Arthur. Bors, Idnerth and Balin stiffened, squaring their shoulders and staring hard at Arthur. 'All Octha wants is to trade a few insults to buy his warriors time to form up. If he can, he'll challenge you, Bors, or you, Balin, to single combat.'

'I'll happily fight him,' Bors bristled. 'I'll cut off his head and use his beard for an arse wipe.'

'I know you would, Lord Bors, but whilst you fight him, the rest of his men form ranks and every man in our army must kill two Saxons for us to win. Half of our men are of the levy. Can an Elmet farmer kill two Saxon warriors? Even ones weakened by hunger and running bowels?'

'My brother is there somewhere,' said Balin. 'They all have to die. We do as Arthur says.'

'I'll talk to Octha. Whilst I do, wheel the army around so that we flank them. I want the bend of the river at their backs so they have nowhere to run. Idnerth, advance with your legionaries the moment I turn back from the parlay. Keep our proper warriors in the front ranks and the levy in the rear with their bows. We march in ranks fifty across, to keep ourselves compact. Hurry and get them lined up now. We kill them today, and drive them into the river.'

Arthur didn't wait for questions. He nudged Llamrei with his knees, but kept the stallion at a slow trot as he went to meet Octha. His men needed time to form up, but not too much time. Cavall bounced along at Llamrei's flank, barking occasionally at the Saxons, tongue lolling over his white teeth. Arthur was the commander of the army, named *dux bellorum* by King Gwallog and entrusted with Excalibur by Merlin. Arthur trusted Idnerth and Dewi to execute his orders, and though refusal to allow Bors to have the pre-battle exchange of insults with Octha might have stung Bors' pride, the champion of Gododdin would forget it once his axe found Saxon necks.

Octha's horse stopped beside a clutch of long, wild grass and bent its neck to crop at it. As Arthur came close, Octha glowered at him with barely concealed hate. His broad chest heaved as he breathed, and his slab of a face was as hard as the cliff behind him. His clothes and armour were filthy with grime and his eyes sunken and skull-like from thirst and sickness. Octha was so huge that he dwarfed the horse beneath him, like a giant astride a pony. Arthur allowed Llamrei to amble close to Octha's horse, and the stallion shook his great head, and snapped his teeth at Octha's mount, and the beast shied away, almost tipping Octha from his riding blanket until the Saxon warlord sawed on the reins and brought his horse under control. Arthur fought to hide his smile at the petty victory, and he called Cavall to him, as the war dog growled at Octha's horse, frightening the beast even more.

'You'll need more than a fancy horse to beat me, pup,' Octha growled in his guttural Saxon tongue, his mouth turning up at the corners to reveal a set of stone-like teeth.

'Have you come to surrender and beg for the lives of your men?' Arthur asked, and smiled cheerfully.

'No druid here to darken the sky? No *galdr* contraptions to toss fire over our heads? Your *Volva* took my hair and used it to curse me. Perhaps you have finally come to fight like a man?'

'Surrender. Kneel to me now and beg forgiveness for the people you have killed and all you have stolen. Give me your oath that you will send your men east to sail back across the narrow sea and your men can live.'

Octha savaged his horse's reins and opened his mouth to reply, but then a wracking cough barked out of him, creasing his body, forcing the mighty warrior to wince. 'Woden curse you, pup, and your band of bandy-legged shirkers. We'll butcher you all here today, if it's a fight you want. When it's done, I want you alive. I'll keep you as my slave. You can empty my shit pail and clean my clothes. I'll geld you, if you aren't gelded already, and cut out your smart tongue. Women will laugh at you, and men will throw scraps from their plates for you to grapple over with the hall dogs in the floor rushes of my hall.'

'Except you don't have a hall. You have no lands, no kingdom. Nothing. Octha, lord of nothing but a band of starving men dying of the shit sickness. Maybe we won't fight you today, maybe we'll just keep you here and watch you die of hunger. We'll feast on roast duck, honey, drink freshly brewed mead, and laugh as you eat your horses, and then the grass, and then die lying in your own excrement. Octha the Unlucky, they'll say, died slathered in turd, loser of battles, master of Loidis for less time than it takes to move sheep from one pasture to the next.'

'I'll kill you, pup. You and all your men. Fight me now, here. You and I. Let's see who is the champion. Fight me, coward!'

'I'll fight you on the field when our armies clash. You can find me in the front rank. Look, my men form up, ready for battle. Are you ready to fight, Octha the Unlucky?'

'You won't be so cocksure when my axe comes for you.'

'Send Balan the traitor out here. My scouts tell me he has

returned to you. He can fight his brother whilst we ready ourselves for battle. You have cowards and turncloaks in your army, Octha the Unlucky. It's little wonder you run from me like a whipped dog.'

'Octha does not run.'

Arthur smiled again at Octha's increasingly reddening face, which enraged the warlord even further. Though Arthur noticed a slight tightening of Octha's eyes at the mention of Balan. Arthur peered over the big man's shoulder and could see no sign of the Briton or his twelve traitors in Octha's camp. There were few horses amongst the Saxons, Octha's own and perhaps six others. All of Balan's men rode, which meant Balin's brother had retreated south to his home and given up on his mercenary's pay, which seemed unlikely given the state of Octha's army and the defeat at Loidis. Or Balan was somewhere else, which, given Octha waited at the borders of Deira and Lindsey, made Arthur uncomfortable. Had Balan gone to seek Cwichelm or Clappa to request aid?

'Octha runs like a child from a scolding mother. Begone now, Octha the Unlucky, and prepare to die.' Arthur whistled, and Cavall barked, bounding towards Octha's horse, and then snarling and snapping at its legs. Octha bellowed with fury as his horse bucked and lurched into a frightened canter away from Arthur and his war dog. The Britons roared with delight to see Octha so humiliated by Arthur and his hound, and Arthur grinned at Octha as he struggled to stay astride his horse. To fall would be yet another humiliation for the Saxon, who had surely already lost the confidence of his warriors.

Arthur strapped on his bright helmet with its plume of raven feathers. He cantered towards his army, sure that he had poked and prodded Octha's pride, the pride all warriors held deep within their core, enough to enrage him to fight. And there must be a fight, because Idnerth was right. If the Saxons fled the field, the battle would stretch for miles, and eventually the Saxons would overwhelm the pursuing Britons. Britons desperate to punish and slaughter the enemy who had come across the sea to kill their people, enslave their wives and children, and take everything from them. So it must be battle, the horrors of the shield wall, blood, slaughter and mayhem.

20

Idnerth's legionaries made a magnificent sight marching to the battlefield. Two hundred soldiers of Elmet who still went to war as the Romans had, with red cloaks, oval shields, pilum spears and shining helmets. They marched in time, stomping through the grass, spears held at the same angle, Idnerth barking orders, calling to his men to defend the honour of Elmet, to find their courage and destroy the enemy. Idnerth's men were a match for three times their number, and Arthur wished to Neit and Andraste that he had two thousand legionaries of old Rome. With such a force, he could crush the Saxons and drive them from Britain forever. For a moment, Arthur wondered how his people could have resisted an entire army of Romans, when they had first come to Britain's shores in their tens of thousands.

The carnyx blared, like a metallic beast's call reverberating across the battlefield. It stirred the war-fury within Arthur, a kindling of anger sparking deep inside him. The long bronze tube and its rearing dragon's head sang to the Britons of war. It was their ancient call to arms, and the black cloaks' own signal that battle was afoot. It was time to fight. Arthur drew Excalibur and held the blade aloft. He rode along the forming ranks and the warriors roared their acclaim, faces staring hopefully up at him, eyes wide with fear. Arthur rode forward and back, so that every man could see both him and the sword. They shook their spears and bellowed from the depths of their lungs. They cheered not only because Arthur was their leader and they were proud to fight for him, but also to give themselves confidence, to build up the courage it took to march into the massed ranks of Saxon axes, shields and seaxes, fully aware that those blades were poised to hack and chop at them. Every man in Arthur's army had seen friends, brothers, fathers and comrades killed. Worse than death, though, were those who lived, gravely wounded by an axe blow to the head, chest or stomach. Such wounds made men fearful, the awful pain, the infection, the sweating and finally death.

Arthur found Bors with Lancelot, Dewi and Balin. The black cloaks formed up behind the legionaries alongside the men of Gododdin, grim-faced, ready to fight and die to protect their fellow Britons. Arthur climbed off his horse and gave Llamrei's reins to a camp-boy who led the stallion to the rear, but Cavall would not go. Arthur whistled at him, pointed, shouted at the dog, but the beast stayed at Arthur's side. He was a hound bred for war, trained to it by his former Saxon masters, and eventually Arthur relented, and Cavall took his place in the line of battle beside him.

'Octha wants to fight, then?' asked Bors with a smirk.

'He does now,' Arthur replied. Nervous excitement rose from the army, the emotions palpable, making Arthur's heart quicken. The army lined up as Arthur had instructed, and as Octha's men came down from the hill to form up opposite their enemies with the river at their backs, Arthur ground his teeth, fear beginning to curdle his guts. Fear was necessary to drive his anger, to give him the courage required to face the Saxon foe.

'For a man who commands an army of experienced warriors,' said Balin, 'he lines up for battle like he has never fought before.'

'Good.' Arthur wanted Octha mad, enraged, so maddened by his defeat at Loidis, by Merlin's druidic magic, by everything that had gone against him, that Arthur's goading forced him to fight without thinking. Octha brought his men down from the crag's shadow to form ranks opposite Arthur's men. With the river at their back, Octha had the greater numbers, and could have stretched his army out in long ranks to envelop the Britons. Or he could simply engage Arthur's army with similar numbers in similar sized ranks, then send the rest of his men around Arthur's flank to attack him from the rear. If only Octha had seen that chance, had calmed himself from his hubris, from the humiliation of defeat by the *Wealas* he so despised, then the blood of Arthur's men would have soaked the fields beneath the high, dark crag.

Octha prowled in front of his men like a great, shaggy bear. His champions lined up behind him, the big men with their round linden-wood shields bossed and rimmed with iron, spears in their fists and axes at their belts. He lifted his axe and his men chanted their Saxon war music, beating spears on shields like war drums. Arthur understood then, as he watched Octha rouse his men for battle, men who were starving and riddled with dysentery. With the river at their backs, there was nowhere to run, no retreat. Only battle and victory, or death. Arthur's attack gave Octha a chance to redeem himself. If he could drive his men to victory here before the river Dubglas, Octha could restore his damaged reputation and win the kingdom he so desperately desired. War and glory lived and died on the edge of the sword blade, victory and defeat possible in such fine margins, life and death waiting to embrace men when the shield walls clashed.

'Attack now,' Arthur called, 'crush them before they make the shield wall.'

Idnerth's men marched first in their formidable Roman order, the Primus Pilum behind them marking marching time, urging his men on to kill. Arthur shouldered himself into the front rank of his own men, between Lancelot and Balin. Dewi and Hywel took their place on either flank, using the butts of their spears, and bellowed orders to keep the men in good order as they trudged towards the enemy, shields raised and spears ready. Becan handed Arthur his spear and shield and scurried back into the third rank, too young and inexperienced to stand amongst the hard men, the savage killers who fought front and centre where the fighting was most brutal. Excalibur rested in its scabbard, and Arthur overlapped his shield with Balin's and tucked it in behind Lancelot's.

'Did you see my brother?' Balin asked as they marched ahead.

'He is not with the army, my friend, but his time will come.'

Balin fell silent and Arthur shifted his grip down his spear's smooth ash-wood shaft. He rested the head over the shield's lip, its leaf-shaped blade pointed ahead towards the enemy who came on in a broiling mass of furs, leather, mail and iron. Octha howled at the sky and raised his enormously muscled arms as though he implored Woden to grant him favour and carry his warriors to victory.

'No mercy,' Arthur called to his men. 'Cut the dogs down and drive them in the river to drown or die.'

The Britons roared and clashed their weapons against the shields.

'Are you ready to fight?'

'Aye!' five hundred men called in response.

'Kill! Kill! Kill!' Arthur bayed, blood rushing in his ears, pounding around his head.

'Who do you fight for?' Dewi called from the left flank.

'Arthur! Arthur Arthur!' came the reply, and so they did.

Octha could not wait for the Britons to cross the field. He was too angry, too worked up into the battle rage. He charged like a maddened bull, and his first line, his picked champions, surged forwards to keep up with him. Idnerth ordered his men to halt, and the legionaries stopped as one, red cloaks flapping in the breeze.

'Ready spears,' Idnerth called, and a line of arms cocked, pilum spears poised and ready to throw. Idnerth held them there as Octha and his screaming, bearded killers thundered towards his men, their oval spears painted with the nailed god's cross. Arthur's men came within ten paces of Idnerth's rear, and the Saxons closed the gap to within twenty paces.

'Throw!' Idnerth bellowed, and two hundred seven-foot-long Roman pilum spears launched from his battle line. The long iron shafts flew like crows' beaks against the sky. They hurtled low and flat and smashed into Octha's front rank with a crunch of wood, a rending of iron and the cries of Saxons impaled by two feet of Roman iron.

'Gladius!' Idnerth ordered, and his legionaries reached down to their right hips and whipped short swords free of their scabbards and brought blades up, ready to fight. The Saxon charge paused as the Roman spears ripped into them, the iron tips bending as they crashed into shields or tore through bodies. 'Forward, march.'

The legionaries marched forward in perfect time, steady and relentless, left foot first and shields levelled. The first of Octha's champions, the men unharmed by Idnerth's shower of deadly pilum spears, thundered into those shields, but Idnerth's well-drilled warriors took one step to the right and let them through. They simply parted to let Octha's champions flow through them like water across rocks. Before the big Saxons had time to turn and hack into the legionaries' unprotected backs, they came face to face with Arthur and his black cloaks. The legionaries were so tightly disciplined that they trusted Arthur and his black cloaks to be there, and so Idnerth's warriors marched on without looking back. Shields steady, gladius swords poised to strike. Arthur threw his spear, but a Saxon caught it with his shield and snarled in defiance. Arthur drew Excalibur, his fingers brushing against the round dragon-set pommel before grasping the leather-wrapped grip. But before Arthur swung at the Saxon, Lancelot was already there, impossibly fast, smashing his sword into the Saxon's shield with so much power that the Saxon, though a full head taller even than Lancelot himself, fell to one knee beneath the onslaught. Balin killed the man, battering his axe into the Saxon's face with brutal savagery.

'Forward!' Idnerth ordered, and the legionaries marched into the waiting Saxons. Octha himself crashed into their shields, his vast bulk bending the line like a willow branch, but the legionaries held. The Saxons howled and roared, hacking with axes and spears, their own shield wall shoving into the Roman oval shields as the pushing match began in earnest. The Saxons struck over their shields, trying to hook their bearded axe blades over shield rims and drag them down so that a spear or seax could strike at a legionary's unprotected face and neck. But the legionaries struck low, their short gladius swords pumping back and forth at hip level like the teeth of a great monster. They ripped and tore at groins, bellies and thighs and men began to die. A legionary fell out of line, gurgling and clawing at his slashed throat, and the Saxons fell like wheat beneath the brutal efficiency of Idnerth's men and their Roman fighting method.

'Charge, now!' Arthur called to his men. The Elmet legionaries had not just held the Saxon line, but were driving the enemy backwards. An enemy who had not eaten properly since their flight from Loidis. 'Now is our chance. Charge!'

Arthur drove into the gap left by the dead legionary, stepping over his corpse and the wide blood-black slash in his throat. He struck overhand with Excalibur, sliding the sword's flat edge over a

Saxon shield rim and into the face of the man behind it. He twitched away screaming and Arthur charged between the legionaries, bullying his shield into the space, shoving his shoulder into the hole behind the boss and heaving forwards. The legionaries paused, their part in the attack complete as black cloaks and warriors of Gododdin took their turn. Bors tore into the enemy, his enormous axe ripping an enemy open from neck to groin. The Saxons struggled away from him, splashed by their friend's blood and terrified by the horrific injury. Lancelot broke shield-wall discipline and drove low, charging into the Saxons at waist height until he was amongst them. Blades struck at his back and torso, but the prince of Benoic trusted his lamellar armour to hold the blows. He rose, sword moving in short, ruthless slicing motions, and Saxons struggled to get away from him as the edge of his sword opened gashes in their arms, chests and backs. Blood flowed, men screamed, and the Saxons fell back from the vengeful Britons.

A spear drove into Arthur's shield and the metal rim banged into his mouth, slicing his lips and staining his tongue with the iron tang of blood. Arthur pushed back and drove Excalibur at the Saxon, a short man with feral eyes and a thick beard. He swerved away from Arthur's sword, and then died as Balin's axe chopped into the back of his skull. The battle raged around Arthur. He took steps forward to hold the line, pushing and heaving the Saxons inexorably towards the river. Octha reared up suddenly in front of Arthur, his flat, broad face spattered with crimson and his cruel mouth set firm. His axe crashed into Arthur's shield with terrifying force, so hard that for a moment Arthur thought the Saxon warlord had broken his forearm. Octha wrenched his weapon free of the splintered shield boards, dragging Arthur close. He head-butted Arthur hard in the nose before he had a chance to defend himself and then struck him again with the haft of his axe. Arthur's vision turned black. He stumbled, held up only by the press of men fighting around him.

'Fight me, pup. Come and fight with Octha,' Octha's voice growled somewhere in the darkness. Arthur panicked, the heat of it burning in his chest and throat. Black gave way to flashing white spots. Octha struck again with his mighty axe and Arthur just raised his shield in time to parry the blow, which would otherwise have smashed his chest into bloody ruin. Arthur let go of his shield this time, before Octha dragged him close again. He was a huge man, reeking of sweat and blood. A ferocious warrior, his axe soaked with the blood of men already fallen to his savagery. 'Where are your words now, *Wealas* dog?' Octha rejoiced, triumph in his voice.

Arthur shook his head, and his vision cleared. He lunged with Excalibur, but Octha batted it aside contemptuously with his forearm and hefted his war axe for the killing blow. Arthur readied himself, prepared to die, hoping that he had done enough for his men to see out the battle and finish Octha and his army for good. Axe lifted, Octha's eyes gleamed with joy, and then Lancelot appeared like a demon from the underworld. Lancelot shouldered Arthur out of the way and parried Octha's axe with his sword. The clang of those two weapons rang loud enough to shake the very sky and Lancelot pushed the Saxon warlord back, matching him strength for strength. He had saved Arthur's life, and now the prince of Benoic and Octha traded blows, swinging and parrying, punching, kicking and slashing. Men moved out of their way, Saxon and Briton alike gawping at the battle between champions. Their weapons moved in a blur, each man's face set firm in grim determination.

The fight gave Arthur the chance to glance along the battle line, and the pain in his head subsided as he realised that Dewi and his flank had driven the Saxons into the river where they splashed and cried in terror as Dewi's men hacked at them from the blood-slick riverbank. Lancelot grunted as Octha clubbed him in the face with a fist the size of a shovel, and then it was Octha's turn to wince with pain as Lancelot smashed the hilt of his sword into the side of the Saxon's shaggy head. Octha swung his axe in a wide sweep aimed to cut Lancelot's head from his shoulders, but Lancelot ducked and as the axe swept over his head he sliced the edge of his sword across Octha's thigh. The big Saxon stumbled backwards and Lancelot rose and kicked him hard in the chest. Octha fell on his arse in the mud and blood-churned battlefield. His men gasped with horror to see a Briton had felled their lord, their leader and champion.

Octha glanced about him, his once hard face turned to strained despair. His army died around him, both flanks pushed into the river and his centre retreating ever closer to the fast-flowing waters. Idnerth's legionaries rejoined the fight, coming about Arthur, Lancelot, Balin and Bors to envelop Octha's centre like the folding wings of an eagle, and their short swords cut through fur and leather to kill Octha's men like slaughtering cattle. Octha's fall broke the Saxons. They were gaunt, sickened by dysentery and hunger, stinking of the shit which ran down their legs, and whatever last drain of strength they had summoned to meet the Britons in a fight for their lives ebbed away. They ran for the water, halted at the bank, afraid to leap into the deep waters where they saw their comrades flailing, drowning and dying beneath the Britons' spear-points.

'No mercy,' Arthur shouted to his army, 'these men are slavers, rapists and killers. Kill them all, no mercy!'

Octha glowered up at him, kneeling on the grass with Lancelot's sword point resting on his gullet. It was over. The Saxons were beaten, and Arthur raised Excalibur aloft and released a primal howl of relieved joy. His men followed, and they cheered and laughed as the Saxons died. It was a desperate victory over a larger enemy, a wild and bloody triumph over a hated invader. Every man in Arthur's army had a story of a wife, mother, daughter, father, son or brother slain by the Saxons. Men who had left their own homes to come across the sea with their axes and seaxes to kill and steal the Britons' homes. So Arthur's men killed with wild abandon, and he did not stop them. His god was not the nailed god who urged men to peace and forgiveness. Arthur's gods were as cruel and hateful as men. They were Neit, Andraste and Manawydan, and Arthur hoped they rejoiced to see their people win.

Saxons died by the dozen, and the battlefield ran red with their blood. Octha watched it all from the end of Lancelot's blade and the battle of the river Dubglas was over. Balin searched amongst the slain, lifting men by the hair, searching in vain hope for his brother Balan. Bors led the men of Gododdin along the riverbank to kill any of Octha's men who tried to swim downriver. Just as Arthur believed his victory was total, and Octha's power destroyed forever, a long, lowing war horn sounded from the north. Men paused their weapons in mid strike to search from where the sound came.

'God save us,' said Idnerth, taking off his helmet as he stared across the battlefield.

Arthur shook his head in disbelief, because a second Saxon army had come to the river Dubglas. They massed beside the crag where Octha's men had camped. Spear-points glinting in the sun, helmets shining, triangular banners daubed with animal sigils fluttering in the breeze, a score of mailed sword-carrying warlords sat astride fine horses in front of hundreds of Saxon warriors swathed in furs.

'Balan,' Balin hissed, and then Arthur saw him amongst the riders. Balin's hated brother had come to the battlefield with a new army, a fresh force of Saxons from Deira or Lindsey, and Arthur despaired, because his glorious victory was about to turn into a bloody slaughter. The enemy leaders rode forward, their horses trotting but made skittish by the smell of blood and battle.

'They want to talk,' said Idnerth, the relief palpable in the old warrior's voice.

Arthur turned to Lancelot and gripped the big man's arm. 'Have the men guard Octha. Find Dewi, Hywel and Anthun. Get the men organised. Form them up. Shields and spears. If this new force attacks us, we are doomed. But we won't go down without a fight.'

Arthur gathered Balin, Idnerth and Bors to him, and together they went to meet the new enemy. Arthur sheathed Excalibur and wiped blood from his face. He spat a gobbet of bloody spit, mouth aching where Octha had pounded his face. Bors limped and blood flowed from a wound on his side. Idnerth too carried a wound at his shoulder, and he cast his red cloak about him to hide the cut.

The enemy riders drew close and reined in before reaching the battlefield's carnage. Balan smiled at Arthur and shook his head in disgust at Balin. The rest of the riders were all Saxons, warlords in wolf furs, with silver and gold at their necks and wrists. The man at their centre sat proudly upon a dappled grey mare. He was broad-shouldered with a circlet of silver upon his brow and a long golden braid hanging over one shoulder. Next to him was a woman with raven-black hair, and when Arthur's eyes fell upon her, his jaw dropped like a simpleton. The woman was beautiful with milk-white skin. She stared at him with a sad look in her eyes, and Arthur couldn't take his eyes off her. He was astonished, because it was Lunete, his lost stepsister.

21

Lunete met Arthur's gaze with an unnerving calmness. Her face remained impassive, eyes cold, and she gave away no flicker of joy to be reunited with him. Arthur just stared at her, unable to find the right words. A new enemy force stood before him, five hundred warriors ready to pounce on his army. But to see Lunete with the Saxon leaders was astonishing. It took Arthur's breath away to see her alive, well, with his enemies. Conflicting feelings of joy, confusion and anger played out in Arthur's mind whilst he kept his face cold and impassive in the face of his enemies.

Saxon warlords stared down at him from the backs of their horses, with an army of grim-faced warriors behind them. At the stroke of their hand or the bark of an order, those men would thunder across the field and attack Arthur's force, his men who had already fought a brutal battle that day. Arthur had not had time to tally the wounded and dead, he did not know if he had lost twenty men or two hundred, for the fighting had been vicious though the Saxons had given way once they saw Octha fall. The river had swallowed much of Octha's force, their mail, leather and iron dragging them beneath the brown churning waters as they tried to escape the Britons' spears on the riverbank.

The Saxon lords stared down at Arthur, hard men with severe faces, and Arthur could not summon the words he needed. His warriors needed him, he was their leader, their *dux bellorum*, it was for him to speak to the Saxons as though he were their equal, which he was in terms of his command and authority, but he did not feel that in his heart. He was just Arthur, and before him was the sister he had grown up with. His beloved sister who had been missing and whom he had searched for relentlessly for over a year. He must find the cunning tongue, the words to save his men, for they could surely not fight again and win, and win they must if they were to survive.

Arthur glanced around at his warriors kneeling with exhaustion, men cradling wounds, other staring at him with terrified eyes. They were men with families who wanted to live as much as they wanted to fight the Saxons. Octha was beaten. That must be enough. It was Arthur's responsibility now to get his men away from the river alive, so that they could withdraw with Elmet's border safe and his warriors free to fight again another day. Arthur tried to speak, but the words would not form. His mouth was empty because all he wanted was to race across the distance between them and embrace Lunete, to laugh with her like they had when they were children. But she shared the Saxons' grim demeanour as though she was one of them. Which she must surely have become, because few women marched with a Saxon army, and for a woman to ride with their warlords was unheard of.

'Is Octha dead?' asked Balan in Saxon. He leant over his horse's neck, fixing Arthur with his one eye, and his oily smile oozing with threat as his gaze slipped to his brother.

'Octha lives,' Arthur said, finding the words he sought as

Balan's sick grin steeled him for what must be done. 'But his army is destroyed.'

'This is Arthur ap Nowhere, the leader of this rabble.' Balan turned to the Saxon lords beside him, gesturing at Arthur and Balin. 'With him are my brother, also a lord of nowhere and nothing, Lord Bors of Gododdin whom I think you know, and Idnerth the commander of King Gwallog's warriors.' Balan pointed to the Britons with a wave of his hand as though they were the runts of a sheep's litter he planned to sell at market. 'This is King Clappa of Deira.' Balan inclined his head to the man next to him, a wiry old warrior with a lined, gaunt face, a grizzled beard and a thick silver chain looped twice about his neck. He carried a sword at his hip and wore a coat of shining mail over a finely woven green tunic. 'I believe you know Prince Theodric of Bernicia.'

The warrior with the silver circlet upon his brow raised an eyebrow at Arthur, and Arthur recognised him then. From the battle at the Glein and from the escape of Dun Guaroy. He looked so much like his father, King Ida, but much younger. His flaxen hair shone like gold and Theodric was handsome and of a similar age to Arthur. Theodric glanced at Lunete and back to Arthur.

'You killed my brother,' Theodric said, fixing Arthur with flint-like eyes.

'I killed Ibissa,' Arthur replied, 'and I cut off your father's hand. Now, I have defeated Octha and will send his soul screaming to the underworld before this day is done. This is not your fight, Prince Theodric, or yours, King Clappa. Though the traitor and coward Balan has brought you to it, when he should have fought beside Octha, who paid him silver and hoped the traitor of Bernicia would help him find victory.'

Balan bristled at Arthur's words, but King Clappa raised a finger to quieten the traitor before he spoke. 'This is my land,'

Clappa said, his voice quiet and filled with gravel. 'Across the river is Lindsey, but where you now stand belongs to me.'

'And Octha led me to this place, so I killed his men here, lord king. He attacked King Gwallog in Loidis, and now he pays the consequences.'

'Prince Theodric is my guest, and we were celebrating his marriage when Balan came to my hall to request my aid. Why shouldn't I kill you where you stand, Arthur?'

Shields clattered and boots squelched in the mud as men shifted behind Arthur. Idnerth and Dewi marshalled the black cloaks, the levy of Elmet and the legionaries into battle order. 'You can try. You have five hundred men, so do I. We have fought one battle already today, and my men are not yet tired of killing Saxons.'

Clappa smiled and cast a clever old eye over Arthur's warriors. Their numbers were well matched, but Clappa and Theodric's five hundred were all warriors, where half of Arthur's men were of the Elmet levy. King Clappa took all of that in, considering what it would cost him to attack Arthur. 'You are weak after your fight with Octha. I should kill you. I have heard of your legend. It gives your people hope. If I let you live, Arthur of Nowhere, will you attack me in Deira?'

'We came for Octha, and his army is vanquished. Deira is yours, lord king. Though the lands you rule once belonged to Britons. Octha attacked us, and we pursued him. It was he who marched into your land. If men attacked your home in Deira, would you not punish them? Now that is done, we shall return to Elmet.'

'You will return to Elmet if I allow it. My kingdom did once belong to your people. Land belongs to the man upon it, and unless he can protect that land from any who wish to take it, he won't rule it for long.'

'I will not beg you for my men's lives, King Clappa. We have earned our victory with our blood, and Octha's men have paid for their ambition with their lives. I wonder, if it were Octha stood before you now and not Arthur, what would you do? Is not an Octha with an army of two thousand warriors more of a threat to you than Arthur and his men who will march away from Deira this very day? I ask nothing of you. We don't need food or ale, we don't need protection. We can just march away. Or we can fight. But I promise you this, lord king, fight us today and we shall kill two of your Saxons for every dead Briton. I am not afraid to fight you, and I will look for each of you on the field.'

'You speak well, for a *Wealas*,' said Clappa.

'We should kill them,' said Balan, dropping his hand to his sword hilt. 'Kill them now whilst they are weak.'

'Quiet, brother,' Balin said. 'If you wish to speak, you and I can talk over yonder. Bring your sword.'

'Soon, brother. Soon.'

'Are you pleased to see your sister, *Wealas*?' said Theodric, his dark eyes meeting Arthur's. 'She is my wife, and a princess of Bernicia.'

'Long have I searched for you, Lunete,' said Arthur. 'You look well.' Arthur couldn't say any more. There were simply too many questions, and now was not the time. It was enough that she was alive, for so many times over the last year he had grieved, worried she was dead, enslaved, suffering somewhere in the dark.

'I am wife to Theodric now,' Lunete said in the Britons' tongue, her face a mask, calm and unflinching. It seemed that the fondness which she had held for Arthur had disappeared to be replaced with a coldness in her eyes. She wore a leather breastplate decorated with shells, amber and jet. Her black hair fell loose about her face and she carried a seax at her waist. 'His warrior-bride. I grieved for my father, but am glad to see you alive, Arthur.'

'How did you come to marry the son of Ida? I thought you were dead?'

'Not dead. But close to it. The tale must wait for another day, when we do not face each other on a field of battle.' She leant over and whispered something in Theodric's ear and said no more.

'What will it be, King Clappa? Peace or death?' said Arthur in Saxon. Bors shifted his monstrous axe and rested the blade upon his shoulder, the blade still filthy with dead men's blood, as though Clappa needed a reminder of the slaughter so close to where they traded words like men on a break from cutting wheat.

'You can go, Arthur of Nowhere,' said Clappa. Balan flinched with anger, but the king of Deira ignored him. 'Today is not the right day to fight. But fight we must, I think. Octha will live, as shall whatever remains of his army. I was a man such as he once. I came here with nothing but my seax, and now I am a king. Our gods reward bravery and daring, so Octha lives.'

'Then I must come back and kill you all.' Arthur spoke with the hardness he felt. He realised in that moment that defeating Octha was not enough. Not when he had risked so much to kill the Saxon warlord. With five hundred men, he could do little to stave off the inevitable Saxon invasion of Elmet, Rheged, Gwent and beyond. Despite the blood and defeat of Octha's army, leaving Octha and Balan alive felt to Arthur like a defeat. He stared up at the shifting sky to calm himself and remembered one of Merlin's many lessons. A warlord must stand back from his base desires and see the war in its entirety, not only the shield wall before him. Bile rose in his throat at what he must do, his heart longed for Octha and Balan's death, he must live to fight another day, a day when he could fight the Saxons on equal terms. The hard truth was that beyond Arthur's vengeful fury, even if he killed Octha, there would be another warlord to replace him. More brutal warriors coming across the sea to seek land and women. It could not be over until the Saxons were crushed or cowed so badly they could never rise again. There must be a slaughter so harrowing that word of it travelled across the narrow sea and the boats stopped coming. To do that, Arthur needed a proper army. He needed three thousand warriors, which only the Pendragon himself could muster. Arthur needed Merlin, and he needed the legend. The Saxons before him were implacable, ferocious men, who understood nothing but peace made by violence. Lunete was one of them now, married to a prince of Bernicia, but her husband would never be a peaceful king. When Ida died, Theodric would seek war, just as Clappa and Octha would never stop. So war it must be.

'We shall wait for you, then.' Clappa pulled on his reins and his horse walked backwards. Theodric and Balan followed. Lunete went with them, and Arthur longed for her to turn and gallop back to him, to tell him what had happened to her on that fateful day when she disappeared. But she did not even turn back to look at him, and King Clappa's five hundred warriors left the field. Fifty men waited to escort Octha and his survivors to safety, and the big warlord marched with his head bowed, fists balled, and he flashed a malevolent look in Arthur's direction as he and his beaten men tramped across the battlefield towards Deira. One of the fifty warriors waiting for Octha removed his helmet to reveal a young, familiar face.

'Arthur,' said the Saxon, and he smiled broadly as though they met to share ale at a summer festival.

'Oathbreaker,' Arthur growled, because it was Redwulf. 'Have you come to return to my service?'

Redwulf chuckled. 'No. I have the favour of Lord Theodric now and am now the captain of these fifty men. You saved my life, but I had to return to my people.'

'You betrayed me and caused the deaths of many good men. You broke your oath, so your life is forfeit.' Arthur remembered well the day he had defied Balin and Merlin and asked for Redwulf the Saxon's life after a fierce fight when Arthur was nothing but a lowly spearman.

'You have brought me good fortune. I own two slaves now, this helmet, a seax, and have men sworn to fight for me.'

'And all it cost you was your eternal soul. Don't you Saxons have an underworld for oathbreakers, thieves and murderers?'

'We do, but I shall go to Valhǫll for the services I have done for my lord. It was I who recognised your sister in the slave pens. She was captured and brought east for sale, but I saw her. A raven-haired rose amongst thorns, and I whispered of her to my Lord Theodric, and he took her to be his bed slave first. She must have worked hard, Arthur, for before long, your sister was his favourite whore. Now, she is his wife and will be queen of Bernicia one day.'

Arthur fought to hold his temper, to resist the urge to whip Excalibur free from her scabbard and take Redwulf's head. Redwulf's words stung him like a whip. Lunete, his foster sister, Ector's daughter, Arthur's childhood friend, whored by the hated Saxons. It was almost too much to bear, and Arthur shuddered at the thought of it. 'One day I shall kill you, Redwulf Oathbreaker, and send you screaming into your Saxon helworld.'

'But not today, eh?' Redwulf laughed, and his men laughed with him. Lazy, mocking laughter to make Arthur's blood boil. Redwulf waved cheerfully to Arthur and led his men behind Octha's, marching away from Arthur's wrath.

'I thought we were dead men,' said Idnerth as he watched them go.

'We must return,' Arthur said, his face contorting with hatred as Balan, Octha and Redwulf marched away. 'With enough warriors to crush the Saxons.'

'Such a force doesn't exist,' said Bors, spitting after the Saxons and making the sign to ward off evil. 'But the fight is coming, whether or not we want it. Could be in Elmet, or at home in Gododdin. Theodric and Clappa together looks like an alliance between Bernicia and Deira to me, and that should frighten us all.'

'The force does exist. But to marshal it, we need the Pendragon.'

'So what do we do?'

'Let Merlin have his way. Allow the legend to flourish and the people will rally to it. They will follow Excalibur. Merlin is right. There must be a reckoning between us Britons before we can defeat the Saxons. Our kingdoms must fight as one. We can never win fighting with my black cloaks and your brave men of Gododdin alone. And we must win. I will crush the Saxons. I swear it on this sword and on this land.'

'A reckoning how? It is for the kings and the Pendragon to summon their armies. What can we do, Arthur?'

'I ride for Dumnonia and Uther Pendragon. We must have war, and the army of Britain to win it.'

22

Arthur, Merlin and Nimue rode hard for Dumnonia, stopping only to rest horses or sleep. Merlin's druidic privileges ensured their safety upon the Roman roads, and the paved roads of the Fosse Way sped them south-west. They slept at way stations along the stone road, which served ale and provided lodging and stables for merchants and bards. Llamrei ate oats and fresh hay in musty stables, whilst Cavall stood guard beside the horse and ate whatever scraps Arthur kept for him.

They crossed a Britain alive with the talk of war. Folk upon the road knew Merlin and showed him deference, and at every opportunity Merlin and Nimue spoke to crowds and introduced Arthur as the warlord Britain had been waiting for. News of the war for Elmet flew south as though carried on a bird's wing, and people clamoured for the tales of Arthur, Bors, Balin of the Two Swords, King Gwallog and the legionaries. They hissed and covered their mouths as Merlin described Octha the brute and his vast horde of murderous Saxons. Arthur played along, showing the crowd Excalibur, letting the people see Llamrei and Cavall, giving the tale of the battle of the river Glein, the escape from Dun Guaroy and the battle for Loidis where Merlin turned the midday sun black. Merlin used Gwallog's epithet, and everywhere they went, he addressed Arthur as Britain's *dux bellorum*. Folk cheered and marvelled at the sword, and the people of southern Elmet, of Gwynedd, in the borderlands now ruled by Saxons, came to hear Merlin talk. They brought spears and shields and clashed their weapons when Merlin roused them into fervour, which he did day after day. Nimue sang for them, promising of the gods' love, even in places where the nailed god ruled. She begged them to give up their crucifixes and to cast aside their fear of priests and bishops and return to the old gods. She sang of Lleu Law and Andraste, of the old tales, and filled their hearts with hope. Merlin asked the people to make ready, to await Arthur's return north with the army of Britain, where they could bring their spears and their anger to strike at the Saxons and win so great a victory that people would talk of it for a thousand years.

Where before the legends had irked him, Arthur now embraced them. When Merlin spoke of the sword in the stone, Arthur raised the blade high and watched as the farmers, potters, woodsmen and fisherfolk gaped with wide eyes and open mouths. He sat astride Llamrei in his shining chain-mail and his helmet topped with raven feathers, and commoners with grime-streaked faces, bent backs and mouths full of rotting teeth gaped at him as though he were a god of war. Merlin told them how he had dimmed the sun to strike fear into Saxon hearts, they had seen the sun disappear and marvelled at Merlin's power.

It took two weeks to travel from Loidis to Dumnonia, and every night Arthur worried he would miss the fight. He longed for Guinevere and feared for her safety. Arthur feared that King Clappa and Theodric would march to war before he returned. His nightmares howled with visions of Octha fighting beside the lords of Deira and Bernicia and their combined armies, that he would return to Elmet to find it a Saxon kingdom and his friends and warriors slaughtered. But there was no other way. There could be no victory without the Pendragon. Only he had the power to order the kingdoms of Britain to rise, and only then could there be the battle Arthur craved.

The three riders reached the Roman town of Durnovaria, where Uther Pendragon kept his summer court, on a hot day where the sun shone between pregnant, dark clouds. It was a day of blistering sun interspersed with periods of driving rain, and Arthur's leather chain-mail liner sat cold and wet against his skin, whilst his brow sweated beneath his helmet. Arthur rode into Uther's fortress, known as the Fist of Dumnonia, in his war finery because he came to meet a king. Men holding shields daubed with the dragon of Dumnonia lined the road, and they bowed in reverence to Merlin, Nimue and Arthur. Arthur recognised some men who had marched north to fight beside him at the river Glein. Arthur made sure he nodded to those brave warriors and called out their names where he knew them. They straightened with pride, those burly men in green cloaks who carried the marks of that fearsome fight upon their faces and arms. Men with warrior rings, heavy beards and the backs of their skulls shaved bald, as was the custom for warriors of Dumnonia. Arthur needed them. If there was ever to be a victory to truly turn back the Saxon tide, then the men of Dumnonia must fight.

A ring of Roman stone walls circled the Fist and twin oak gates broke its north-facing wall. The town comprised the palace, barracks, feasting hall and dwellings within the walls, and then ramshackle houses of wattle, thatch and turf clung to the outside of the walls like tumours. That outer settlement sprawled beneath a cloud of smoke, reaching to a winding river with its smithies, brothels, seers, pigs, chickens, urchins and goats. A ditch surrounded the walls, and spear-points glinted in the sunlight as warriors patrolled the fighting platform inside the high Roman walls.

'Welcome to the Fist,' called a familiar voice as the three travellers reined in before the gate. A big man strolled through the gate, hands on his hips and a green cloak thrown back over his broad shoulders. He was long-faced with a short beard and his dark hair hung in two braids about the sides of his face, with the back of his head shaved in the Dumnonian fashion.

'Well met, Malegant,' said Merlin to the captain of Uther Pendragon's warriors. 'Is King Uther at the Fist?'

'He is, Lord Merlin. He rarely leaves these days. Though he may not greet you with the welcome you expect.'

Arthur jumped down from Llamrei's back and gripped Malegant's forearm tightly in the warrior's grip, and a smile cracked Malegant's face.

'I do not expect a warm greeting,' Merlin said, and slipped from the back of his horse as though he were a man a third of his age. 'But we must speak with the king today.'

'King Uther does not take kindly to orders, even from a druid.'

'But a druid I am, and Uther will hear me. Time is not on our side. Malegant, war waits for no man and every moment we delay gives the Saxons a chance to muster their armies.'

'I know it well enough. But beware. You know Uther, and he does not grow kinder as the years pass. He has thrown a dozen bards out of his hall for singing songs of Arthur and Merlin. Uther is the Pendragon, the high king of Britain, and though old, he still has the beating heart of the dragon we carry upon our shields.'

Merlin glowered as Malegant led them through the twist of cobbled pathways towards Uther's hall. Faces stared out at Arthur from the limewashed buildings topped with a patchwork of fresh golden thatch, and older rotting grey thatch. Priests in brown tunics hurried from lanes to peer at Merlin and Nimue, making the sign of the cross and babbling to the gathering crowds of pagans and God's will. Merlin had prepared Arthur for what must happen in Durnovaria, and Arthur was ready. Dumnonia was a kingdom devoted to the nailed god and Uther allowed priests and bishops to swarm his country, gifting them land and power in return for their god's favour. Arthur ignored them, his jaw set firm on what must be done. Nimue hissed at the priests, and the people of Durnovaria pointed and whispered at her frightening appearance.

Rain fell again, pounding the cobbles and hammering against the metal of Arthur's helmet. People huddled beneath overhanging roofs to stay dry, and Merlin pulled his hood over his head to keep his white beard and head dry. They reached Uther's hall with hundreds of people clamouring behind them. Though they whispered in awe at the druid, the *gwyllion* and the hero of which there were so many legends, the collective sound of their voices rumbled like the sigh of the sea. Uther's hall loomed above the old city, a lofty building with high walls and a red-tiled roof patched here and there with brown clay tiles. Malegant led them along a sheltered walkway flanked by white pillars with ivy climbing across the cracked, finely chiselled stone.

They entered a wide hall, airy and clean, and with the summer heat there was no roaring hearth. Arthur treaded lightly upon the scene etched into the floor by thousands of tiny tiles, fearful of his heavy boots breaking the faded but startlingly brilliant picture of fish leaping around a man in a chariot. Tall windows and square holes cut into the whitewashed walls cast bright sunlight into the room, where men and women in finely woven garments of red, green and blue peered at Arthur as priests wove about them whispering prayers and making the sign of the cross across their chests as though it would in some way ward off the evil pagans who had come amongst them.

'Wait here,' said Malegant, and he hurried across the hall to disappear through a small door.

Merlin scowled at the priests, and Nimue grinned at a bishop in a tall mitre, flashing him a peek at her stone-encrusted teeth. Arthur fought to keep his face as still and hard as the surrounding walls. He needed to piss, and his underarms sweated beneath his leather and chain-mail. Merlin had prepared him to face Uther. Both Nimue and the druid had hammered it into him on the long road south. How the meeting with Uther would unfold, not to fear the priests and their sour faces, how to do what must be done. Arthur steeled himself to it. He had stood in Uther's hall before, had fought single combat upon its very floor against Mynog the Boar and won. Uther was a fearsome man, the high king, a warrior of famous strength and cruelty. Arthur knew what to expect, but he still feared it. His mind still gnawed at him to turn and run for the door, find Llamrei, ride away and hide. But he could not hide. He was Arthur.

The rear door creaked open and Malegant strode through it, followed by a man in the same white Roman sheet King Gwallog wore. The man carried a brass-coloured trumpet and Arthur clenched his teeth. He forced himself to recall the hate he felt for Redwulf, Octha, Balan, Ida and the Saxons. He thought of the unthinkable hardship Lunete must have endured as Theodric's bed slave, and how that would have broken Ector's heart. So much death, so much pain, and Arthur had to end it.

The trumpet blared, as loud and shrill as the carnyx in the enclosed hall.

'King Uther of Dumnonia, Pendragon of Britain,' the trumpeter called, and every person in the hall bowed their head in reverence. Six warriors marched through the small door. The biggest of them carried the Roman imperial fasces, a long-handled axe tied about with wooden rods which had once symbolised the authority of old Rome, but was now the symbol of the Pendragon's power. A command delivered by a man carrying the fasces was to be obeyed. Recognised across Britain as Uther's word. To defy it was to die. The warriors' boots stomped upon the tiles and filled the hall with their echo. They stopped, formed a column and lifted their heavy shields bearing the snarling dragon of Dumnonia. A thick-set figure lumbered from the doorway's darkness into the bright sunlight. His broad shoulders rolled, and though hunched and limping badly, he was as wide as two men and, even in the winter of his days, Uther Pendragon emanated strength and power. He had a bull-like head which seemed almost too big for his body and he winced every time his left foot touched the floor. His long white hair had grown thinner since the last time Arthur had seen him, and it stood out from his spotted scalp, wispy and frail like a dandelion in the wind. Uther's skin was as dark as seasoned oak, and as cracked as old leather.

Uther's single eye found Arthur and glared at him, but it was the stark cave of his dead eye which seemed to bore into Arthur, penetrating him with an unnerving feeling of malevolent violence. He slumped onto his high throne, set on a raised dais before a finely woven tapestry. Uther raised his hand, which the battle had ripped three fingers from, and beckoned with the two curled remaining claw-like fingers for Arthur to come closer. Arthur took two long steps towards the high king, and Merlin went with him.

'If it isn't the war hero, I should be honoured,' Uther groaned, and was rewarded with nervous chuckles from the courtiers about the hall's pillared edges. 'I gave you men, *Comitatus* Arthur, and won you a great battle. Now, you return to me a man of reputation. There isn't a bard in all Britain who does not sing of Arthur and his deeds. Though I fear Lord Merlin himself sends them on that errand. You came to me as a snot-nosed boy with a famous sword, and you return to me now as a man of power. A man to fear, perhaps. I would not have sent Malegant and my warriors north if I knew the monster my generosity would create.'

Merlin growled and banged his long black staff down hard on the floor tiles. It thudded like a stone falling into a deep well, silencing the vast room.

'Lord king,' Merlin said, his voice carrying to every corner of the hall, filling its high celling, the cracks in its stone columns so that even the mice between the walls heard the power of his words. 'We come to you with a tidal wave of war about to crash across our island, and we have no time to bandy words.'

'Saxons stir in the north, Merlin. I know it, I hear of it daily. But I cannot remember a summer when the Saxons did not stir. They seek trouble, land, glory. There is nothing new about that. But the fighting is in the north, not here.'

'The Lord our God keeps us safe from heathen blades, lord king,' said the bishop, a red-cheeked man with heavy jowls and a protruding belly. He shuffled closer to Uther's throne and stared at Merlin.

'Your god is generous to keep you so well fed, and to hang you with so much silver and gold, priest,' Merlin snapped. 'Do not interrupt us again, or I will make you understand the power of our gods.'

'Don't make threats in my hall, Merlin,' Uther barked, his shout so loud and sudden that the bishop jumped.

'Already we waste time. You are the Pendragon and you must summon the kingdoms to war. All of them, Uther, it is time to meet the Saxons in battle once and for all.'

'Is it, Merlin? Is it your place to give me orders, druid? Your gods have no power here, and I only suffer your presence to honour the old ways.'

'I am a druid, and though you surround yourself with these cross-wearing rats, men who grow fat and rich on your kingdom's wealth, deep in your heart you fear Neit and Manawydan, you know the gods are in every rock and stream of Dumnonia, in our hearts, in the trees, the sky and the surrounding sea.'

'Careful, Merlin. Uther fears no man.'

'Again we tarry, haggling like women at market. The Saxons grow ever more powerful and we must stop them before they cannot be stopped. Give the order, Uther, call the banners, let the Britons fight our enemies with an army to crush them forever.'

'You forget, Merlin. We have been here before. It was my brother Ambrosius who stood beside you then with Excalibur. We had an alliance, and we marched to war. We won a battle and lost a war. My brother died, and Igraine...' Uther stopped himself, slamming the fist of his ruined hand down upon the arm of his throne. His head trembled, bottom lip moist and drooping like a fish.

'Do you wish to share what happened back then with everyone here? I do not think so. You and I know both know why we failed and how the Great War was lost. We know, because it was you and I who let it fall through our fingers. But again, there is no time to go through old regrets, to pore over those dark days when we came so close to winning our island back forever. Now is the time to fight. Raise the army.'

'I am the Pendragon, not you. You think I have lost my wits in my old age? You would have me raise a great army and name your pup here as its commander? Do not think to manipulate me with your stories and cunning. You want to usurp me and put this thing next to you on the throne of Dumnonia. This mere *comitatus*, leader of a ragtag bunch of thieves and raiders given power and legend by you alone. But I have an heir now, Merlin, a son who will succeed me as king. I have a young wife and bonny son. So take your dark cunning and your warlord and leave Dumnonia, never to return.'

'So be it, Uther.' Merlin turned to Arthur and blinked, because it was time.

Arthur's stomach clenched, and he stared into the old king and his terrifying face. 'I challenge you, Uther, for the title of Pendragon. I challenge you to single combat.'

Uther sat back in his throne, and his dead eye seemed to pulse with hate. Arthur felt it like a scream inside his skull, but he kept his face cold and hard. Gasps shook Uther's hall, and the bishop's mouth flapped open in disbelief.

'And now we have it,' Uther cackled. 'The mask slips. How can this boy be the high king of Britain? Would Letan, Urien, Cadwallon Longhand or Brochvael the Fanged take orders from him? He is not even a king, Merlin. Send him to my stables to muck out the stalls and leave my hall. You have lost the run of yourself, druid. Begone, back to the forests, your mushrooms and your potions.'

Arthur drew Excalibur, its steel scraping on the scabbard's wooden throat. He held the sword aloft so that everyone there could see its patterned blade and the ancient writing wrought into its bright steel. 'I am Arthur, warlord of Britain. I pulled the sword from the stone and cut the hand from Ida of Bernicia himself. I am the man who will lead our armies to victory, not an old king who spends his days groping his new young wife. It is time for war, and to win we need a battle-king, not a man who thinks only for his own throne and interests. I am a man of no kingdom, with no concern other than the fate of our people. I fight for you, your sons and daughters, for our future and to free our land of Saxons. I shall be Pendragon, and if you dispute it, Uther, then meet me with sword and shield and defend yourself.'

The hall exploded, noblemen and warriors shouting, waving their arms in outrage at Arthur. Malegant grabbed the hilt of his sword and his eyes shifted from Arthur to Uther, the shock of

Arthur's words too much for him to understand. Arthur held firm and showed them all Excalibur's blade, and even though his insides broiled and churned, he kept his face cold. Merlin and Nimue had prepared him, and they had prepared the kingdoms of Britain for Arthur's rise. Of course he had not pulled Excalibur from a stone, nor done half of the sorcery-infused tales of Merlin's cunning, but they bound the people to Arthur, the legends gave the people belief that they could defeat the Saxons, that a higher power would grant them victory, that the gods had sent them a champion to return the land to its people. Arthur had seen too much suffering to deny the legend, and so he embraced it and let it envelop him like a warm cloak of possibility.

Arthur had voiced his concern about the legends to Merlin and Nimue on the road south, but Merlin had dismissed him like an annoying puppy. But one night, whilst Merlin slept, Nimue had drawn close to Arthur. The campfire spat and crackled around damp twigs and green wood, its light dancing on her painted face as she whispered to him of the gods' power.

'This land must return to the old gods,' she had said. 'The nailed god will be banished, and we shall return to the golden time, the time before the Romans came and filled our heads with false gods and greedy priests. It is only in lands under the nailed god's sway where a man who is not brave enough to lift a spear can become powerful through the words and fear of a god who the Romans nailed to a cross. It is enough, and that time is over. You will lead us to victory, Arthur. You and Excalibur, the god-forged blade. To do that we must use every tool at our disposal: warriors, *seidr*, kings. But know this, Arthur, the people are ready, they need the legends, they crave to believe in something greater than themselves. It is hard for a boy raised within the walls of Caer Ligualid to understand, but for a man or woman born and raised in the marsh, the fens, on a hillside in Powys or in the shadow of a forest in Elmet, the gods are everything. The gods decide if a newborn baby lives or dies, if the harvest will flourish or fail. The gods decide if your mother will die of the coughing sickness or if your barley will rot. Most folk never travel more than three miles from the hovel in which they are born, they struggle in mud, rain and sleet to scratch a life from the soil beneath our feet and they fear the brutal men who come to rip whatever paltry life they have away with spears and shields. You say the legends are lies, but when lies make love with fear, they become the father of belief. Our people are afraid, and you will make them believe in themselves and in this land. We need the legend and the people need you.'

Nimue's words stuck with Arthur, and so he stood strong, even under the withering fury of Uther Pendragon, high king of all Britain.

'The challenge is made,' Merlin called, and the hall fell silent again. 'I am Merlin, druid of Britain, and I support Arthur's claim. Face him, Uther, or relinquish your title here and now. You shall remain king of Dumnonia, but Arthur will be Pendragon.'

'I have never relinquished anything in my life,' Uther said. Arthur heard a note of sadness in the old boar's voice. He ran his claw hand down his beard and his one eye closed as though his great, heavy head hurt. 'But I know the old ways as well as you, and I cannot refuse your challenge, even though it shames both you and I to have the high king fight a man not of royal blood for the title of Pendragon.'

'Royal blood? Your grandfather's grandfather was little more than a bandit, a commander left behind by the legions who used his men and his weapons to gain power over common folk.'

'You go too far, druid. I can trace my roots all the way back to...' Uther paused and glanced with a sharp frown at the bishop.

'The challenge is made,' the bishop cut in before Uther uttered his claim of descendancy from Neit, god of war, a god he neither acknowledged nor believed in. 'But there will be none of your pagan pageantry at the standing stones, Lord Merlin. You can have your challenge, in respect of our old customs, but we are a Christian people, so there will be no bale fires, no howling at the moon, none of your tricks with sunsets or sunrises. I will say a mass to the flock who come to witness Uther defeat Arthur.'

'You will not bring your nailed god to the stones erected on our land by the gods themselves!' Merlin said, and he levelled the amber tip of his spear at the fat bishop. 'Provoke me again, lackwit, and you should find your innards turned to serpents and your eyes to stone.'

Uther smiled, his pale tongue flickering across his lips and the stubs of his remaining teeth. 'It shall be as the bishop says, or not at all.' Uther sat back, grinning, enjoying the conflict playing out on Merlin's face. Merlin needed the challenge if Arthur was to become Pendragon, but the standing stones at Sorviodunum's great plain were ancient, huge rocks carved and placed there by the gods in the time when they roamed the earth. To allow the bishop to preach his god's word there was sacrilege.

'It cannot be,' Nimue hissed, sensing the conflict in Merlin. 'We cannot foul the place of our gods with their Christian totems. Better to die than allow this.'

Merlin shook his head, pale hand flexing around his staff. He glanced at Nimue and then at Arthur, and for the first time since Arthur had met Merlin, he looked old. His eyes turned rheumy, full of red lines, his skin pallid and creased like a dry riverbed. Merlin sighed, reaching a decision inside his cavernous mind.

'We must have Britain back,' Merlin whispered, half to himself and half to Nimue. 'The Saxons must be defeated.'

'No,' she said, and slunk back from Merlin, face contorting in horror. 'The land must be returned to the gods. That is why we fight. That is what we live for. Do not surrender to their nailed coward of a god, Merlin. What are we if we allow more to flock to the cross?'

'So be it,' Merlin said to the bishop, the corners of his mouth turned down as though he had eaten something foul. 'The challenge will take place at the ancient stones, and there will be no ceremony to honour our gods, though doing so desecrates both the stones and the land beneath them.'

Nimue screeched and ran from the hall, tearing at her hair as though betrayed by the man she so revered and loved.

'So we shall fight, and God will decide our fate,' Uther said, leaning forward and scowling at Arthur. 'But if you lose, Arthur ap Nowhere, I will butcher you like a dog for your impudence. I shall flay the skin from your bones and cover my shield with your hide.'

'We meet in three days at the standing stones of the old folk,' said Merlin.

23

'I had to choose the fate of Britain,' Merlin said, chasing Nimue along the Fist's cobbled street. Merlin's robe flowed as he went, giving unflattering glimpses of his boots and pale arms as he tried to keep up with her.

'You gave the great stones up to the Christians,' Nimue snarled over her shoulder. 'Stones erected by our gods for our people. I live only to restore the gods to power, and I thought you did too. What have you done? We have our summer and winter festivals there, and people can witness the power of the gods as the sun sets into the bosom of those stones too heavy to lift even for the Romans. You surrendered like a dog, and that fat priest will babble of his false god with their crosses and their prayers, in the most sacred of places. It is a knife to the heart of everything I have fought for.'

'It is one concession for the greater good. Wait, Nimue, please.'

Nimue stopped and turned on her heel, teeth showing in her anger-twisted face. 'When you stand there, listening to them preach of their nailed god, it lessens your power. You are Merlin, one of the last true druids. We despise the Christians. We live to restore this land to the true gods. What are we if we allow their priests to preach at our holy places? We are nothing. You gave up the stones' power, and any respect, any love I had for you, died with that surrender.'

'When Arthur is Pendragon, the stones will be ours again.'

'He will do what he must to defeat the Saxons. Will Arthur declare war on the church when he has hordes of Saxons to fight?'

'We must defeat the Saxons first, and then the Christians. You must see that?'

'I see nothing but an old fool, driven to stupidity by his mistakes of old. You would do anything to right your failure in the Great War. To show that Aurelius didn't die in vain, that Igraine did not suffer for nothing.'

'You need me, Nimue.' Merlin held out his arms, and he was suddenly just a man. A man who loved Nimue just as Arthur loved Guinevere. The cloak of invincibility granted by his druidic status fell away to reveal an old man desperate to hold on to the woman he loved.

'I have learned everything I can from you, Merlin.' She drew close to him, her dark eyes exploring his face with distaste, her fingers drawn into tight fists. 'I let you leer and slather over me to glean your knowledge, harvesting the knowledge of Britain. Now, I have the secrets of Ireland, of the Saxons, and of Britain. There is nothing you can teach me now, old man. I go to wage war for the gods, to serve them only, whilst you serve yourself.'

Merlin grabbed Nimue's arm and tried to pull her close, but she shook him off and laughed as though he were a pitiful beggar. She strode away and left Merlin, hunched and forlorn. Merlin would not talk of it as he and Arthur rode to Sorviodunum and its ancient stones piled high like gallows. Ring forts of old banks, ditches long ago filled in by time and overgrown with grass, littered the plain around the standing stones, and Arthur could feel the power in the place as if it leaked from the land itself.

Merlin rode in sullen silence and rebuffed Arthur whenever he tried to open conversation. Until the day when King Uther arrived with his long column of warriors, priests, his bishop and hundreds of courtiers and common folk come to see a warrior challenge a king. Their column of wains, riders, warriors, lords in fine cloth and flapping cloaks twisted away along the rolling chalk plain. King Uther's dragon banner flew in a wind which whipped briskly across the flatlands.

'We'll have the challenge today,' Arthur said. 'We have delayed too long already. Let the bishop say his words and let's have at it.' Every night when he lay beneath his cloak, Arthur feared that King Clappa would march west before he returned, or, worse, that Theodric would bring Ida's army to join with Clappa, and then Octha, Theodric and Clappa would crush Elmet beneath the heel of their joint force. The thought of those banners, of those warriors marching in wolf and fox fur to crush Elmet, Rheged, Gododdin and the rest of the kingdoms in their path, kept Arthur awake. Guinevere remained at Loidis, and the city could surely not stand up to another attack. If the Saxons arrived in overwhelming numbers, the city would fall, and Guinevere's fate might match Lunete's, and that he could not bear.

'Today,' Merlin agreed, his voice wan and distant.

'Will Uther fight me himself or name a champion?'

'He'll fight you, and you might have to kill him. But if you do, you cannot become king of Dumnonia. The lords and landholders would not stand for it. You shall be the Pendragon who is king of nowhere but warlord of everywhere. You shall have the power to command kings, but no kingdom of your own. Uther's infant son Madoc will be king of Dumnonia and you his protector. Beware, Arthur. Uther may be old, but he was once the stoutest, most brutal fighter in all Britain. I once saw him kill a dozen men on the battlefield and still hunger for more blood.'

'I must win. Octha must fall. Balan must die.'

'Just so. Though we pay a high price for you to be Pendragon. Perhaps too high a price. So kill him, Arthur, and lead this country to war.'

'If I do this thing, Merlin, I will need more than skill with a blade and the ability to lead men. Will you teach me the lore you hold in that cavernous mind of yours? I wish to know how the Rome folk fought and what they knew of battle, teach me how to bargain and talk to kings, princes and queens.'

A slight flicker played at the corner of Merlin's mouth. 'If you become Pendragon, I will teach you as much as I can. I give my word.'

'One last thing.'

'Enough questions, destiny approaches and you must steel yourself to the task.'

'Do I fight my father today?' Arthur spoke almost as a whisper. Ector, Arthur's spear-father, had quashed any rumours of Arthur's royal parentage and told Arthur he was the son of nobody, a lost child taken from his forgotten parents as a substitute for Igraine and Uther's dead baby.

'Do not concern yourself with that.' Merlin leant close, fixing Arthur with his bright, clever eyes. 'We have spoken of it before. I hold the truth of it, and when the time is right I will tell all. But don't let rumours and fears cloud your mind, they will slow your blade and curb your savagery, and you will need it when you fight to become Pendragon.'

Merlin looked away as the king's procession drew close. Arthur wanted to press the druid, to understand finally the truth of his birth, but Merlin was not a man to be pushed and the high king of Britain approached. Uther's bishop rode beside the king on a fine roan mare, silver and gold shining at neck and wrists and a huge silver cross about his neck. A score of priests hurried behind him, a gaggle of piglets in their brown smocks and tonsured heads. They camped on the plain within sight of the mighty stones. Each one was as tall as five men. Many lay toppled on the ground, but some stood tall and proud as a testament to the gods' power. As the king's men threw up sailcloth tents and started campfires, Arthur walked amongst the old stones, hoping to find Merlin there, but instead found only the huge, silent rocks and their sense of ancient power. Arthur laid his hand upon one, coarse and cold to the touch, and was surprised to find the stone almost blue in its deep grey hue. Merlin was nowhere to be seen. His deep sadness appeared to have overwhelmed him. He had surrendered the stones, and lost both Nimue and his chance to show the power of his gods over the nailed god as pagan Arthur fought Christian Uther.

Arthur was alone in a crowd where nobody wanted him to win. The people of the south had no sense of the horror of war which plagued the northern kingdoms, but Arthur knew it better than most. He drew Excalibur and laid the blade upon the stones, and he shuddered, as though the old gods knew it was there and channelled their ancient strength through the blade. He closed his eyes, preparing himself to fight and kill a great king and become what he must for the people of Britain. Arthur sheathed the sword and watched the priests hurry about the stones, erecting crosses cut from fresh pine, preparing the place for the bishop's sermon.

Uther was in the camp somewhere, the old bull preparing himself to fight. Arthur wondered if he was about to fight his own father, or if that tale really was another of Merlin's legends. Ector had no reason to lie about it, nothing to gain by making Arthur believe he was the son of a forgotten mother, perhaps a churl, a whore or a slave. If Uther was his father, would he curse himself by killing him? Arthur waited for the stones or the gods to answer, but the ancient rocks remained silent.

A shrill trumpet sounded, and people flocked from the makeshift camp to gather about the standing stones. Dozens of them came, and an air of excitement hung about the crowd for they were about to see something to tell their children's children about. Malegant led two lines of green-cloaked warriors into the ring of stones, and in between them strode Uther Pendragon. Uther wore a heavy coat of mail belted at the waist, carried a shield bearing the Pendragon banner of a clawing dragon, and a sword belted at his hip. Arthur waited patiently in his mail, his raven-feathered helmet, and with his hand resting on Excalibur's hilt.

'Welcome all!' the bishop boomed, his hand held up with two fingers raised. 'Welcome to Chorea Gigantum, as the Romans called this place, once home to false pagan gods, where now we shall hear the word of our Lord God. If the druids and pagan beliefs are true, then let their false idols strike me down now, for I am the messenger of Christ and the servant of God in heaven.' The bishop paused and looked about the tall stones and then smiled at his congregation. 'See? The old gods have no power in this place now. We shall bless it with holy waters and say prayers to the one true faith...'

The bishop went on, but Arthur let the words drift away. He took his place at the stones' centre and drew his sword. There was no fear in that moment, not like he had felt inside the Fist. He was calm, accepting of his fate. If Uther killed him, it was over and he would pass to the afterlife as a servant of the gods. But if Arthur won, then he would become the lord of kings, and he could feel that destiny calling him through Excalibur's grip, could almost hear it screaming at him from the home of the gods beneath the earth and high in the sky, whispering to him in the wind rustling across the grass. Destiny. So he waited alone between the monstrous standing stones until the bishop finished preaching and Uther's warriors marched into the circle.

Uther drew his sword and turned to his people, who cheered the old king, and then he limped towards Arthur, cheeks puffing and sweat gleaming on his brow. Malegant and his men formed a protective ring around the stones, and the crowd fell silent so that it was like Arthur and Uther were alone in stones which had stood since the dawn of time. Arthur rolled his shoulders to loosen the tension from his muscles. It was as though the entire world watched him, like time stood still and the gods parted the sky to watch him fight the king of kings. Uther drew close, breath wheezing from his cruel slash of a mouth.

'There was a time I could fight all day,' Uther croaked, gesturing with his shield and sword, 'and these weighed no more than a willow wand.'

'You cannot fight me, lord king,' Arthur said, suddenly feeling pity for a man who had once strode across battlefields, feared and mighty, but was now just an old man draped in a warrior's panoply. A man who had achieved great things, who was the most powerful man in Britain. 'So why agree to the challenge?'

'I had no choice, as Merlin knows well. Anyone can challenge the Pendragon, that is the way of it. The Pendragon must be the strongest.'

'Have a champion fight in your stead?'

Uther straightened. 'It's my time. I have an heir. Your star is rising. I knew you would come for me. I saw it in your eyes when you killed Mynog the Boar in my hall. Men tell me you could be my son. Are you Igraine's boy?'

Arthur's shoulders sagged, the weight of not knowing suddenly pulled him down like one of the enormous stones around him. Arthur opened his mouth to reply, but Uther suddenly exploded into life. He snarled, had stunned Arthur by giving word to the mystery of Arthur's birth, and Uther's sword came up in a blur followed by a flash of stinging pain on Arthur's face. Arthur reeled away as a jubilant cry went up from the crowd. He panicked, slashed skin flapping against his face where Uther's sword had torn open his mouth and cheek.

'Bastard!' Uther shouted, and he smashed his shield into Arthur, driving him backwards. The iron rim battered into Arthur's ribs and shoulder and he almost fell, scampering away as the sword flew at his neck but found only fresh air. Arthur ran backwards four paces and raised Excalibur. 'Come, pup, come and fight.'

The tiredness had fallen from Uther as though he had worn a disguise. He was now powerful and full of rage, a hulking warrior advancing with murder in his eyes. He had feigned old age, pretended to be resigned to his fate, hoping to buy himself one chance to kill Arthur before the fight had even begun. But he was old, and Arthur was determined to win. Arthur lunged forward, and Uther parried the blow with his shield. The high king's sword came around in a wide arc, grip strapped to his maimed hand by strips of leather. Arthur ducked beneath the blow and dragged Excalibur's edge across Uther's thigh. The king roared in pain and anger. Uther had found strength and savagery in his old bones, but he faced a warrior forged hard by endless skirmishes and recent battles. Uther tried to swing his sword again, but Arthur was quicker, and he stepped in, two hands on Excalibur's hilt, and he ripped Uther open from neck to gut. Chain-mail links shattered, and the king staggered as blood sheeted down his front.

Uther Pendragon fell to his knees, staring down at the terrible wound. The king's new queen shrieked in horror and the gathered folk gasped as one. Arthur stood within the ancient stones and it seemed as though the world itself shifted, the gods granting a change of power. His chest heaved, muscles imbued with strength, head swimming with the conflicting feelings of victory, glory and fear of what must come next.

'Don't kill my son,' Uther said, the words coming out as strained gasps.

'Madoc will be king, and I will protect him. But I am the Pendragon now,' Arthur said, the words marred by the savage wound on his face. Arthur deftly cut Uther's throat with Excalibur's edge and the old king slumped dead, his lifeblood soaking into the earth, melding with the ancient power of the mighty standing stones.

Arthur raised his sword, but nobody cheered his victory. Gaping faces stared at him from beyond the stones, people who had witnessed the death of a great king, and the birth of a new one. The king of kings lay dead at his feet, but a shadow fell over Arthur's heart. Had he just killed his father?

'Behold!' said Merlin, appearing from behind a huge monolith. He locked eyes with Arthur, and Merlin's gaze blazed with ferocious hunger. 'Arthur Pendragon, high king and *dux bellorum* of all Britain. Kneel to your lord, to the king of kings.'

The crowd all knelt as Merlin commanded, even Malegant and his warriors. A still silence fell over the standing stones as though the world stood still for a moment. Arthur had killed the high king of Britain, and by a sweep of his sword, had become the most powerful man in Britain. Arthur walked to Malegant with his king's blood still bright upon Excalibur's blade.

'Summon every warrior in Dumnonia,' Arthur said, 'and send word to Gwynedd, Kernow, Powys, Gododdin, Rheged, Lothian and Gwent. The Pendragon orders the banners to gather for war.'

24

A week later, Arthur rode north at the head of two thousand warriors. Half were warriors of Dumnonia and Kernow. Landholders and their hearth troops, professional warriors with spears, axes, shields and armour of leather and mail. The rest came from the levy. Summoned to war by Malegant from the verdant fields of Dumnonia and the fishing villages, tin and salt mines of Kernow. It would take much longer than seven sunrises to gather the full strength of those kingdoms, but Arthur could not wait, so on the seventh morning, he marched. Men had flocked to the Fist of Durnovaria to see the man who had killed Uther Pendragon. They kneeled and gawped when Arthur came before them, a man of no kingdom, a warrior who came from nowhere with the power of Excalibur and the backing of Merlin to make himself the lord of kings. Arthur walked amongst them, showing them the Neit-forged blade. He spoke to the hard-faced warriors and the gaping churls of the Saxon threat, and how they as Britons must fight to turn back the tide of war. They cheered his name and Arthur encouraged them, feeling their hope in the legend swell to fervour. He had his army at last.

Merlin rode with Arthur and Malegant at the head of the marching column, and with them rode Prince Tristan of Kernow, the son of King Marc and brother of Lady Morgan. Arthur's wounded face ached, even though Merlin had stitched the wound and tended to its care daily. Uther's vicious blade had left Arthur with a lurid jagged cut which ran from his top lip to below his eye. The stitches raised the corner of Arthur's mouth so that his face became a constant snarl. It was a painful reminder of the cost of Arthur's quest, and a last bitter victory for Uther. From now on, whenever anybody met Arthur, they would see the scar left by Uther's sword, a stark reminder of how Arthur had come to power and which had changed Arthur's face forever. Uther's cruel face came to Arthur each night as he slept, whispering to him of Britain's expectation. The scarred old bull leered at Arthur in his nightmares, showing the faces of small children and their mothers whose future depended on Arthur's victory. Arthur saw those innocent faces as they were today, and then as abused, terror-stricken slaves to brutal Saxon masters. The fate of Britons everywhere if Arthur lost the war. Every night Arthur woke in a cold sweat, surrounded by an army of campfires, the weight of expectation impossibly heavy like one of the mighty standing stones of Sorviodunum. Had he killed his father to become Pendragon? Arthur did not want to know. He had enough to worry about, a head full of battle, soldiers, Saxons, and Guinevere.

A dark melancholy hung about Merlin like a storm cloud. His usual busy aloofness vanished with Nimue and her wrath to leave Merlin brooding and sullen. He did not protest that the warriors of Dumnonia and Kernow wore crosses at their necks. He even acquiesced when Malegant requested that priests accompany the army to shepherd men's souls and receive their prayers. The Merlin Arthur knew would rail against the Christians, curse them and forbid their presence, but this Merlin seemed to accept their inevitability as something that must be endured for the sake of victory.

'Your men grumble, Lord Malegant,' said Prince Tristan. He rode a white horse and was a tall man with flowing chestnut hair worn loose and long. Tristan had a long face with bright blue eyes and was a respected commander of his father's warriors. He spoke slowly with a heavy Kernow accent, the words rolling around his mouth as though it were full of pebbles.

'They wish to mourn their king,' Malegant replied, and did not bother to hide his frown.

'Was Uther loved by his people?' Tristan leant back with a raised eyebrow.

'He was not a kind man. I know that well enough. But he was a good king, victorious and respected. He was king before I was born, and our people know of no other king but Uther. They mourn the change, and they fear for the future.'

'There will be no mourning in Kernow. We remember too well Uther's raids, his tin tax and his cruelty. Will our new Pendragon be any different, I wonder? Now that Lord Arthur has been confirmed quickly as steward of Dumnonia and protector of Uther's heir.'

'A king must be both cruel and kind, he must rule and provide justice for his people. The people of Kernow were lucky to enjoy so many years of peace behind the safety of Uther's shield. Let us hope that Lord Arthur rules in the same way.'

'My sister can surely attest to his statesmanship. How fares Lady Morgan in the north, Lord Arthur?' Tristan's voice dripped with scorn.

Arthur ignored Prince Tristan's probing. Morgan's name jabbed at his conscience, pricked at the shame festering in his heart for what he had done to the princess of Kernow. He had given no thought to what the Pendragon would do when the fighting was over. He only thought of the title as a means to an end, a tool to give him an army. Arthur grimaced at the thought of ruling Britain as its high king. It was a problem for another day. If he lived. If they won. Arthur thought only of the battle to come, of the difficulties of marching with so many men, how to keep them fed, where to camp, where and how the battle against the Saxons would unfold. After Uther's death Malegant had knelt before Arthur and sworn an oath to serve him truly, as had his green-cloaked warriors with their shaved skulls. There was bitterness there, and sorrow for their dead king, but they accepted Arthur's right to challenge and his new title. Arthur had sworn before Merlin and the lords of Dumnonia to be young King Madoc's protector until Uther's son grew old enough to rule as king of Dumnonia in his own right. Madoc would be king, but all would bow to Arthur, and as Arthur led his army north he wondered how Urien, Letan Lyddoc, Gwallog and the rest of Britain's kings would react when forced by tradition and Arthur's victory to acknowledge him as their overlord.

'Uther was a great man. You remember him only as he was at the end,' said Malegant, wrestling with the reins as his horse sensed his anger. 'He was once the greatest warrior and king in all Britain.'

'They can mourn Uther for as long as they like when the fighting is over,' Arthur snapped. The lords and champions of Dumnonia and Kernow were cold to him. They respected his title of Pendragon and did not challenge his authority, but Arthur ate alone and found no warmth from the men under his command. He found companionship with Cavall, who bound along beside Llamrei on the march, and slept beside Arthur at night. Arthur had not challenged and killed Uther for friendship. He had done it to build an army to save Britain from its enemies. He longed for Guinevere, to hear her laughter and to feel the touch of her warm skin against his own, but Arthur steeled himself against gentle thoughts and bent his mind to war. 'How many messengers did we send out?'

'A dozen, Lord Arthur. Good men on swift horses.'

'Then we shall meet the warriors of Gwynedd and Powys on the road. Malegant, you ride on ahead with Merlin and a score of warriors to make sure the men of Gododdin, Rheged and Lothian, who march south, know where to find us. Tell them to march to Loidis.'

As Malegant and his men nudged their horses into a canter to follow Arthur's orders, Merlin drew close to Arthur and leaned in, his eyes scything deep into Arthur's own.

'Remember to show them the legend,' Merlin said through clenched teeth. 'We have risked much and lost more for you to be Pendragon. Use it wisely.' With that, he rode after Malegant and left Arthur alone with the army.

Five hundred men of Powys and five hundred from Gwent met Arthur where the Roman road turned east along the winding banks of the river Abona. They waited inside a wide bend in the river where it hooked around fields of golden wheat on one bank and butted up against coppiced forest on the other. The warriors clamoured around the road as Arthur approached, and he wore his helmet with a fresh plume of raven feathers, his black cloak, chain-mail armour and Excalibur strapped to his side. Malegant rode beside him, carrying the dragon banner of the Pendragon and the fasces of power resting upon his shoulder.

'Make way for Arthur Pendragon!' Malegant barked, brandishing the fasces. Warriors shuffled away from the roadside, bowing their heads, but sneaking peeks at Arthur as Llamrei trotted past the crowds. A grim warrior named Einion led the men of Powys. King Brochvael himself stayed in his own kingdom but sent his oath with Einion that he respected Arthur's position as Pendragon. King Tewdrig of Gwent sent his men under the command of a short, barrel-chested man named Maccus who also passed on Tewdrig's respects to Arthur. Arthur accepted their oaths, and without delay pushed north. Arthur led three thousand men to Viroconium, a once large Roman city now fallen to crumbling ruin in the borderlands where Saxon raids came north from their southern kingdoms, and struck east from Lindsey. There, in the shadow of Roman *civitas,* Prince Maelgwyn of Gwynedd waited with four hundred spearmen, each carrying a cross painted upon their shields.

'Lord Pendragon,' Maelgwyn said when he rode out to meet Arthur on the road. He wore a fine wool tunic and a long red cloak, and a heavy silver cross bounced against his chest as he rode. Maelgwyn was a pinch-faced man, balding though he had seen barely twenty summers, and carried neither spear, axe nor sword. But a monstrous brute of a man rode at his flank, a scarred warrior with rumples of skin gathered at the back of his bull neck and a short forehead above a malevolent face. 'I come from my father, King Cadwallon Longhand. I am a man of God and do not wield a blade, but Orin here will lead our warriors into battle.'

'I count only four hundred spearmen,' Arthur replied. 'Surely Gwynedd, one of the largest kingdoms in Britain, can muster more?'

'Time is short, and we are hard-pressed by raiders from Lothian. My father has spared all he can. But Orin here is a stout fighter, and we shall do our bit. Have no fear.'

Arthur camped the army for a night in the shadows of Viroconium, where they ate a sparse meal of dried fish and roast pork.

Supplies ran low and men complained of hunger, so Arthur sent Einion ahead with a detachment of two hundred men to forage for food, ale and water, and to leave those supplies in wagons guarded by warriors. After that, the men ate well as they pushed north to Loidis. Arthur kept to himself, riding alone at the head of the long marching column. He heard daily reports of men fallen ill after drinking from a river, of wagons full of arrows losing wheels, of men hung for raiding villages on the road, and his head swam with the complexity of keeping the army moving. Their progress slowed under the myriad problems of marching so many men north, but Arthur drove the men onwards, allowing their column to stretch behind him for miles along the Roman roads. He sent scouts ranging up and down the column, ranging east in case the Saxons attacked Arthur's men on the road. No attack came, and the worst Arthur had to deal with was a brawl one night between the men of Powys and Gwynedd after a wrestling match gone bad.

King Gwallog and Prince Ceretic came from Loidis to meet Arthur, and Gwallog could barely contain his excitement at the vast army come to do battle with the Saxons who threatened his borders. Idnerth and his legionaries lined the road leading to the city gate. Common folk lined the walls cheering with wild abandon because they saw safety and hope in Arthur's three and a half thousand men. Hope at last, after living so long in the threatening shadow of fresh Saxon attacks. They were people who had fled Loidis when Octha captured the city, and the survivors who had tarried and become slaves to Octha's warriors. Arthur was their hope, and he carried that with him, strengthening his resolve as much as Excalibur strengthened his sword arm.

'You've been busy, then?' said Balin, in typically laconic fashion. He came to meet Arthur inside the city gate with Dewi, Hywel, Becan, Anthun and Bors.

'I don't know whether to kneel, fart, or get you some ale,' said Bors, and the men laughed.

Arthur laughed with them, enjoying the moment of levity after long weeks of impossible tension. 'Ale would be good,' he said, 'but you keep your cabbage farts for yourself.'

'What do we call you now? Lord, boy, Pendragon, king? Or what was it Octha called you? Pup?'

Arthur smiled. 'Nothing has changed between us. I am the Pendragon now, but we are still brothers. Don't forget that. But we have a hard fight ahead, and now we must take the fight to the Saxons.'

'You have a new scratch.' Bors winced and pointed to the livid gash on Arthur's face.

'A gift from Uther's blade.'

'They are gathering, lord,' said Dewi, after taking Arthur's forearm in the warrior's grip. 'Our scouts report long hundreds of Saxon warriors marching south from Bernicia with Theodric to join forces with King Clappa's men.'

'So they have between two and three thousand men?' Arthur guessed, unsure of the strength of Deira and Bernicia combined.

'Could be,' said Balin. 'We don't know for sure. My brother is with Clappa. But worse news is reports that King Cwichelm of Lindsey also sends men to join the Saxon alliance.'

'How many?'

'We don't know. They march through the fens, and our scouts cannot count them in the marsh and floodwater.'

'We have close to four thousand men ourselves, with the warriors of Gododdin, Rheged and Lothian yet to arrive.'

'It's the largest army of Britons since the Great War,' said Bors, and the big man stared at each one of them in turn. 'Time to crush the fur-wearing bastards at last.'

Arthur called the captains, princes and warlords to meet in

King Gwallog's hall that evening. King Gwallog's stewards set a seat for Arthur on the raised dais next to Gwallog's own throne. Arthur waited in the chamber behind the hall, pacing the stone floor, thrumming his fingers on Ida's sceptre. Gwallog had offered Arthur a silver circlet to wear on his brow as a symbol of his new status, but Arthur refused. He did not feel like the high king. He didn't own any land of his own, not even the smallest field or meanest hovel, but now the kings of Britain must pay him homage because he had killed an old man in Dumnonia. The oak door creaked open and Becan's head poked through the gap.

'They are all gathered inside, lord. Waiting for you,' he said, and gulped. 'So many great lords.'

'Thank you, Becan,' Arthur replied and took a deep breath. This was what it meant to lead them. This was what it took. He feared standing before their judging eyes just as much as he feared facing the Saxon horde, but again he summoned the memories and the blood to steel him to what must be done. Arthur strode through the door with his black cloak about his shoulders, and his chain-mail polished by Becan to a shine. He stepped up onto the dais, boots banging upon the wooden stairs and the buzz of conversation in the room died, so that Arthur could hear the creak of leather and the cough of a warrior at the back of the hall. A hundred eyes settled on him, men wondering how the man before them had clawed his way from nothing to become the Pendragon of Britain. Arthur felt those eyes boring into him. Warriors and champions wondered if they could defeat him in single combat, asking themselves if he was worthy of his title.

Gwallog rose from his throne and smiled. 'Arthur, *dux bellorum* and Pendragon of Britain,' he said, and gestured to Arthur.

Arthur stared at the crowd, using his cold stone face, and he met their eyes, staring belligerently at them with the confidence a warrior and leader must possess if men were to respect him. A few heads bowed, then more, and Arthur waited until every man in the hall bowed their heads in deference. Only then did he take his place next to Gwallog. More silence, men swaying as they stood below him, waiting to hear what the new Pendragon would say of the war to come.

'Tomorrow we march east to face our enemies,' Arthur said, fighting to keep his face stone calm as his own voice echoed back to him from the rafters.

'We face your enemies,' shouted a voice from the back.

'The Saxons are the enemy of every man in his hall. The enemy of every man, woman and child in Britain!' Arthur shouted. The comment thrown at him was impertinent. Would the man have questioned Uther Pendragon so?

'What becomes of our homes whilst we are here fighting your war? Saxons from the southern kingdoms could attack Dumnonia whilst we are gone. What then?'

'Then we march south and crush those men, too.'

'How shall we feed so many men here in Loidis? Is there bread for all?' A different voice this time.

Arthur stood and drew Ida's sceptre from his belt. 'We fight for each other. We fight for our people. Let the warrior who moans of hunger rejoice that his empty belly is the greatest of his worries. That his wife and children sleep safe in their beds because we march east. I have gathered you here to fight a war that will keep our borders safe for a generation. Defeat the Saxons now and they shall fear us. Fewer ships will come across the narrow sea when they hear how hard the Britons fight, when they understand what it will cost them to win the land they so desperately crave. We march tomorrow. So gather your warriors in the fields east of the city walls. We march to war, men of Britain, and we must fight as one. The next man who barks up at me without respect shall meet me in single combat this evening.' Arthur waited, letting his eyes swoop over the crowd, meeting the gaze of hardened warriors, warlords and princes. They remained silent. 'Go now and prepare your men. Princes Tristan and Maelgwyn, Balin of the Two Swords, Primus Pilum Idnerth, Lord Bors, Lancelot of the Lake, Einion of Powys, Maccus of Gwent and Orin of Gwynedd, stay.'

The men filtered out of the hall and Arthur stepped down from the dais, followed by Gwallog and Ceretic. Arthur waited until all were gone except for the men he had called by name.

'This shall be our war council,' Arthur said. 'Scouts report that Saxons muster in the east, a combined force of Bernicia, Deira and Lindsey. This will be the greatest battle since the Great War, and we must win. Or Elmet and the rest of our kingdoms shall surely fall.'

'We have the numbers to match them,' said Maccus, arms crossed before his barrel chest.

'What news of the warriors I called for from Gododdin, Rheged and Lothian?'

Men in the hall exchanged glances, some nervous, others with belligerently curled lips and shrugs. Bors cleared his throat loud enough for everyone to know he meant to speak.

'King Letan will not ignore the Pendragon's call to arms,' Bors said, the set of his jaw daring any man to disagree with him. 'The road south is long, and once the warriors of Gododdin are assembled, they will march, I am sure of it.'

'We cannot wait. We march anyway. King Gwallog, Prince Ceretic and Primus Pilum Idnerth. Your warriors bore the brunt of Octha's invasion this year, so your brave fighters shall remain here at Loidis to protect your kingdom in case the enemy attack around our flanks. If more Britons come from the north, send them east to join us there. We march tomorrow before noon.'

Arthur ate with Guinevere alone that night, and their reunion filled Arthur's heart with joy. He pulled her to him, and her fingers caressed his wounded face, her touch like something from a dream. King Gwallog had graciously given her a spacious room in his fortress and his stewards brought them a meal of fish, bread and cheese. It was a simple meal, but it was the best Arthur could remember eating in his life, because he ate with his wife. Since their wedding, there had been precious few moments to enjoy together. They shared their meal together, but their closeness was tainted by the knowledge that Arthur must leave again in the morning. They sat beside a fire and Guinevere embraced him. She traced Uther's cut across Arthur's face with her soft fingers and he closed his eyes. She was so gentle and fair, a world away from the dirt and cold of sleeping on the march and the company of warriors.

Guinevere said, 'What have they done to you, my love,' as she touched where Arthur's lip now bore a permanent scar, her touch lingering on the puckered skin. 'You seem older somehow. Angrier. The scar makes your face a constant scowl.'

'Do I repulse you now?' he asked.

'Of course not. You are everything to me. My husband is the Pendragon of England, and I am a queen, of sorts, I suppose. I just wonder what toll the war, Merlin, your men and your new power take on you. Come back to me when it's over, Arthur. So that we can find time to be together, to be husband and wife. Much has been sacrificed already for this war.'

Morgan's fate lived as an unspoken but shared secret between them. It was thing both understood, accepted, but never spoken of. Like a family secret buried, but shared in glances, sad memories and subtle references. He pulled her close, and they lay together beside the warm fire, lying on soft furs. It was a night of love and comfort before the brutal war to come. In the morning, Arthur woke whilst Guinevere still slept. He kissed her cheek and pulled on his chain-mail. He strapped on his heavy sword belt, slid Excalibur into her scabbard and his seax into the sheath at the small of his back. The smell of iron and leather replaced the gentle aroma of Guinevere's hair. Cold steel and the hard stone sceptre replaced the warm touch of her skin. Arthur left his wife in warmth and safety and went to fight a horde of savage Saxon warriors to decide the fate of Britain.

25

Arthur and his army marched due east of Loidis, marching across the mountainous back of Britain, across scree-covered hills, over high peaks barren of all but rock, and down into steep valleys, glass-like tarns, through purple heather and hillsides thick with sheep sent up to the high ground for summer grazing. He had not waited at Loidis for news of Merlin and Malegant and their journey north, and no news of Lothian, Rheged or Gododdin came as the army came down from the mountains into Deira. The Saxon army massed close to where Arthur had fought Octha at the confluence of the Ouse and Trent, where the two rivers joined to become the wide and brown-watered river Dubglas. Arthur sent Hywel and Balin ranging ahead of the army to find the enemy's exact location, and they returned two days later to report three thousand warriors moving eastwards away from the Britons, following the wide river towards the narrow sea.

The river Dubglas cut through eastern Britain like an axe blow, its waters carving deep into the land. Its waters ran murky and brown with silt and sediment carried down from the high mountains into the Ouse and Trent and out towards the rolling tidal estuary. At the ebb, the river flowed as fast as a cantering horse, churning and powerful as it drained its waters into the narrow sea. The river slowed in flood, becoming gentle as the waters sat heavily amongst the salt marshes and mudflats on its south bank. Arthur's Britons marched deep into Lloegyr to the border where Deira met Lindsey and Arthur called them to halt on a damp day. They rested on a hillock where an ancient willow tree sprawled across the summit, its broad, weeping canopy reaching like crooked fingers to stroke the soggy earth as though it mourned for the lost lands like a dead king of old.

'What are they waiting for?' asked Bors, as the war council met beneath the willow tree to eat a meal of cheese and hard bread. 'If the bastards flee any further east, they'll fall into the sea.'

'The Saxons aren't running,' said Einion, his voice as rough and weathered as the bottom of a fisherman's boat. 'They seek a place to fight. A battlefield where six thousand men can stand and fight.'

'A field of their choosing,' said Orin, leader of the warriors of Gwynedd, now that Prince Maelgwyn had stayed at Loidis and the comforts of King Gwallog's court.

'They run like Gwynedd men before Powys spears,' said Einion, chewing slowly, waiting for Orin to take the bait.

'Or Powys men towards a field of sheep,' Orin replied, and Maccus bleated like a sheep. All but Einion laughed.

'They seek a place to fight,' Arthur said once the laughter had died down. He smiled at the jest, sharing the moment with his men. 'The Saxons want the fight as much as we do. They see a chance to crush our combined forces, and a victory that would open up Britain for conquest. These are their lands, and they have food and ale and grow stronger as we grow hungrier and weaker.'

'Our scouts report fresh warriors swell their ranks daily, coming south from northern Deira and Bernicia,' said Balin.

'So we must force the fight. We can't keep three and a half

thousand men in the field for much longer before we must retreat in search of food.'

'Fight without the men we are waiting for?' asked Bors, conscious that his own countrymen were yet to answer the Pendragon's call.

'We fight with what we have. I want to meet the enemy whilst we are strong, not with pinched bellies and weak spear arms.'

'How do we do it?'

'We pick a fight. Don't let them choose the battleground. Clappa and Cwichelm are kings because they are the strongest of their people. They came here with nothing and made themselves kings. Their rule depends on their reputation and their strength. They can't afford to look weak in front of their warriors. Both will have strong men in their ranks waiting to take their place, ambitious men who criticise and undermine them at every turn. That is the nature of a war-king. So, we make the challenge and force the fight.'

'Where are they now?' asked Lancelot.

'A day ahead of us,' replied Balin. 'We killed three of their scouts today. We can catch them by tomorrow night if we rise with the sun and push hard. It's boggy there, marshland. No flat fields to fight on. A few hills which might be large enough for a battle.'

'We could send men further along the river,' said Maccus, 'find some boats, sail two hundred of our best around their rear.'

'We fight in the bog,' said Arthur. 'We meet them head on and slaughter them on the banks of the river Dubglas. I won't split our forces unless we have to, but if you see any coracles and canoes they use in these parts to navigate the fens, take them and bring them with us. We make the shield wall and hack them to pieces, just as their warriors have done to us for years, going all the way back to the Great War. My black cloaks and Bors' men will take the centre of our battle line and we'll hold them using their own shield-wall tactics. If we win, we have peace and safety for our people.'

Einion said, 'But if we are defeated, Elmet will surely fall, and our kingdoms will be next,' and the rest of them accepted that hard truth with silence.

The army slept beneath a malevolent night sky where clouds shifted fast and silent to hide stars and moon alike. Arthur woke before the sun. He fed Llamrei and sat with Cavall, staring at the distant hills, hoping to see Merlin come riding across the peaks with another thousand warriors from the northern kingdoms, but the druid did not come. Men rose with yawns, stretches, coughs and complaints about the morning chill and Arthur went amongst them, sharing a joke about the cold, accepting a drink of hot nettle tea from one campfire, and a piece of flatbread from another. It was not so long ago that he had been a warrior himself, one of Ector's war band marching through dew-wet grass, spear in hand, and he enjoyed the men's banter. Arthur led them east through lands where Britons had once lived. Villages where people once worshipped Manawydan, Maponos, Neit and Andraste. It was like marching through a foreign land. Lloegyr had been changed by the invader, with houses dug into the earth in the Saxon fashion, whorls and beasts carved into hall gables. The land even smelled different. The folk there had already fled before the advancing Britons, leaving cows, sheep and pigs in the fields as they ran east seeking the protection of their warriors.

Arthur rode with thoughts of Guinevere swirling in his mind. He tried to concentrate on the fight to come, to stay focused on the conflict, but her face constantly fought its way through to the forefront. He was no longer a simple warrior and leader of a small war band, Arthur was a husband. As much as he longed for victory and to see his people restored to their lost lands, he longed to be with Guinevere. It was a simple desire, one that made him feel guilty for allowing it to stand alongside the fate of Britain. Arthur dreamed of summers spent riding with her in green fields, of laughing and talking beside babbling brooks beneath a bright sun. He dreamed of winters beside a roaring fire, of the touch of her skin, the shine of her hair and the brightness of her eyes. To die in battle would rob him of that future, and now Arthur had more than his own life to fear when he faced enemy blades and malice on the battlefield.

Arthur found the Saxons just as Balin had predicted, on the evening when a red sunset lit the sky the colour of flame. Thousands of Saxon warriors tramped about in the marshes, spread out in small groups who clung to patches of dry ground between the channels, creeks and pools of brackish water. Arthur's men gathered on a long hummock overlooking the marsh and watched the Saxons hurry away from them, men shouting to warn their comrades of the Britons' arrival. The Saxons splashed through foul water, gathering in the islets between the salt beds, mudflats and reeds. It was a landscape of islands amongst the wet. It stank of brine and rank mud and it was the place Arthur would fight for the future of his people.

'The stupid turds don't know what to do,' said Bors, grinning behind the bush of his beard. 'No room for a shield wall in these parts.'

'A fight here won't be a battle,' Einion replied, tutting at the wetlands and the Saxons struggling to find order.

'It'll be a hundred fights on a hundred islands,' said Orin. 'Tide looks like it's going out, though.'

'So the islands will soon grow larger and many of the waterways between them will disappear,' said Arthur. 'That's how we'll kill them. Wait here and form up for battle in ranks.' He stared up at the sun, already sinking close to the hazy mountains behind him in the west. 'When the tide is far enough out for sure footing, we attack.'

'They won't have time to form up.' Lancelot grinned. 'We'll attack an army in broken formation.'

'But every little group of the scum we fight, we have to attack uphill,' Einion said. 'Each hill and small island we approach poses a threat. We must break our own line to march across it in boots wet from the marshes. We'll be fighting uphill whilst they strike at us from above.'

'If the Powys men are afraid,' said Maccus of Gwent, 'you can wait at the back and cook us a meal for when the fighting's over. Wash our clothes perhaps, shovel away the shit we leave behind.'

'Watch your cheese hole, Maccus,' Einion growled, his knuckles whitening around his spear. 'Another cross word about Powys and I'll crack your skull here on this hill and dance in your blood.'

'You couldn't crack an egg.'

'Enough,' Arthur barked. 'We hold them until the tide ebbs, and then we attack.'

'They come to talk,' said Lancelot, jutting his chin to where half a dozen Saxons in furs and carrying spears and shields picked their way gingerly across the islets towards the Britons.

'A chance to stall them,' said Arthur. 'Come, let's see what they have to say.'

Prince Tristan laughed. 'These parlays are tiresome. Insults, posturing and threats. But a useful way to delay, as you say. We must have our fight this evening because we have little food left, even if darkness might fall before the tide washes out. Can we fight in the dark?'

'They'll die well enough, whether it's light or dark. Tell the men to raise the banners. I want the enemy to see the dragon banner and the sigils of your kingdoms so that they know the warriors of Britain have come.' Arthur led his war council down the hillock, going slowly to keep his footing on the damp earth. To fall in front of his army would be an ill omen.

If darkness fell, the battle would become a treacherous mess. Impossible to read, a bloody slaughter where neither side could be sure of victory or defeat. So Arthur reached for Igraine's disc at his neck and asked the gods for luck. The tide must go out before the sunset. If not, Arthur would have to camp in the marsh without shelter, food or ale, and his men would fight the following day tired, hungry and thirsty, against a savage army of Saxons fully rested, supplied and ready to fight. The battle must be now and it must be fast.

King Clappa, Octha, Theodric, Balan and King Cwichelm waited on an islet separated from the hummock by a thin stretch of water running quickly over long grass. Octha scowled at Arthur, his hulking frame heaving as though the rage would burst from him at any moment. Lunete stood beside her husband, Theodric of Bernicia, and the two of them shone, handsome and beautiful between the grim, scarred warlords bristling with weapons and hate. Theodric was golden-haired and blue-eyed, and she raven-haired and darkly beautiful. Lunete stared at Arthur with dead, uncaring eyes, and it was a struggle not to smile at her, his lost sister who had come so far that she stood with Saxon lords and kings to parlay before a battle.

'Remove your army from these lands,' King Clappa shouted in guttural Saxon across the water. 'There is no firm ground to fight upon. Do you know nothing of war?'

'We know what you have taught us, Saxon,' said Arthur. 'You fear us. I can smell it on you, like corruption on a dying man. Submit to me now. Surrender, take your ships and leave these shores forever. Kneel to me, Arthur Pendragon of Britain, and let your men live. Do it not, and you shall all die here today.'

'Pendragon? You?' scoffed Balan. 'Are you drunk? You expect us to believe you have succeeded Uther of Dumnonia?'

'He is the Pendragon,' said Balin, 'and you are a cowardly traitor.'

Balan laughed. 'You look a little better than the last time I saw you, brother.'

'I say we fight,' Octha growled, teeth bared, desperate for revenge after his defeat.

'Arthur,' Lancelot whispered in Arthur's ear. 'The tide.'

Arthur glanced across at the river, and sure enough, the channel between Arthur's hillock and the islet upon which the Saxons stood grew thinner. The tide had begun to ebb.

Balan peered over Arthur's shoulder at the triangular flags raised high on spear points, he saw the dragon banner of the Pendragon, the cross of Elmet, the stag of Gododdin, all flying beside the fluttering banners of Powys, Gwynedd, Kernow and Gwent. He understood then that the army of Britain had come. Balan licked his lips and his wet boots shuffled on the damp marsh grass.

'Will you surrender?' Arthur asked again and rested his hand upon Excalibur's hilt.

'Impudent dog!' Octha snarled, the tension palpable. The Saxon warlord seemed to have recovered some of his old strength and he lifted his double-bladed war axe and pointed the twin bearded blades at Arthur.

Balin shifted to stand beside Arthur and placed his hand on Arthur's forearm.

'You saved my life,' he said, smiling sadly up at Arthur. Arthur shook his head, unsure of what to say. The Saxon war leaders stood opposite and Balin spoke as if they were alone at a fireside. It was a strange moment, awkward, completely out of place amidst such an important parlay. 'Thank you, you are the *dux bellorum*, the Pendragon, and I am honoured to call you friend. What I do now, I do because I cannot bear my brother's existence any longer. If we are to fight, then let it be now.'

Before Arthur could react, Balin howled like a madman and broke into a flat run. He whipped his axe free from its loop at his belt and leapt over the small river and onto the Saxon's islet. They had no time to react. Balin's charge was so sudden, so unexpected. Balin's boot slipped on the damp ground, and he rose snarling, dragging a long knife free from a sheath with his left hand. Octha reacted first and swung his monstrous axe at Balin. Balin swerved as fast as an otter and the axe blade slapped into the ground, and Balin of the Two Swords was amongst them. King Cwichelm leapt backwards and Theodric grabbed Lunete and hauled her away from the murderous Briton. Balan stumbled backwards, desperately snatching at the hilt of his sword, but Balin was upon him, axe swinging to take his hated brother's head. The blade came around in a wide arc, but the clang of steel split the evening air as King Clappa blocked Balin's axe with his spear blade.

'Die!' Balan hissed, sword in his hand, grinning as Clappa thwarted his brother's mad charge.

'Charge!' Arthur roared, and he ripped Excalibur from her scabbard and charged at the Saxon leaders. The carnyx sounded behind him, shrill and fearsome, and three and a half thousand warriors charged behind their Pendragon to attack the Saxon invaders. The islet turned into a sudden, furious welter of flashing blades and howling war cries.

Balin kicked Clappa out of his way and the king of Deira fell flat on his arse, bellowing at his warriors to charge into the fray. Balin hacked at his brother, but Balan parried the axe blade with their father's sword. Orin charged at Cwichelm, lumbering like a bear, and Arthur paused, sword in hand, chest heaving but conscious that he had to think. He had to control the battle. Victory was paramount. The Saxons must be defeated. Hot liquid spattered across Arthur's face and he turned just in time to see Octha's axe cleave open Maccus of Gwent's chest, carving through leather breastplate, breastbone and into the gore beneath. Octha roared with hateful defiance and turned to face Arthur.

'I have you now, pup,' Octha growled, and he came at Arthur with huge sweeps of his war axe.

Arthur swayed away, the twin blades singing past his face with the iron stench of Maccus' blood heavy on their steel. Octha splashed into the receding river as Arthur stepped away from him, and he stumbled as his boot caught in the underwater grass, anger turning to fear on his flat face, and Arthur stabbed at him, ripping open his bicep with Excalibur's point. Octha staggered and Arthur drove his shoulder into the bigger man and pushed him off balance, and then whipped the seax free from its sheath at the small of his back. Arthur stabbed the wickedly broken-backed blade at Octha's face, but the warlord caught it with his hand. He had let go of his axe to catch the long knife and blood oozed between his fingers as he held the point away from his face and a gust of Octha's fetid breath filled Arthur's nose. Arthur pushed and Octha growled as the knife sliced into his hand.

A cry snapped Arthur's attention to where Balin reeled away from his brother with a cut to his shoulder bleeding freely. Arthur let go of the seax and swung Excalibur at Octha, an enormous blow to take the enemy's head from his shoulders, but he found only air. Octha had rolled away on the wet grass, and he surged to his feet. Octha turned to run, and met Anthun charging at him, spear levelled, bellowing in anger. The Saxon warlord batted the spear away with his forearm and grabbed its shaft with his bloody paw. He wrenched it from Anthun's grip, spun it around him in a blur and drove the point up under Anthun's chin. The black cloak quivered on the spear like a landed fish and Octha tossed him aside like an old rag. But Arthur closed the gap between them in four great strides and swept Excalibur across Octha's knees. Octha shrieked and fell on his front, clawing at the marshy bog, desperately trying to crawl away from Arthur's wrath. Arthur swung Excalibur with two hands on the grip, bringing the blade down like he was chopping wood. Octha turned just as the bright sword hacked into his face, carving his skull open like a rotten log. Teeth, skull and filth burst from his split-open head and Arthur dragged his blade free from the harrowing death-wound.

A figure slumped beside Octha, terror-stricken by Octha's horrific death. Arthur recognised Redwulf, and charged at him with Excalibur raised for the kill. Redwulf ran like a stag, leaping across the islet and running towards the advancing Saxon force and away from Arthur's sword.

'Hold the line, hold here!' Arthur shouted, calling Orin, Einion, Prince Tristan and Lancelot back as they ran after the fleeing Saxon lords. They paused, and Orin hauled them back to stand at Arthur's side. The army of Britain came down the hillock in a controlled march, Dewi at the centre of the black cloaks holding the line, calling marching time as the men came on with shields raised and spears levelled. They stopped just behind Arthur and the Saxons formed up in front of them, their battle line broken into two dozen groups vying for position on islets which grew ever larger as the tide ebbed away into the wide river.

Balin and Balan circled each other as six thousand men faced off on either side of them. The evening sea breeze whipped battle standards taut, war horns howled from the Saxon ranks, and the clanking of thousands of spears and shields filled the estuary with the sound of war. Balan lunged at Balin, and he parried the blow, but Arthur's friend laboured as he moved, wincing at the pain in his injured shoulder. Balan pointed his sword at the cut and laughed like a madman, and then charged at his brother, hacking wildly with his sword. Balin stepped in, but moved too slowly and Balan drove the sword point first into Balin's stomach. Chain-mail links shattered and sharp steel punched into Balin's guts. He coughed a gout of blood and Arthur gasped in horror, appalled that Balan, betrayer, coward and traitor, was about to kill his brother.

Balin roared. The feral, blood-curdling sound of a man summoning the last of his life's strength. Balin howled at the sky, desperate to kill the brother who had raped his wife and killed his children. Balin twisted, the sword sawing into his guts, and swung his axe in a desperate strike. The bearded blade thudded into Balan's shoulder, biting deep, like a cleaver chopping meat, and Balan the traitor let go of his sword. He fell to his knees, staring down in horror at the axe embedded in his shoulder and chest. Balin dragged the sword from his own stomach, staggered, and turned the blade around. He crumpled as blood oozed from his wound to soak his legs, righted himself and held aloft his father's sword. The sword his ancestors had used to rule their swathe of land in Bernicia for generations before the Saxons came. And Balin wept. He cried like a bereaved father and husband, like a man who has seen his land and people slaughtered and his own brother turn against him in the worst possible way. Balin took one nimble step and swept the head from his brother's shoulders. He took his brother's head and fell to the marsh.

Arthur ran to him, rushing to the side of his dying friend whilst two armies faced off around him. Balin smiled at Arthur, tears rolling down his hard, scarred face.

'It's over,' Balin said. Arthur nodded and held Balin in his arms as his friend died, finally avenged on the cruel world. Balin was at peace, but his death left Arthur feeling alone, even though hordes of baying warriors surrounded him. The journey from boy, to warrior, to war band leader, to high king, was a road to loneliness. Arthur had fewer friends now than he had when he was a boy running through the fields of Caer Ligualid. Balin, though cold and fierce, was his friend. They had shared many campfires together, marched and ridden together across the hills and dales of Britain and, as he looked at his dead friend's face, Arthur wondered if that was the fate of all men of power. To be alone, to be looked upon with fear and reverence, perhaps even hate. Would he ever have anybody to talk of the small things, to laugh and share a joke with? Time slowed as Arthur looked for the answers to those questions in the scars of Balin's face. Destiny and expectation outmatched the need for friendship, the pain of Balin's hard life showed how much the people needed Arthur, and he understood then that the needs of Arthur the man must die at the altar of his responsibility, and his ambition.

Arthur hauled Balin's body back towards his ranks. Becan and three black cloaks burst from the shield wall, seized Balin and forcefully dragged his corpse into the massed warriors. They carried his body to safety, intending to bury him with honour once the battle was over.

'Are you ready to fight for Britain?' Arthur shouted to his men, Excalibur held aloft and Balin's blood staining his hands.

'Aye!' the army shouted behind him.

'Who do you fight for?'

'Arthur! Arthur! Arthur!'

'Then let me see you do it.' Arthur took his helmet from Dewi and strapped it quickly around his chin. He took his shield and shouldered into the front rank between Dewi and Lancelot. Bors,

Orin, Tristan and the rest of the commanders joined their own men.

'Charge!' Arthur roared, and the Britons advanced towards thousands of baying Saxons, each of them clad in fur, iron and leather. Axes, spears, seaxes and shields waited for them. Blood and death called across the salt marsh as the battle of the river Dubglas began.

26

The battle raged beneath a setting sun, its red hue turning the river the colour of blood as men hacked and stabbed at one another. Britons and Saxons fought with hate and fury across wetlands where briny water mixed with the blood and offal of the dying and slopped around their boots. They fought like animals, clawing, lunging, stabbing and slashing. Arthur's shield hung from his left arm in a half-moon, the rest of it sheared away by a Saxon axe in the furious shield-wall clash. Battle lines dissolved into smaller fights. The Saxons pushed back across dozens of islets as the army of Britain cut them down with merciless blades.

Arthur lost sight of the remaining Saxon leaders in the furious fighting. He scrambled from one islet to the next, Dewi and Lancelot beside him, killing Saxons with Excalibur's terrible blade. The Saxons rallied and formed a line on a long shelf of silted mud exposed by the retreating tide, and it was against that line of warriors Arthur and his men faced off as twilight embraced the shore. Black cloaks gathered about him, other smaller conflicts broiling on either flank, but the main Saxon force had come together on that spit of land to make their stand against the army of Britain.

'As one,' Arthur ordered. 'Hold the line. Advance on me.' He marched forward, spears and axes bristling around him. The Saxon shield wall formed with a cracking of wood and iron-bossed shields coming together like s ship's hull crashing onto a stone beach. Arthur and his men closed the gap, Saxon eyes peering at him, snarling faces and spitting mouths so close he could smell the ale on their breath. But just as Arthur was about to charge, his line faltered and men called out in alarm. They were almost upon the enemy, poised to drive into them with all of their might, and Arthur craned his neck to see what caused the confusion. His helmet impeded his sight, so that Arthur had to fully half turn to see across the battlefield, and as he did, Arthur's stomach turned over as though punched.

'It cannot be,' he gasped. Hundreds of Saxons came charging from the south. Fresh men, new to the battle, shouting their war cries as they came for Arthur's flank.

'Cwichelm's men,' Lancelot said, wiping gore from his face with the back of his hand. 'The men they were retreating to wait for. The rest of Lindsey's warriors answering their king's call.'

'If they flank us, we are all dead men,' said Dewi, his face drawn long with terror.

'Hold them here,' Arthur said, banging his shield into Dewi's, snapping him out of his fearful daze. 'Do not charge. Let the Saxons charge our lines. I'll hold the flank.'

Arthur drove through his men, their muddy, blood-spattered faces looking to him for hope, eyes showing fear of injury and death. A new enemy came for them, shaking them from the cusp of victory. Arthur bullied his way into his army's right flank, where Orin the champion stood with the men of Gwynedd.

'Form a new front rank facing the charge,' Arthur ordered. 'So we have two fronts, one facing the silt bank, and one facing the new enemy.' Orin nodded and gave the order. The Gwynedd men shifted, presenting a wall of shields to the newly arrived warriors of Lindsey. 'Now. Let them come.'

The Saxons charged. They broke into a flat run, spears shaking and mouths snarling with feral bloodlust. King Cwichelm ran from the main Saxon force with hundreds of men to join his newly arrived warriors, and Arthur could not count the foe. He guessed there were at least seven hundred men facing his flank, and still thousands on the silt bank and fighting amongst the islets. The sun had almost reached the horizon. Night came, and if he could not secure victory soon, the battle would be over. A stalemate, forcing him to retreat in search of food, shelter and water. Nothing would change, and the Saxons would crush the kingdoms of Britain as the Pendragon's authority dwindled, compromised by Arthur's inability to win the battle.

The Saxon charge thundered across the march and Arthur shuffled down the line, keeping his eye on King Cwichelm, the old warrior's grey hair flowing out behind him like a horse's mane. Arthur stopped in line with the king's charge and braced himself.

'Take the first charge and hold fast,' he called to the men of Gwynedd. 'Then we kill them.'

Orin and Lancelot flanked Arthur, the scarred Gwynedd man raising his spear to lead his countrymen in an undulating war cry. The Saxons came like an inexorable tide of blades and anger, and they crashed into Arthur's shield wall with the ear-splitting crunch of breaking bones and shattering shields. King Cwichelm himself came at Arthur, their shields clattering together and the old man spitting insults as he drove Arthur backwards. But Lancelot shoved them back, his extraordinary power not only absorbing the Saxon charge, but throwing them back from his shield as though they were children.

Orin's spear tore out a Saxon's throat and Cwichelm's shield tipped off balance, driven in by Lancelot's strength, exposing his left side. Without hesitation, Arthur stabbed Excalibur low and hard into the king's ribs. Cwichelm tried to twist away but the press of warriors behind him drove their king's body onto Arthur's sword. Arthur stepped in, headbutted the old king twice with the rim of his helmet, tearing Cwichelm's face to a bloody pulp. Arthur yanked the sword back and punched the tip forward again, this time stabbing into Cwichelm's groin. The king grimaced in pain, staring at Arthur with wide, fearful eyes, and then died as Orin thumped his spear into the king's gullet, and with a savage twist spilled Cwichelm's blood across Arthur's battered shield.

The men of Lindsey fell back in horror, the news of their king's demise rippling through the ranks like a plague. Their line collapsed and Arthur charged after them. That fight became a slaughter, a desperate pursuit where Britons chased Saxons down like dogs, men they hated with the upmost intensity, and butchered them in the mud, salt and stinking foulness beside the river Dubglas. Arthur killed until his arm ached. His mail, sword and arms became slathered in blood and filth. He and Lancelot slashed and stabbed until they collapsed in exhaustion. Orin's men destroyed the Lindsey Saxons, for a fleeing army is where men die. The shield wall is a place of pushing, shoving, shouting, where few men lose their lives. When one side breaks, backs are laid bare, and men in heavy armour carrying weapons run, only to fall, slip and have their skulls and hearts shattered by enemy blades.

Arthur forced himself to rise from the butchery and cast his eyes about the battlefield. His black cloaks still fought the main Saxon force, alongside Bors and the men of Gododdin, and Einion and his Powysian warriors. Arthur stumbled forward, searching for the strength he needed to join that fight, still desperate for the resounding victory. One king was dead, as was the traitor of Bernicia, but Theodric and Clappa yet lived and, even though the sun fell beyond the western hills, Arthur needed to fight on.

'Arthur, look!' Lancelot cried, and pointed his blood-smeared sword towards the river. Boats pounded across the Dubglas under oars, a dozen boats filled with helmeted warriors and spears held high so that it appeared that a forest came across the river turned orange in the dimming twilight. 'By Andraste's tits, please do not let it be more Saxons.'

Arthur squinted, spotting a banner flying from the lead ship. His heart lifted and new-found strength flooded his tired limbs. The banner showed a growling bear, and Arthur grabbed Lancelot by the shoulder. 'Rheged has come.'

Arthur and Lancelot ran towards the fight, leaping over dead bodies, skirting around wounded men who reached for them, men holding in their own innards, crying out for help. Many were Saxons, but some were Britons who had sacrificed their lives to fight for Britain, and Arthur could not let those men die in vain. A great cheer went up from the Britons as the boats crashed into the riverbank. Arthur reached the shore just as Kai leapt from the lead ship's bow and hurled himself at the enemy.

The men of Rheged poured from their ships and thundered into the Saxon right flank, and the enemy line buckled from the pressure as Arthur led his men in a charge from the front. Orin broke through the enemy front rank like a hero of old, clearing Saxons away with great sweeps of his axe. Lancelot surged into the gap behind Orin, driving a wedge into their beleaguered warriors, and the Saxons collapsed.

Arthur threw his head back and shouted to the heavens, roaring his victory into the creeping darkness. Then he remembered Lunete. She was there somewhere with Theodric, amongst the last horde of Saxons who tried to cut their way free of slaughter. Arthur ran, leaping through his men, panic killing the joy of victory. He surged past Einion, who had his sword resting at King Clappa's throat, and Lancelot, who hacked into the enemy like a demon from Annwn. Arthur peered at the dead and dying on the damp earth but saw no sign of Lunete. He charged around the flank, bursting into the men of Rheged until he found Kai fighting at the front against Theodric's Bernicians. Theodric was there, his golden hair plastered to his head by sweat, and Arthur leapt between the Rheged blades and the enemy.

'Hold! No more, no more!' Arthur bellowed, because Lunete was there, staring at him over Theodric's shoulder. Her raven hair tousled and her dark eyes full of fear, she held a bow in her hand and Britons lay dead and wounded before her with white-feathered arrows jutting from necks, chests and guts. Although she fought beside the enemy and had become one of them, Arthur couldn't bear to see Lunete hacked to pieces by blades. The riverside ran red with blood, and night descended like a cloak across the land. Arthur stood between Kai's men and the enemy, beneath the encroaching darkness, and before his beloved foster sister.

'Kill them all, Arthur,' Kai pleaded, shouting at Arthur with his sword poised to strike at the enemy.

'Look, brother,' Arthur replied. Kai saw her then, and the battle was over.

27

Lunete screamed and clawed at Kai as he dragged her away from the Saxons. Theodric had not wanted to give her up, but Lunete's return to the Britons was the price of Theodric and Clappa's lives. The surviving Saxon leaders gave Arthur an oath there would be no fighting for an entire year, and Arthur took a dozen of their champions and lords as hostages, along with Lunete.

'Take their weapons, and anything of value, and let them go,' Arthur said, masking the tiredness in his voice. His body screamed with pain, aching from the exertion of battle. Shields had clattered him, spear staves and axe hafts battered him, blades had scored his mail, slicing cuts to his forearms and legs. 'All but them.' He pointed Excalibur at a half-dozen men crouched on an islet between the shimmering waters. Men with shields bearing the faded sigils of lost Briton kingdoms, the survivors of Balan's twelve traitors. 'Hang those men from the nearest tree as a warning to all traitors.'

'Don't let the others go, lord,' pleaded Dewi, his face sheeted in blood from a deep cut on his forehead.

'They are beaten, and we have our peace, for now. We have

killed over two thousand of their warriors, and Bernicia, Deira and Lindsey won't be strong enough to attack us for years. Night has fallen and we can fight no more. That is victory. Octha, Balan and Cwichelm are dead. We have beaten them, Dewi. If we fight on, how many more of our men will die? Lose too many and we shall be too weak to fight the next horde of Saxons who will surely come across the sea next summer. If we slaughter them now and lose too many of our own men, we condemn ourselves to defeat next year. If we keep our strength, we can march again next year and drive the enemy back across the narrow sea.'

'Becan is dead.' Dewi held a spear broken a foot below its blade and he pointed the blade to where young Becan lay sprawled with his face down in a thin river of water between two islets. His cut throat gaped open, washed clean by the river. A small silver amulet bobbed in the water about his cut throat, the charm Nimue had pressed into Becan's hand to protect and watch over him. Arthur slumped, despairing at the price of victory and the death of a youth who had put so much faith in Nimue's gods. So many lay dead or had suffered wounds that would kill them in the days following the battle. But he had won.

'You came,' Arthur said, finding Kai with his men close to the boats.

'I could not leave you to fight alone. Though King Urien forbade me to come.'

'I called the banners to war. Urien should have sent Owain and every warrior of Rheged to heed my call.'

'Urien does not recognise you as the Pendragon. Merlin came to him, and still he refused. As did Lot of Lothian and Letan of Gododdin.'

'I thought Letan at least would come.'

'I cannot return to Caer Ligualid. Urien would kill me. These few hundred men are all I have.'

'But you came, and we won. Thank you, brother.' Arthur took Kai's arm in the warrior's grip and together they turned to stare at Lunete, who stood between two of Kai's men, arms folded across her chest, tears staining her cheeks.

'You are Theodric's wife?' asked Kai.

'I am, and I will be a queen,' Lunete snapped. 'Let me go with him. Let me go before they are gone.'

'They captured you, sister. We searched for you. How can you choose them over us?'

'Saxons took me from under your nose and sold me into slavery. I will spare you the horrors that befell me in those days, before Theodric found me and raised me up. I am an important woman now. With power. My husband asks for my advice and heeds it. I ride, hunt, fish and fight. He is a great man, the man I choose. My choice, not yours, or Arthur's or Urien's or even my father's. Let me go.'

Arthur thought of Guinevere and her escape from Urien, and then of Morgan. He gestured to the warriors to stand aside, and the anger fell from Lunete like an old cloak. She smiled at Arthur, and then at Kai, suddenly their sister from Caer Ligualid once more.

'We are enemies, brothers, but I love you still. Theodric is my husband now, and his people are my people. I am happy, and I am not sorry.' She flashed a half-grin and loped off after Theodric. Her calfskin boots splashed in the marsh and she called to her husband, who turned and cried out for joy as she leapt into his arms.

'I would not keep her against her will,' said Arthur.

'My sister married to the enemy, and me a masterless man. The warp and weft of this war is cruel.'

'You are not a masterless man, Kai. You will be my man now, a warlord of the Pendragon.'

'Your man? I can still best you, no matter how far you've come.'

They laughed, but Arthur meant it. He was Pendragon now, steward of Dumnonia, and would rule lands of his own. He would build a fortress and gather warriors to him and fight the Saxons until Britain was free and ruled by its own people once more. Guinevere waited for him at Loidis, and there must be time for love and rest. But the kings of the north had rebelled against his command, and so there must be war amongst the Britons before Arthur could fight the Saxons again. But fight them he would. Bors caught Arthur's eye across the blood-soaked battlefield. The giant looked away, for he understood the heft of his king's refusal to heed Arthur's call, and what it must mean for their great friendship forged in the struggle for Britain's survival.

'Is Merlin still at the Bear Fort?'

'He left under a storm cloud after a furious row with Urien. Nimue is there. She is Urien's pet now, and she and Merlin are not friends.'

'Come with me, brother, and we shall restore Britain to its former glory.'

Kai nodded and took Arthur's arm and shook it warmly. 'Urien may soon soften. Do you remember his bride? Lady Guinevere's companion?'

'Princess Morgan?'

'Yes, she is with child. It happened so quickly, the old brute must be as virile as a bull. Nimue says it will be a boy, already named Mordred before the babe is even born.'

Arthur shuddered and thought of his mistake, his drunken night with Morgan, and how he had sacrificed her for Guinevere's hand. He closed his eyes and smelled the sea air, eyes stinging with exhaustion, shoulders heavy with the weight of all he had accomplished, and what he had done to get there.

He left Kai and strode across the battlefield. Arthur's men chanted his name across the corpses, blood and ruin, and he held

Excalibur aloft, drinking in the power and the glory. He was their high king, and the thrill of their adulation coursed through his veins. The warriors had their legend, Arthur, wielder of Excalibur. So much sacrifice, so many dead, but Arthur was the warlord of Britain, Pendragon, king of kings.

Octha had fallen. Balan was dead. Arthur had won.

GLOSSARY

Annwn – Celtic underworld.
Bard – Professional storyteller in Celtic culture.
Caer Ligualid – Roman city in what is now Carlisle, Cumbria.
Cameliard – Brythonic kingdom in Brittany.
Civitas – Roman towns based on pre-existing Brythonic territories, with streets and imposing administrative buildings like forums and recreational buildings like amphitheatres and baths.
Druid – High-ranking priest or shaman in Celtic culture.
Excalibur – Arthur's legendary sword.
Fasces – Roman symbol of power, an axe wrapped in rods, used to symbolise a Roman magistrate's civil and military power.
Fetch – Ancient word to describe a ghost or apparition.
Gwyllion – Welsh word for a witch or spirit.
Lorica segmentata – Type of Roman armour with overlapping plates riveted to leather straps.
Pilum – Roman spear.
Scop – Poet.
Seidr – Ancient word for magic.

Volva – Seeress or witch.

Wealas – Saxon word for Britons, which also means slaves.

Ynys Môn – Island of Anglesey.

HISTORICAL NOTE

Pendragon is the follow-up to *Excalibur*, the first book in this Arthurian series. In that novel we met a young Arthur finding his way in a crumbling Britain. A country under a veil of darkness following the Roman departure in the first decade of the fifth century after four hundred years of rule. *Pendragon* continues to explore Arthur's myths and legends, taking inspiration from early texts, such as 'Y Gododdin', an elegy for warriors of the Gododdin tribe from a region in south-east Scotland, Bede, the *Historia Brittonum* (History of the Britons), written by Nennius, and the medieval work of Geoffrey of Monmouth and Chrétien de Troyes.

Nennius wrote his *Historia Brittonum* sometime in the ninth century. It begins with the story of Adam and recounts the founding of Britain and a history of its kings. Nennius gives Arthur the Roman title *dux bellorum*, or lord of war, and provides the details of Arthur's twelve battles. We saw the first of those battles in *Excalibur* at the river Glein, and we follow Nennius in *Pendragon* as Arthur fights two battles at the river Dubglas. Dubglas can be interpreted as black water, and there has been much debate over its location, but I have placed the battle on the south banks of the river Humber.

One of Taliesin's poems provides the spell that Merlin chants at the eclipse before the walls of Loidis. Taliesin was a sixth-century poet mentioned by Nennius, who is said to have written the *Book of Taliesin*, a collection of some of the oldest poems written in Welsh. They cover topics as diverse as praising the rule of King Urien of Rheged to a satire and a song about mead. The poem I have Merlin chant in this novel is from a section where Taliesin talks of birth and rebirth, and being in touch with the cosmos, which lends itself well to Merlin's use of an eclipse to put fear into Saxon hearts. Arthur challenges Uther for the title of Pendragon at Stonehenge, the prehistoric megalithic structure found on Salisbury Plain. In the book, Stonehenge is called Sorviodunum, which was the Roman name for Salisbury. The Romans called the stones *Chorea Gigantum*, and given what we know about the standing stones and their significance to the summer and winter solstices, the ancient monument must have been of huge significance to the druids and people of Britain. The Pendragon title Arthur fights Uther for means head dragon in the Brythonic language, much like the later Anglo-Saxon kings fought over the title of Bretwalda, or high king, of England.

The stone-throwing machines Merlin builds to hurl flaming boulders over the walls of Loidis come from the works of Vegetius, the fourth-century Roman writer of *De re militari*. Vegetius writes on Roman military organisation, how to fortify a camp, how to train troops, how to march and handle a battle engagement. He writes in detail on siege craft, and describes how to construct an *onager* stone thrower, torsion catapults and battering rams. That military technology was lost to the Britons of Arthur's day, but it is not inconceivable that Merlin could have discovered a copy of *De re militari* in one of the many Roman *civitas*, or cities, in Britain.

Morgan is a well-known character of Arthurian legend. She appears as Morgen in Geoffrey of Monmouth's *Life of Merlin* and as Morgan Le Fay in Malory's *Morte d'Arthur*: Arthur's half-sister and the daughter of Igraine and her first husband, Gorlois. Morgan is a character linked to Merlin in the mythology, and we shall see that aspect of her character develop in future novels in this series.

Arthur's dog, Cavall, is a feature of Arthurian legend mentioned in Nennius because his footprint was preserved in rock whilst the hound pursued a great boar known as Twrch Trwyth. Like Arthur's horse Llamrei, Cavall appears in medieval Arthurian texts and so I include him in the novel as Arthur's faithful hound.

Arthur's twelve battles are far from finished, and he must march again to defend Britain against the encroaching Saxon threat. In the next novel, we shall see more of Lancelot, Guinevere, Morgan, Nimue and Mordred as Arthur continues his journey from spearman to legend.

ACKNOWLEDGEMENTS

Thanks to Caroline, Claire, Nia, Ross, Gary, and all the team at Boldwood Books for their unwavering support and belief in Arthur's story.

ABOUT THE AUTHOR

Peter Gibbons is a financial advisor and author of the highly acclaimed Viking Blood and Blade trilogy. He originates from Liverpool and now lives with his family in County Kildare.

Sign up to Peter Gibbons' mailing list for news, competitions and updates on future books.

Visit Peter's website: www.petermgibbons.com

Follow Peter on social media here:

- facebook.com/petergibbonsauthor
- x.com/AuthorGibbons
- instagram.com/petermgibbons
- bookbub.com/authors/peter-gibbons

ALSO BY PETER GIBBONS

The Saxon Warrior Series

Warrior and Protector

Storm of War

Brothers of the Sword

Sword of Vengeance

The Chronicles of Arthur

Excalibur

Pendragon

Printed in Great Britain
by Amazon

52672632R00187